Virgil, born in 70 BCE, is best remembered for his masterpiece, *The Aeneid*. He earned great favor by portraying Augustus as a descendant of the half-god, half-man Aeneas. Although Virgil swore on his deathbed that *The Aeneid* was incomplete and unworthy, it has been considered one of the greatest works of Western literature for more than two thousand years.

Born in India of a British army family, **Patric Dickinson** served as poetry editor of the BBC, wrote many radio plays, and received an Atlantic Award in literature. He was the author of four books of poems as well as translations of Plautus's *Pseudolus*, *Trinummus*, and *Amphitryon*, among others.

Matthew S. Santirocco is Professor of Classics and Seryl Kushner Dean of the College of Arts and Science at NYU. He has written on Greek and Roman literature and edits the journal *Classical World*.

THE AENEID

Virgil

A Modern Translation by
Patric Dickinson
With a New Introduction by
Matthew S. Santirocco

SIGNET CLASSICS

To J.L.R.
In gratitude and affection
and to my son
David

SIGNET CLASSICS
Published by New American Library, a division of
Penguin Group (USA) Inc., 375 Hudson Street,
New York, New York 10014, USA
Penguin Group (Canada), 90 Eglinton Avenue East, Suite 700, Toronto,
Ontario M4P 2Y3, Canada (a division of Pearson Penguin Canada Inc.)
Penguin Books Ltd., 80 Strand, London WC2R 0RL, England
Penguin Ireland, 25 St. Stephen's Green, Dublin 2,
Ireland (a division of Penguin Books Ltd.)
Penguin Group (Australia), 250 Camberwell Road, Camberwell, Victoria 3124,
Australia (a division of Pearson Australia Group Pty. Ltd.)
Penguin Books India Pvt. Ltd., 11 Community Centre, Panchsheel Park,
New Delhi - 110 017, India
Penguin Group (NZ), 67 Apollo Drive, Rosedale, North Shore 0632,
New Zealand (a division of Pearson New Zealand Ltd.)
Penguin Books (South Africa) (Pty.) Ltd., 24 Sturdee Avenue,
Rosebank, Johannesburg 2196, South Africa

Penguin Books Ltd., Registered Offices:
80 Strand, London WC2R 0RL, England

Published by Signet Classics, an imprint of New American Library, a division of
Penguin Group (USA) Inc. Previously published in a Mentor edition.

First Signet Classics Printing, October 2002
First Signet Classics Printing (Santirocco Introduction), February 2009
10 9 8 7 6 5 4 3 2

INTRODUCTION:
READING VIRGIL'S *AENEID*

Every classic conveys a sense of its own inevitability—but perhaps none more so than the *Aeneid*. Virgil's great poem is, after all, the epic of the West and has shaped not only our understanding of Rome, but also of what a hero is, what an epic poem ought to be, and how poetry should be read. And yet such a classicizing view, bred of long familiarity and adaptive reuse, misrepresents the true greatness of the poem, most especially its novel, almost experimental, poetics and the highly contingent nature of its political and philosophical content.

To appreciate the *Aeneid*, both as a work of art and as a component in our Western cultural formation, we must have some familiarity with the complicated historical background that self-consciously underlies the text (section I below). We also need to know something about its literary background, in particular the tradition of Homeric epic, which Virgil appropriated, distorted, and forever transformed (section II). Then, we need to appreciate the subtleties of Virgilian poetics, the symbolic way in which Roman history is grafted on to Greek myth (section III), and the way in which the clear moral structure of the poem is in tension with the sympathies it evokes in us (section IV). Finally, the way in which the *Aeneid* resists closure demands that we approach it with an openness to its multiple and changing meanings, which have enabled the poem to transcend its particular historical moment and to speak at a level more philosophical than political to people of all times and places (section V).

I. Historical Background: The Roman Civil Wars and the Augustan Settlement

When Virgil[1] was born in Mantua in 70 BCE, Rome had boasted of a republican form of government for hundreds of years. The small city-state established in central Italy in 753 BCE (the traditional date for the city's founding by Aeneas' descendants, Romulus and Remus) had gradually subsumed, largely through conquest, all of the Italian peninsula and many contiguous Mediterranean states, including those of Greece, Sicily, Carthage (in North Africa), and even some of Asia. Lately, however, the social and political fabric had begun to unravel, as the class struggle, always an important factor in Roman politics, turned particularly violent. This tendency was abetted by structural weaknesses in the machinery of government and also by the expansion of Rome's empire by military conquest, which offered ambitious generalissimos opportunities for ruthless self-promotion.

Virgil had just turned twenty-one when this process culminated in a bloody civil war that put Julius Caesar into power. Although the traditional governing institutions were still nominally intact—the senate, assembly, magistracies, and courts—much actual power resided in this one man who packed these institutions with his partisans, retained control of the army, and had himself voted dictator for life. Amid rumors that he planned to take further constitutional liberties and make himself king, Brutus and Cassius led a conspiracy: on the Ides of March 44 BCE Caesar was assassinated in the Senate.

The death of Caesar did not, however, bring about a return to the good old days, if such had ever existed. Instead, control of the state passed to a triumvirate consisting of Marc Antony (Caesar's former colleague in the consulship), Octavian (Caesar's great-nephew, adopted son, and heir), and Lepidus (Caesar's master of horses). In 42 BCE, the triumvirate defeated Brutus and Cassius at Philippi. But then, only a few years later, Antony and Octavian initiated another, and even bloodier, civil war against each other. This ended in 31 BCE at the battle of Actium, where Octavian defeated Antony and his ally, the Egyptian queen Cleopatra, and established himself as the sole ruler of Rome—*princeps*, a word that literally meant only "first citizen" but which would eventually acquire the monarchical and dynastic connotations of our cognate word "prince."

The birth of the principate confirmed what had, in

fact, been under way for a century, the death of the republic. But Octavian, who subsequently (in 27 BCE) took the name Augustus ("the august one"), did not want his actions to be understood in such terms. Just how he wanted to be viewed can be seen from his autobiography, the *Res Gestae* ("Deeds"), which is preserved on a monumental inscription found in Ankara, Turkey.[2] Looking back to the earlier years in which he came to power, Augustus names neither Antony nor any other opposition figure (he speaks only of a "faction"); instead, he downplays the memory of the civil wars in which so many citizens had died, and when he deals with military matters he prefers to enumerate less objectionable triumphs over foreign foes. Having learned from the mistakes of his adoptive father, Augustus asserts that he refused all extra-constitutional arrangements. He downplays the actual sources of his power—his command over large standing armies; his access to the wealth of Egypt, which had become an imperial province after Cleopatra's death; and his possession of the tribune's capacity to influence legislation. Instead, he attributes his preeminence in the state simply to his moral and personal authority (*auctoritas*), which all men acknowledge (*consensus*). His essential boast is not that he established a new form of government but, rather, that he restored the republic. Indeed, much of this extraordinary document is concerned not with proclaiming change but affirming continuity. Thus, Augustus boasts of restoring the ancient temples that had fallen into disrepair during the civil wars, of initiating religious and moral reforms to call the people back to their ancestral piety, and, finally, of bringing peace back to Italy and to most of the Roman world.

Historians from antiquity onward have debated the extent to which this account is true or false. In all fairness, though, what the Augustan principate replaced was not a republic in our sense of the word, where all citizens have a share in representative government; rather, it was closer to an oligarchy, in which the major offices were usually controlled by a few important families. In addition, the old machinery of government had become inadequate to the needs of a far-flung empire and Augustus' reorganization not only improved efficiency but also guaranteed stability and prosperity for centuries to come. Finally, there was at least some legitimacy to Augustus' claim that he restored peace after the civil wars, although that boon was achieved at great cost.

II. LITERARY BACKGROUND: ROMAN EPIC AND HOMER

It was not just in his autobiography that Augustus sought to project a positive image. He did so also in the artistic, architectural, and urban planning projects that he commissioned and in the secular and religious ceremonials over which he presided. In addition he sought to capture the imaginations of the best poets, sometimes through the brokering of his friend Maecenas (whose name has become synonymous with enlightened patronage of the arts), and sometimes directly.

The *Aeneid* is the most ambitiously "Augustan" of all these literary works. We know that Virgil was already in the imperial circle since his earlier work, the *Georgics* (discussed briefly below), is dedicated to Maecenas. The biographical tradition preserves a letter from Augustus to Virgil asking to see a section or outline of the *Aeneid*; we have an account of how Virgil later recited parts of the poem to the imperial family; and the emperor is said to have countermanded Virgil's deathbed wish that his poem be burned (although few scholars today credit this story). It would be misleading, however, to regard the *Aeneid* as the product of external pressure. Poets at Rome had always enjoyed greater artistic freedom than other craftsmen who depended on explicit commissions. In addition, there is no evidence of any centralized direction of thought or expression during this period. Moreover, propaganda implies a large audience, but the audience for serious non-dramatic literature at Rome was necessarily limited owing to the modest diffusion of literacy and (even more) of the sort of education necessary to appreciate its subtleties. Finally, and most important, the works of the major poets of the period simply do not read like propaganda.

In fact, many of the ideas in the *Aeneid* had already

found expression in Virgil's earlier pre-Augustan works—
the *Bucolics*, a selection of ten pastoral poems that pre-
date the Augustan settlement,[3] and the *Georgics*, a four-
book didactic poem purporting to be a farming manual,
that was published in 29 BCE but was actually begun
several years before Actium. Both works unfold against
the backdrop of the civil wars as endured by those who
dwell on the land. Theirs is an experience of untold
hardship, of suffering and personal loss. In the first *Bucolic*, for instance, a farmer laments that his property
has been confiscated to be given as payment to a returning soldier; and in the *Georgics* the landscape has
been damaged by the fighting and only hard work can
render it fertile again. In both poems, though, there is
hope. Another rustic in the first *Bucolic* expresses gratitude that an unnamed but godlike man has restored his
land to him; the fourth (or "Messianic") *Bucolic* prophesies the birth of a child, again unnamed, who will bring
about a new cosmic order; and in the *Georgics*, as later
in the *Aeneid*, it seems as if this savior is retrospectively
identified as Augustus, the leader whose achievements
have made possible agricultural (and social) renewal.

It is noteworthy that, at the very midpoint of the
Georgics (3.8–48), Virgil announces that his next work,
which he imagines as his masterpiece, will be an epic
about the new leader. He then uses an architectural met-
aphor to describe this future poem as a temple, on which
will be represented Augustus' actual and imagined triumphs over such foreign foes as Britain, Egypt, and Par-
thia. These words seem to situate Virgil's next work, the
Aeneid, within the dominant tradition of poetry at Rome,
nationalistic historical epic, i.e., long narrative poems
that celebrated great events in Roman history, particularly military victories, and the statesmen and generals
who accomplished them and who were often the poets'
patrons. Most major pre-Augustan leaders were the subjects of such panegyrics—although poor Cicero could not
find a willing bard and had to write his own!

The problem, however, was that such poems were
both artistically and politically constraining. By now a well-
worn form, historical epic offered little scope for artistic
innovation. In addition, it posed very real risks, since

praise poetry that was too overt could diminish not only its author (who might appear sycophantic) but also its subject (who might inadvertently appear ridiculous and take umbrage).[4] Finally, and perhaps most important, such poetry offered little opportunity for independent, much less critical, reflection about persons and power.

Virgil's solution to this problem was brilliant. Rather than deliver on the promise he made in the *Georgics*, he turned to another, even older form of poetry, not the historical epic popular at Rome but the mythological epic of archaic Greece, in particular Homer's *Iliad* and *Odyssey*. Of course, Roman literature had always depended on Greek precursors, and one of the earliest works in Latin had been an adaptation of the *Odyssey* by Livius Andronicus (third century BCE). Similarly, those Roman historical epics discussed above had all imitated Homer's lofty style and many of his poetic devices—lengthy descriptive passages (*ekphrasis*), dramatic speeches, catalogues, battle narratives, invocations to the muses, divine interventions, comparisons by simile, and the like. But Virgil went one step further: he adopted not just the style but also the setting and the time frame of Homer. The *Aeneid* begins not in Augustan Rome but over a millennium earlier in Troy, and its hero is not Augustus but his mythical ancestor Aeneas, one of the Trojans who managed to escape their city's destruction and, after much wandering, arrived in Italy as fate had decreed.

The *Aeneid* is full of close verbal echoes of the *Iliad* and *Odyssey*, many of its scenes are closely modeled on specific Homeric episodes, and even the overarching structure of the poem depends on these Greek models. Thus, the first six books, in which Aeneas escapes Troy, wanders through many lands, has a love affair, and visits the underworld, correspond to the *Odyssey*, whose hero, Odysseus (Ulysses in Latin), has similar postwar adventures during a difficult journey home. Then, the next six books in which Aeneas must do battle to settle in Latium and to win the hand of the native princess Lavinia correspond to the *Iliad*, which focuses on Achilles, the preeminent hero of the Greeks when they fought at Troy to recover the abducted Helen.

Upon closer examination, however, these correspondences are not exact. Indeed, it is precisely in the dissonances between Virgilian text and Homeric subtext that we can divine something of the *Aeneid*'s meaning and its originality. Thus, while Aeneas resembles the wandering Odysseus in the first half of the poem, he differs from that Greek hero since his difficult journey is not a homecoming, but an exile: having lost his home and wife at Troy, he must now move toward an unknown future in a western land that remains perpetually elusive. Similarly, in the second half of the poem, Aeneas may resemble Achilles in his military prowess; but he is motivated to fight not by the Homeric hero's quest for individual glory (*kudos*) but rather by a deeper sense of responsibility to society and the gods (*pietas*, discussed further below).

III. Myth, History, Symbol

Virgil's decision to mediate Roman history through Homeric myth not only offered great artistic flexibility but also enabled him to bypass overt celebration of Augustus in favor of a more subtle and honest exploration of the historical and moral significance of Rome and of its current ruler. For although the poem is set more than a millennium earlier, historical Rome and its contemporary leader everywhere underlie the text in at least three ways—through genealogy, prophecy, and what we may call, for want of a better word, symbolism.

At the most basic level, genealogy, Aeneas is represented as the literal ancestor of the Romans. Fighting for the right to settle in Italy, he and his Trojan followers merge with the native population to create a new race. Not himself the founder of Rome, Aeneas sets in motion a process that will, centuries later, lead to Rome's founding by his descendants, Romulus and Remus, and that will, later still, culminate in the rule of another descendant, Augustus.

Beyond genealogy, Rome finds its way into the poem by being mentioned explicitly in three major prophecies about the future. In Book I, Jupiter reassures his daughter Venus that her son Aeneas will survive the wrath of

Juno and that a mighty empire will one day be ruled over by a Caesar, who will trace his ancestry to Aeneas and who will bring peace to the world. In Book VI, Aeneas visits the underworld, where the ghost of his father, Anchises, shows him a procession of Roman heroes yet to be born, including Augustus, who is destined to reestablish a Golden Age and to extend his empire to the stars. Finally, in Book VIII, Aeneas prepares for battle by taking up a divinely manufactured shield on which are depicted scenes from Rome's future history, and at its centerpiece are Augustus' victory at Actium and his triumph at Rome.

But more important than either genealogy or prophecy is one other technique by which Greek myth provides a cover for Rome's past and present. Throughout the poem key characters and episodes suggest parallels to real persons and events. The most obvious case is, of course, Aeneas: deferring to the will of the gods, battling the forces of violence, restoring peace, and establishing a state, he stands in symbolic equivalence to Augustus. This symbolism extends even to particular scenes. To take just one example: the famous episode of Aeneas and Dido in Book IV is not just a personal love story but also has political resonance. Dido, the queen of Carthage, for whose sake Aeneas is initially willing to set aside his divinely appointed mission, surely calls to mind Cleopatra, another foreign queen who had recently sought to distract a Roman general (Antony) from his duty. And when Aeneas, obedient at last to the gods' command, abandons Dido and she kills herself in grief, he corresponds to Augustus, whose defeat of Cleopatra at Actium drove her to suicide.

At this point, however, two observations about the symbolism of the *Aeneid* are in order. First, it is not an allegory in which every element of the plot has one, and only one, precise object of correspondence. In her death Dido may resemble the contemporary queen Cleopatra, but the deathbed curse she places on relations between Aeneas' people and her own also foreshadows an earlier event in history, the Punic Wars, in which Carthage was eventually destroyed by Rome (in 146 BCE). Similarly, if Aeneas stands in a symbolic relationship to Augustus

throughout the poem, Augustus is also suggested by
other figures—by Neptune, for example, whose calming
of a storm at sea is explicitly compared to the efforts of
a statesman quieting a mob in a civil war (I.142–56=
157–173 Dickinson), and by Hercules, whose rescue of
Evander's people from the monster Cacus calls to mind
the way in which Augustan propaganda cast Augustus'
victory over Antony as a Herculean triumph (VIII.184–
279=235–347 Dickinson).

If, then, the symbolism of the *Aeneid* operates at many
levels, the second point worth noting is that the symbolism is also pervasive and even systematic. Not only do
the characters and events point to Roman parallels, but
these parallels are themselves worked into a larger the-
matic structure. Specifically, the entire plot revolves
around the basic contrast of *pietas* and *furor*—piety and
violence, calm and passion, order and disorder. The action of the poem can be seen as the triumph of the
forces of *pietas*, in the person of *pius Aeneas* and his
followers, over the forces of *furor*, who interfere with
his divine destiny—chief among them the goddess Juno,
his mistress Dido, and his enemy Turnus. The contemporary political relevance of this is, again, unmistakable,
calling to mind Augustus, who also triumphed over the
forces of *furor* in the civil wars and whose accomplishments are thus assimilated to the Trojan myth.

IV. STRUCTURE AND SYMPATHY

So far, so good. But as the poem progresses, this symbolic structure is subtly undercut by the way in which
the reader's sympathies are poignantly evoked. It is no
accident that for many readers the most moving line of
the poem (and also the most difficult to translate) has
always been *sunt lacrimae rerum et mentem mortalia tangunt* (I.462): "Life is full of tears and mortal matters
touch the soul." While, on the structural level, Aeneas'
victory represents the triumph of *pietas* over *furor*, on a
more personal level the reader is emotionally drawn to
those characters whom Aeneas' *pietas* or their own *furor*
destroy—Dido, for instance, in the grip of a pathetic
passion; Aeneas' helmsman, Palinurus, who is innocent

but whom the gods nonetheless demand as a sacrificial victim; and Turnus, whose delusion is nonetheless invested with the nobility of failure. Indeed, reading the battle scenes in the second half of the poem, we are increasingly moved less by the bravery of Aeneas (who, as the fighting progresses, becomes more brutal) than by the pathos and suffering of all those perished youths, Trojan and Italian alike—Nisus, Euryalus, Lausus, Camilla, and Pallas—who capture our imagination not (as some critics have claimed) because of anachronistic and romantic preconceptions we bring to the text but because Virgil by word and image has drawn sympathetic pictures of them.

But then, in the very last scene of the poem, something much darker and unexpected occurs, as the moral structure of the poem, already challenged by our wayward sympathies, is allowed to dissolve before our eyes. Aeneas has finally caught up with Turnus, who surrenders and begs for mercy. Aeneas hesitates, about to grant the suppliant's request. But then he spots on his enemy's chest the shoulder belt that Turnus had stripped as booty from the corpse of Pallas, his ward and the son of his ally Evander. At that moment all humanity deserts Aeneas and he hesitates no longer (XII.945–52=1134–45 Dickinson):

> Aeneas' eyes
> Drank in the sight—emblem of bitter grief.
> His fury [*furiis*] overflowed and in a terrible voice,
> "Do you think to slink from my grasp—you, you
> Clad in the spoils of my friend? It is Pallas, Pallas
> Who with this blow makes you his sacrifice!
> It is he who exacts his vengeance with your blood,
> You accursed fiend!" As he spoke he plunged his sword
> In fury deep into his enemy's heart.
> But as for him his limbs lay slumped and chill
> And his soul flew, resentful of its fate,
> Down to the Shades, with many a sigh and groan.

This passage is disturbing in so many ways, not the least of which is that it ends the epic abruptly, without any sense of satisfying closure. The corresponding scene in the *Iliad*, the death of Hector at the hands of Achilles, does not end that poem. Instead, after the killing, the Trojan king Priam risks his life to beg Achilles to return his son's corpse; Achilles weeps with the old man, relents, and recovers his humanity; and a temporary ceasefire is called to allow both sides to mourn their dead. By contrast, Turnus himself asks Aeneas to return his corpse to his people and that this action does not happen within the poem's time frame is, in a sense, Virgil's way of calling attention to the drastic foreshortening of his poem.

Next, the death of Turnus is, strictly speaking, unnecessary to the plot on either the human or the divine level, since Turnus in the previous lines had already surrendered and since the goddess Juno had already put aside her long-standing opposition to Rome's foundation (XII.808–842=958–1005 Dickinson). In addition, Aeneas' brutality in this scene, though greatly provoked, nonetheless violates important societal and religious norms, such as the expectation that suppliants will be shown respect and the prohibition against human sacrifice. Aeneas also disobeys here the advice that he had received from Anchises in the underworld, advice that pointedly called to mind Augustus' claim to be a man of peace, viz., "to impose upon the nations / The code of peace; to be clement to the conquered. . . ." (VI.851–853=1100–1101 Dickinson).

Finally, and most important, the ending of the *Aeneid* shatters the moral structure of the poem, which had until now depended on the polarity of *pietas* and *furor*. Already undercut by the reader's sympathies, that carefully wrought structure at last collapses upon itself. Aeneas who, until now, had been the champion of *pietas* and had sacrificed all his personal desires to that overarching value, at last surrenders to *furor* and in so doing becomes indistinguishable from his enemy.

V. The Virgilian Achievement

What can this possibly mean? That personal rage is sometimes legitimate, even necessary, to bring about a preordained good? Or that a good man, even one "so patently pious" (I.1.10=13 Dickinson), can succumb at a crucial moment to passion and irrationality? And what bearing does this have on our understanding of Augustus, to whom Aeneas stands in a symbolic relationship? Was the real Augustus the ruthless youth who came to power in a civil bloodbath, or the leader who restored peace and displayed selective clemency? Finally, what bearing does this have on our judgment of Rome, or any other empire, that exerts a profound civilizing influence on its world but does so by abridging individual freedoms and committing unspeakable acts of violence and aggression?

Over the past several decades the interpretation of the *Aeneid* has increasingly turned on this last scene and, in particular, on the recognition that here, as everywhere in the poem, at least two voices are in counterpoint: the public or panegyric voice, which celebrates Rome's triumph, but also the personal or elegiac voice, which laments the human cost of such success.[5] Some critics hear Virgil's authentic voice in the celebratory aspects of the poem, others in the epic's pervasive sense of regret and loss, and still others in a delicate balance—or perhaps we should call it a standoff—between the two. That critics can differ so strikingly on this reflects not only their personal experiences and political beliefs but also the poem's own openness to interpretation.

Indeed, one of the most striking features of the *Aeneid* for a modern reader is its radical indeterminacy. It is not just that, like all great works of literature, it is amenable to multiple interpretations; rather, it goes further and explicitly problematizes its own meaning. Our reading of the poem so far has focused on its personal and political relevance. But the poem also operates at a philosophical level, calling into question what we know and how we know it.[6]

Throughout the poem Aeneas fails to grasp—often through no fault of his own—the full significance of ob-

jects and oracles. Whether neglecting to recognize the
threat implicit in the scenes of the Trojan War on Juno's
Carthaginian temple (they are evidence of her vindic-
tiveness, not of compassion), or hoisting upon his shoulder
Vulcan's shield without understanding the significance of
his gesture or of the images on the shield, Aeneas mis-
reads the world around him. Similarly, confronted with
a surfeit of prophecies that offer a glimpse of the future,
his own and that of Rome, Aeneas either misinterprets
them and makes the wrong decision or the prophecies
are themselves deceptive and he is misled. Faced with
the necessity of reading or interpreting his world, Aeneas acts and (more frequently) is acted upon without
full understanding of the signs around him.

But the same could be said for us as readers. In Book
II, for instance, the Trojan horse is described at one
point as made of fir, but elsewhere of maple, and elsewhere still of pine. Which is it? Or again, there are two
conflicting accounts of the death of Palinurus, the narra-
tor's account of his falling overboard at the end of Book
V and then the victim's own account to Aeneas in the
underworld in Book VI. Which story are we to privilege?
Of course, it is possible to come up with solutions to
these conundrums—different parts of the Trojan horse,
for instance, could have been made up of different sorts
of wood, and the two accounts of Palinurus' death
could be evidence of the poem's unrevised state. But
too many of these problems exist for them to be dis-
missed so easily.

Perhaps the best and certainly most famous example
of this sort of interpretive conundrum is one that con-
fronts both Aeneas and the reader simultaneously, the
status of the prophecy of Rome's future greatness that
Aeneas receives from his father in Book VI. Here, as in
Book XI of Homer's *Odyssey*, the hero descends into
the underworld. But whereas Odysseus encountered the
ghosts of his past life, Aeneas encounters the future, the
major figures of Roman history who are yet to be born.
This is a stirring panorama, and after Anchises delivers
detailed commentary on each individual as well as custo-
mized advice to his son, Aeneas takes his leave of the
underworld. He exits, however, through the gate of ivory,

the gate (Virgil pointedly tells us) through which false dreams are sent to men. What is Aeneas to make of this? What are we?

Here, as in so many other places, the poem puts the reader in the same interpretive bind as Aeneas; the same difficulties he has interpreting his world we encounter interpreting the poem. This aspect of the work—its philosophical (as opposed to personal or political) dimension— is one of the poem's most distinctive characteristics. The *Aeneid*'s resistance to hermeneutic closure enables it to transcend its immediate historical context or political relevance and necessitates constant rereading and reinterpretation. It is in this way that Virgil effectively rivals Homer, whose own epics also transcend (albeit in different ways) the historical circumstances of their composition and engage us continually in reflection on timeless questions about the human condition.

Even though Virgil only rarely intrudes into the impersonal third-person narrative, there is perhaps one passage in which he covertly comments on his achievement. Aeneas learns from Anchises in the underworld that the future Romans' greatest accomplishments will not be intellectual but institutional, that they will excel not in the cultural realm but, rather, in war and governance (VI.847–53=1093–1102 Dickinson):

> And there are others, assuredly I believe,
> Shall work in bronze more sensitively molding
> Breathing images, or carving from the marble
> More lifelike features; some shall plead more
>   eloquently,
> Or gauging with instruments the sky's motion
> Forecast the rising of the constellations:
> But yours, my Roman, is the gift of government,
> That is your bent—to impose upon the nations
> The code of peace; to be clement to the conquered,
> But utterly to crush the intransigent!

Those others who will excel in the visual arts (here represented by bronze and marble sculpture), oratory, and science (here represented by astronomy) are, of course, the Greeks, whose excellence in these areas the

Romans anxiously acknowledged and proudly sought to emulate. What is most striking about this prophecy is that one major art form, Virgil's own, is missing. The absence of literature from this catalogue of Greek achievement subtly suggests that in this area Greece is not supreme, that Rome has at last found a poet to rival Homer. Even allowing for the indeterminacy introduced by the gate of false dreams, it is safe to say that this prediction at least has come true.[7]

—Matthew S. Santirocco

NOTES

1. The correct spelling of the name is Vergil (from the Latin, *Publius Vergilius Maro*). The alternative spelling, Virgil, is an easy linguistic change and was later "explained" by reference to a tradition according to which the poet was a magician (*virga* was a magic wand) or maidenly (*virgo*). The folk belief that Virgil had magical powers derived from the Christianizing interpretation of his fourth or "Messianic" *Bucolic*, in which the prophecy of a birth of a child was taken to refer to the Messiah.

2. For convenient text, translation, and commentary, see P. A. Brunt and J. M. Moore, *Res Gestae Divi Augusti: The Achievements of the Divine Augustus* (Oxford: Oxford University Press, 1967).

3. These works are also known as the *Eclogues* ("Selections").

4. Virgil's contemporary and friend, the poet Horace, discussed these risks in his *Epistle to Augustus*. Augustus was so sensitive to this that he once paid a poet *not* to write about him!

5. The classic exposition of this is Adam Parry, "The Two Voices of Virgil's *Aeneid*," *Arion* 2.4 (1963) 66–80, reprinted in S. Commager (ed.), *Virgil: A Collection of Critical Essays* (Englewood Cliffs, NJ: Prentice-Hall, 1966), 107–23; more recently, see R. O. A. M. Lyne, *Further Voices in Vergil's* Aeneid (Oxford: Clarendon Press, 1987).

6. Particularly relevant to the following discussion are the important studies by J. J. O'Hara, *Death and the*

Optimistic Prophecy in Vergil's Aeneid (Princeton: Princeton University Press, 1990) and, more recently, *Inconsistency in Roman Epic* (Cambridge: Cambridge University Press, 2007).

7. I want to thank the Corporation of Yaddo for the residency during which I completed this essay; Michèle Lowrie, Michael Peachin, and Michael Putnam for sage advice; Tracy Bernstein for her patience and careful editing; and, most especially, my colleague and friend, Marcelle Clements, for stimulating discussion of Virgil and so much else.

SUGGESTIONS FOR FURTHER READING

For an overview of the historical background and also of aspects of Augustan art, literature, and culture, the following collections of essays are useful: F. Millar and E. Segal (edd.), *Caesar Augustus: Seven Aspects* (Oxford: Clarendon Press, 1984); K. A. Raaflaub and M. Toher (edd.), *Between Republic and Empire: Interpretations of Augustus and His Principate* (Berkeley: University of California Press, 1990); and K. Galinsky, *The Cambridge Companion to the Age of Augustus* (Cambridge: Cambridge University Press, 2005); see also Galinsky's own study, *Augustan Culture* (Princeton: Princeton University Press, 1996), and P. Zanker, *The Power of Images in the Age of Augustus*, trans. A. Shapiro (Ann Arbor: University of Michigan Press, 1988).

Among the best short introductions to the *Aeneid* are Commager's edited volume (cited in note 5 above), especially his own introduction and the essays by Clausen, Parry, and Poeschl; W. A. Camps, *An Introduction to Virgil's* Aeneid (Oxford: Oxford University Press, 1969); W. R. Johnson, *Darkness Visible: A Study of Vergil's* Aeneid (Berkeley: University of California Press, 1976); and K. W. Gransden, *Virgil: The* Aeneid (Cambridge: Cambridge University Press, 1990). Particularly influential for the interpretation of Virgil are the many books and articles by M. C. J. Putnam, who has written on all of this poet's works; on the *Aeneid* see especially *The Poetry of the* Aeneid: *Four Studies in Imaginative Unity and Design* (Cambridge, MA: Harvard University Press, 1966) and *Virgil's*

Aeneid: *Interpretation and Influence* (Chapel Hill: University of North Carolina Press, 1995).

Informative collections of essays include: S. J. Harrison (ed.), *Oxford Readings in Vergil's* Aeneid (Oxford: Oxford University Press, 1990); C. Martindale (ed.), *The Cambridge Companion to Virgil* (Cambridge: Cambridge University Press, 1997), N. Horsfall, *A Companion to the Study of Virgil* (Leiden: Brill, 2000); and J. Farrell and M. Putnam (edd.), *The Blackwell's Companion to Vergil* (forthcoming).

More specialized studies of certain aspects of the poem include not only the works cited in the footnotes above but also: V. Poeschl, *The Art of Vergil: Image and Symbol in the* Aeneid, trans. G. Seligson (Ann Arbor: University of Michigan Press, 1962); G. Williams, *Technique and Ideas in the* Aeneid (New Haven: Yale University Press, 1983); K. W. Gransden, *Virgil's* Iliad*: An Essay on Epic Narrative* (Cambridge: Cambridge University Press, 1984); P. Hardie, *Virgil's Aeneid: Cosmos and Imperium* (Oxford: Oxford University Press, 1986); W. Clausen, *Virgil's* Aeneid *and the Tradition of Hellenistic Poetry* (Berkeley: University of California Press, 1987); J. D. Reed, *Virgil's Gaze: Nation and Poetry in the* Aeneid (Princeton: Princeton University Press, 2007); and F. Cairns, *Virgil's Augustan Epic* (Cambridge: Cambridge University Press, 1989).

Finally, there are numerous studies of Virgilian reception. For the influence of Virgil on later Roman epics see P. Hardie, *The Epic Successors of Virgil: A Study in the Dynamics of a Tradition* (Cambridge: Cambridge University Press, 1993). For other periods see D. Comparetti, *Vergil in the Middle Ages* (London: George Allen and Unwin, 1908; repr. with intro. by J. M. Ziolkowski; Princeton: Princeton University Press, 1997); C. Kallendorf, *In Praise of Aeneas: Virgil and Epideictic Rhetoric in the Early Italian Renaissance* (Hanover, NH: University Press of New England, 1989); T. Ziolkowski, *Virgil and the Moderns* (Princeton: Princeton University Press, 1993); and Sarah Spence and Michèle Lowrie (edd.), *The Aesthetics of Empire and the Reception of Vergil*, a special issue of the journal *Literary Imagination*, vol. 8, no. 3 (Fall 2006).

CONTENTS

BOOK I

Of arms I sing and the hero, destiny's exile,
Who came from the beach of Troy and was the
  first
To make the Lavinian landfall, Italy;
Who in the grip of immortal powers was pounded
By land and sea to sate the implacable hatred
Of Juno; who suffered bitterly in his battles
As he strove for the site of his city, and safe
  harboring
For his gods in Latium (himself the father-founder
Of his race, of the Alban chiefs, of the towers of
  Rome).
Then, Muse, remind us what was the root-cause   *10*
Of the goddess's wrath, what had he done that
  a Queen
Of heaven should break, on such wheels of
  disaster,
A man so patently pious? Is it a god's nature
To nurse an abiding fury?
There was an ancient city, a colony of Tyre,
Which stood on the African coast fronting across
  the sea
The mouth of the Tiber and the port of Rome;
A wealthy city, with a war-tempered army,
A city Juno favored of all the world the most,
Her Samos even was second; and here she kept   *20*
  her arms,
And here she kept her chariot, and here,
If the fates allowed, she yearned to see a city
Ruling the world; and in her heart already
She was furthering, fostering this. But she had
  heard

Of a race to spring from the blood of a Trojan lord
That in due time would wreck that Tyrian
   stronghold
And down its throat of empire swallow Libya.
She feared this, Juno, and remembered still
The old campaign against Troy she had prosecuted
30   So vigorously in her affection for Argos.
Rage and chagrin boiled in her breast unabated,
The judgment of Paris rankled as bitterly—
That insult to her beauty, that hated people,
That stolen Ganymede loaded with honors!

So those poor refugees, the remnant left by the
   Greeks
And brutal Achilles, were tossed on the mid-sea
   surges
As she kept them off from Latium: thus for years
They quartered the unmapped water, flotsam of
   fate—
To found the Roman people so titanic an effort
   was needful.
40   Just out of sight of Sicily, full sail with a fair wind
The ships were scudding along, the bright spray
   flying,
When Juno nursing the quenchless wound in her
   heart
Said to herself: "Am *I* to be defeated?
Deprived of my spoil? Am *I* to be impotent
To prevent this Trojan princeling landing in Italy?
Simply because the fates appear to forbid it?
Did not Athene burn the Argive fleet
And drown their sailors, and for no more reason
Than the frenzy of Ajax? Did she not dare, herself,
50   To hurl Jove's instant thunderbolt from the clouds,
Smash the ships, whip up the sea with a whirlwind,
And suck the man up, lightning-struck to the heart
As he gasped out the fire, and impale him on a
   rock-point?
But I who am Queen of heaven, sister and wife
To Jove, must *I* battle for years with a single
Nation? Who will worship me for the future,
What suppliant lay a gift on my failing altar?"

The caldron of her indignation still
Seething, the goddess came to storm-inhabited
Aeolia, native region of raging gales,   *60*
For it is here that King Aeolus holds in thrall
The rampant moaning tempests shackled
  imprisoned
In a colossal cave. In muffled fury
They chafe and rumble in the mountain's bowels
While Aeolus sits, scepter in hand, above
On his high battlement soothing and calming them.
Were he to fail, they would sweep away land and
  sea
And even the vault of heaven itself into thin air!
Aware of this, Jove the King thrust them down
Into subterranean dark, heaped mountains on   *70*
  them,
And over them set a lord whose genius lay
In his power to adjust them to the nicety
Of his King's wishes: and to him it was
That Juno, speaking humbly, made her plea.

"Aeolus, you were granted by the Father
Of Gods and King of men the faculty
Of calming wind and wave. Now listen to me. A
  people
I abominate are afloat on the Tuscan sea,
Bearing to Italy Troy and its conquered Gods:
Now, lash the sea to frenzy, shatter their ships and   *80*
  sink them,
Scatter them utterly, sow the deep-sea furrows
With all their bodies! I have twice seven nymphs,
All beautiful, most beautiful Deiopea,
And for this favor she shall be yours for life
In proper marriage, and bear your family."
Aeolus answered: "Goddess, it is your destiny
To ensue your will; my duty is to obey it,
My kingdom is in your gift, my place at your feasts;
You make me sib to almighty Jove, my dominion
Over storm and cloudburst emanates from you."   *90*
When he had said this he turned his stave over
And dug it into the ribs of the mountain; then
The winds snuffing an outlet, as if in assault order,

Swirled out and swept the land in a hurricane,
Whirled on the sea and whisked it deep to its bed,
From every quarter hurling the breakers
    shoreward.
Oh cries of sailors! Groan of straining tackle!
In a flash the flying wrack had masked the sky
From Trojan sight, darkness swagged on the deep,
100   Thunder shackled the poles, the air crackled with
    fire,
Everywhere death was at the sailor's elbow;
Terror played fast and loose with Aeneas' limbs
And he moaned and lifted his arms to the stars
    in prayer
Crying: "Oh, three- and four-times lucky, my
    friends
Who died in their fathers' sight under Troy wall!
O Diomede, bravest of all the Danaan tribe,
Why could not I have died by your strong hand
There on the plain, where Hector is stretched stark
From Achilles' spear, by huge Sarpedon's hulk,
110   Where the Simois trundles, down its stream,
So many shields and helmets and heroes' bodies?"
But even as his lament poured out, a sudden blast
Howling out of the north struck the sail square
And the waves towered to the stars; the oars
    were smashed,
The bow yawed, she wallowed, and a huge
    mountain
Of toppling water battered her sheer on the beam.
In the bow they seemed to poise on a wave-
    pinnacle,
In the stern the wave-trough gaped to the naked
    bottom
Swirling among the sands. The south wind seized
    three ships
120   And impaled them upon a hidden reef, a ridge
Rising far out to seaward half-submerged,
(The Italians call them The Altars). Another three
The east wind drove to shore and to shallow and
    quicksand—
A pitiful sight as they floundered on the shoals
And foundered under a weltering wall of sand.

A huge sea struck the Lycians' ship with their
    leader
Trusty Orontes; in a flash, as Aeneas watched her,
She was pooped, and the helmsman flung,
    headfirst, overboard.
Three times she spun in the swirl, pinned on the
    vortex,
Then the whirlpool gulped her down its greedy   *130*
    throat.
Survivors were spotted struggling in the waste;
Wreckage of heroes' arms and of Troy's treasures
Bobbed through the waves; and now the storm
    had conquered
Ilioneus' stout vessel and the ship of brave
    Achates,
And now it was Abas', now old Aletes' turn.
The bolts gave way, the seams opened, the sea
Swilled in. But in the meanwhile Neptune
    became aware
Of the storm that had been raised, for the
    surface roared
And the still deep was stirred, and he was
    gravely troubled.
High from the surface he lifted his calm face   *140*
And scanned the ocean. He saw Aeneas' fleet
Scattered about and the Trojans crushed between
    sea and sky
And the hatred and cunning of Juno was obvious
    to her brother.
He called the East and the West wind to his side.
"Have you so great a faith in your birth, O winds,
That you dare to raise this turmoil, this melee
Of land and sea without consulting me, the
    sovereign godhead?
As for *you* . . . But first, it is best to calm
The seas you have raised—when that is duly
    accomplished
You shall pay for your offenses far otherwise.   *150*
Now off with you! And bear these words to your
    king:
The Lordship of the sea, and the awesome trident,
Were not allotted to him. They are my sway.

His to hold the great cavern that is your dwelling.
You Eastern wind, let Aeolus lord it there
In his own halls reigning; in the wind's prison!"
These were his words, and even as he was
    speaking,
The seas fell, the clouds dispersed, and the sun
    came out.
At the same time Cymothoe and Triton
160 Strove to push off the ships from the fangs of rock,
The God himself levered them with his trident,
Opened the huge quicksands, and skimming the
    surface
Calmed all the sea as he drove his gliding car.
And just as in a great crowd where tempers are
    high
And the rowdies are milling and sticks and stones
    are flying
(For rage finds weapons to hand), then if by
    chance
They see some man who has won true respect
They quieten down and are ready to hear him
    speak
And by his argument he will soothe their passion,
170 So fell to silence the tumult of the deep
As the Father of Seas looked out across his
    kingdom,
And then with a cloudless heaven above his head
Gave loose rein to his horses and let his chariot
    rip.

Aeneas and his men, dead-beat, attempted
To make for the nearest shore, and Libya was
    nearest.
There is a harbor there at a long gulf's narrows
Where an island makes a bar against the tide
And divides the flood in navigable channels.
Great rocks, twin crags, lunge upwards to the sky
180 And under their sheer scree is a safe harbor.
Inland a stubble of thick woods threatens darkness
And terrible shadows. But at the foot there lies
A cavern with stalactites and a fresh spring,
Seats cut from the live rock, a nymph's dwelling.

No cable is needed here to moor a ship
Weary of deep sea, no fluke to bite the bottom.
It was here Aeneas came with the seven ships
Spared from his convoy and oh, with what a longing
To foot dry land the Trojans disembarked
And molded the dry beach with their sopping   *190*
  bodies!
Then first Achates struck a spark from his flint,
Caught the dry leaves, and fed the brittle flotsam.
There was warmth; and they brought the mushed
  sea-sodden grain—
Themselves as soaked and mushed, utterly
  downcast—
And the utensils of the corn goddess, as is meet,
And tried to dry the rescued grain by the fire
And grind it in a millstone and make bread.
Meanwhile Aeneas climbed a high lookout to see
If anywhere he could spy more Trojan ships—
Phrygean Antheus with his storm-tossed biremes,   *200*
Or Capys, or Caicus with his tall painted rudder.
There was not a ship on the sea, but on the shore
Three meandering stags and a whole herd
  following them
Spread out in file grazing along the valley.
He took his stance; in a flash his aide-de-camp,
Faithful Achates, handed him his bow
And his speedy arrows, ready for such an
  occurrence.
And first Aeneas sniped the leading stags—
Brow, bay and trey, with antlers big as trees—
Then scattered all the herd and peppered them   *210*
With arrow-volleys among the leafy groves.
He did not cease till he had brought down seven—
Seven prime bodies—one for each of his ships—
Then back to the port and the division of game!
Add this: the wine kindly Acestes stored
For the departing heroes on the Sicilian shore:
This he divided too, and to their gloomy spirits
Offered this comfort:

             "My friends we must not forget
What we have suffered before—and there has
  been worse,

220 But the Gods will grant sometime an end to it.
     You have looked on Scylla and heard her rocks
       re-echo
     Her rabid shrieks—you have passed your pilot's
       ticket
     In the Cyclops straits— Cheer up my friends,
       fear not!
     One day you may look back on these memories
     As pleasant memories. Whatever happens,
     Whatever sort and share of luck we have,
     Our aim is Latium; where Destiny has ordained
     A quiet house: where Troy will rise again
     As it is meet she should; then, friends, endure,
230 Keep yourselves fit for the end, the good days to
       be."
     Such were his words and his face was a mask of
       hope
     That hid the terrible boding in his heart.
     His men prepared to deal with the spoils and the
       feast to come.
     They stripped the pelt off the ribs and laid bare
       the flesh.
     Then some cut it up and spitted the quivering
       steaks,
     Some set up caldrons on the beach and laid fires,
     And all rekindled their spirits with the food
     And, filled with old wine and venison, relaxed
     Outstretched on the grass: and when they were
       satisfied
240 And the feast cleared away, they took to discussing
     Their long-lost comrades, wavering in between
     Hope that they might be still alive and fear
     That they were dead and gone beyond their ken.
     Noble Aeneas brooded over Orontes,
     He mourned Amycus and wondered what awful
       fate
     Lycus had met, brave Gyas or Cloanthus.

     Now all were spent: but Jove himself looked down
     From the height of heaven and saw the sail-
       flecked sea

And the spread of earth and the manifold of its
  people
And his eagle eyes came to rest on the realm of   *250*
  Libya.
And Venus, more grievously concerned even
  than he
As he considered all that was at stake,
Spoke to him through a mist of crystal tears:
"Oh Ruler of Gods and men with laws eternal,
Who wields the terrible thunderbolt, now tell me
What crime have my Aeneas and the Trojans
Committed against you? What can they have done,
Who have suffered so many deaths, and now it
  seems
The entire world is a barrier against
Them reaching Italy, and yet you promised   *260*
In the full course of time the rule of the world
To the Romans, a people sprung from Trojan
  blood.
What has changed your will? For this far-off event
Solaced me, in Troy's wreck—that another fate
Should be balanced against that ruin, yet ruin still
Pursues these ever ruin-hounded heroes.
O God of Gods, when will you grant them an end
Of their sufferings? Consider how Antenor
Slipped through the fingers of the Greeks and
  reached
The gulfs of Illyria safely and the realms   *270*
Of the Liburnians, and Timavus' source—
The stream through whose nine mouths comes
  flooding in
The main with a rock-throated roar and the fields
Are inundated with the surf—and here it was
He founded a colony for the Trojans, and built
The city of Padua, and walls to hang up the arms
Of ancient Troy, and lapped in tranquillity he
  rests there.
But we, your very own kin, and given the freedom
Of the high citadel of heaven at your nod,
Because of the wrath of One are betrayed utterly;   *280*
Our ships lost, cut off from Italy's coast.

Is this the just reward of our piety—this
How you restore the kingdom promised to us?"
Smiling down at her with the smile that calms
A heaven of storms, the sower of Gods and Men,
Kissed the lips of his daughter and spoke to her.
"Have no fear, Cytherean; the destiny of your
    people
Remains unaltered, you shall see your city,
And see Lavinia's walls as I have promised.
You shall bear great-heart Aeneas to the height
Of the highest of heaven's stars.
                 I have no thought
Of a change of mind. But since you are so
    consumed
With anxiety for Aeneas I shall turn forward far
The hidden pages of fate and speak of the future.
He shall conduct a great campaign for you
And conquer all Italy and its haughty peoples.
He shall impose laws on his own people
And build walled cities for them; the third summer
Shall see him rule in Latium, the third winter
Of warfare see the Rutulians subdued.
But his son Ascanius to whom the second name
Iulus is now added (when Ilium stood he was Ilus)
It is he who shall consolidate your power—
For thirty years with all their turning months;
Then shall he move his capital from Lavinium
To Alba Longa, which he shall fortify
To the uttermost; and there a line of kings,
The seed of Hector, for three hundred years
Shall reign and reign till Ilia, a priestess
Of royal blood, bear twins begotten by Mars;
And one of these, Romulus, fostered by a she-wolf,
And joyfully wearing her tawny hide, shall rule
And found a city for Mars, a new city,
And call his people Romans, after his name.
For them I see no measure nor date, I grant them
Dominion without end. Yes, even Juno
Bitter as she has been, who harries heaven,
And land and sea cower under her lash,
Even she will mend her ways and vie with me
In cherishing the Romans, the master-race,

290

300

310

320

The wearers of the Toga. So it is willed.
And an age shall come in the course of measured
    years
When the House of Assaracus shall subdue
Even Phthia and famous Mycenae and conquer
    Argos
And rule there. And then shall be born Caesar
Of the great Trojan line, and his rule shall extend
To Ocean itself, his fame to the last star—
Julius named, and truly, from his forbear great
    Iulus,
And you shall surely receive him safe to your
    bosom,
Welcomed to heaven laden with all the spoils   *330*
Of the East, and men shall invoke him in their
    prayers.
The bitter centuries of war shall cease then,
The world grow mild at last. And white-haired
    Faith,
Vesta, and Romulus with his brother Remus
Shall make the Laws and the grim, iron-bolted
    Gates
Of War shall be closed and within them the fiend
    of Fury
Throned upon weapons lethal as himself
Rage impotently, his arms and his hands pinioned
Behind his back with a hundred brazen shackles,
Roaring from his blood-boltered throat in vain."   *340*

Such was his prophecy, and he sent the son of
    Maia
Down from on high, to ensure that the realm of
    Carthage
With its new citadel should welcome open-armed
The Trojan refugees—for Dido could not know
The design of fate and might summarily expel
    them.
Down flew Mercury winging through the air
And swiftly alit on the Libyan shore and
    immediately
Imposed upon the haughty Carthaginians
The Divine Will and softened their rugged hearts.

350   And most of all their Queen was inspired with
            thoughts
        Of kindness and good will towards the Trojans.
        But steadfast Aeneas spent the night mulling
        His many problems over and soon as dawn
        Offered him light enough he set out to see
        What sort of terrain it was that they were
            wrecked on,
        And whether inhabited, for it looked wild
        And desolate and he was determined to come back
        With some report to his men. (He had concealed
        The ships under an overhang of the cliff
360   In a woody cove shut in with gloomy trees.)
        So off he went with no one but Achates,
        Two iron-tipped spears at the ready in each hand.

        In the midst of the wood he met his Divine Mother
        In the guise and mien of a girl, with a girl's
            weapons,
        Silent as a Spartan—or Thracian Harpalyce
        Outpacer of flagging horse after flagging horse,
        Outpacer of even the racing currents of Hebrus.
        Slung huntress-fashion from her shoulders she
            carried
        A handy bow, and her hair streamed out loose
370   In the wind, her knees were bare, her tunic
            caught up
        Close in a knot. She hailed them, "You, there,
            my lords!
        Have you seen anyone wandering in these parts
        Who might be my sister—wearing a spotted lynx-
            hide,
        With a quiver of arrows—she might be in full cry
        After a wild boar?"—So questioned Venus.
        Aeneas answered, "No, we have seen or heard
        Nothing of any sister of yours. . . . O maiden . . .
        How am I to address you . . . ? For your face
        Is not of earth, nor is your voice a mortal's.
380   You are a goddess. . . . Are you Apollo's sister?
        Or kindred of the nymphs? Whoever you are,
        Be kind, and take the weight off our minds. Tell us
        Where in the world we are? For driven here

At the mercy of wind and sea, we are wandering
In total ignorance of the clime or people.
Tell us, and we will sacrifice to you
Many and many a victim on your altar."
Then Venus said: "I cannot claim such honors.
Any Tyrian girl will dress in a like style
With a quiver and such purple hunting boots.   *390*
But what you see is the realm of the Phoenicians
Who come from Tyre—which is Agenor's city.
The Libyans live on our frontiers, they are fierce
Unconquerable tribes: Our queen is Dido—
She fled here from Tyre—escaping from her
    brother—
But this is a long and intricate tale of troubles—
I will give you the gist of it. Her husband's name
Was Sychaeus—indeed he was the wealthiest
Of all the Phoenician landowners—and Dido
Loved him devotedly, poor girl, she was a virgin   *400*
When given in marriage to him by her father.
But she, alas, had a brother Pygmalion,
Who was king of Tyre, an utterly evil monster.
A quarrel broke out; and then Pygmalion lurked
By the very altar—his impiety blotted out
By his blind lust for gold—and as Sychaeus
Unwarily worshiped, he stabbed him in the back
Without a thought for his sister or her love:
For a long time he kept the murder secret,
And fobbed her off with lies and cheating hopes,   *410*
But then the ghost of Sychaeus, still unburied,
Appeared to her in a dream, his face alight
With a supernatural pallor, displayed his wounds,
Revealed the deed of defilement at the altar
And the whole evil crime within the house.
He bade her fly the country with all speed,
And to that end disclosed a hidden treasure.
Shocked to the marrow, Dido and her friends
Prepared for flight—all whom their fear or hatred
Of the tyrant had united—they seized some ships   *420*
Which happened to be ready for sea—they loaded
The treasure on board—and greedy Pygmalion's
    wealth
Was spirited overseas! And who was the leader

Of all this enterprise? Dido, a woman!
They reached the site where now you will see the
     walls
And citadel of Carthage rising—a new city—
For they bought the land—as much as could be
     encompassed
By a bull's hide, and 'Byrsa' it still is called.
But tell me who are you? Where have you come
     from?
430 And where are you journeying to?"
With a sigh from his deep heart's core Aeneas
     answered:
"Goddess, if I began at the beginning,
If there were time to detail our tribulations,
Evening would fall on Olympus before I had
     finished.
We are from ancient Troy—does the name of
     'Troy'
Mean anything to you?—there is not a sea
We have not traversed—but now we have just
     been wrecked
On the coast of Libya. I am Aeneas the steadfast,
And I bear my peoples' gods snatched from the
     foe,
440 They are with me here in our ships. I am a name
Bandied among the stars and beyond. I seek
My destined land of Italy; there my posterity,
Offspring of Jove, is to be born. With twenty
Ships I launched in the Phrygian sea: my goddess
Guiding and guarding my fate: only seven ships
Shattered by gales from the East have weathered
     the storm.
A beggar, a nameless creature, I probe this desert;
A refugee from Europe, from Asia, I
Am come to Libya, as you tell me it is, and . . ."
450 Venus broke in; she could bear his woes no longer.
"Whoever you are, I do not believe the gods
Abhor your existence, for still you breathe the air
And have reached this Tyrian city. Be on your
     way, now,
Go straight ahead, you will come to the Queen's
     palace.

And I can give you news: the winds have changed
And brought your fleet and all its company here.
If this is not the truth, my parents failed
To teach me the art of augury: look up
At those twelve swans flying carefree in line—
Just now an eagle stooped from a height to harry   *460*
   them—
But now some have landed, some look down as
   they fly
And flock together and flail their wings for sport,
And some go circling round in the height and utter
Cries of delight—so some of your ships already
Lie safe in port and some with port in sight
Crowd on all sail—but as for you, simply
Fare forward where the road leads." So she spoke.
And turning away from him her neck glowed
With hues of rose, and her ambrosial hair
Wafted a heavenly scent, her garment flowed   *470*
To her very feet and her gait revealed her a
   goddess.
As soon as he knew he started after her crying:
"Why did you mock me with these false disguises?
I your son? Oh why are you so cruel?
Why may we not join hands and speak together
As our true selves?" So he upbraided her
As he went his way with Achates to the city.
But Venus enwound them in a swathe of mist
And fold upon fold of cloud, that none should see,
Touch, or waylay them or ask them why they   *480*
   came.
The goddess then took wing to Paphos, happy
To return to her favorite haunt where stands her
   temple
With incense rising from a hundred altars
And fragrance of fresh garlands, ever renewed.

The two meanwhile pushed on where the path led,
Then climbed a hill commanding most of the city
And the rising citadel. Aeneas was amazed
At the grandeur of the buildings—once mere
   hutments.
He marveled at the gates, at the general bustle,

490 At the stone pavements, at the mill of workmen
Laying the walls, uprearing the citadel,
Manhandling every stone.
                            Some were siting the houses
And making the sites with trenches. Others were
    busy
Framing the Constitution and electing leaders.
Some were digging out dockyards, others the deep
Foundations for a theater, some cutting from the
    quarries
Huge pillars to adorn the stage to be.
It was like watching bees in summer tireless
In the flowering fields under the high sun;
500 —And out come the new generation ready to work
And they squeeze more honey into the bulging
    cells
Swollen with nectar, or relieve their loaded
Foragers of their spoils or gather a party
To drive the idle drones from their community;
And the work glows, and thyme and honey-scent
    mingle—
"O lucky people, whose city already rises,"
Aeneas sighed as he looked across the rooftops.
Then clothed in his miraculous sheath of cloud,
He went clean through the crowds and nobody
    saw him.
510 Now, there was a grove in the center of the city
Sweet in its coolth of shadows, and it was here
That the Carthaginians, first freed from storm
    and whirlwind
Unearthed the Token Juno had bidden them
Be sure to seek for, the head of a lively war-horse,
An earnest of prosperity and success
In war, and harvest, for centuries to come.
And there Queen Dido of Sidon bid be founded
An enormous temple, richly enwrought and
    redolent
Of the Goddess's presence; and steps of bronze
    led up
520 To a threshold bronze-inlaid and doorposts bound
With rivets of bronze and great bronze hinges
    creaking

In the bronze doors. And it was suddenly here
That for the first time a pang of hope
Shot through Aeneas and a seed of trust
In the future rooted in his afflicted heart.
For, as he waited for the queen, his eyes
Slowly explored the details of all the wonders
Under the huge roof of the temple, and he
   marveled
At the good fortune of a city that could call
Upon such craftsmen, each expert in his trade.   *530*
He saw a mural of the Trojan War—
And all its battles in order (so world-renowned
Had it become already). There were the Atridae,
And Priam, and their mutual foe Achilles.
He stood and wept: "Achates, is there a place
Left in the world not full of our miseries?
Look, there is Priam! Even here there is
   recognition
Of a man's worth, even here there is compassion
For human fortunes, they are touched by the
   common lot
Of mortal men. We must put off all fear.   *540*
Our very fame will bring us means of safety."
He spoke and sighed and pored on the inert
   picture,
Tears coursing down his cheeks, reliving the
   whole scene
In the depths of his soul. They were back in the
   thick
Of the fight round Pergamus, and the Greeks
   were flying,
The Trojans hot on their heels. There were the
   Phrygians
And, hunting them, Achilles in his chariot
His tall crest waving.

Still weeping he saw next the snowy canvas
Of Rhesus' tent betrayed to Diomede   *550*
As its inmates slept their first deep sleep, and the
   slaughter,
And the warrior steeped in blood, driving away
Their fiery horses to his own encampment,

Before they had tasted a blade of Trojan pasture
Or drunk from the Xanthus— And, oh, there
   was Troilus
Unlucky youth, no kind of match for Achilles—
His weapons lost he lolled from his chariot
Still gripping the reins, but still his horses bolted
And his neck and hair went trailing along the
   ground
560 And the dust was scored by his down-pointed
   spear.
Meanwhile with loosened hair the Trojan women
Beating their breasts in weeping supplication
Were bearing to the Temple of Athene
The offering of a robe, but She was biased,
And held her face averted, her eyes on the ground.
And there was Achilles dragging poor dead Hector
Those three grim circuits round the Trojan Walls,
And, final insult, selling his corpse for gold.
At this Aeneas gave a groan of anguish:
570 The spoils, the chariot, the very body
Of his dead friend, he saw them before his eyes
And Priam stretching out his helpless hands.
Then there he was himself among the chiefs!
There was the battle-line from the Orient
And the standard of swarthy Memnon. Fire-
   eating Penthesilea
Was leading her Amazons with their moonlike
   shields,
In frenzy among her thousands, her naked breast
Clasped in a golden circlet, a war-queen,
A maiden against men, and keyed for the combat.
580 While Aeneas stood in trance with his wondering
   eyes
Riveted on these pictures the stately Queen
Most beautiful in her presence entered the temple
With a great retinue of attendant youths.
—Picture Diana dancing beside the Eurotas
Or on the slopes of Cynthus with a thousand
Oreads gathered from every place—and picture
Quiver on shoulder how she towers above them,
A Goddess of goddesses and Latona's breast
Beats silently with joy. So it was as Dido

Bore herself in triumph through the throng,   *590*
The key to the creation of her state.
Then opposite the threshold, the Goddess's entry,
Under the midmost arch of the vaulted temple
Fenced by her bodyguard she took her seat
On a throne and set herself to dispensing laws—
Assigning her subjects tasks in fair proportion,
Or else by lot—and suddenly Aeneas
Saw Antheus and Sergestus coming in
And brave Cloanthus, the whole body of Trojans
Whom the black storm had scattered and driven   *600*
   off
To other shores. He and Achates were stunned
With joy and fear and longed to seize their hands,
But still they were confused by the mystery,
Still withdrawn in their hollow cloud they waited
To hear what had befallen, where their comrades
Had beached their ships—for this was a deputation
From every ship come to the temple to beg
For clemency and crying aloud for mercy:
They entered and Dido gave them leave to speak.
Then Ilioneus the oldest with calm self-control   *610*
Began to speak: "O queen to whom Jove has given
Leave to found a new city and powers to bring
The savage under the rule of Laws and Justice,
We unhappy Trojans
Driven by every storm across every sea
Entreat you: forbid the firing of our ships;
Have pity on us, we are god-fearing people.
Consider our case more closely. We come not
To wreck or raze your Libyan homes with the
   sword,
Nor loot and carry our loot off to the shore,   *620*
We have no such violent plan, we are not pirates—
It is broken men you see.

                              There is a place,
The Greeks called it Hesperia, a land
With a long history, powerful and prosperous:
The Oenotrians settled there, but we have heard
It is called Italy now, after one of their leaders.
We were carried there when suddenly cloudy
   Orion

Boiled up a storm and wrecked us on hidden
   shoals.
He drove us at the wind's will and the seas',
630 By rock and reef scattered and overborne,
And some few of us finally reached your shores.
But what sort of people are you that you allow
The barbarian usage that we have had? We are not
Even allowed to land, and threatened with death
If we so much as set foot upon your shore.
It may be you have no respect for your fellow
   mortals,
But remember there are gods who are concerned
With right and wrong. Our king was named
   Aeneas,
And no man in the world is finer or more steadfast
640 Or a greater warrior— Oh, if he *is* alive,
If the fates have favored him and he has not gone
Down to the cruel dark—we need not fear,
Nor you regret you were the first to show us
Some courtesy! In Sicily too we have cities
And arms; and a ruler there, Trojan Acestes
Of noble blood. Allow us to lay up
Our storm-wracked fleet and cut ourselves from
   the woods
Timber enough for repairs and boughs to shape
   into oars—
We ask no more, if our king and our comrades live
650 And we are restored to each other, than to sail
For Italy and Latium—there lies our happiness.
But if our king our father lies at the bottom
Of the Libyan sea and we have no chance of
   salvation
And Iulus, our hope for the future lies drowned
   beside him,
We still could make for the Sicanian straits
Whence we began the voyage that has ended here;
We have a welcome there and houses ready,
And Acestes could be our king." So Ilioneus
Finished his plea and the Trojans shouted accord.
660 Then Dido with covered eyes made brief reply.
"Trojans, Oh fear no more! Put by all these
   anxieties!

My kingdom is new; we are in constant danger,
It is imperative to guard my frontiers,
I have no other course. But who has not heard
Of Aeneas, of Troy, of its heroes and their exploits
And the blaze of that great war? We Carthaginians
Are not so obtuse as that, nor so benighted—
Whether you choose famous Hesperia, once
The kingdom of Saturn, or the region of Eryx
And its king Acestes, I will escort you safely   670
And give you stores; or would you prefer to settle
With me in my kingdom here? I give you the
    freedom
Of this city I am building; beach your ships—
I make between Trojan and Tyrian no distinction!
If only Aeneas driven by that same gale
Were with you here—I will send picked men to
    search
Along all the coast and to the ends of Libya
And bid them look for him—he may be wrecked,
And wandering lost in some city or some forest!"

Then lordly Aeneas and brave Achates craved   680
To break from their cloud, and now these words
    kindled
Their spirits to such a pitch that Achates said:
"O Son of a goddess, what burns in your mind?
You see all safe, our fleet and all our fellows:
One comrade is lost—we ourselves saw him sink
In the mid-sea, but all the rest are here,
As your mother said." Hardly were these words
    out
When their surrounding wrack suddenly vanished
Dissolving to clear air. There glowed Aeneas
Shining on head and shoulder like a god,   690
For his mother Venus had graced him with a head
Of translucent hair and the warm radiance
Of youth and eyes shining with gay delight,
Such gloss as artists impart to a fine ivory
Or silver or Parian marble inlaid with gold.
Then suddenly, to everyone's amazement
He addressed the Queen. "I, whom you seek, am
    here!

Standing before you! I, Trojan Aeneas,
Snatched from the Libyan sea! And you, O queen,
700 Alone have pitied Troy in its unspeakable travails
And offered us, the relicts of Greek fury,
Us utterly spent by the batterings of storm
And the twists of Fate, succor and household
    here—
We can never repay such a debt of gratitude
Nor could a Trojan anywhere in the world.
Oh Dido, if there are anywhere any gods
That reward Goodness, if anywhere there is Justice
And an all-seeing Mind that knows the Right
—Then may you be rewarded!
710 What golden age were you born in? What parents
    bore you,
What gods or mortals? While rivers run to the sea,
While shadows sweep along the mountain crags,
While the sky feeds the stars—so long your name,
Your praises and your honor shall endure,
Whatever the land that calls me to its heart!"
His words rang out; he offered his right hand
To Ilioneus, his left hand to Serestus;
Then to brave Gyas, Cloanthus and the rest.
Dido was awestruck first by the hero's aspect,
720 Then by the enormity of his sufferings.
"O Son of a goddess," she questioned him,
    "what fate
Has hounded you, and hurled you on our coasts?
Are you in truth Aeneas whom beautiful Venus
Bore to Dardan Anchises by the stream
Of Phrygian Simois? Why, I remember
Teucer's coming to Sidon, driven to exile
From his own land and seeking a new settlement
With my father Belus' help—it was when my father
Was conquering rich Cyprus for himself.
730 Since then I have known the story of Troy's
    disaster,
And known your name and the Greek princes'
    names.
Even my father spoke well of the Trojans
And wished that he himself had sprung from
    their blood,

Enemy though he was. So come, my friends,
And settle here with us! I understand you,
For I have had ill fortune and sufferings
Like yours before I found this place to rest in.
I am no stranger to sorrows and they have taught
    me
To succor those in misery and distress."
So saying, she led Aeneas into the palace   740
And bade thanksgiving be rendered to the gods
In the temple, and she also gave command
For twenty bulls to be sent to Aeneas' company
Down by the shore, and a hundred bristling hogs,
A hundred lambs with their ewes, in prime
    condition,
And plenty of wine, the god's gift of delight.
Inside, the palace was sumptuously appointed
And in the great hall a banquet was being laid:
Embroidered cloths of marvelous purple, silver
That weighed the tables down and golden vessels   750
Enwrought with the deeds of all the nation's
    heroes
From the remote beginning of their history.

But his father's love disturbed his equanimity,
So Aeneas sent Achates to the fleet
Posthaste to tell Ascanius how things stood
And conduct him back to the city, for all his
    anxieties
Were centered upon Ascanius—and in addition
He ordered gifts to be brought—some treasures
    salvaged
From the wreck of Troy: a cloak that hung stiffly
Because of its gold embroidery—a veil   760
With a pattern of yellow acanthus as a border—
The marvelous clothes that Argive Helen had
From her mother Leda when she left Mycenae
For Troy and her unhallowed marriage bed.
There also was the scepter that Ilione
The eldest daughter of King Priam wielded,
And a necklace of pearls and a two-tiered coronet
Of solid gold and precious-stone-encrusted.
Off went Achates posthaste to the fleet,

770 To carry out his command. Meanwhile the
         Goddess Venus
     Was reviewing in her mind new plans of action
     And this seemed best. Cupid her son, assuming
     His form and feature, must replace the charming
         Ascanius
     And as he gave the presents to Queen Dido
     Inflame her desires and pierce her to the marrow
     With passionate love. (For she could not but
         mistrust
     A palace full of duplicitous Phoenicians).
     The thought of Juno's anger racked her too
     And as night fell her anxieties redoubled,
780 So she addressed Cupid. "My son, my strength,
     My only source of power who even derides
     The Typhoean thunderbolts of almighty Jove,
     I fly to you and beg your divine aid.
     Your brother Aeneas has been brutally storm-
         tossed
     On every sea enflamed by the persistent
     Malice of Juno. You know this well enough
     And often have shared my grief. And now Aeneas
     Lingers and listens to Dido's blandishments
     As she begs him stay—and I am apprehensive
790 Of any part which has Juno's blessing—
     This is a crucial moment, she will not be slow
     To seize her opportunity: I must forestall her,
     I know, and put the queen in such a blaze
     Of passion for Aeneas, she shall be mine
     And no god make her change. Your part is this:
     The boy-prince, at this moment, is preparing
     To go to the city—my best beloved boy—
     (His loving father has sent for him) to bring
     Gifts to the queen that have survived the sea
800 And the fiery last of Troy. I shall lull Ascanius
     Into a deep sleep and spirit him off and hide him
     In the heights of Cythera or at Idalia
     In my holy temple: then it cannot be possible
     For him to be ware of our plot or spoil it in the
         middle.
     Now you, for this one night, must assume his
         features,

His tricks of speech and gesture, his very essence,
(You both are boys) and then when enraptured
  Dido
Embraces you while the feast is at its height
And the wine flowing, and she pins you down
  with kisses
Breathe into her passion unwitting and poison   *810*
  her heart."
Cupid obeyed his beloved mother's commands
And shed his wings and walked in Ascanius' shoes
With relish, but as for Ascanius, Venus
Laid upon all his limbs an all-pervading languor
And bore him on her breast to the high groves
Of Idalia where the soft amaracus lapped him
In flowers and sweet shade-haunting scents.
But Cupid went with the royal gifts for Dido,
Achates leading him, and when he arrived the
  Queen
Had settled herself upon her golden throne   *820*
In the midst of the hall. And then Aeneas the chief
And the Trojan retinue arrived and took
Their places on the purple coverings.
Then servants offered them water to wash their
  hands,
Proffered them bread from baskets and brought
  them napkins
Close-woven and soft. Within were fifty maidens
Whose task it was to see the storerooms stocked
And light the household fires. A hundred others,
And a hundred serving men of the same age,
Were there to pile the food upon all the tables   *830*
And set the wine cups. A crowd of Tyrian guests
Thronged through the festive doorways and took
  their places
On the embroidered seats allotted to them.
They marveled at the gifts Aeneas had brought,
They marveled at Iulus—for Cupid's godhead
Glowed in his features and in the conversation
He feigned for the boy; they marveled at his
  mantle
And the scarf picked out with a yellow acanthus
  border.

Infelix – in-starred

But most of all, now singled out for disaster,
840   Unhappy Dido could not slake her thirst
For gazing upon the boy and upon the gifts—
And gazing only fueled her craving to gaze the
      more.
The boy clung to Aeneas embracing him,
His arms about his neck in an access of devotion
To his pretended father, then made his way
To the Queen's lap. She was obsessed with him,
She had eyes for no one else and her whole heart
Went out to him, and often she hugged him tight—
Poor ignorant Dido! She was not to know
850   How great a god was possessing her, to what cost.
But he kept well in mind the adjurations
Of his Acidalian mother and little by little
Began to expunge from Dido's heart all thought
      of Sychaeus *—First husband*
And tried to arouse to her heart, so long inert,
A living passion; and stimulate her mind
So long a stranger to all thoughts of love.
When they arrived at the first pause in the feasting
The tables were removed and in their stead
Were set great bowls of wine filled to the brim.
860   The palace rang with talk, the voices rolled
Through the long spaces of the halls; lamps hung
From the gilded ceilings and a blaze of torches
Turned night to day. Then it was that the Queen
Demanded a heavy golden cup encrusted
With jewels and filled it full with unmixed wine,
—As was the wont of Belus and every king
From Belus onward. Silence was commanded
Throughout the palace. Then she spoke these
      words:
"O Jove, for you are said to have made the Laws
870   For host and guest, grant that this day may be
A day of rejoicing both for us Tyrians
And for the voyagers from Troy, a day
To be remembered by posterity!
May Bacchus giver of gaiety, may kindly Juno,
Smile on us here; and you, my lords of Tyre,
Grace with your blessing and goodwill this feast."
She spoke, and poured a libation onto the table;

Then having done so, put the cup first
To her own lips, then handed it to Bitias
And chaffed him at his hesitation—then eagerly   *880*
He drank the foaming bowl at a draught and
   drenched himself
From the full golden cup!—and after him
Drank other Tyrian nobles. Then Iopas,
The long-haired bard, took up his gilded lyre—
Mighty Atlas himself had been his master.
He sang of the wandering moon and the toils of
   the sun;
He sang of the making of man and of the
   creatures;
Of rain and fire; of Arcturus and the Hyades
That bring the rain; he sang of the Twin Bears.
He sang why the suns of winter make such haste   *890*
To dip in Ocean, and why the nights are long
And move so slowly.
            The Tyrian nobles gave him
Round upon round of applause and the Trojans
   followed them.
Unhappy Dido stretched the hours of night
With varied talk, drinking long draughts of love.
She plied Aeneas with a stream of questions—
About Priam; about Hector; what were the arms
Aurora's son had worn when he came to Troy;
How many horses Diomede had; how tall
Achilles was. . . . "But come, dear guest," she   *900*
   cried,
"And tell us the whole tale from the beginning—
Of the cunning of the Greeks, of your country's
   ruin,
Of your wanderings—it is now the seventh
Summer of wandering you have had to bear
On all the lands and seas of all the world."

BOOK II

☕

They were all silent then, and every face
Was raptly turned to Aeneas. And now the chief
Began to speak from the eminence of his couch:
"Great Queen, the tale you bid me tell again
Recalls a throe too terrible for speech:
The tale of how the Greeks reduced to ruin
The power of Troy and its empire to be lamented
    for ever.
And I myself saw with my own eyes
The tragedy unfold, and I myself
10   Had no small part in it. In such a recital
Who could refrain from tears? Why even a
    Myrmidon,
A Dolopian, or a henchman of heartless Ulysses
Would weep his fill. And now the dews of night
Are falling fast from heaven and setting stars
Prompt us to sleep. Yet if your eagerness
To learn what ills we suffered and to hear
In brief the tale of Troy's last agony
Be insatiable, although my whole mind blenches
At the remembrance and flinches at the pain of it,
20   I will begin.

                    Broken by war and flouted
By fate and seeing so many years slide by
The Greek Commanders had a horse constructed
With ribs of interlocking planks of firwood.
It stood high as a mountain and Minerva
Divinely inspired its fabrication: the reason
They cunningly put about, which became
    widespread,
Was that this horse was an offering to procure
A safe voyage home. It seems they then drew lots

28

And secretly hid selected troops inside
In its dark void, till its whole huge cavernous belly   *30*
Was stuffed with men at arms.
       Within sight of Troy
Lies Tenedos, an island that in the days
Of Priam's Empire was most prosperous,
And all men knew of it—but now nothing
Is there but the mere bay, a treacherous roadstead:
And thus far sailed the Greeks and hid their ships
On its desolate shore. We thought they had gone
 away
And running before the wind made for Mycenae.
So the whole land of Troy was shed of the load
Of its long agony. The gates flew open   *40*
And oh! What joy it was to wander where
The camp had been and find the whole place
 empty
And the shore quite deserted! Here the Dolopians
Had had their quarter—here relentless Achilles
Had pitched his tent: here were the ships'
 moorings;
Here was the accustomed battlefield.
Some of us stood and gawped at the gift of
 disaster,
The horse for the unwed Goddess Minerva, and
 marveled
At the bulk of the beast. I remember it was
 Thymoetes,
Whether from treachery or because Troy's fate   *50*
Was already sealed, who first encouraged us
To drag it inside the walls and set it up in the
 citadel.
But Capys and several others of saner judgment,
Regarding a Greek gift with the deepest suspicion
And scenting a trap, advised us to pitch the thing
Into the sea, or fire it from underneath
And burn it up or pierce the hollow sides
Of the womb and tear it open. The rest of the
 people
Wavered and plumped for one side or the other.
But there, in front of us all, with a great crowd   *60*
Following at his back, Laocoön thrust

In a heat of passion down from the citadel
And from far off he cried 'My unhappy
    countrymen
What height of folly is this? Do you really believe
The enemy has sailed? Do you really think
Any gift from a Greek is guileless? Have you
    learnt
Nothing from knowing Ulysses? Either the Greeks
Have hidden some men inside this wooden
    monster
Or in itself it is a foul contrivance
70 For overthrowing our walls, somehow designed
To spy into our homes or menace Troy
With its height, or there is some other trick in it.
Whatever it be, I am nothing but apprehensive
Of the motives of Greeks, even as givers of gifts!'
As he spoke these words he lunged with all his
    might
And plunged his mighty spear into the horse's
    body,
Into the tough woodwork of its ribbing
And there it quivered, while a hollow echo
Rang chattering round the curving emptiness
80 Of its cavernous womb and rang and rang again.
If the leaden steadfast will of the gods, if the
    featherweight
Of our human powers had not been set awry,
He would have had us gore and gouge the horse
With swords of massacre, into the Greek ambush,
And Troy would still be a city and Priam's
    citadel standing.

But behold! some Trojan shepherds now appeared
Haling before the King, with a loud clamor,
A stranger with his arms pinioned behind him,
A young man who had thrown himself upon them
90 In eager surrender:—it was his firm resolve
To open Troy to the Greeks—it was either that
Or his own death, and he had the cool resource
To meet whichever befell. The youth of Troy
Came jostling up to peer at the prisoner
Outmocking each other in his mockery.

Now let this one example be the proof
Of the whole pattern of Greek perfidy.
For there the prisoner stood, all eyes upon him,
And seemed in a defenseless dither and let
His panic eyes flicker along their faces *100*
As the Trojans had their stare; and then cried out:
'Alas, alas, is there coign of earth or sea
Anywhere, anywhere, that I could hide in?
I am stretched to the utmost on the rack of
    misery—
What is there left me?—I have no place
    whatsoever
Among the Greeks, and the Trojans pursue my
    blood
With a bitter animus!'

                      This pitiful cry
Chastened our mood and checked our urge to
    violence.
We encouraged him to explain—to tell us his
    nationality;
And what he aimed to accomplish by this essay *110*
Of trusting to surrender. After some hesitation
He seemed to lay his fears to rest and answered:
'Great King I will tell you all, whatever it cost me.
This is the truth: I am Greek; I will not deny it.
That for a start: it may be Fate has wrung
The last drop of its malice out of Sinon,
But never let it be said it has made of him
A cheat or a liar. Never let that be said!
It may be that in some random gossip the name,
Palamedes, has come to your ears, of the house *120*
    of Belus,
A man of untarnished fame in the field whom
    the Greeks
Accused on a trumped-up charge and condemned
    to death,
Though he was innocent, simply because he
    censured
This war—and now he is dead they regret his loss:
I was his kinsman: my father was not wealthy,
And when I was very young he attached me to
    Palamedes

To be his page in war: and while he retained
His royal state and his seat in the Council of Kings
I, too, enjoyed my due of respect and dignity.
130   But after Ulysses in his jealousy
Had worked his crooked will (you know the story)
And removed my master from the world of men,
I was cast down to the dark, my days dragged by
In misery and I ate my unhappy heart out
In fury for the fate of my innocent friend.
I was so crazed I could not hold my tongue
And I kept on swearing that if I had the chance
And ever came in triumph back to Argos
I would avenge him, and my violent words
140   Drew down a storm of hatred on my head.
This was the first step in my downfall; Ulysses
Thenceforward never ceased to harry me
With charge after charge and dropped his sinister
          hints
Among my fellows and deliberately
Planned how to kill me. Nor did he ever relax
Until, with Calchas aiding and abetting—
But what is the point of my continuing?
My story can be nothing but disagreeable.
Why should I waste your time if you lump all
          Greeks
150   Together in one mold? I am a Greek.
What more do you need to hear? You should have
          killed me
When first I said so. It is the very thing
That would please Ulysses, and the sons of Atreus
Would give you a large reward for such a deed.'

This, of course, made us intensely curious
To question him and elicit all the facts—
We had no conception of what wickedness
And cunning art the Greeks were capable.
So he stood there and quaveringly continued,
160   Out of the hypocrisy of his heart:
'Often, because they were wearied by the duration
Of the war, the Greeks intended to abandon it
And beat a retreat from Troy. I wish they had!
But equally often the violence of the weather

Prevented their embarkation and contrary winds
Scared them from going. And especially
When this horse stood completed, with its skin
Of maple-planks, the firmament was filled
With thunderous storm. In our perplexity
We sent Eurypylus to the oracle of Apollo 170
To question it and he brought back from the shrine
This dreadful answer: "Greeks, it was with blood
You appeased the winds on your first setting sail
To Troy, the blood of the maiden Iphigenia;
With blood it is you must buy your passage
      home—
And only the blood of a Greek will suffice for
      payment."
When these words reached the common ear, cold
      fear
Clutched every heart, a shudder of horror thrilled
To the marrow of their bones: on whom would fall
The sentence of Fate? Whom would Apollo 180
      choose?
And now Ulysses propelled our prophet Calchas
Before us all in the midst of a great clamor.
We insisted on knowing how these divine
      directions
Should be interpreted. And already many were
      saying
That I would be victim of the cruel plot
And silently they foresaw the end to come.
But for ten days the prophet would not speak
And kept to his tent, refusing to utter a syllable
That might result in anyone's sacrifice.
At last when he was driven beyond endurance 190
By the persistent hectoring of Ulysses
He agreed to his proposals and made a
      pronouncement
Condemning me to the altar. All the rest
Assented, only too glad that the fate each feared
Might fall on him had fallen, poor wretch, on me.
The day of doom soon came. The sacrificial
Instruments were set ready; the salted meal cakes,
And the ribands to be bound about my forehead,
And then—I am safe to admit it now—I burst

200 From my bonds and snatched myself from the jaws
    of death.
That night I hid myself among the reeds
In the mud of the marsh: they should have sailed
    that night
And I had to think there was just a chance they
    would.
For I had no hope at all I should see again
My dear old homeland, my beloved children,
Or the father I so longed for: and now the Greeks
Will likely avenge themselves on those poor souls
For my escape and expiate my guilt
By taking their innocent lives. In the name of the
    Gods,
210 And the guardians of the truth when it is spoken,
In the name of faith unsullied, if anywhere
Among men there is such a thing as unsullied faith,
I beg you have pity for the enormity of my
    sufferings,
Have pity for one who has borne sufferings none
    should bear!'

For this pathetic appeal we gave him his life,
And our hearts went out to him. Priam himself
Was first to order the man to be set free
From his manacles and shackles and spoke to him
With friendliness: 'Whoever you are, forget
220 The Greeks—they have all gone from here;
Be one of us. Now answer me fully and truly:
What did the Greeks mean when they set up
This huge bulk of a horse? Whose idea was it?
What was their purpose? Has it religious
    significance?
Or is it an engine of war?' The prisoner
With all a Greek's adept duplicitousness
Raised his unfettered palms to heaven and cried,
'You eternal Fires of heaven, Godhead inviolable,
Now bear me witness, and you altars and knives
230 Set for unspeakable deeds from which I escaped;
You holy ribands donned for the sacrifice
I am empowered, by right, to break the bonds
Which were sacred as between me and the Greeks,

I am empowered, by right, to exercise
The hatred they have engendered in my heart
And to disclose their secrets: I am beholden
No more to my country's laws. But it is for you
To keep to your word, you Trojans (if you are
    saved,
And I am your savior and tell you all the truth
And repay you well): do not break faith with me!   *240*
Right from the beginning of the war
The confidence of the Greeks, the sum of their
    hopes
Resided in Minerva— But as for that:
After impious Diomede and Ulysses, fertile
In the invention of new crimes, slunk up
To steal from your hallowed temple the guardian
    image
Of Minerva of Troy, cutting the throats of the
    sentries
Who guarded the citadel, and seized the statue
And dared to defile with hands still dripping blood
The virgin riband round the goddess's head,   *250*
The hopes of the Greeks went ebbing, slipping
    away,
Their strength was broken, the goddess set
    against them.
Nor was there any doubt about the portents
That evidenced her change of mood—for hardly
Was her image set up in the camp when spurts
Of flame flashed from her staring eyeballs, a salty
Sweat poured from her limbs and, miraculous to
    relate,
Three times of its own volition her statue leaped,
Shield, quivering lance and all, clean off the
    ground.
Calchas immediately divined the omen.   *260*
We must take flight across the sea; no longer
Could we expect to capture Pergamus
With our Greek arms: we must return to Argos
And seek renewal of those holy powers
Which brought us here, at first, in our curved ships.
Their present expedition to Mycenae
Is to recruit new forces and a new dispensation

Of the divine favor; then cross the sea again
And fall on you unforeseen: —This was the
    prophet's
270   Interpretation of the omens. As for this effigy,
He advised them to erect it to atone
For the rape of Minerva's image and expiate
The onus of their guilt. It was Calchas too
Who bid them rear the beast to the vast
    proportions
You all can see, plank after plank of oak—
Till it nearly touched the sky, so that you Trojans
Should not be able to get it through your gates
Or hoist it over the walls, and the people again
Live in the tutelage of the old religion;
280   For if your hand defiled this gift for Minerva
A terrible holocaust, he said, would ensue
For Priam's Empire and the Phrygian people—
(Let the gods divert it onto Calchas first!)
Yet if the horse should ascend into your city
With the help of your own free hands, then Asia
    has
Carte blanche to launch an invasion in full force
To the very walls of Pelops—and that would be
The destiny that awaits our Greek descendants.'

Such was the cunning, such was the subtle skill
290   Of the perjurer Sinon that led us to believe him.
There we were, conquered by his tricks and the
    tears
He could summon at will, whom neither Diomede
Nor Larissaean Achilles, nor ten years
Of warfare nor a thousand ships could conquer.
But now another event of a far more terrible
    nature
Was forced on the attention of my poor
    countrymen
And threw their simple minds into further
    confusion.
Laocoön, drawn by lot to be priest of Neptune,
Was sacrificing a mighty bull at the proper altar
300   When suddenly—and I shudder to recall to it—
Two serpents were to be seen swimming across

From Tenedos breasting the calm sea waters
In ring upon vast ring swirling together
Towards the shore. Their blood-red hooded heads
And necks went towering up above the waves,
The rest of their length went thrashing through
     the water
Squirming colossal coils, churning the sea
In a breaking foamy wake—then they made the
     shore,
Their bloodshot eyes ablaze, the flickering forks
Of their tongues playing about their mouths. We   *310*
     scattered
In every direction white with fear at the sight.
But they made straight and purposefully on
Towards Laocoön: and first each serpent
Seized one of his little boys and wrapping itself
In squeezing coils around him snapped and
     swallowed
The wretched limbs. Then as he rushed to their
     rescue
Waving a weapon they seized on him and
     enwound him
In their huge spirals. Twice around his middle
And twice around his throat and still they reared
Their heads and necks above him. He in his turn   *320*
Strove wildly with his hands to wrench at the
     knots,
His priestly garland sodden black with blood
And poison, while his cries of agony
Were terrible to hear as they rang to heaven,
Like the bellowings of a bull when the sacrificial
Ax has not fallen true and he shrugs it off
And bolts away from the altar. But now the
     serpents
Withdrew and glided off to the citadel,
To the temple of implacable Minerva,
And there they disappeared by the feet of the   *330*
     goddess
And behind the round of her shield. And then,
     indeed,
Into every terror-stricken heart a new
And deeper terror struck, and all men said

Laocoön deserved to pay for his crime
Because he had profaned the sacred woodwork
With his spear-point when he hurled his sinful
   spear
At the horse's back. And all began to clamor
For the image to be hauled to its place in the
   temple,
And prayers be said to appease the might of
   Minerva.
340 We breached the walls and opened our defense
   works,
All braced themselves to the effort; under its feet
We inserted rollers to make it easy to move,
And hempen ropes were knotted round its neck.
So the doom-laden engine climbed the walls
With its womb full of death—while round it boys
And unwedded girls went chanting sacred songs,
Thrilled with delight even to touch its ropes,
And on it went and slid to a sinister halt
Right in the heart of our city. O my country!
350 O Ilium home of gods, O Trojan ramparts
The seat of so much glory! Why, four times
On the very threshold of the gates the horse
Came to a stop, four times within its womb
We heard the clank of weapons and we stood
Blind in our frenzy, mindless; then pressed on
And set the baleful horror in position
In our hallowed citadel. Then, too, it was
That Cassandra, whose own deity had decreed
That never a Trojan should believe her words,
360 Opened her lips and prophesied the truth
Of the fate in store for us, while we—poor dolts—
We spent that day (which was to be our last)
In decking every shrine, in the whole city,
With festal boughs.
              Meanwhile the sky turned round
In its course and from the Ocean rose the Night
Enfolding in its single cloak of shade
Earth and high heaven and Greek treachery.
The Trojans, stretched in sleep about the ramparts,
Resigned their weary limbs and made no sound
370 And the Greek fleet in ordered line had already

Put out from Tenedos and was heading straight
For the shore they knew so well, under the friendly
Connivance of the still moon's quietude.
And suddenly, see! from the royal ship the flare
Of a signal, and Sinon under the shelter of Powers
Opposed to Troy crept stealthily to unpin
The pinewood hatch and loose the pent-up Greeks:
The horse stood open; they opened their lungs to
  the air,
And joyfully leapt out of their timber cavern—
Thessandrus, Sthenelus, and ruthless Ulysses   *380*
Slid down the rope they dropped out of the horse;
Then Acamas, Thoas, Neoptolemus
Of Peleus' line and, to the fore, Machaon
And Menelaus and the inspiration
Of the deceit of the horse Epeus, and all made free
To ramp through a city drowned in wine and sleep.
They killed the sentries, they flung wide the gates,
They admitted all their comrades, they all joined
  forces.
It was the time when the first flush of sleep,
That gift of the gods, infuses in mortal souls   *390*
Its balm to ease their frailties; and its onset
Is too ravishing to resist. But in my sleep,
Before my sight stood Hector in utter sorrow,
A torrent of tears, still in the semblance
Of that far day when he was dragged and mangled
Behind the chariot, caked with dust and blood,
His feet still swollen where the thongs had
  pierced them.
Oh! what a grievous sight! alas! How changed
From the Hector strutting back with spoils of
  Achilles
Or flinging our firebrands among the enemy ships!   *400*
His beard was matted, his hair clotted with blood,
And livid upon him all the weals and wounds
He had suffered for his country and our walls.
I thought in the dream I was the first to speak,
As heavily weeping as he, at this strange meeting:
'O light of Troy and truest hope of the Trojans,
What has kept you so long? Dear, longed-for
  Hector

From what clime have you come? After so many
Deaths of your kinsmen, after so many travails
410 Of the folk of our city, we who regard you are
     weary—
What cause unworthy of your powers has branded
The beauty of your countenance, oh why
Do I see these wounds?' He did not answer a
     word.
He took no heed of my vain questions. None.
But heaving a deep half-strangling sigh he said:
'Son of a goddess, oh fly, fly, and escape
From the conflagration: the enemy hold your
     walls!—
Troy from her highest tower is tumbling down,
The end has come for Priam and our country!
420 If Pergamus could be held by any hand
Mine would have held it. But now Troy entrusts
Her gods and her holy ordinances to you:
Take them with you to share your destiny,
Find them a fortress site, and found it, as you
     shall do,
After a mort of wanderings over the sea.'
He spoke and with his very own hands drew forth
The holy garlands, Vesta and her powers,
And the ever-burning fire from the inmost shrine.

Meanwhile from the city cries of agony rose
430 Louder and louder, although my father's palace
Stood back secluded by a screen of trees;
The clamor swelled and the horrible clash of
     combat.
I started out of sleep and climbed to the rooftop
Listening with my ears skinned—what I heard
Was like the sound of sparks that catching a
     cornfield
Are fanned by a fierce south wind; or like the
     roaring
Of a mountain torrent scouring the flooded
     pastures
Felling the ripening crops, the bullocks' labors,
Uprooting woods in its onrush, and up on a crag
440 A shepherd hears in amazed perplexity.

There was no room for doubt: we saw only too
  clearly
The naked treachery of the Greeks. Already
Deiphobus' great mansion lay in a charred
Ruin before the all-mastering might of Fire,
And next to it, Ucalegon's was ablaze—
The broad Straits of Sigeum reflected the fire.
Men shouted, trumpets pealed. Out of my mind,
I sprang to arms—not stopping to reason why—
More than to muster to me a band of fighters
And rally with them to the citadel.   *450*
Rage, fury, mastered me; I had in my mind
No thought but death in battle and its glory!
But see! Where Panthus came escaping the
  Greek weapons,
Panthus the son of Orthrys, the priest of Apollo's
  temple
Up on the citadel, running madly for our doorways
And trailing along somehow his defeated gods
And his little grandson. 'Panthus!' I called to him.
'Where is the core of the battle? Where best shall
  we make our stand?'
My words were hardly out when he sighed and
  answered:
'This is our last day, the final inescapable   *460*
Moment of reckoning for all us Trojans:—
Trojans we were: Troy was a city—once!
We have had our hour of glory: relentless Jove
Has given us over to Argos and all that is ours.
The town is on fire and the Greeks are masters
  of it.
High in the heart of the city stands the Horse
And warriors pour from inside it—Sinon swaggers
His conquering way fanning the flames as he goes.
There are others thronging at the open gates—
As many thousands as came from mighty Mycenae,   *470*
Some are blocking the streets with a bristle of
  weapons
Ready for all who come, their naked blades
Glittering in a murderous hedge of steel.
Only the guards on duty at the gates
Have attempted to fight back, blindly at that.'

I heard these words of Panthus, I felt the
    prompting
Of heavenly powers and plunged into fire and fight
Where the black lust of vengeance led me, where
The din was loudest, and the shouting cracked
    the sky.
480 Rhipeus came to my side, and Epytus
That mighty warrior clattered out of the moonlight
And Hypanis and Dymas and young Coroebus
Added their numbers to my band, Coroebus
Had come to Troy quite lately, as it chanced,
In a rage of frantic passion for Cassandra
And pressing his suit with Priam by bringing help
To the Trojan cause— Poor luckless boy you gave
No heed to the ravings of your bride to be!
Seeing them in a body and ready to fight to the last
490 I addressed them: 'Comrades! bravest of the brave
But all in vain! If you wish with your whole hearts
To follow a man who dares all, even to death,
Then follow me—you see the state of affairs.
Our gods have left us, every one, their altars
And shrines are deserted, the prop and stay they
    gave
To our Empire are no more. The city you go to
    succor
Is a blazing shambles—come then, let us die!
Let us charge into the thick of things—the
    defeated
Have but one hope of safety—not to hope for it!'
500 My words worked on their valor, their hearts
    were stirred
To fighting madness. Then like wolves on the
    prowl
In a black mist of night driven blindly on
By the intolerable pangs of insensate hunger,
Whose famished cubs await them in their lair,
We took the road to certain death among
The enemy javelins making our way straight
To the center of Troy under the dark wing
Of shadowy night—that night! Who could describe
The holocaust, the hecatombs of the dead?
510 An ancient city after so many years

Of pride and power was in her final throes.
The dead lay everywhere about the streets
In moveless mounds—they lay in the houses,
 they lay
On the temple thresholds hallowed for so long,
Nor was it Trojans only who paid the price—
Even in this last hour the defeated felt
New courage surge up in their hearts and Greeks
In the flush of victory fell. And everywhere
Was agonizing grief and terror and death
In a myriad forms.   520
                         The first of the Greeks to run
Foul of us with no small force at his back
Was Androgeus and stupidly he mistook us
For some of his own supporters and called out
A friendly greeting: 'Hurry up, my men,
Why are you late, dawdling along like this?
Pergamus is on fire and others are looting it—
Have you just disembarked from the tall ships?'
He spoke and then immediately realized,
When there was no response, that he had
 blundered
Right into enemy forces. So he recoiled   530
And bit his words back; he was like a man
Who unawares has put his foot on a snake
Among the brambles and starts back in alarm
As it rears up in anger its steely neck.
So did Androgeus tremble at sight of us
And try to retreat. But we rushed in and penned
His men in a circle of steel and being ignorant
Of the ground they fought on they were seized
 with panic
And we slaughtered them: fortune had smiled on
 us
In our first encounter. And here Coroebus cried 540
In the flush of success and his own exuberance,
'Friends, let us take this hint from fortune and
 follow
Wherever she leads and shows herself our ally:
Let us change shields, let us fit ourselves
With Greek equipment: courage or cunning—
Who cares which, when dealing with the foe?

They shall arm us themselves!'—and as he spoke,
He put Androgeus' crested helmet on,
Took up his shield with its noble device and
    strapped
550 A Greek sword to his side. Then Rhipeus, Dymas
And all our youthful company followed suit
In gay good humor—and each armed himself
With weapons stripped from the newly dead.
    And so
We went our way and mingled with the Greeks,
Under auspices not ours, and many the combat
We fought in the blindness of night and when we
    fought
Many the Greek we sent down to the Shades.
Some broke and fled to the ships, hoping for safety
If they could make the shore, some utterly craven
560 Climbed back into the Horse and hid in the belly
They knew already.

                    Alas! it is not for a man
To trust in the gods if they will not accept his trust.
Before our eyes Cassandra daughter of Priam
Was being dragged by her loose-streaming hair
From the Temple, from the very Shrine, of
    Minerva.
She could but yearn up with her flashing eyes,
Her eyes toward heaven; her delicate hands were
    chained.
This piteous sight was too much for Coroebus
And mad with fury he ploughed into the ranks
570 Of the Greeks to certain death—and we all
    followed,
Charging in close order, armed to the teeth.
Now for the first time, from the lofty top of the
    temple
We were subjected to a shower of weapons
From our own side—and the most pitiful
Slaughter ensued—our crests and the shape of
    our arms
Made them mistake us for Greeks. The Greeks
    themselves
Fuming with rage at the rescue of Cassandra
Rallied from every side and set upon us.

Fiercest of all was Ajax, then Menelaus
And Agamemnon and all the Dolopian army—   *580*
It was like the outbreak of a whirl of storm
When the winds clash from every quarter, west,
And south, and east exulting in his team
Of the horses of dawn; the forests crack and
  Nereus
In a whirl of foam lashes the waves to fury
Wielding his trident and stirs up the sea
Right from the bottom.
                        Why, and those very men,
Whom we tricked in the dark and harried through
  the shadows,
And chased all over the city, again confronted us
And they were the first to recognize our trick   *590*
Of shield and weapon, and note that our speech
  was alien.
All was lost: we were crushed by weight of
  numbers.
Coroebus was first to fall—Peneleus killed him
Beside the altar of the Goddess of Arms.
Rhipeus went down, the justest man of us all,
And the most zealous and scrupulous for Right;
(Who knows the canons of heaven? They are
  simply other than men's).
Hypanis, Dymas fell, run through by their
  friends—
Nor, Panthus, could you escape for all the
  devotions
You paid to Apollo and his holy garland   *600*
Bound on your brow! O ashes of Ilium!
O final flame destroying all I loved,
Witness that in your fall I never shrank
From any weapon, from any close encounter!
Had I been marked for death, I earned my death
At the hands of many a Greek!
                           We were separated:
Iphitus clove to me, and Pelias—
Iphitus, slow with age, and Pelias
Maimed by a wound from Ulysses. Drawn by the
  shouting,
We made for Priam's palace, and there indeed   *610*

The fight was fiercest—nowhere else in Troy
Was carnage to touch this or death on such a scale.
We were face to face with naked war and we saw
The Greeks charging towards the house and
     milling
About the entrance, a wall of close-knit shields.
Scaling ladders were reared against every wall
And men were climbing close to the very rooftops
Their left arms thrusting out their shields to
     protect
Their bodies from blows, their right clutching the
     coping.
620 Against them the Trojans tore up roof and turret—
These were the weapons they used instead of
     spears,
In their death throes, so they sought their defense,
And hurled down gilded rafters, ancestral glories,
While some with drawn swords packed the doors
     to guard them.
We felt our spirits lift with our resolve
To help the palace, relieve the beset defenders
And breathe new vigor into vanquished hearts.

At the back of the palace there was a hidden
     postern
Which gave on a passage connecting two wings of
     the household,
630 And often Andromache, poor soul, made use of it
When she went unattended on a visit to Hector's
     family
Or to show little Astyanax to his grandfather.
I went through here and climbed to the rooftop
     where
The wretched Trojans were hurling down their
     weapons
All to no purpose. Now, there was a tower
That reared its height to the stars from another
     house
With a sheer drop, and from it you could see
All Troy spread out below, and the Greek camp
And their fleet beyond. We chopped at it all round

Where the top stories offered gaps in their   *640*
    framework
And we wrenched it out from its eminence and
    canted it
And suddenly down it crashed with a rumble of
    ruin
Tumbling onto the Greeks in widespread havoc.
But others took their place and the hail of stones
And weapons of all sorts never abated.
In the front of the entrance in the very gateway
Pranced Pyrrhus, all a glitter of steel and bronze.
He was like a snake that has come out after a
    winter
Lived underground and bloated from a diet
Of poisonous greenery and now prinks in the light   *650*
And sloughs his skin and rears his head to the sun
Glistening in new vigor and youth renewed,
Flexing the fluid coils of his back and frisking
His three-forked tongue. And with him was
    Periphas,
A huge man, and Automedon charioteer
And armor-bearer to Achilles, and all
The youth of Scyros pressing up to the building
And lobbing firebrands onto the roof. Pyrrhus
Among the leaders with his two-edged ax
Was battering down the door, and cleaving through   *660*
The bronze pins of the hinges: and soon he hacked
A hole through the tough oaken planking turning
The door into a window—the whole inside
Of the house was nakedly exposed and the Great
    Hall.
The ancestral home of the House of the Kings of
    Troy
Lay open wide and standing within the entrance
Its last guard of armed warriors.
                        From within
The stricken palace rose the pitiful sound
Of grief and panic—the desolate cries of the
    women
Echoed from every room: a keen went up   *670*
To the golden stars. The terror-stricken women

Dithered from room to mighty room, and clung
To the pillars in close embrace and kissed them
  with passion.
But Pyrrhus moved inexorably on,
True son of his father Achilles—no bolted door
Nor guard could stem his irresistible onset.
Under a hail of blows the doors collapsed
Both hinge and hinge-post belabored till they
  burst.
Force found its way—the approaches were
  overrun,
680 The guards killed and the Greeks came flooding in
And occupied the building in full force.
They were more violent than a river in spate
That bursts its banks and tumbling over the dikes
In the swirl of its flood water runs amok
Over the cornfields, and over the whole champaign
Sweeps the cattle away and their stalls with them.
With my own eyes I saw Neoptolemus
In his full killing fury, and through the gateway
Stormed the two sons of Atreus. I saw Hecuba
690 With the wives of her hundred sons. And Priam
  defiling
With his own blood the altars whose holy fires
He had lit himself. Those fifty marriage rooms,
The glorious promise of such progeny,
The pillars gleaming with barbaric gold
And proud with plunder,—all sank down to dust.
The Greeks were masters wherever the fires were
  not.

Perhaps you would like to ask of Priam's doom.
When he saw his city fallen, his city sacked,
And the gates of his palace broken down and the
  foe
700 In the heart of his own home, with the trembling
  hands
Of an old man he struggled into his armor,
So long disused, and girded on a sword
He was too weak to wield and turned his steps
Towards a certain death in the thick of the fighting.
In the central courtyard open to the sky

Stood a great altar and an ancient bay tree
Bending above it, and cradling in its shade
The household deities. Hecuba and her daughters
Were huddling here in helpless hope of sanctuary,
Like doves that have dived for safety from a storm,   *710*
And their arms tight round the statues of their
    gods,
But when she saw Priam accoutered in the arms
He had worn as a young man, she cried 'My
    dearest,
My wretched husband, what mazes your mind
To do a thing like this and arm yourself?
Where are you off to? In straits as dire as ours
This is not the help we need, no, not if even my
    Hector
Were still alive to help us: come to us here; this
    altar
Is our defense in common—or let us face
A common death.' She drew the old King close   *720*
And made him crouch beside her, at the altar.
But see, Polites, one of Priam's sons
Escaped from the murderous blade of Pyrrhus,
    fleeing
Through the enemy storm down the long corridors
And crossing the empty courts was lurching
    wounded
And Pyrrhus pursued him like a running flame,
Poised for the kill and all but clutching him,
His spearpoint inches away. At last Polites
Staggered within his parents' sight and there
Before his eyes fell dead in a pool of blood.   *730*
At this old Priam, though death hemmed him
    about,
Could not restrain himself but roared in anger:
'For a crime such as this' he fulminated,
'For such an outrage may all the gods of heaven,
If any still have any sense of Right
And mark such wrongs as these, give you the
    thanks
You merit and pay you back in your true coin—
You that have killed my son before my eyes
And smirched a father's presence with this blood.

740 Not even Achilles whom you lie in calling
Your father dealt with me, his enemy, thus.
He could blush crimson at the dishonoring
Of a suppliant's claims, he returned to me
  Hector's corpse
For burial, he gave me safe conduct back
To my own kingdom!' So the old man cried
And hurled his feeble spear without the power
To inflict a wound and it was fended off
By the ringing bronze and hung there uselessly
From the end of the shield-boss. Pyrrhus
  answered him,
750 'You shall be my messenger, then, to my father
  Achilles
And report all this to him: remember to tell him
Of my disgraceful deeds—how degenerately .
His son behaved. Now die!' As he said these words
He dragged the trembling dotard, slipping and
  sliding
In the pool of his own son's blood, towards the
  altar,
He clawed his left hand in Priam's hair
And with his right he raised his glittering sword
And plunged it in his side up to the hilt.
So ended Priam's fortunes, such was his fate
760 After seeing his Troy fired, his Pergamus flattened,
He who had once been the proud sovereign
Of so many Asian lands and people. He lay,
His mighty body abandoned on the shore,
Head severed from the trunk, a nameless corpse.

Then, for the first time, I was seized with utter
  horror.
The image of my beloved father rose
Before my eyes when I saw the King (for both
Were the same age) breathing his last, his life
Drained by that dreadful wound. I saw my love
770 Creüsa and my house sacked and the fate
I had exposed my little Iulus to.
I looked back, I looked everywhere to see
What forces were with me still. All had forsaken
  me.

In utter exhaustion they had slumped to the
   ground
Or thrown themselves on the fires in sheer despair.
I was alone, alone. It was then I saw her—
Helen the daughter of Tyndareus lay cringing
Silently shrinking into the darkest corner
Of the Temple of Vesta: by the flare of the fires
That lit my ranging steps and my roving eyes   *780*
I saw her: she who was equally terrified
Of Trojan hatred for the fall of Pergamus,
And Greek revenge in fury for her desertion
Of Menelaus, she the scourge alike
Of Troy and her own country, and there she had
   hidden
Her hateful hated self beside the altar.
My blood boiled; I was filled with an
   overmastering fury
To avenge my country and make her pay in full
For the crimes she had committed: was she indeed
To go safe to see Mycenae, land of her birth,   *790*
And Sparta again? And queen it as a queen?
And see home, husband, parents, children—she
With a retinue of Trojan lords and ladies
To wait upon her? And Priam put to the sword
And Troy burnt to the ground and the shore so
   often
A sweat of blood? No, never. To kill a woman
Will never make a name: no fame nor honor
Springs from a conquest such as this—but I
Shall get my due for having blotted out
A sin like this, and executed justice   *800*
Where it was long deserved. And I shall relish
Feeding my fires of vengeance and satisfying
The ashes of those I love! Such were the ravings
Formed on my lips by the ravings of my mind.
But there before me and never before so clear
To my sight, appeared my mother in her grace
And tender beauty canceling the night
With her pure radiance, in all her divinity,
With the same mien and stature as she wears
Among the Heaven-dwellers, she took my hand   *810*
And held me back, enhancing this restraint

With these words from her lips of rose: 'O Son,
What intolerable weight of agony
Can rouse in you such uncontrollable anger?
Why are you frenzied? And where has disappeared
Your love for me? Will you not first attend to
Your father Anchises? where have you left him
   worn
With age as he is? Will you not see if your wife
Creüsa is still alive and your son Ascanius?

820 Everywhere, all around them, are Greek patrols;
They had been dead by now or burnt alive,
Had I not kept them safe. It is not the hateful
Beauty of Spartan Helen you must blame,
Nor even Paris—it is the gods—the implacable
Enmity of the gods that is wrecking Troy
And hurling her empire down to utter ruin.
Look! I will peel off all the glaucous mist
That dulls the vision of mortals in gloom and
   darkness.
But you—fear not to obey your mother's bidding,

830 Follow her instruction. Here, where you see
Masses of rubble and stone wrenched from stone
And a smother of smoke and swirl of dust—
   Neptune
Is prodding the walls down with his mighty trident
And undermining the city's deep foundations;
There Juno in full spate of fury is guarding
The Scaean gate and sword at hip is driving
Reinforcements up from the ships. Oh look
   behind you!
There is Minerva already on her throne
High on our citadel hissing from the cloud

840 Of her Gorgon headdress— There is Jove himself
Nerving the Greeks to a new recourse of courage,
Rousing the very forces of heaven against the
   Trojans.
There is a time to flee, my dearest, to resign
A hopeless struggle—never shall I desert you,
Safe shall I bring you to your father's doorways.'
She vanished into the black abyss of night.
And huge and mighty forms, that do not live

Like living forms, I saw encompassing
The obsequies of Troy.

                    I saw all Ilium
Dissolving in the fires, all Neptune's city   *850*
Toppled to its foundations—like an old rowan
On a peak a gang of farmers hack and hack at
With iron axes trying to dislodge,
Till it begins to shudder; the topmost branches
Quiver and threaten and in the end it creaks
And groans and falls to a final stroke and crashes
Down the fellside and leaves a wake of havoc.
I climbed down from the roof and the goddess
    led me
Safely through fire and foe: the flames withdrew,
The weapons glanced aside.   *860*
                    But when I won
To that old house I knew so well, my father's,
Whom first I wished to bear to a place of safety
Upon the mountains—he refused to come!
He refused to go on living in banishment
After the sack of his city. 'You are young,
Your blood is not clotted yet, you are in the
    fullness
Of your strength and spirit—it is for you to flee.
But as for me if the Heaven-dwellers had wished
To extend my days they would have saved my
    home.
It is enough to have witnessed and survived   *870*
One sack of my city— It is here, it is here
You must leave my members and bid me last
    farewell—
I shall find my death in my own way—the enemy
Will show me pity: graspingly for my spoils.
The lack of a tomb is a thing I can lightly bear;
I have suffered long enough from heaven's hatred,
Long enough have I dragged a useless life out,
Since the All-Father blasted me with the winds
Of his thunderstroke and laid the finger of flame
Upon my body.'   *880*
                He was adamant
For all the entreaties of our tearful hearts—

My wife Creüsa, my son Ascanius
And all the household—though we appealed to
  him
As head of the family not to drag us all
Down to disaster with him and lend his weight
To the doom that hung so heavily already
Over us all. He refused utterly.
He would not budge from the house or change
  his purpose.
So again I prepared to arm myself and in
  desperation
890 Launched on the sea of death—what could I do?
What other course was open? 'Truly, father,
Did you suppose I should up with my heels and
  bolt
And leave you behind?' I said, 'Could a father's
  lips
Let fall a thought so shocking? If the Immortals
Have willed this mighty city to be crushed
To an utter cipher, and if it be your pleasure
To add the deaths of you and yours to Troy's—
That door to death is open wide—yes, Pyrrhus
Fresh from the bath of Priam's blood will be here,
900 The killer of his son before a father,
The killer of that father at the altar.
Sweet mother, was it for this you rescued me
From fire and sword? Simply to see the foe
In the heart of my own home—see my Ascanius,
My father, and my wife Creüsa butchered
In pools of mutual blood like sacrifices?
Come, heroes, bring my arms—it is the light
Of our last day calling the conquered! Get me to
  grips
With the Greeks again, let me go back to the
  battle!
910 We shall not all die unavenged this day!'

So I was strapping on my sword again
And easing my left arm into position
In the harness of my shield and about to sally
Out of the house when at the very doorway

There was my wife and she clasped me by the feet
And held out little Iulus to me, his father.
'If you are going to death,' she sobbed, 'then take
    us with you
To all that may befall—from what you have seen,
If you have any faith in a further stand,
Then make it here protecting your own home!   *920*
To whom else are you leaving little Iulus,
Your father, or your wife—as you called me once?'
The house was ringing with her piteous cries
When suddenly appeared a miraculous portent.
For there between his parents' hands and faces,
As they stood grieving over him, the very top
Of Iulus' head was seen to burst into flame
And glow with a fiery light, that harmlessly
Played round his silken hair and upon his
    forehead.
We in a pother of alarm and hurry   *930*
Shook out his blazing locks and tried to quench
The holy fires with water. But my father
Anchises raised his eyes to the stars in rapture
And stretched his hands to heaven and prayed
    aloud:
'Almighty Jove, if my prayer has power
To bend your iron resolve, look down on us
This one and only time, and if by our piety
We have earned any reward, grant us your help
And affirmation of this omen.'

                                        Scarcely
Had the old man finished his prayer when   *940*
    thunder pealed
Suddenly on the left and a shooting star
Slid down from heaven trailing a brilliant tail
And flashing through the dark. We saw it pass
Over the top of our house and marked the
    gleaming
Course of its flight till it fell and disappeared
In the woods of Ida. Over a great stretch
Of the sky it scored a shining furrow of light
And over the earth a cloud of sulfur smoke.
This sight convinced my father utterly.

950   He made obeisance to the holy star,
He raised himself heavenward, he addressed the
    Gods:
'No more delay, no more! Gods of my country!
I follow, and where you lead there I shall be!
Preserve my house, preserve my little grandson!
Yours is this sign and under your sway is Troy.
For my part I give way, my son. I am willing
To come with you now.'

                    And now we heard the roar
Of the fire grow louder and louder through the
    town
And the waves of heat rolled nearer ever nearer.
960   'Come then, dear father, up onto my back
I will bear you on my shoulders—you will be
No burden to me at all, and whatever befall us,
One and the same peril will face us both
And there will be one and the same salvation!
Little Iulus, you must walk at my side,
And you, Creüsa, follow in my footsteps.
Now you, my servants, attend to what I say:
As you leave the city there is a mound and upon it
An ancient shrine of Ceres long abandoned,
970   And by it grows an aged cypress tree—
For many years our forebears held it in
    reverence—
And here we shall rally—each of us arriving
By different routes. You, father, take in your hand
Our holy relics and our country's gods—
I cannot do so without sacrilege,
Hot as I am from the moil of war and drenched
In the fresh blood of slaughter, till I have cleansed
My body in running water.'

                    Having spoken
I bent my neck and shoulders down and cloaked
    them
980   In a tawny lion-skin, and took up my burden.
My little Iulus clutching my right hand
Kept at my side with his quick little steps.
My wife followed behind. So we set out
Creeping along in the shadows. As for me
Though never till that moment had I flinched

From any weapons the Greeks could hurl against
  me
Nor at the knots of those picked men who barred
My way against me, now a breath of wind
Was enough to scare me, I jumped at every
  sound—
Equally fearful for the load I carried   *990*
And the little thing I led. And now I had nearly
Reached the gates of the city and thought I had
  made
The whole long way in safety when suddenly
We seemed to hear the tramp of hurrying feet—
Feet hurrying our way and my father peered
Through the shadows. 'Son,' he cried. 'Quick
  quick, my son!
They are on us; I can see the glint of shields
And the flash of swords!' What hostile powers
  robbed me
Of my wits in this extremity and stress
I cannot tell, for as I dodged away   *1000*
Out of the streets I knew I lost my bearings
As I fled over trackless country, and Oh, alas:
Creüsa—she was torn from me—what happened
  to her?
Did she stop or stray or sink down in exhaustion?
I was never to set my eyes on her again.
Never had I looked back when first she flagged,
Never gave her a thought before I came
To the mound and the Shrine, such ages dedicated
To the cult of Ceres; here we were all gathered,
But she was not. She was lost to us for ever,   *1010*
Her husband and her son and all her companions.
I went out of my mind, there was not a god,
There was not a man that lacked the lash of my
  curses!
In all the sack of the city, what had I seen
More fraught with agonies unspeakable?
Ascanius and Anchises and the Gods
Of our country I committed to the care
Of my comrades, leaving them in safety hidden
In a curving dip of ground, whilst I myself
Needs must return to Troy. Again I clad   *1020*

Myself in my shining armor. I was resolved
To answer every challenger again, to retrace
My every step through Troy, to expose my life
Once more to every danger. First of all
I sought again the wall where the dark gate
Had let us out and carefully cast my eye
Over the ground and tracked my footsteps back
Through the black night. Everywhere on my senses
Pressed horror, the very silence made me shiver.
1030 Then I turned homeward hoping against hope,
Hoping against all hope, that she had gone there.
The Greeks were everywhere—they had occupied
The entire house: but all was lost for the greedy
Tongues of the hungry fire fanned by the wind
Licked round the roof and mounted ever higher,
And the heat fumed up to the sky. So on I went
And visited the citadel again
And Priam's palace. Here in the empty cloisters,
In Jove's sanctuary, Phoenix and grim Ulysses
1040 Had been set guard and were standing over the
    plunder.
Looted from every burnt-out Temple in Troy
Here lay a pile of treasure—holy tables,
And mixing bowls of solid gold and vestments.
Trembling mothers and little children stood
In a long line beside them. I even dared
To call out through the darkness, I filled the streets
With my unhappy cries—all to no end—
Calling Creüsa! Creüsa! again and again.
As I was combing the city frenziedly,
1050 There before my eyes the unhappy phantom
Of my Creüsa appeared but taller far
Than ever she was in life this image stood.
I was struck dumb, my hair stood on end, my voice
Died in my throat, but then she spoke to me
And calmed my fears: 'Sweet husband, why do
    you choose
To indulge yourself in such extremes of grief?
Not without heaven's cognizance is the scope
Of these present plans. That you should take
    your Creüsa
Upon your journey is forbidden: it is opposed

To what is Right, and the Mighty Ruler of Heaven   *1060*
Forbids you also. You have years of exile
And untold leagues of ocean to plough—but at last
You will come to the Western Land where the
  Lydian Tiber
Rolls softly through the rich acres of rich men.
There you will find happiness and a kingdom
And a royal bride awaiting. Do not weep
For Creüsa your beloved. I shall not suffer
The pride of Dolopian or of Myrmidon
Lording it in their homes; or be the slave
Of some Greek mother. I am Dardan begotten   *1070*
Of the royal blood and my mother was Venus
  divine:
And it is the Mighty Mother of gods who is
  keeping me
Safe in these coasts. And now farewell. Keep safe
In your loving care the son of our own love.'
These were her words and she departed from me
And vanished into thin air for all that I wept
And longed to say so many things— Three times
I tried to fling my arms about her neck;
Three times in vain, the phantom slipped through
  my hands
Like a breath of wind or the fleeting of a dream.   *1080*
So passed the night and I returned to my
  comrades.
When I arrived I found to my amazement
Their numbers swelled by a great multitude
Of new arrivals, mothers and warrior-husbands
And young men, mustered for exile; a pitiful
  concourse.
From everywhere they had gathered, their minds
  made up,
And their resources ready at my disposal
To have me lead them over sea to whatever
Land I might choose. And now the morning star
Was rising over the highest ridges of Ida   *1090*
Bringing the day. In Troy Greek sentries blocked
Every gate of the city. There was no hope of help.
I turned my back, I hoisted my father on it,
And made tracks for the mountains."

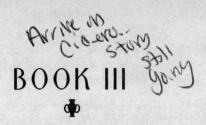
Arrive on
Cicero...
story
still
going

BOOK III

"After the overthrow of the Asian powers
Was seen to be the manifest will of the Gods,
After the overthrow, though they were guiltless,
Of Priam's people and proud Ilium's fall,
And Neptune's Troy was a flattened smoking
   waste,
We were driven on by auguries from the gods
To scour the empty regions of the world
For a home of exile, and beside Antandros
Under the first slopes of our Phrygian Ida
10   We built a fleet,—but where the fates would
   carry us
Or where it would be granted us to settle
We had no clue, but we mustered our men, we
   were ready,
And scarcely had summer begun when my father
   Anchises
Bid us set sail before the winds of fate.
Weeping I left my country's shores and the port
And the plains where once Troy was: I was
   borne out
Onto the deep, an exile with my comrades,
My son, and my household gods, and the Great
   Gods of my people.

In the distance lies a terrain owned by the War
   God
20   And its wide plains are tilled by Thracian
   farmers—
Once it was ruled by the cruel king Lycurgus;
We were bound by ties of friendship and alliance
From times of old, when things were well with us.

60

There was I borne, and on a curving line
Of the coast I chose the site for our city walls—
(An ill beginning as it proved) and named it
Aeneadae, after my own name.
                              I was sacrificing
To Venus my mother and to the other gods
That they might bless the work I had embarked on;
And to the Monarch of all the Heaven-dwellers   *30*
I was about to slay a glossy bull
On the seashore. Now there chanced to be nearby
A mound whose top was thick with a scrub of cornel
And myrtle shoots as stiff and sharp as spears.
I went there and I tried to uproot some greenery,
To grace the altar with a leafy canopy,
When I was met by an awesome and ghastly marvel:
From the first tree I wrenched at, tearing it off
At the roots, blood welled up in black drops
And sullied the earth with its spots. A chill shudder   *40*
Convulsed my body and my blood froze with fear.
I tried again and tugged at the stubborn stems
Of a second tree, to try and find out the cause
Of the mystery. Another gout of blood
Broke from the bark. In a moil of puzzled wonder
I began to pray to the nymphs of the countryside
And Father Mars, the god of Thrace; I besought them
To turn the vision to good and to purge off
The horror of the omen: but when I tried
To uproot the third stem, straining with my knees   *50*
Dug into the sand and my whole body braced
For a greater effort—oh shall I dare to tell
What happened, or keep silent?—from the depths
Of the mound I heard heartrending moans and I heard
A human voice: 'Aeneas,' it cried out, 'why
Must you tear me apart, suffering as I am?
Let me alone, at last, in my grave—stain not
Your innocent hands with guilt. I am no stranger;
I am of Troy—it is Trojan blood you see

60   Weep from that branch. Fly from these cruel lands!
      Fly from these misers' shores! I am Polydorus.
      And here I lie where an iron crop of spears
      First laid me low, and out of my buried body
      Shoot stems as weapon-sharp.'
                             Then indeed I stood
      Dumfounded in a maze of doubt and dread.
      My hair stood up, my voice stuck in my throat.
      For Polydorus it was that luckless Priam,
      When he began to despair of Trojan arms
      And saw the city in a noose of siege,
70   Had secretly despatched, with a great hoard
      Of gold to the King of Thrace—and he when he
        saw
      Troy broken, her power and prosperity
      Melted away, he turned his coat and sided
      With the victorious arms of Agamemnon;
      All laws of Right and Equity were shattered.
      He murdered Polydorus and seized the treasure
      By main force— O accursed lust for gold!
      To what will you not force the hearts of men?
      After that panic had ceased to grip my marrow
80   I summoned my father and a chosen few,
      Acquainted them with this miracle of the gods
      And asked for their opinion. One and all
      Agreed to quit this land of villainy,
      And cut all contact with a place which so
      Had smirched the laws of amicable conduct.
      We must set sail whatever wind was blowing.
      Therefore we reburied Polydorus
      And heaped upon him a huge pile of earth;
      We raised up altars to the Shades below
90   Somber with mourning garlands and black
        cypresses,
      And women of Ilium with their hair loosed
      In customary fashion attended them.
      We offered bowls of new warm foaming milk
      And vessels of consecrated blood and committed
        his spirit
      To rest in its tomb and lifted up our voices
      In last farewell. Then in the first calm spell

When the sea was smooth and a gentle breeze
   from the south
Invited us, our crews hauled down their ships
And the shore was crowded. Then we put out from
   the harbor
And lands and cities dwindled in our wake.   *100*
In the midst of the sea there lies the island of
   Delos
An inhabited and a most holy place,
Well favored by the Nereids' mother and Neptune;
Apollo, the archer-god, had found it drifting
From shore to shore about the seas and had
   moored it
Between the crags of Myconus and Gyarus
And offered it as a fixed dwelling-place
And potent to defy the winds. He did this
In deference to his mother. There I sailed,
And in its sheltered harbors my weary men   *110*
Found gentlest welcome. We landed and paid
   homage
To Apollo's city. Anius temporal king
Of his subjects and at the same time priest of the
   god
Hurried to meet us, his temples wreathed in
   garlands
And hallowed bay-leaves: he recognized Anchises,
His friend of old: we shook each other's hands
In mutual esteem and approached his dwelling as
   guests.
In the temple built of ancient stone I worshiped
And spoke this prayer: 'Grant us, O God of
   Thymbra,*
A home of our own. Grant walls to us weary   *120*
   mortals,
Grant us descendants and an enduring city.
Keep safe for Troy a second citadel—
All that was left to us by the Greeks and brutal
   Achilles.
Who is our guide? Where do you bid us go?

*Apollo.

Where found our home? Father, vouchsafe a sign
And fill our hearts with the knowledge of your
    presence.'

My prayer was scarcely finished when it seemed
That a tremor passed through everything—even
    the door
Of the temple and the bay-tree of the god.
130 The whole mass of the mountain shook, the shrine
Flew open and the hidden tripod tolled.
We flung ourselves face downwards to the earth
And a voice sounded in our ears.
'O Dardan people strong to endure, the land
That cradled first your race, from whence you
    sprung,
That land shall take you to her joyful breast
On your return. Seek for your ancient mother.
From there the house of Aeneas and the sons of
    his sons
And all that are born from them shall hold dominion
140 Over the whole earth.' So spoke Apollo.
There was a great burst of jubilation
And a wild uproar as each man asked his fellow
Where was the walled city? Where did Apollo
    intend
Us wanderers to return to? What did he mean?
Then spoke my father turning his thoughts back
To the traditions of our ancestors:
'Listen, you lords of Troy, and learn where lie
Your hopes. There lies in the middle of the sea
The isle of Crete—the isle of almighty Jove.
150 A Mount Ida is there and the cradle of our race.
The Cretans live in a hundred splendid cities
And the land is very fertile; it was from there,
If I remember rightly what I have heard,
That Teucer, the founder of our people, went
To the coasts of Troy and chose a site for his
    kingdom.
Not yet was Ilium built nor the citadel
Of Pergamus; the people lived in the valleys.
Cybele our Mother Goddess came from this isle
With the ritual dances of her Corybants,

Clashing their cymbals in the Grove of Ida; *160*
From here, the silent awe in which we worship;
And the lions harnessed to her Queenly chariot.
Come, then, and let us follow out the road
The gods have bidden. Let us propitiate
The winds and set a course for the realms of
    Knossos—
It is no long way—if Jove show us his favor
The third day ought to see us touch the shores.'
Such were his words, and standing at the altar
He offered the due sacrifice—a bull
To Neptune, and to you, beauteous Apollo, *170*
Likewise a bull; and a black lamb to the Storm
    Wind;
A white lamb to the gentle westerly breezes.

There was a rumor widely and speedily
Being put about that King Idomeneus
Had been exiled from his father's kingdom of
    Crete;
That we should find the shores deserted and the
    houses
All standing empty and meet no opposition.
So we put out from the harbor of Ortygia
And sped over the deep—we shaped our course
Through racing channels in a sea dotted with *180*
    islands,
By NAXOS where the bacchantes reel on the
    hilltops;
By green Donusa; Olearos; and Paros
White with its marble; by the Cyclades:
And sailor shouts encouragement to sailor
As each bends to his task in rivalry,
'Crete and the land of our fathers! On to Crete!'
A following wind sprang up and helped us on
And at last we glided in to the ancient coasts
Where the Curetes live. Then eagerly
I began to raise the walls of the city we all *190*
So craved for, and I called it Pergamea.
My people rejoiced at the name and I urged
    them on
To love their homes, and erect a defensive citadel.

Our ships were nearly all laid up securely
Above the tide-line, our young men and women
Were busy with marriage and the cultivation
Of their new farms, and I myself was busy
Allotting houses and formulating laws,
When suddenly from some poisonous region of
　　heaven
200 A pestilence fell upon our wretched frames,
A killing blight on man and crop and tree,
And that year death was the only yield we had.
The people died, they surrendered their sweet
　　souls,
Or dragged their wasted bodies just alive,
And the Dog Star shriveled the fields to
　　barrenness;
The grasses withered, the blighted crops denied us
Our sustenance. And then my father urged me
To sail back to Ortygia, to the oracle
And pray for Apollo's pardon and ask the god
210 What term he would set to our weary struggle,
　　and whence
Did he bid us seek for aid in our tribulation
And whither we should direct our course.

　　　　　　　　　　　　　　　　It was night;
And every living creature upon the earth
Was in the grip of sleep. But in my sleep
The sacred figures of the Gods of Troy
Which I had carried off from the midst of the
　　flames
Seemed to appear standing before my eyes,
Clear-cut in a flood of light the full moon poured
In through the window slits, and they spoke to me
220 And with their words relieved me of my cares:
'We are here at Apollo's bidding, he has sent us
Of his own will to your very door to give you
The prophecy he was prepared to give you
If you sailed to Ortygia. Since Troy was consumed
We have followed you and your arms; we have
　　been with you
Through every trough, on every crest of ocean
Your fleet has weathered, and we it is shall raise
Your posterity to the stars and give to your city

Its mighty sway. Do you make ready the walls,
Great walls for the great and do not flinch from   *230*
  the long
And grinding toil of exile. You must move
Your habitation—it was not these shores
Apollo of Delos commended nor did he bid you
Settle in Crete—there is a place the Greeks
Have called Hesperia—the western land—
An ancient country powerful in war
And rich of soil: the Oenotrians once lived there
But now they say their descendants have called
  themselves
"Italians" after Italus—one of their leaders.
There lies your true home—it was from there   *240*
That Dardanus came and Iasius your founder.
Come now, arise, and joyfully repeat
This message true, beyond all doubt of truth,
To your aged father—tell him to seek Corythus
And the lands of Italy.' I was stunned
By such a vision and the divine voices.
For it was not sleep—I was in their very presence,
We were face to face and I saw their braided hair
And the movement of their lips, and a cold sweat
Broke out all over my body. I sprang from bed   *250*
And stretched my hands to heaven and breathed
  a prayer
And poured upon the hearth a libation of
  unmixed wine:
I performed this office and then joyfully
Told every detail of the occurrence to Anchises.
He called to mind then our double pedigree
And the two rival branches of our stock
And saw that he had muddled the location
Of the two ancient countries of our source:
'O my son versed in the destinies of Troy,
Cassandra's was the only voice to foretell   *260*
Such an event to me. I remember now
This was the prophecy she made about our people
And often and often she cried out "Italy!"
"Hesperia! There is our destined home!"
But who could believe in Trojans ever having
To travel to the shores of the Western Land?

And who believed Cassandra's ravings then?
Let us yield to Apollo and being guided by him
Follow a more favorable course.'
270 So spoke Anchises and we all with acclamation
Seconded his pronouncement. So on we moved
From here as we had moved from Thrace, leaving
A handful of our folk behind, and sped full sail
Over the waste of waters in our ships.

When we were truly out on the high seas
And no more land was in sight—when there was
    nothing
But sky and sea and sky wherever you looked,
An ink-black storm-cloud gathered lowering
Over our heads, a brew of night and tempest
280 Whipping the sea to curling crests of darkness.
At once the gusts made all the surface seethe
And the waves rose mountains high. Our fleet
    was scattered
About the heaving deep. Clouds dimmed the
    daylight
And sodden night blotted the whole sky.
Bright tongues of lightning split and split the
    clouds.
We lost our bearings and blindly groped our way
Over the blind waste. Palinurus himself
Could not tell night from day by observing the sky
Nor plot a course in this void of open sea.
290 For three whole days (they were hard enough to
    reckon)
We lurched about in this dank oblivion—
For three whole nights with never a star to guide
    us.
At last on the fourth day we sighted land
With distant mountains and smoke curling upward.
Down came the sails, it was all hands to the oars!
There was no hesitation, every sailor
Pulled with a will, dipped deep in the dark blue
    surface
And made it boil with foam. Saved from the waves,
It was on the shores of the Strophades first I
    landed.

The Strophades—as the Greeks have called   *300*
   them—are islands
In the great Ionian sea and there the appalling
   Celaeno
And the rest of the Harpies have lived since the
   house of Phineus
Was closed against them and they were driven by
   fear
From the tables where they had gorged themselves
   in the past.
No more disgusting monster nor plague more cruel
Nor agent of heaven's anger more dire than these
Was ever thrust up from the Stygian waters.
They were birds with the features of young girls,
   their droppings
Were utterly nauseous, their hands had talons,
Their faces eternally pinched and pale with hunger.   *310*
Here we made landfall and when we entered the
   harbor
We saw rich herds of cattle everywhere
At graze about the plains and goats at pasture
With none to guard them. So we rushed upon
   them,
Weapons in hand, and called upon the gods,
Even great Jove himself, to share our plunder.
Then we spread seats along the curving shore
And addressed ourselves to a delicious banquet.
But suddenly with a horrifying swoop
Down from their mountain eyries swooped the   *320*
   Harpies
With a great clattering of wings and ripped
The feast in fragments and fouled everything
With their filthy contact—they stank revoltingly,
And screeched appallingly—. So once again
We set our tables, moved our altars and kindled
Their fires in a deep recess hidden beneath
An overhang of rock and hedged in by trees
But once again, from a different quarter of sky,
The raucous flock swooped down from their
   hidden lairs
And fluttered round their prey with their hooked   *330*
   claws

And fouled the feast with their mouths. Then I
    commanded
My comrades to take up arms: we must wage war
On the loathsome tribe. Obedient to my orders
They unsheathed their swords, hiding them in the
    grass,
And covered up their shields. Then, when the
    sound
Of their swooping wings was heard along the shore
Misenus blew a trumpet blast from his lookout
High on a rock. My comrades charged and engaged
In a new form of battle—trying to wound
340   These disgusting birds of the sea. But however
    hard
They struck they could not even mark their
    feathers
Nor inflict wounds on their backs—they simply
    escaped
By soaring quickly into the sky and leaving
Half-eaten food and a trail of filth behind.
But one of them, Celaeno, perched on a spur
Of rock, and spoke—a prophetess of woe.
'You have slaughtered our cattle, you have felled
    our bullocks—
Do you mean to make war to justify your deeds,
True kindred of Laomedon? To make war
350   And drive us Harpies, blameless as we are,
From our ancestral home? Listen to me!
Take heed of my words and fix them in your
    minds!
This prophecy the Almighty Father Jove
Imparted to Phoebus Apollo and he, Apollo,
Imparted it to me, chief of the Furies,
And now it is mine to impart the words to you.
Your course is set for Italy. Summon the winds,
They shall obey, to Italy you shall go,
You shall be granted entry to a harbor.
360   But you shall not put one stone upon another
To encircle your fated city with its walls
Before the utmost pangs of ravenous hunger
Force you to gnaw at and wolf your very tables
In payment for your brutal assault upon us!'

So saying she flew off and swiftly fled
Into the wood. My comrades' blood went cold
With sudden dread. They had no more heart to
    fight
But bid me sue for peace with prayers and vows—
Whether these creatures were goddesses indeed
Or vile and disgusting birds. My father Anchises   370
Lifted his hands from where he stood on the shore
And invoked the Mighty Powers—instructing us
In the due ritual for the sacrifice.
'Great gods, forfend this menace; Great Gods
    avert
Such evil case as this, but graciously
Look down on us your faithful worshipers
And shield us from all evil.' Then he bade us
Cast off, uncoil the sheets and hoist our sails,
And they filled with a good southerly breeze and
    we sped
Over the foaming waters where their slant   380
And the pilot chose. And soon there came into
    view
The wooded isle of Zacynthus, then Dulichium
And Same and Neritus' rocky cliffs.
We escaped the rocks of Ithaca, the realm
Laertes ruled, and cursed the land that nourished
Cruel Ulysses. And soon the storm-crowned
    summit
Of the headland of Leucata hove in sight
And Apollo's shrine, the dread of every sailor.
But we were exhausted, it was there we made for,
Cast anchor from our prows, drew up our sterns   390
Along the shore and entered the little town.

So now, beyond all our hopes, we had made port;
We performed our due ritual to the Almighty
And kindled altars to repay our vows.
Then on the shores of Actium we held games
In the Trojan manner—my comrades stripped,
    and slippery
With olive oil they wrestled using the holds
That are traditional with us. We all rejoiced
To have passed safely by so many settlements

400   Of Greeks, to have held the course of our escape
Through such a crowd of foes. Meanwhile the sun
Rolled on through the circuit of the enormous year
And winter brought the ice, and northerly gales
Lashed up the seas. I fastened upon the portal
Of the temple a hollow shield of brass once borne
By Abas, that mighty man, and celebrated
The deed with an inscription: 'Aeneas offers
This armor won from his Greek conquerors.'
Then I bade my crews to their place upon the
    beaches
410   And gave my sailing orders and out we put,
Striking the sea in rhythmic strokes and striving
Each ship with the next in line. Nor was it long
Before Phaeacia's heights sank down astern
And we coasted along Epirus and put in
At Chaonia and approached the high-built city
Of Buthrotum.

              —Here a truly incredible story
Came to our ears: we were told that Helenus,
Son of Priam, was ruling over Greeks
In the cities here—sitting upon the throne
420   Of Pyrrhus, Achilles' son, and having for wife
Andromache—who thus became again
The wife of a Trojan. I was flabbergasted.
I burned with a strange overpowering compulsion
To question my old friend and hear from him
The story of such an astounding train of events.
Leaving the shore and the fleet I was coming up
    from the harbor
At the very time when Andromache, in a grove
Near the city by a stream she had called Simois,
Was celebrating her yearly rites of grief,
430   Her customary sacrifice to Hector:
She was pouring her libation to his ashes
And calling on his spirit by a mound
Of green turf which was empty, but consecrated
To his memory with two altars—she had raised
As a place where she could weep in holy peace.
She saw me coming and wildly she saw me coming
Clad all in Trojan arms and she was shattered
By this fantastic shock, she stiffened, went cold,

Her eyes glazed and she swooned: it was long
  before
She whispered, 'Is it you? Is it truly you?   *440*
Is it real news you bring me? Son of the goddess,
Are you alive? Or if the blessed light
Of life has withdrawn from you, Oh where is
  Hector?'
She burst into a torrent of tears, her sobs
Filled all the grove. She was so beside herself
I had little chance to answer and worked my words
Haphazardly between her bouts of grief.
'Why, truly I am alive, though I pass my days
At the stretch of suffering—but I *am* alive,
No doubt of it—your eyes tell you the truth.   *450*
But, alas, what chance has befallen you—cast down
From such a height of married happiness?
O wife of Hector! Andromache! Has fortune
Blossomed upon you such a second spring
As you deserve? Are you still Pyrrhus' wife?'
With downcast eyes she said in a low voice:
'Supremely happy was Polyxena,
Beyond all others, being doomed to death
By an enemy's tomb at the foot of Troy's high
  ramparts.
She was not chosen to be a slave by lot,   *460*
Or pleasure her master with her captive body!
But I saw our city burnt, I was carried off
Far overseas to suffer the scorn and pride
Of Pyrrhus, Achilles' son, and in my slavery
I bore his child: but soon he turned from me
To lust after Leda's grandchild Hermione
And make a Spartan match—and he fobbed me off
On Helenus—for he too was a house slave.
But Orestes who was still being harried by the
  Furies
And himself in a fever of love for Hermione   *470*
Whom Pyrrhus was now intending to snatch from
  him,
Ambushed and murdered him at his father's altar.
Then, after Pyrrhus' death, part of the kingdom
Was passed to Helenus and he called the plains
The Chaonian plains and the whole realm Chaonia

After the Chaon in Troy and built our Ilium
A citadel on that spur and called it Pergamus.
But tell me about yourself—what wind, what fate
Has blown you here? What god has driven you
480 Onto our shores not knowing we were here?
How is your son Ascanius? Is he alive?
Is he still nourished on the upper air?
He was there with you in Troy— Was he too
    young
To remember now the mother he lost that night?
Does he yet realize whose son he is?
That Hector was his uncle? And, if he does,
Is he inspired with the valor of olden times
And the virtues of true manhood?'
Weeping she plied her questions, weeping and
    moaning
490 Her long and fruitless tears when Helenus
The heroic son of Priam issued forth
From the city walls with a bevy of followers.
He recognized his kindred and joyfully
Conducted us to the gate, his every word
Borne on a flood of tears. As I went onward
I recognized this little Troy—its Pergamus
Built to resemble its magnificent namesake;
Its Xanthus, a dry rivulet—why, indeed,
There was a Scaean gate and I embraced it!
500 My Trojan comrades, one and all, were made
Free of the friendly city—the king received them
In a spacious cloister—and there in the midst of
    the hall
They poured libations to the god of wine
From the bowls in their hands, and found a
    banquet set
On plates of gold.

              And now day followed day;
And the winds wooed our sails, the canvas bellied
In the warm southern airs. So I approached
King Helenus (he was a seer) and put these
    questions:
'O Trojan-born, interpreter of heaven,
510 You know the true godhead of Apollo,
His tripods, and his bay-tree there at Clarus;

You know the signs in the stars, the tongues of
  the birds,
And can divine the secrets of their flight.
Come, speak (for I have been fostered on my
  voyage
By happy auspices and all the gods
Have urged me with all their powers to make for
  Italy,
And to make trial of those remote domains,
Save only Celaeno the Harpy who foretold—
It is a sin even to speak of the horror—
A monstrous portent and bitter tides of wrath   *520*
And famine beyond imagination) tell me,
  therefore,
What dangers must I principally avoid?
What precepts must I follow to overcome
The tremendous tasks ahead?'

                Then Helenus
First by the ritual sacrifice of bullocks
And by prayer besought the clemency of the gods,
Then loosed the garland from his sacred brow
And took my hand, Apollo, and led me straight
To your temple-door in an ecstasy of possession,
And opened his sacred lips, priest that he was,   *530*
And made this prophecy. 'Son of the goddess,
Beyond all doubt it is clear that you plough the
  deep
With the good will of the Great Powers:—for so
The King of the Gods ordains the lot—events
Go forward at his behest, such is the order of things—
I shall reveal to you only a few of the many
Truths I am free of: such as will make your passage
The safer through alien waters and securer
Your homing to an Italian harbor—the Fates
Either forbid me knowledge of the rest   *540*
Or Saturnian Juno forbids me utterance.
First, as to Italy which you imagine close,
And ignorantly think a voyage direct
To one of its harbors a simple matter—No!
For you the way is far over seas uncharted
And leagues of coastland. First you must ply
  your oars

In Sicilian waters, your ships must cross the expanse
Of the Italian seas, you must pass by
The Infernal Lakes and the isle of Aeaean Circe
550   Before you can find safe land to found your city.
I shall tell you the signs: so keep them clear in
      your mind.
When in a time of anxiety you find on the bank
Of a remote river under ilex trees
A huge white sow stretched out along the ground
That has just farrowed thirty piglings all
As white as she—there is the site for your city,
And rest assured from all your length of labors.
And do not blench at the thought of being reduced
To gnawing at your tables: the fates will find you
560   A way out—so will Apollo if you invoke him.
But you must shun the lands along this shore,
This coast of Italy washed by the ebb and flow
Of our own waters: for every city-fortress
Is inhabited by Greeks. Here Locrians
From Narycium have built—here Idomeneus
Of Crete has pitched his camp and occupies
The Sallentine plains—here is little Petelia,
The base of Philoctetes the Meliboean,
With its bastion-wall. But when you have crossed
      the sea
570   And your fleet lies at anchor—build your altars
And offer prayers of thanksgiving on the shore.
Swathe your head in the folds of purple robes
Lest while at worship, and the holy fires
Still ablaze, some prying eye should see you
And annul the holy sympathy of spirit:
Let all your comrades too observe this custom
And your descendants keep it in their rubric
Of their purest observances.
                              Now, when you depart
And the wind bears you close to the coast of Sicily
580   And the narrows of Pelorus open wider,
Make for the shore to port though it means a long
And circuitous route over open waters—avoid
The land and sea to the starboard. Long ago
This region suffered the throes of a ruinous
      earthquake

And its unbroken mass was torn asunder
(So great a power to encompass change
Has the long lapse of centuries). The sea
Poured violently between and with its current
Severed the Italian from the Sicilian side
Thrusting the narrow tongue of its racing tide   *590*
Between fields and cities sundered now for ever.
To starboard Scylla lies athwart your course,
To port Charybdis the insatiable
Who three times in a day swills down huge waves
To her vast whirling maw, then hurls them as high
And stripes the stars with spray. But Scylla lurks
In the hidden gloom of a cavern whence she
    thrusts
Her hungry mouth and sucks ships onto the rocks.
She is human to the waist, a maiden with
    beautiful breasts,
But below she is all sea-monster with dolphin tails   *600*
Growing from wolfish bellies. Take my advice:
Accept the long and tedious grind you must make
To double Cape Pachynus in Sicily,
Better it is than to look once more where the
    monster
Scylla skulks in her cave and the rocks yelp
With her deep-blue dogs. And add to this, if
    Helenus
Has powers of divination, if you give
Any credence to his prophecy, if his well
Is brimming with the truth of Apollo, listen;
O son of the goddess, one particular thing   *610*
There is above all else, one absolute obligation
You must fulfill—of paramount importance—
And let me repeat this warning again and again:
You must worship mighty Juno; it must be Juno
Above all others to whom you offer your prayers—
Placate her; submit your *will* to her; win her
By every means of piety and honor:
For only so may you successfully
Leave Sicily behind and head for Italy.
When you have finally reached there you must visit   *620*
The city of Cumae with its ghostly lake
Among the whispering glades above Avernus.

There you will see a prophetess in trance
Who from the hollow depths of a cavern intones
The decrees of the Fates, and commits her
    prophecies
To leaves—and all the runes that she has written
She puts in order and stores them secretly
In her cave—and there they stay, unmolested, still,
    in order.
But if the hinge be turned and a breath of air
630 Ruffle or rustle them, if the opening door
Disturbs their thistledowny sequence, the
    prophetess
Is never afterwards concerned for a single instant
In catching them as they drift about the cavern
And reassembling them coherently.
Inquirers, therefore, go away unanswered
And curse the sibyl and her seat of prophecy.
Now I adjure you, however your comrades chide
    you,
However fair the wind blows for your voyage,
Let no delay, no loss of time prevent you
640 From visiting this prophetess and you must persist,
You must badger her until she answers you,
Of her own free will, in her own utterance!
Then she will tell you of the nations of Italy,
The wars that you must fight and how to escape
Or withstand the shock of every trial to be.
She will grant you a prosperous passage if you
    revere her.
These are the counsels which I am permitted
To give in answer to your prayers—go!
Exalt great Troy to heaven by the glory
650 Of the deeds you do in her name!' So spoke the
    seer
And then in kindness of heart he ordered gifts
To be carried to our ships, great ingots of gold
And carven ivory; he crammed into our holds
A weight of silver and caldrons from Dodona,
A cuirass of chain mail three-plied with threads
Of gold and a splendid helmet coned and crested,
The armor of Pyrrhus once. And there were
    particular

Gifts for my father. He also furnished us
With guides and horses; rearmed our company
And filled our emptying benches with new   *660*
    oarsmen.

Meanwhile Anchises bid the fleet up-sail,
Determined we should not miss a favoring wind;
And dutifully Helenus, priest of Apollo,
Addressed the old statesman with profound
    respect:
'Anchises, counted a fit mate for Venus,
Anchises for whom the Gods had special care,
Whom twice they saved from the fall of Troy—see
There is the land of Italy—make all sail!
But first you must take your course and sail
    straight on—
It is on the further coast of Italy   *670*
Apollo intends your landing—Go!' he cries,
'Glad in the gift of a son so dutiful!
But why do I go on? I keep the winds
In custody while I talk!'

                                    Adromache
Was no less sad, now it was time to go,
And no less generous—giving Ascanius
Garments with designs in golden thread
And a Trojan cloak, and as she heaped on him
These gifts of woven raiment she said to him:
'Take these, my darling, take these gifts as well,   *680*
To remember me by, and what my hands can do—
A memento that Andromache, wife of Hector,
Offered you love. Oh my dear, take these last
Presents from your own kindred, all that is left
Of my own lost boy Astyanax—you are his age—
And your hands, your eyes, your face, are so like
    his—
His every movement was so like yours—had he
    lived
He would be just your age.' I left them there,
My own eyes blind with tears and said to them,
'Live happily, prosper long, your perils are past,   *690*
You have won your rest; but we must face our fate,
Blow upon blow—you have no wastes of sea

To traverse as we have, no land of Italy
Ever receding as we seem to approach it,
Your eyes feed on your make-believe River
   Xanthus,
On a Troy your own hands have built— A Troy
With happier hopes and no more fear of invasion
And Greek destruction—if ever I reach the Tiber
And the lands on its banks and see at last
700   The city-walls my people are promised—then
We will make two kindred states, two mutual
   cities,
One in Epirus, one in Hesperia,
With Dardanus our common founder and both
With a common history—we shall be Troy, one
   Troy.
Let our descendants preserve this faith in
   common!'

We sailed to sea holding a course that took us
Close by the Ceraunian headland whence the
   distance
Over the water to Italy is the shortest.
Meanwhile the sun set and the mountains were
   shrouded in darkness.
710   So we put in to shore, and a watch on the oars
Was drawn by lot, and the rest of us were glad
To stretch ourselves on the lap of kindly earth
Close by the waterside. And scattered about
On the dry sand we eased our weary limbs
And refreshed our bodies in the balm of sleep.
But night, in its passage of hours, had not yet
   reached
The middle of its cycle when Palinurus,
Who was ever watchful, arose and cocked an ear
For a wind from any quarter: he marked the
   movement
720   Of all the stars as silently they wheeled
Across the silent sky: there was Arcturus,
There were the Hyades that augur rain,
There the two Bears; and as his eye ranged round
He marked Orion on his arms of gold.
He satisfied himself that all was calm

About the sky, then standing up on the stern
Gave the signal to embark, so we struck camp,
Resumed our voyage and spread the wings of our
   sails.
And now at the first blush of dawn when the stars
Were put to flight we saw dim hills in the distance   730
And a low coastline, 'Italy!' Achates
Was the first to shout it out; then a cry of joy
Broke from my comrades, 'Welcome, Italy!'
My father Anchises twined a garland round
A mighty bowl and filled it with pure wine
And standing up in the high stern he made
This invocation: 'Gods of land and sea!
Powers that rule the storms, look kindly upon us,
Give us a fair wind, a breath to speed us!'
In answer to his prayer the breeze freshened,   740
A harbor opened its arms as we drew nearer
And on the heights a temple of Minerva—
My comrades furled their sails and swung inshore.
The harbor had been eroded into an arc
By easterly seas and lay concealed within
Projecting cliffs dripping with salt spray;
The temple lay well back above the tideline.
Here on the meadowgrass I saw four horses
Cropping the pasture—they were white as snow,
And the first indication of heaven's will.   750
My father Anchises then pronounced these words:
'Strange land, it is war you offer—it is war
These horses are equipped for—it is war
These creatures threaten. But it is also true
That these fourfooted creatures can be trained
To draw a chariot yoked in harmony
And happily harnessed—so there is also hope
For peace!' And then we offered up our prayers
To the holy goddess Minerva, the weapon-clashing,
The first to welcome us in our first flush of   760
   rejoicing.
We stood before the altars our heads muffled
In Trojan cloth and with due ceremony
Paid homage to Argive Juno in accordance
With Helenus' insistent admonitions.
We did not linger; as soon as our vows were paid

We swiveled our yardarms so that our sails could fill
And left that region being chary of anywhere
That Greeks inhabited. Next in its bay we saw
Tarentum—the city, if the tale be true,
770   That was visited by Hercules, and, opposite,
Lacinian Juno's temple reared its glory
And the fortress of Caulonia and Scylaceum
Where ships are wrecked. Then, far away in the
    distance,
Rising out of the sea, Sicilian Etna;
And we heard the melancholy mighty roar
Of the sea shattering on rocks, and a jangled
Noise from the shore, and then saw the waves
    leap up
And the smothers of sand in the turbid maelstrom.
My father Anchises cried, 'This is Charybdis,
780   The dreaded Charybdis without any doubt.
Those are the frightful rocks that Helenus
Forewarned us of. We must keep free at all costs,
Comrades! Jump to your oars and pull together!'
They did as they were bidden and the first
To force his roaring prow to port and out
To open water was Palinurus—and after him
The whole fleet followed, straining oars and sails.
On the crest of the wave we seemed to touch the
    sky,
Down in the trough we wallowed deep as Hell,
790   Three times the rocks rang back their hollow echo,
Three times we saw the sky through sheets of spray
And a screen of lathered foam. We were exhausted,
We were bereft of wind and the sun deserted us—
Our course was lost and we ignorantly floated
To the shores of the Cyclopes. There is a harbor
Spacious indeed and free from the winds' onset
But Etna is close by, rumbling and erupting
With terrible destruction and now and then
Thrusts up to heaven a cloud of utter blackness,
800   A whirling column of smoke and molten ash ·
And puts forth tongues of flame to lick the stars.
And now and then it vomits rocks which it roots
Out of its very bowels and with a roar
Whirls lumps of white-hot stone into the air

And seethes to its inmost base. The story goes
That the body of Enceladus who was blasted
By a thunderbolt lies crushed under the bulk
Of mighty Etna which is piled upon him
Breathing out flame from its erupting fires,
And that as often as, from weariness,   *810*
He turns his body over to his other side,
All Sicily quakes and groans and draws a pall
Of smoke over all the sky. That night we lay
Hid in the woods and having to endure
The weirdest manifestations—but we could not
See what produced the sound—there was no starlight,
No heaven glittering with its bright array,
But the firmament was filmed with a murk of cloud
And the night confined the moon in a cell of storms.

Just at the crack of dawn the following day   *820*
When the first rays had made their way among
The dewy shadows of the height of the sky
There suddenly burst from the woods a fantastic figure—
A strange man, shaggy and starved to a skeleton,
Who stretched his hands towards us and the shore
In supplication. We looked him up and down.
His state of filth was appalling, his beard straggled,
His clothing held together with thorns. But still
It was clear he was a Greek who in his time
Had been to Troy in the campaign and worn   *830*
The country's arms. Poor fellow, when he saw
Our Trojan garb, our Trojan arms, from afar
He checked for a moment in sheer terror—then
Dashed for the shore in a volley of entreaty:
'I implore you by the stars, by the gods above
And the light of heaven we breathe, take me away!
Oh Trojans, take me to any land you choose:
That is all I ask. I know, I admit I sailed
With the Greek fleet, I confess to making war
On your Trojan homes. And if my crime was such   *840*
That I deserve it, scatter me in pieces
And drown me deep in the sea. If I am to die,
To die at the hands of ordinary men

Will be a source of happiness.' So he pleaded
And clung to our knees and cringed. But we
   encouraged him
To tell us who he was, from what race he came,
And the fortunes that had been meted out to him.
After a little pause my father Anchises himself
Offered his hand to the young man—a gesture
850 Which reassured him greatly so that at last
He laid aside his fears and spoke these words.
'I come from Ithaca. I was a comrade
Of the ill-starred Ulysses and my name
Is Achaemenides—I am the son
Of Adamastus, a poor man, whom I left,
To.sail for Troy. Oh, how I wish we had let
Things be as they were—and I was marooned here
In the huge cave of the Cyclops—my friends
   forgot me
In their panic haste to escape from its murderous
   threshold.
860 Inside it is dark and enormous and revolting
From its bloody orgies—the Cyclops is so gigantic
He towers to the stars (Gods, keep the world
Of men from such a monster!). He is hideous
To look upon, nor can his mind be moved
By human speech. He feeds upon the entrails
And the dark blood of his unhappy victims.
With my own eyes I have seen him snatch up two
Of our number in his colossal hand and brain them
Upon a rock without the need to move
870 From where he lay. I have seen all the floor
Awash with spurting blood. I have seen him crunch
Their limbs up dripping with dark blood
And their joints warm and twitching still as his jaws
Closed over them. But he did not go scot-free:
Ulysses was not the man to brook such deeds,
Nor did his great resource fail him in such a crisis.
For as soon as the Cyclops, sated with food and
   drink,
Sagged down in drunken stupor and sprawled his
   length
Over the cave with his neck bent, and retching
880 As he slept gobbets of meat and wine and blood,

We offered prayers to the Powers and then drew
   lots
For our places in the action, then as one man
We thrust in to surround him and with a sharp
Weapon jabbed out his eye—his one huge eye
Sunk deep in his frowning forehead and as big
As an Argive shield or the very sun of Apollo.
So we avenged with relish the ghosts of our poor
   comrades.
But you, poor people, fly, oh fly! cast off
Your ropes from the shore—there are a hundred
   other
As huge and hideous Cyclopes as this   890
One Polyphemus who pens his woolly flock
And milks them in the spaces of his cave,
And they live all along this curve of coast
And stride about the mountain-tops. It is now
For the third time that the moon is filling her horns
With light, and for so long have I eked out
My days in the woods among the desolate
Lairs of wild beasts and in terrible trepidation,
Keeping a watch on the huge Cyclopes
From behind a rock and shivering at the tread   900
Of their feet and the sound of their voices. I
   have fed
On what I could gather from the branches—berries
And stony cornel-seeds—I have rooted grass up
To allay my hunger—I have kept constant watch,
But yours are the first ships I have seen put in
   here.
Whatever the outcome might be, I decided
To trust myself to you—it would be enough
If I escaped this execrable race—
Rather than them—I would let you take my life
With any death you choose!'   910
                 He had scarcely ended
When we saw Polyphemus mountainous
As the mountain whence he was driving down his
   flocks
To the familiar shore—a ghastly monster,
Repulsive, huge, and his one eye put out.
To guide himself and steady his steps he had

A pine-tree he had trimmed into a staff.
His fleecy sheep accompanied him—his sole
Delight and solace in his evil case.
After he had felt for and found the sea,
920 He waded out into the deep and groaning
And grinding his teeth he washed away the blood
That dripped from the socket of his put-out eye,
Then he strode through the deeps of the sea but
    the water
Never reached his towering thighs. In our alarm
We took aboard the suppliant—he deserved
His rescue—and stealthily we cut our cables
In a flurry of departure and flung ourselves
Onto our oars and raced each other seaward.
He was aware of something and turned his steps
930 In our direction because of the sounds we made,
But he had no scope to lay his hands upon us
Nor could he hunt us clean through the Ionian,
So he raised a gigantic roar and the whole sea
Shuddered through all its depth and Italy trembled
To its midland core, and Etna bellowed too
Through all the winding systems of its caverns.
Now the whole tribe of Cyclopes was raised
And rushed from the forest and the mountain
    heights
Down to the shore: and there we could see them
    standing
940 Each with the baleful menace of his eye.
But impotent to harm us, a grim gathering
Of towering heads, this brotherhood of Etna,
Like oaks that point to the sky or coniferous
Cypresses in a mountain forest of Jove's,
Or in a grove of Diana. Terror-goaded
We hoisted sail whatever way we could,
Freeing the sheets to any wind that blew,
Oblivious of our course. But Helenus
Had bidden us otherwise: he had given us warning
950 Not to hold on a course that took us through
The narrows of Scylla and Charybdis—a passage
So close to death and destruction either side,
So we decided to put about: but suddenly
A north wind rose from over Pelorus Head.

We skirted Pantagia's rocky river mouth
And the bay of Megara and low-lying Thapsus.
Achaemenides named these places for us
As he retraced the course of his wanderings'
When he was sailing with ill-starred Ulysses.
Stretching in front of the Sicanian bay   960
Plemyrium lies, an island which in old times
Was called Ortygia, with its ruff of surf.
The story goes that Alpheus, river of Elis,
Thrust through the sea his invisible currents here
To join Sicilian waters, Arethusa,
At your own mouth—and here in obedience
To the command we worshiped the High Gods.
Then we passed by the rich soil of Helorus
Built on its marsh and round the jutting rocks
Of the headland of Pachynus. Camerina   970
Which, said the oracle, must never be moved,
Came next and the plains of Gela, and Gela itself
Grim Gela mocked by the name of its laughing
    stream.
Acragas on its hill with its high walls
Seen far and wide, that was once a breeding place
Of bloodstock; then with favorable winds
I left Selinus with its palms and threaded
My way through the hidden rocks by Lilybaeum;
From there I made the port of Drepanum—
Oh, without any joy in memory: 980
For here, after such batteries of storm,
Alas, my father died, my dearest Anchises,
My prop and stay who had lightened my every care;
You left me lorn and weary, best of fathers
Saved from so many dreadful perils, in vain!
Among the appalling catalogue of travails
The seer Helenus foretold was never
Never this grief—nor did that foul Celaeno.
This was my last disaster—this the term
Of my long wanderings—from there it was   990
The gods, on my departure, drove me here."
So did the chief Aeneas tell the story
Of his voyagings at the behest of Heaven
And every face was fixed intent upon his,
Till at last he ceased, his saga at an end.

BOOK IV

But the queen so long distraught with her load
    of anguish
Yet fed it with her heart's blood, all the time
Being consumed within as with a bog fire. But still
    the aspects
Of her hero throbbed and pulsed back to her mind.
His noble blood and state, his face, his voice
Were branded upon her breast, forbidding sleep.

The Nymph of the new day was gilding earth
    already,
Dawn loosing their dewy mantles from the Poles,
When Dido, almost out of her wits, sought
10 Her sister, whose instinctive sympathy
Was never-failing, and said

                                "O Anna, sister,
What dread terrors hold me sleepless? Who *is* he?
This new guest sown and rooted in our midst—
So brave his bearing, such his strength and
    prowess,
How can I see him but as a god? And truly
I see him so. Fear is a mark of ill breeding;
But he has told us of his harrying by the fates,
And war to the utmost limit of endurance. . . .
Were my mind not made up, if I had no wish
20 To keep the vows I swore to my first love
Whose single infidelity was with death,
If I had not lost the inclination to marry,
It may be I would give myself this once
To this man. I tell you Anna, never
Since Sychaeus died, never since the household
    gods

88

Dripped with my brother's murder has anything
Had power to rouse my soul from its torpor—to
   impel it—
Yes! I feel again some trace of love's first fires!
But oh! Let the earth gape open to its core,
Let God Almighty dash me with thunderbolts   30
To the darkness, the blank of hell, to uttermost
   night,
Before I lie with another man and break
My vows to the man I married. He has my heart,
It is his to hold, it is his alone—let him keep it
There in the tomb. . . ."

                She faltered, her voice failed;
Her gathered anguish burst in a flood of tears.

Anna said, "I love you more than the light,
You poor lonely darling, but must you mourn for
   ever
Your frozen youth, refuse the joys of children,
And the comforts of a bed—do you really think   40
The dead, the dust and ashes, care at all?
Ages ago, in your grief, you rejected them all—
Whether from Tyre or Libya, all those princes—
You loathed Iarbas and every other chief,
Though glutted with the riches of Africa.
Why struggle now against a love you want?
Think where we are; in whose territories we have
   settled.
One side there is Gaetulia, unconquerable in war,
The Numidians on the rampage all around us;
The Syrtes hostile to shipping, and inland   50
The dry throat of the desert, where the Barcae
Range in their violence; there is war fermenting
   in Tyre,
Pygmalion is threatening—perhaps it was
For this very reason the Trojans were blown here,
If the gods favor us and Juno fosters our cause.
O Dido! What a city, what a kingdom
Could swell from such a husband—to what heights
Of power would Carthage rise with Trojan aid!
First ask the Gods for grace and if you get it,
Exploit this visit! What patterns of delay   60

Cannot you weave from winter and Orion's
Tempestuous light on the lifting sea and the ships
Straining and shaken and the sky lowering?"

These words set fire to Dido. Her chastity melted
In a furnace of desire and she made up her mind.
So first they went to the shrines and sought
    placation
From every altar according to the rubric.
They sacrificed a sheep to Ceres the Lawgiver,
To Phoebus, to the Father, but primally to Juno
70   Whose province is the sanctity of marriage.
How beautiful Dido was, the cup in her right hand
As she poured the libation down between the
    horns
Of a milk-white cow—before the gods were alive
To their heaped altars, she had hallowed the day
With gifts, and into the riven breasts of the beasts
She peered with parted lips in divination
Of the quivering live-yet entrails. Alas for the
    purblind,
The sycophantic seers! What oaths, what shrines
Can minister to a mind diseased? The fires
80   Slinked mining through her marrow, the tacit
    wound
Sucked inward from her breasts. Unhappy Dido
In frenzy staggered and reeled through the whole
    city,
Like a wild doe in the mountain groves of Crete
A shepherd has shot at a venture, at long range,
And does not know his lucky shaft has stuck
And the flying barb clings like a burr in its
    wound—
And through the woods and plains of Dicte it reels,
The deadly weapon fast in its dying flank.

Now she paraded Aeneas the length and breadth
90   Of the city, displayed Sidonia and all its wealth,
Opened her lips to speak, halted in mid-word,
And as the day wore on she yearned for yesterday
And its banquet, and wildly begged to hear the
    story

Of Troy again and hung on every syllable
Of the twice-told—thrice-told tale. Then he had
  gone.
She was alone in the occluding moonlight,
The glittering stars invited her to sleep but still
She patrolled the empty house and groveling lay
On the couch he sat on; though he had gone she
  saw him,
She heard him still; she fondled young Ascanius,   100
So like his father she pretended he was,
And vented on him the love she could not speak.

Half dead at the top the half-built towers stood,
The young neither paraded nor built defenses,
Everything now hung fire, the threat of the walls
  and these engines,
Was like an empty frown on the vacant sky.

As soon as Jove's belovèd wife divined such a
  turmoil
In Dido's heart and realized neither her vows
Nor fear for her repute stood as a bar
To this overriding passion—she, Saturn's daughter,   110
Approached Venus and said: "I congratulate you!
I have reason to! You and your boy have got
Reward enough—it is a nine-day wonder
When one poor mortal woman is overcome
By the conspiring of two gods! But I am not so
  blind
To your concern for my Carthage and its walls.
Very well, then. What is to happen? What is the
  outcome?
Why not make peace? Will you not then
  accomplish
All that you had a mind to, by a marriage?
Dido is made with love to the mid-marrow;   120
Let us two rule this people together, then;
Let her be slave to a Trojan husband—yes!
And make her Tyrians over—to you, for dowry?"

Venus saw perfectly well the guile in her mind—
How she hoped to fend that Kingdom of Italy

Off to the Libyan shore. She saw this, but she said:
"Would anyone be so mad as to refuse?
Choose *you* to fight?—So long as good luck stems
Out of your proposals?—I am the fool of Fate.
130   If Jove has willed the city to be the Tyrians',
In league with the Trojans, if indeed he approves
Them joined in treaty . . . if . . . who am I to
    tell . . . ?
It is your office to test him with entreaties:
Try. I shall follow you." Queen Juno answered,
"It is my office. And how we shall accomplish it
I briefly propose to tell you: here and now.
Aeneas and unhappy Dido plan
To hunt tomorrow in the woods as soon
As the sun is up and the earth bathed in its beams.
140   I shall loose on them, from above, a cloud
Heavy with hail and shaken up with thunder.
Their comrades shall disperse, as if benighted.
Then Dido and Aeneas shall take shelter
In the same cave. I shall be there. I needs
Must have your help to count on; there I shall
    join them
In bodily love, and pronounce it lawful marriage,
Their Hymeneal Day." Then, smiling, Venus
Nodded assent, aware of Juno's sleight.

Meanwhile the dawn from its ocean bed had leapt
150   And the young chivalry went through the sunrise
    gate
With wide-meshed nets, close snares, and iron-
    tipped spears.
The Massylian huntsmen jogged with their pack
    of hounds.
But the Carthaginian nobles lagged at the threshold
Of their Queen who lingered still within her
    chamber
While her own charger, purple-and-gold
    accoutered,
Stamped and champed at his slavered bit. At last
With all her retinue she emerged swathed
In a Sidonian purple-bordered chlamys.
Her quiver was gold; her hair broidered with gold,

A clasp of gold retained her purple robe.   *160*
Happy Iulus and the Trojans followed;
Aeneas last, most handsome of all the rout,
Grafted himself to the morning cavalcade.

v. rjl doesn't say when switching took place

simile

Just as Apollo leaves his winter quarters,
In Lycia where the River Xanthus flows,
To visit Delos, dwelling of his mother,
And there inspires the Spring Rites; and the
    Cretans,
Dryopes, and painted Scythians dance,
And the god strolls upon Mount Cynthus binding
His flying hair with a wreath, and interweaving   *170*
Fillets of gold to hold it firm, and his armor
Rings on his shoulder, so Aeneas strode
No less inspiring—no less an effulgence flowing
From his princely mien; so to the woods they went,
The heights, the trackless terrain, and saw the wild
Goats hurtle down from pinnacles of rock
And rattle away—and there went the flushed stags
Full tilt across the open, trailing their gathering
Dust cloud, down from the heights, rushing away!
There, young Ascanius, fresh as his horse,   *180*
    delighted
To pelt along the valleys overtaking
Now one, now another hunter, eagerly hoping
Among such feeble game for a rough customer—
A wild boar or a red-gold mountain lion.

But soon black mutterings trepidated the sky,
A line-storm lashing hail gathered and flashed,
And Trojan and Tyrian helter-skelter scattered
Seeking whatever cover they could, in terror.
Dido, Aeneas, together alone found shelter
In the same cave.   *190*

description of storm, hunting

                    The Gods, Primeval Earth,
And Juno convenor of marriages give their signal;
The lightning streaks; they couple; the skies
    shudder;
The vault of heaven feels that mortal surge;
The nymphs from their hilltops shriek the cry of
    Hymen.— *male god of marriage*

Day of disaster and woe; first day of doom!
But Dido was oblivious—she has no care
For her name or her repute nor feels the amour
A furtive one—she conceives it to be "marriage"
And hides her deed of shame behind a word.
200   Then Rumor ripped through all the cities of Libya,
What is more foul? more swift? Rumor that
      feeds on
Speed and bloats in her going—at first, minute,
From fear, but soon swelling—swelling—swollen
With every wind and treading the earth baring
Her head to the clouds and still goes growing—
      growing—growing.
Earth bore her, people suppose, an ugly sister
For Coeus and Enceladus, to spite the gods.
Swift-foot, foul-wing, a monster to appall
With an eye under each feather—and a tongue
210   (Believe who can) and a mouth and an ear pricked
Under each feather and every single one.
Midway between earth and sky she flies by night
Whispering, hissing, and never a wink of sleep;
By day on the peak of a house or a high tower
She perching puts whole cities on the sweat,
So potent a champion of the lie she is
So steadfast against truth.   .

And so from mouth to ear from mouth to ear
Her tattle went with no respect for truth.

220   *"Aeneas, they say, is a prince of the Trojan blood,*
      And Dido our lovely queen, oh she'd marry him,
      She is good enough for him they say, and all the
            winter
      Letting their kingdoms go to pot, idling, fiddling
      There in the palace, lapped in luxury and
      Of course you know what they do. . . ." these lies
            the creature
Poured in all ears, and in the end she came
After how many twists and turns to King Iarbas:
Rage drove him frantic, as it was bound to do.
Iarbas, son of Almighty Jove and a nymph
230   The god had raped on Garamantis, —Iarbas

Had built a hundred temples to the god
In his wide domains and at a hundred altars
Had kindled watch-fire sentinels for the gods.
Now, roused to frenzy by the bestial rumor,
The thresholds flowering with votive garlands,
The altars wet with sacrificial blood
And fruitful tilth, he is said to have gone on his
    knees
A suppliant with every godhead round him
And prayed with upraised hands:

"Oh God Almighty for whom the Moors feasting   *240*
On painted couches pour libation now:
Look down upon me! When you hurl thunderbolts,
Do we cringe for nothing? Are those fiery
    rumblings
That terrify our souls no more than drunken
    belches?
Here is a woman. She strayed into our dominions
And founded a meager city—at a price.
We granted certain leaseholds. She disdained our
Offers of marriage—but makes Aeneas Master
Of her city and herself and now with his mincing
    minions
Like Paris with a Maeonian coif keeping his chin   *250*
    up,
With his crimped hair, he lords it over his leman—
And she gives him everything:—and all we do
Is worship in due obeisance and all we give is
Rumor its head."

                    Great Jove heard him praying,
Grappling the altar in his agony.
Then he turned his gaze upon the royal walls
And the oblivious lovers and summoning Mercury
Gave him this ukase:
"Come now, my lad! Rally your winds and glide
On your quickest wing down to this Trojan Prince   *260*
Who dallies in Carthage there and has no care
For the cities fated for him. Speak to him,
Bear my words through the quick air; acquaint him
That he seems not of such mettle as his beautiful
Mother promised and by her promise twice

Saved him from Greek swords. And if he indeed
    should be
That man ordained to be king of an Italy
Pregnant with lands to win by war, and rule,
And pass the blood of Teucer on unblemished
270 And bend the world to his laws—if he be that man,
Yet no ambition spurs him nor desire
To see himself renowned for his own deeds—
Even so—would a father's love begrudge
Ascanius his due, the Roman inheritance?
What is he doing? In hope of what does he loiter
Among a hostile tribe? Has he no respect
For his Ausonian stock nor the fields of Lavinia?
Let him set sail! That is all. My message be
    delivered!"

Mercury leapt to obey the Great Father's order.
280 First he bound his golden sandals on
Which, winged, carry him high over land or sea
With the same despatch. Then he took up his
    wand.
With this he can summon a spirit up from Orcus,
Can post another down to Tartarus,
Give or withhold sleep, open the eye after death;
With this cleave cloud, dog-drive the wind. Now,
Volplaning down he saw the summit and flanks
Of grumly Atlas who upholds the heavens
With his head, whose locks of pine are shrouded
290 In circlets of black cloud and bristle with wind
    and rain.
Snow cloaks his shoulders, rivers pour in spate
Down his cold chin, his beard is daggered with ice.
Here Mercury folded his wings and rested; from
    here headlong
He dived to the wavetops like a cormorant
That round the shores and round the fishy rocks
Flies low along the water; and when first
He landed upon his winged feet among
The suburbs—there was Aeneas building
Towers and houses. He had a jeweled sword
300 That gleamed with jasper—he glowed in Tyrian
    purple—

Dido had given them to him. The mantle hung
  from his shoulders
Embroidered with rich designs of golden thread.

Unroman
via
overdressed

Mercury speaks to him without preamble:
"Aeneas! laying out for your mistress a great city
Here at Carthage! you forget, it seems,
Your kingdom, your destiny! Now Jove Almighty
The absolute monarch of the Gods has sent me,
He who holds heaven and earth in the palm of
  his hand,
Has sent me from Olympus not unknown.
It is his behests I bring through the quick air.   *310*
What are you doing? In hope of what do you loiter
In Libya? If no ambition spurs you, nor desire
To see yourself renowned for your own deeds—
What of Ascanius, earnest of your line?
The realm of Italy, the Roman inheritance
His due, and—"
                in mid-sentence he vanished clean;
Into air, into thin air, he disappeared.
Cowed by this apparition, terrified Aeneas
Was dumb; his hair stood on end; his tongue clove;
He burned to escape, to quit these lotus-lands;   *320*
Thunderstruck with this stark ultimatum
From the god of gods. Oh God, what can he do?
With what words mollify the queen's fury?
His quick mind ran through the possibles of the
  possible.
Then he decided. He sent for Mnestheus,
Sergestus and bold Serestus: *Prepare the fleet*
For sea secretly; rally the sailors armed
To the shore; give no reason for this new move.
(Dido knows nothing—how should she believe
Such love could be broken? There will be a time   *330*
And he will pick the time and mood and mode.)

They were delighted to obey—but the queen
Raw to the least pain was quick and aware—
(Who can trick a lover?) She felt the first
Wave of the flood to be; though seeming-safe
But fearing-all and that same Rumor brought

To her frenzied senses— *"The fleet's to be manned;*
Its course is set." In mad frustration of mind
She fumed, and ramped through the length and
   breadth of the city
340 Like a Bacchante blind with the holy rites
Of the triennial festival when they hear
The cries of Bacchus nightly, daily, nightly.

At last she confronted Aeneas. She *must* speak:
"You traitor! Did you hope to mask such treachery
And silently slink from my land? Is there nothing
   to keep you?
Nothing my life, our love, has given you
Knowing that if you go—I cannot but die?
And you launch your fleet under a wintry star
Into these northerly gales? Why, if Troy still stood,—
350 Would you seek Troy across these ravening waters?
Is it unknown lands and unknown homes you seek
Or is it from me you flee? You see me weep.
I have nothing else but tears and your right hand
To plead with, and our bodies, once at one,
Our marriage rite performed—if you ever loved me,
If you ever found in me any sort of sweetness,
Pity me now! My life, my power seeping.
If prayer has any potency, change your mind!
Because of you the Libyan lords of the desert
360 Detest me; my Tyrians turn a cold shoulder,
My chastity is destroyed, the repute I had—
My immortality insured in the stars—
All, all is gone. And whom do you offer me to?—
A woman bound for death—you my departing
   "guest"—
A word I took to mean a husband. . . . No . . .
What have I to await? My brother Pygmalion
To smash my walls? Iarbas to rape me? Oh
If I'd had a child of yours before you fled,
A little Aeneas to frolic on my floor
370 And remind me of your face, I would not feel
So utterly ruined, deserted and destroyed!"

Aeneas heard her; he strove to harden his heart,
His eyes steady; Jove's command in his ear.

At last he said, "I shall not ever deny
All you have done, you may name each separate
    act;
While I have memory, a breath of life in my body,
I shall remember Carthage; not without pleasure.
But I have this to say; do not imagine
I ever intended to slip away secretly;
Do not imagine either I ever came   *380*
As a prospective husband. If the Fates
Allowed me the life I would choose to live for
    myself—
The city of Troy, the sweet relics of my people,
Would be my foremost care—the towers of Priam
Would rise again—with my own hand I would
    build
Up Pergamus—a restitution
For a conquered race—but now Apollo compels,
His oracles are brookless—to Italy I must go.
There is the fatherland that I must love.
You are Phoenician, yet you dote on Carthage—   *390*
Why then forbid a Trojan his Italy?
It is a human right to seek foreign dominions.
Often at night when the fiery stars appear
The gruff ghost of my father fills my dreams,
Upbraiding me as I lie in a sweat of terror.
And always like a thorn in my mind I feel
How I am cheating my own, my son Ascanius,
Of his Hesperian realm; his fated inheritance.
Now comes an order straight from Jove himself.
I swear by our two lives his messenger   *400*
Brought mandates down through the midday air, I
    saw him
In clear day enter these walls, I heard his words
With my own two ears. Oh, cease tormenting both
Our souls with lamentation—it is not
Of my own free will I must seek Italy."
She heard him out; she turned away from him,
At random roved her eyes and then they fixed him
Head-to-foot in a silent scance and then
Her fury burst.

           "No goddess was your mother!
No noble Dardanus forebear of yours, you scum,   *410*

But the foul Caucasus breached you out of its rocks,
Hyrcanian tigresses gave you suck— What is
   there still?
Is there anything more unbearable than this?
When I wept tears did he not groan for me?
Did not his own eyes fill? Was he not overcome
With pity for his love? What clue have I to hold?
Neither Jove Almighty nor Juno views this straitly—
Nowhere have I any hold on trust.
I took him in shipwrecked—he had nothing,
420 I allotted him part of my realm—I was mad to
   do it;
I saved his fleet, I rescued his retinue—
O God, I am driven raving mad with fury!
So—now it is Apollo's doing—now the Lycian lot,
And now a messenger winging from Jove himself
With detestable commands—indeed it is the ploy
Of the overlords—their pastime is to destroy
Us quiet ones! I shall not keep you. No!
Nor recant my words. Go. Go—seek Italy
On the tempest, seek your realms over the
   storm-crests,
430 And I pray if the gods are as true to themselves
   as their powers
You shall be smashed on the rocks, calling on
   Dido's name;
O, I will shadow your course like a black star
And when cold death possesses my body and soul;
I will haunt you wherever you go, you wicked
   creature,
I will see to your punishment. Report of you
Will filter down to me even among the dead,
And I will—"

                         She broke off in mid-sentence
And shuddered away from him in a dead faint.
Struck dumb, with a mouthful of unspoken
   excuses,
440 Aeneas saw her servants bear off her lolling limbs
To her marble chamber where they laid her down.

But virtuous Aeneas although he longed
To comfort her and suage her grief with words,

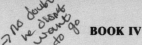

no doubt he didn't want to go

His spirit at stretch with his love, and girning deeply,
Obeyed the god's command and sought his fleet.

Then they all buckled-to: dragged down their ships
On the whole shore, and tested their
    seaworthiness,
And such was their lust to be off, made do with
    oars
Still sprouting leaf, and beams rough-hewn from
    the forest.
Behold them pouring out of every coign of the city   *450*
Like provident winter-minded ants that swarm
Over a heap of grain, stripping it for their store,
That coil their writhing columns across the plains
As they carry their trove through the grass, on a
    penciled path,
And some hoist grains on their backs, their
    shoulders shoving,
Others egg on the sluggards, and the whole path
    teems
With vital energy.

> *O Dido! What did you feel then?*
> *Watching them from your tower in what torture?*
> *Seeing the stretch of shore seething with sailors,*
> *The bay re-echoing with their busy voices.*   *460*
> *O cruel Love, is there an uttermost limit*
> *To your hounding of mortal hearts?* Again she
>   was driven

enlarged narratorial limits?

To tears, to entreaties, to groveling for her love
Lest she should leave one single course untried,
And the death she has set her heart on be in vain.

"Anna, look at the shore! What haste they seem
    to be making,
Do you see them congregating—how every sail
Whistles the wind, and how the happy sailors
Hang garlands on the sterns? Can I sustain
Such a grief, foreseen as grief must be foreseen?   *470*
I suppose I may—but do this for me, will you?
He trusts you, the monster confides in you,
You only know the moods and moments he
    might soften.

Go to him, sister, this proud enemy,
And beg for me. Tell him I never joined
The federation of Aulis against the Trojans,
I never sent a fleet to Pergamus,
I never dug up the ashes of Anchises
Nor his spirit—why should he block his ears?
480 What haste is this? Beg him for this last gift
To his wretched love—beg him, beg him to wait
For a fair wind and favorable weather.
I do not ask him to forgo his realm
In beautiful Latium, by any renewing
Of our old love so brutally betrayed—
No! Only I ask for time, a neutral time,
A rest and breathing space for my love to learn
A way to grieve—if fortune show me any.
Dear sister this is the last thing I shall ask you
490 And I will repay you all—and more—in death."

Again and again her sister was go-between
With suchlike pleas. The hero was moved by none
   of them
No arguments could break his calm resolution;
The Fates forbade and if the hero seemed
Relenting, Jove stopped both his ears.

Just as the Alpine gales with quartering blasts
Compete to uproot an oak in its full prime
And the uproar rings, and leaves from the
   topmost branches
Layer the ground because of the writhen stem:
500 But cleave to the rock it does, and as much as
   the gale
Shivers the top so do its roots thrust down
And clench the underworld—so was the hero
Buffeted by these pleas from every quarter,
In his great heart agony twisted the knife
But his mind was steadfast. All tears rolled in vain.

Then poor Dido crazed by her fate prayed
For death—the arch of heaven was agony
To her sight. Her purpose, secretly set
For suicide, was manifestly strengthened—

Horror! as on the incense-bearing altars   *510*
She laid her offerings, she saw the sacred
Vials turn black, the sacrificial wine
In the very cup curdle to filthy blood.
This she told no one, no, not even her sister.
Add this: there was in the house a consecrated
Altar of marble to her dead Sychaeus—
She nurtured it with a devoted care,
Dressed it with snow-white fleeces and festal
   garlands,
And from this shrine she imagined she heard his
   voice—
Words in the nightwatches. And often a single owl   *520*
On the gable tautened a long note of grief
To breaking point; the sooth of ancient seers
Knocked at her mind with terrible prediction.
Aeneas himself went stalking through her dreams
And always alone she plodded an endless road
Leading her Tyrians to a barren land.
So Pentheus in his madness saw the advancing
Formations of Furies; saw two suns; Thebes
   double;
Or Agamemnon's son, hunted and haunted
By his mother armed with fire and serpents, fled   *530*
From place to place and the avenging fiends
Crouched at whatever door he knocked for help.
So in the throes of grief she spawned her Pursuers;
Was absolute for death, and cunning to that end
With a clear mien, her forehead smooth with hope,
Sidled up to her sister, grievous for her . . .
Words, words. "Dear Anna be happy for me,
I have found a way to win him back to me,
Or be quit of his love for ever.

                 At the world's end
There is a plot between Ocean and the sunset   *540*
Where Atlas hoists the spindle of the stars
Upon his shoulder. There a Massylian priestess,
As I am told, is guardian of the temple
Of the Hesperides. She feeds the dragon,
Preserves the Golden Tree, she drips sweet honey
And sleep-enlisting poppy. She has power
To set the mind care-free with her incantations

If so she choose, or impose inescapable woe.
She can stop the flow of rivers, reverse the stars
550 Raise ghosts in the night—and you shall see the
    earth
Under her foot-sole roar, and the rowan-trees
Leap from the mountain crags. My darling sister
I swear by your sweet life I have no wish
To assume these magic arts.

                        Now if you will,
Build me in the innermost open court,
That winks a secret eye to the sky above,
A pyre, and place on it the hero's arms
Which he, in careless cruelty, strewed about
In our very room, and all his cast-off clothes,
560 Yes, and the marriage bed I perished on.
It is my wish to destroy all traces of him,
And the priestess bids me do what is my wish."

Anna did not detect behind these requests
Her sister composing death—she could not divine
A grief more irresolvable, a frenzy
Worse than befell when her Sychaeus died.
So the pyre was built in the innermost court with
    pine
And hewn oak, and Dido decked the structure
With garlands and a funerary wreath:
570 As crown of the summit, on their marriage bed,
She laid his cast-off clothes, his sword, his image;
She knew the end to be. Altars were set up;
A priestess with lank hair invoked a three hundred
Of Gods: Erebus, Chaos, Hecate and
The thrice-incarnate form of Diana the Virgin—
Holy water was sprinkled—warranted from
    Avernus—
Herbs gathered by full moonlight with bronze
    shears
Rich with the milk of black poison—even
The live-blazon on the forehead of
580 A newborn colt she harpied before its mother
Could seize it. And she with purified hand, for
    death bespoken,
One foot naked, her girdle loosed, knelt

At the altar and prayed to the stars and the gods
   that have
Control of destiny. *If any god have cognizance*
Of the truths that lovers lie to each other: O hear
   her now.

       [Probably Virgil]

Night fell and weary bodies everywhere
Sought rest. The woods and the killing seas were
   still,
The stars mild in mid-orbit—all nature rested,
The beasts and the colored birds and whatever
   widely
The lapsing waters hide or the hard earth holds   590
   in thicket,
All were enthralled in sleep.
                     But Dido, no.
She could not sleep. Nor eye nor heart could close.
Redoubled anguish, unrequitable love
And burning anger pulsed in her soul in turn;
Obsessed, consumed, with room for nothing else.
"What shall I do next? Ogle the neighbors
I mocked before? Go on my knees to seduce
Those desert sheiks I have so often scorned?
Shall I follow the fleet and the flick of a Trojan
   finger?
What will they care that once I helped them, what   600
   will it matter?
And even if I chose to, who would receive me now
Into his proud ship? [one of the builders of Troy. Tricked Hercules]
              Do I *still* not understand
The falsity of Laomedon's foul race?
Shall I go alone then and prostitute my body
To the mocking sailors? Shall I uproot my people?
I emigrated from Sidon and bade them sail
By law to face the vagaries of the winds.
Die as deserve you! Sheathe your grief in a sword!
O Anna, my sister, it was you who forced me
On my foe. I was mad—you made me seem I   610
   was sane.
I broke every law of the essence of true marriage,
I broke them like a beast, my faith vowed to
   Sychaeus,

I broke every vow like a beast: could I escape
    scot-free
And think I would not suffer the uttermost?"
Her heart was bursting with such agonizings.

Aeneas in his cabin, his sailing certain
And everything going well, was simply going to
    sleep.
But the god returned to him, the image of
    Mercury,
His voice, his color, his golden hair, his litheness,
620 And again the vision warned him: "Goddess-born,
How can you sleep now—are you such a fool
You cannot see the dangers that surround you?
Cannot you hear the wind whispering favor?
And she on the spit of her heart is roasting hatred
Evil and cunning, being foredoomed to die!
Fly! Fly at once while you have power to order,
Or you will see the waters threshed with beams
And battering-rams and alive with savage torches;
You will see the coast a chain of fire if the dawn
630 Still finds you loitering here. Wake up! Move!
Women are always changeable and violent!"
His warning given he dissolved in the darkness.

Aeneas truly terrified by the vision
Started from sleep and roused up all his crews.
"Wake up, my friends! Get to your oars! Set sail!
A god from heaven has come with a second
    warning!
There is not a moment to lose— Quick! Cut the
    cables!
O Gods wherever you are, we joyfully follow,
We lucky ones, we obey. Let you be with us
640 And aid us wisely, setting the guiding stars
As each is useful." He snatched his glittering sword
From its scabbard and with the blade severed a
    hawser.
Men all were seized with a like enthusiasm—
They scurried and hurried, pushed off, were in
    open water:

Strongly they strove with the foam and drove for
   the deep,

And now the dawn rose from the saffron couch
Of Tithonus sowing new light on the land;
The queen in her watchtower saw the light growing
And as it grew the glittering white light
Disclosed the fleet full-sail and heading northwards,   *650*
The quays deserted, not a ship, not an oar!
And three or four times she beat her gleaming
   breasts,
And tearing her hair she screamed, "By the Gods,
   shall he go?
Shall a stranger bilk our realm—and we not take
   arms
And the whole city pursue—launching our ships
   from the docks?
Go, quick! kindle the beacons! Arm the people!
Dash in with the oars! . . . What am I saying?
   Where am I?
What madness churns in my mind? O wretched
   Dido
What evils now consume you—when you ruled
You ruled indeed! Now see what has befallen . . .   *660*
My life . . . my dust . . . there goes that man
   they say
Carries the gods of his native land—who carried
His spent father upon his shoulders—and I
Could have seized and scattered him piecemeal to
   the sea,
Could have murdered Ascanius and served him to
   his father
As an appetizer . . . which of us would have
   prevailed?
No one can know. What do I fear in death?
I could have burned his camp down, burned his
   ships,
Killed father and son, his whole house, then
   myself!
O sun that illumines all the works of the world,   *670*
O Juno aware of my woes, O Hecate

Invoked on the city-highways, avenging Fates,
Hear me! It is meet you should. You gods of
  dying Carthage
Give ear to my evil case; O hear my prayer.
If it be fated that this abhorrent monster
Make landfall, if Jove demand it, let this curse
Be set upon him. Bereft of his son's face,
Plagued by a bold foe, let him seek help in vain,
Let his friends die useless paltry deaths about him;
680 Then having made a traitor's unjust peace,
Let him never enjoy his realm, as he would choose,
But let him die before his time and lie
Unburied upon the field!
                                    This is my prayer.
I pour it out with my blood. And you, my people
For ever persecute them—grant that to my dust.
Never let there be love between our peoples,
Never a treaty. But let an Avenger rise
From my bones to harry these Trojan colonists.
Now, or in time to be, whenever the power is
  vouchsafed,
690 Let coast contend with coast, army with army,
Let them fight each other in every generation!"

And now she bent her mind to the final problem:
What was the quickest way to shatter the life
She hated so. She summoned Sychaeus's nurse
(Her own was long dead in her father's country).
"Dear nurse, please fetch my sister, tell her to purge
Herself with lustral water and bring what creatures
We need for sacrifice. So let her come.
And wreathe a holy garland about your brow.
700 I have a mind to complete those sacrifices
To Stygian Jove I have prepared duly;
I have a mind to end my own sorrows
And feed to the flame the pillow he laid his head
  on."
The old woman, with an old woman's zeal,
Bustled away. But poor demented Dido
Wild with purpose, her cheeks interfused
With shuddering blotches, but pale with her death
  to be

Burst in the door into the innermost court,
Frantically mounted the pyre, unsheathed the
   sword
She begged from Aeneas (never to this end),   *710*
She looked at his clothes, at the horrible bed of
   sorrow,
Wept and weeping remembered; pressed her
   breasts to the bed.
"Sweet relics," she wailed, "sweet while the fates
   allowed,
Receive my soul and loose me from my grief.
I have lived. I have run my course as fortune let
   me.   *Vixi = often first word*
Now goes to the underworld the image of my
   greatness.
I founded a fine city. I saw my ramparts.
I avenged my husband, punished my hateful
   brother,
What happiness did I lack? Too happy—if . . .
The ships of Troy had never touched these   *720*
   shores!"
She kissed the bed. "Unavenged I die, so be it,
Thus! Thus! I am pleased to go into the dark. . . .
Let the cruel Trojan in mid-ocean spy
These fires and bear with him presage of my
   death!"

O, as she spoke, she fell upon the sword.
They saw the blood spurt out on the blade, they
   saw
Her hands bloody. The keen rang to the rooftree.
Rumor staggered through the appalled city.
The palace was hollow with the women's howls,
Echoes belabored the air with such a grief   *730*
As if, like Troy, Carthage were overthrown.
Fires leapt from roof to roof of gods and men.

Her sister heard. She scored her cheeks with her
   nails,
She flung through the crowd and called upon the
   dying,
"O sister, was *this* how you sought to deceive me?

The pyre? The altar fires? What words have I?
You should have let me share your fate with you.
And the same hour and the same grief had
    twinned us
Upon one blade. Did I with my own hands build,
740 With my own voice call upon the gods—that you
Should lie there—and I not there? We are all
    dead now.
You, me, the elders of Sidon—all our city,
We are all dead. But let me lave your wounds,
And if a single breath remain, it is mine to claim!"
She climbed the steps, she pressed her half-dead
    sister,
Sighing she stanched with her robe the gouts of
    blood.
Dido struggled to lift her head, sank back.
The wound grides through her breast. Three times
    she strove
To raise up on her elbow, three times she failed.
750 With wandering eyes she sought the light of
    heaven
And shuddered to see it still.
                                        Then mighty Juno
In pity for her long agony sent Iris
Down from Olympus to loose her imprisoned
    limbs,
And grieving soul. Since she was dying not
In the course of Fate or a death deserved, but in
    grief
And before her time in an access of wild passion,
Proserpina had not yet levied from her
That wisp of hair that is key to the Stygian shades.
Therefore did Iris fly, her saffron wings
760 Refracting a thousand colors through the sunlight
And stood at her head.
                            "I bring the word of Dis
I loose you from that flesh." With her own right
    hand
The lock was shorn.
                        All vital power departed—
Her life was gone with the wind.

BOOK V

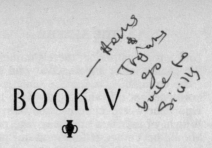

Meanwhile Aeneas was well out from the shore.
He had set his fleet an unwavering course to keep
And they were ploughing through a choppy sea
Blown black by a northerly wind. But looking back
Towards the city he saw the glow of fire—
Poor Dido's funeral fires—but what had caused
So great a conflagration he could not tell.
But as they thought of the bitter agonies
Ensuing from the outrage of great love
And to what lengths frenzy will drive a woman,   10
The Trojans felt in their hearts the leaden weight
Of grim foreboding.

              When the ships were far
Into the deep and land was out of sight—
Nothing but sea and sky and sky and sea—
A scud of raincloud gathered and hung glowering
Above Aeneas' head in stormy darkness
And the sea shuddered in the shadow—even
Palinurus the pilot shouted from the helm:
"Why, why should such a wrack of heavy cloud
Blanket the sky? What are you brewing up   20
For us now, old Father Neptune?" When he had
    spoken
He gave the order to reef the sails and pull
Strongly upon the oars, then set them again
For a different tack and spoke these words to
    Aeneas:
"Aeneas my hearty, not even if Jove himself
Gave me his warrant would I hope to make
Italy with a weather sky like this:
The wind has changed—it has swung into the west
Onto our beam, and it's rising out of the dark

30   And a fog's gathering, there's nothing we can do:
We cannot make any headway and we haven't
   the strength.
Fortune's got the whip-hand—we'd better obey
And steer whatever course she sets: I took
A sight of the stars on the voyage out and if
My memory's not at fault and our present course
Is properly plotted by the same constellations,
I'd say the friendly coast of your brother Eryx
And the harbors of Sicily are in the offing."
Then good Aeneas answered, "I agree.
40   I have noticed for some time what the winds
   dictated
And your vain counter-action. Then trim your sails
And alter course! —No land would more delight
   me,
Nor harbor would I choose more happily
For my weary ships, than where Dardan Acestes
Is safe alive and where my father's bones
Lie buried in the bosom of the earth."
So with a following wind from the west they ran
Full speed for port over the heaving deep
And touched the familiar shores with joy at last.

50   Far off from the top of a lofty spur Acestes
Had marked their coming with amazement and
   grasped
That they were friendly ships and ran to meet
   them.
Dressed in a Libyan bearskin and armed to the
   teeth
He seemed a savage—yet his mother was Trojan;
And his father was the god of the river Crimisus.
His ancestral blood was strong in his veins and
   he welcomed
These men of Troy come back, and joyfully made
   them
Free of his primitive riches and alleviated
Their weariness with every kind of comfort
60   Friendship could offer.
                On the following day,
When the first hint of dawn hunted the stars

Out of the sky, Aeneas called an assembly.
From every part of the shore his comrades
   gathered
And standing on the top of a mound of earth he
   addressed them.
"Great sons of Dardanus, blood-descendants of
   gods,
The cycle of months is complete and come full
   circle;
It is a year now since we committed to earth
The mortal bones of my father, now an immortal,
And consecrated altars to mourn his loss.
Unless I am at fault this is the day,   70
The very day (for so you gods have desired it),
That I shall hallow for ever in grief and honor—
And were this day to find me an African exile
Beside the Syrtes or on the Argive sea
Or in the streets of Mycenae—wherever I was,
Still would I keep my annual vows of observance
In solemn ritual, and pile up on the altar
Its meed of gifts. And now by our own choice—
But not I think without the provenance
And guidance of the gods—we are here present   80
Beside the very grave, my father's bones and ashes,
Having made landfall in a friendly harbor.
Come therefore everyone and take your part
In joyful celebration. Let us pray
For favoring winds and when in the course of time
I have built my city walls and founded its temples
May it please my father I should offer him
These annual rites in his own shrine! Acestes,
True son of Troy, has allotted to the crews
Of every ship two head of oxen—summon   90
   therefore
The household gods of our fathers to the feast
And those our host Acestes worships. And
   furthermore
If the ninth dawn bears up benign to us mortals
And fixes in its light the myriad world,
I shall declare a race to be fought out
Among my Trojan fleet; then next a foot race,
And then a match for those who pride themselves

On their prowess with the javelin or light arrow,
Then boxing bouts for any who believe
100 In their skill with the gloves, come one and all!
Prizes await all those who merit them.
Keep holy silence all, and wreathe your brows
    with leaves."

So saying he bound his brows with his mother's
    myrtle
And Helymus followed suit and aged Acestes
And young Ascanius, and all the rest of the
    Trojans.
Aeneas made his way from the assembly
Towards the tomb with thousands pressing round
    him,
The center of the throng. And with due formality
He poured two bowls of unmixed wine on the
    earth,
110 Two of fresh milk, two of the blood of sacrifice,
Then scattered some bright flowers and spoke
    these words:
"O hallowed father, hail to you once more!
O father saved in vain only to lie
In ashes here, all hail O Shade and Spirit!
It was not granted me to seek with you
The borders of Italy, our destined demesne,
Nor see the Ausonian Tiber—wherever it be."
He had hardly finished when a colossal snake
Slithered its seven coils from the depths of the
    tomb
120 And in seven enormous rings it slid and calmly
Wound round the tomb and gliddered between
    the altars:
Its back was a sheeny pattern of blue markings,
Its scales ashine with gold—like a rainbow catching
The light of the sun and glancing a thousand colors
Onto the clouds. Aeneas stood there spellbound.
And the snake threaded its long sinuous body
Between the bowls and the polished cups sampling
The fare, then, harmlessly, when it had eaten
The altar offering, slipped back to the base of
    the tomb.

Not knowing whether he ought to regard the snake   *130*
As the tutelary Spirit of the place
Or as the familiar of his father, Aeneas
Resumed the ritual of his filial duty
With quickened purpose: he duly sacrificed
A pair of two-year sheep, and then two pigs
And then two black-skinned bullocks; he poured
    wine
From the bowls and called on the soul of the
    mighty Anchises,
And his shade let free from Acheron. His
    companions
Joyfully offered gifts each as his means permitted,
Piling them on the altars and slaughtering bullocks.   *140*
Some set up rows of caldrons. Some brought live
    coals
To the spits and, stretched at ease along the grass,
Roasted the flesh.
                    And now the day they awaited
Had come, and Phaeton's team were harbingers
Of a bright and tranquil dawn. News of the games,
And the magic of Acestes' famous name
Had drawn the folk from all the neighborhood;
And they filled the shore in a jolly holiday crowd
Eager to see Aeneas and his fellows,
And some were ready to enter for the events.   *150*
And first of all the gifts were exhibited
In the center of the ground—the sacred tripods,
The green garlands, the palms—emblems of
    victory,
Weapons and robes dyed purple, and talents of
    gold and silver.
Then from a mound in the middle a trumpet
    pealed
Announcing the games begun.
                            The first event
Was a rowing race: four ships of equal size,
Four ships with heavy oars, were singled out
From the whole fleet. Commanding the speedy
    Pristis
Was Mnestheus with his dashing crew—that   *160*
    Mnestheus

Who was to be an Italian prince, and from whom
The Memmian family take their name; there was
   Gyas
Directing the vast bulk of the *Chimaera*,
She was as big as a city and propelled
By Dardan rowers at three banks of oars;
Sergestus, from whom the Sergii derive
Their name, was captain of the mighty *Centaur*;
And finally Cloanthus—the founder, O Roman
   Cluentus,
Of your house—in the sky-blue *Scylla*.

                     Some way out
170 To sea, off the spray-beaten shore, jutted a rock
Sometimes submerged and pounded by the swell
When the northerly winter wracks blindfold the
   stars;
But now, in the calm, it heaves from the smooth
   waters
A level shelf where the gulls love to bask.
Here lord Aeneas set as a mark the green
Branch of an ilex, a clear sign to the sailors
To tell them where to turn in their long voyage
And strike for home.

               They drew lots for position;
Then at their helms the captains took their stand
180 In dazzling gold and purple, a far-seen splendor;
Their crews were crowned with garlands of
   poplar leaves
And their bare shoulders gleamed with
   embrocation.
They took their place at the thwarts, their
   muscles tensed,
Tensely they waited the signal, their hearts
   pounding
With nervous fear and longing to be the winners.
The trumpet gave the signal. Then in a flash
All shot away from the start; and seamen's orders
Rang to the sky as they drew back their arms,
And the waters boiled. Then they clove through
   the furrows
190 With steady strokes and the whole sea was slashed
By trident-prow and striving oar.

No chariot
Drawn by a tandem team ever shot out
From its starting gate with such a headlong thrust,
Nor charioteer giving his gallopers head
And waving the slack reins above their backs
Leant forward so to the lash. Then all the
  woodland
Rang with the cheers of men and the urgent
  appeals
Of eager supporters—and the high hills resounded
And the sound rolled round the low line of the
  shore.
Amid the tumult and the shouting Gyas   *200*
Had slipped into clear water and the lead.
Cloanthus followed—he had better oarsmen
But the weight of his pine-timbers held him back.
Behind, at an equal distance, *Pristis* and *Centaur*
Struggled against each other and now *Pristis*
Was just in front and then the mighty *Centaur*
Put in a burst, and passing her took the lead.
Then both forged on together bow to bow
Ploughing the salt seaway with long keels.
They were already approaching the half-way mark   *210*
And shaping a course to round the rock when
  Gyas
Who was leading at this point yelled at his helmsman:
"Menoetes! Why are you steering so far to the
  starboard?
Steer *this* way; hug the shore! Let the blades of
  our oars
Feather the rocks to our port—let the others
  indulge
In the open sea!" But Menoetes timorous
Of hidden reefs turned to the open sea.
Again Gyas shouted, "Make inshore, Menoetes!"
And looking back he saw Cloanthus gaining
And pressing him from the inner berth—and indeed   *220*
He snaked his way between the ringing rocks
And Gyas' ship on the port side and passed him,
Rounded the mark, and got into safe waters.
Then a grievous fury welled from the very marrow
Of Gyas' bones, tears stood out on his cheeks,

And blind to his own good name and his crew's
   safety
He tore Menoetes from his timorous helm
And hurled him headlong into the sea and took
The helm himself: he would be pilot now.
230 He cheered his rowers on, and altered course
Closing towards the rocks. But poor Menoetes
Struggled at last to the surface from the depths—
He was old, his clothes clung sodden to his body,
But he managed to grope his way up onto the rock
And collapsed in the dry. The Trojans jeered as
   he fell,
Jeered as he swam, and roared to see him retch
The brine out of his lungs.
                              The hearts of Sergestus
And Mnestheus, the last two, were suddenly fired
With the wild hope of passing the flagging Gyas.
240 Sergestus jockeyed into position first
And neared the rock, but he had not cleared the
   Pristis,
She was only half a length behind and pressing.
So he leapt down among his crew and exhorted,
"Come now, my comrades, fellows once with
   Hector,
You whom I chose in Troy's last throe to follow me,
Rise to your oars with all the dash and spirit
That got us out of the Syrtes and the storms
Of the Ionian Sea and Malea's currents.
I tell you, I do not strive for first place now
250 Nor aim at total victory . . . oh, but I wish . . .
No, Neptune, let whoever you want to, win . . .
But to come in last, think of the shame of that!
My friends, prevent that horror at all costs—
Count that your victory!"
                              They made a supreme effort
The brazen keel shuddered under the pulse
Of their mighty strokes. The sea slipped under
   them.
Their throats were parched, their lungs were
   almost bursting,
Their sweat poured off in streams. And a sheer
   chance

Brought to the heroes the honor they coveted;
For Sergestus, in a fever of excitement   260
Kept bearing in towards the rocks and thrusting
On the inside berth, with lessening room to
    maneuver,
Until he ran, by ill luck, onto a reef.
The very rock juddered; against the jagged
Edges of flint the oars splintered and broke;
The prow hung high and dry. And the crew leapt
    up
Clamoring, from their thwarts at the sudden check,
And seizing iron-bound poles and pointed boat-
    hooks
Grappled their broken oars and fished them out.
Mnestheus now was jubilant and madder   270
Than ever to win and with the wind at his beck
And call and his oarsmen striking a fast rate
He scudded over the open water landward.
As a dove is suddenly startled from the niche
In the lava-rock where she has her nest and the
    nestlings
She loves to cosset, and with a terrified flap
And clatter of wings comes whirling over the
    meadows,
But soon you will see her slide through the
    limpid air
Tranquilly gliding and without a wing-beat,
So in the *Pristis* now Mnestheus skimmed   280
Through the last lanes of water as the way
Of the boat simply propelled her onward.
Sergestus he left behind, still in the toils
Of reef and shallows, calling in vain for help
And learning how to limp with broken oars.
Next he came up with Gyas and the colossal
Chimaera and, being bereft of her pilot, passed her.
So there was only Cloanthus alone and close to
    the finish,
And he pressed after him straining every nerve.
Then truly the cheering redoubled to a roar   290
And everyone urged the pursuer on
And the sky rang with the racket. The leading crew
In a cold sweat of fear that after all

A prize they considered theirs already and honors
As good as won might still be snatched away,
And willing to give their lives for glory—the others
Spurred to a greater effort by success
And the crowd's confidence inspiring theirs.
There might have been a dead heat and the prize
300 Divided if Cloanthus had not stretched
Both hands out over the sea in fervent prayer
And called upon the gods to heed his vow.
"O gods who have dominion over the sea
Upon whose breast I sail, if you hear my prayer,
With joyful heart I shall station by your altar
Upon this shore a snow-white bull: I shall scatter
The entrails into the salt waves, I shall pour
Clear streams of wine." Deep down among the
 billows
His prayer was heard by all the Nereids
310 And Phorcus' troop and the maid Panopea—and
 Father
Portunus himself with his own mighty hand
Gave a boost to the ship as she passed; and on
 she shot
Swifter than arrowflight or the south wind
Towards the land and in the heart of the harbor
Was lost to view. Then duly the son of Anchises
Called all together and in stentorian tones
A herald proclaimed Cloanthus winner! A garland
Of green bay leaves was placed upon his brow.
Aeneas next gave their prizes to each crew—
320 They could choose to have three bullocks,
Wine, or a bulky talent of silver. The captains
Had further special awards: Aeneas gave to the
 winner
A gold-embroidered cloak with a double pattern
In Meliboean purple on its facings,
While on the whole was woven a depiction
First of the young prince Ganymede at his hunting
On leafy Ida, hounding the swift stags
With his darts in sharp pursuit; you could almost
 see
The heaving of his chest, it was so lifelike.
330 Then sweeping down from Ida came that bird

Which is Jove's armor-bearer and snatched him up
In its hooked talons while his agèd attendants
Raised helpless hands to heaven and his hounds
Expended their fury barking into the air.
To him whose prowess had gained him second
    place
Aeneas presented a cuirass of mail
Close-linked and triple-threaded with gold—he
    had stripped it
Himself from Demoleos after killing him
By the banks of the swift Simois under the walls
Of Ilium: and this was the gift he gave   340
To a warrior to have for his own, to be
His pride and defense in battle. Indeed his servants
Phegeus and Sagaris could hardly manage
To carry its many layers on their straining
    shoulders.
Yet Demoleos in his day had worn it
And worn it flashing after fleeing Trojans.
The third prize was a pair of brazen caldrons
And two cups wrought of silver with bas-reliefs.

Now all had received their gifts and were
    strutting off
With purple ribands round their brows exulting   350
Each with his treasure when at last Sergestus
Was sighted—he had just succeeded,
After a painful and protracted series
Of cunning maneuvers, in refloating the *Centaur*:
He had lost some oars and one whole bank was
    crippled
And now he brought her home in a storm of
    catcalls:
She was like a snake, caught on the verge of a road
And run over by some brazen wheel or mangled
And left half dead by a brutal traveler
With a stone in his hand, that writhes but cannot   360
    move;
Its eyes glitter, its neck and hissing head
Are reared upright, and half its sinuous length
Strives to escape but paralyzed by the wound
It flounders impotently writhing and coiling

Back on its stricken half—such was the state
Of the oarage the *Centaur* dragged herself along
   with;
But she broke out sail and made the harbor mouth
In spanking style in the end. So Aeneas gave
Sergestus his promised prize—he was delighted
370 To see the ship safe and her crew returned—
Gave him a Cretan slave girl not unskilled
In domestic matters with twin sons at her breast.
Her name was Pholöe.
                So this event was finished,
And good Aeneas next turned his attention
To a grassy level enclosed on every side
By wooded hillsides curving up and providing
A perfect vantage point for the track in the valley
   below them.
Hither the hero went with many thousands about
   him
And took his seat on a dais in the center.
380 From here he invited any young man of mettle
Who wished to compete in the footrace to come
   forward,
And offered prizes and set them up to the view.
From every side competitors appeared,
Both Trojans and Sicilians and to the fore
Were Nisus and Euryalus—Euryalus
In the April of his youth and beautiful,
Nisus who loved him with a pure devotion.
Next after them there came princely Diores
A sprig of Priam's noble house; and next
390 Came Salius and Patron, both together:
An Acarnanian one, the other Arcadian
Of the stock of Tegea—then two Sicilian youths,
Both adepts of the woodland, Helymus
And Panopes—companions of Acestes
Though he was older, and many more besides
Whose names are dim now and whose fame
   forgotten.
When all were assembled round him Aeneas
   addressed them:
"Attend to my words with care. The gist of them
   will delight you.

No man of all your number shall go away
Without a gift from me. I shall give a pair   *400*
Of iron darts from Crete, agleam with polish,
And a two-edged ax with silver chasing—all of you
Alike shall have this honor. The first three
Shall receive special prizes and have their brows
Wreathed with pale olive garlands. Let the first,
As winner, receive a horse with glorious trappings;
The second an Amazon's quiver fully loaded
With Thracian arrows, and a broad belt of gold
To sling it from, and to fasten it a buckle
Wrought of a polished jewel. Let the third   *410*
Be happy to take this Argive helmet home."
When he had finished they all got on their marks
And at the sudden signal off they streaked
From the starting line and pelted down the course
Like a burst of storm, each with his eye on the
    goal.
Right from the start Nisus was far in front
Leaping into the lead swifter than wind
Or winging thunderbolt. Next after him,
But a long way behind, came pounding Salius,
Then with a closer interval between them   *420*
Euryalus third. Then after Euryalus, Helymus
And right on his heels and hustling up to his
    shoulder
Diores—if the course had but been longer
He would have slipped him—there would have
    been no doubt
Of the outcome of their struggle.
                         And now they were nearing
The end of the course and spent they saw the tape
Almost in reach when Nisus by sheer ill luck
Slipped in a slime of blood that had been spilt,
As it happened, at the slaughter of some bullocks
And still lay soaking into the earth and sticky   *430*
On the green of the grass. And here the poor
    young man
With the taste of victory already on his tongue
Planted his steps and skidded and found no
    foothold
But fell flat down into the muck and blood.

But even then he never forgot Euryalus,
Never forgot his love—heaving himself
Out of the mess he obstructed Salius
And Salius went down, head over heels in the
　　mush.
Euryalus sprinted ahead and thanks to his friend
440　Was cheered to the winning post by the crowd's
　　noisy favors.
Helymus came in second, Diores third.

But Salius filled the whole arena with eloquent
　　protest
Appealing to the elders sitting in front,
Insisting that the prize he had been deprived of
By a trick be given him back. But Euryalus
Had the support of the crowd because of the tears
He shed so becomingly and because of the grace
Of his burgeoning beauty—and Diores backed him
With his own loud appeals—he had won a prize—
450　And if the first place were to be given to Salius
His own position as third would go for nothing.
Then lord Aeneas said to them "My lads,
You certainly keep the prizes you have won:
Nobody can disturb the order once it is settled,
But let me be allowed to commiserate
With a friend for ill luck he did not so deserve."
So saying he presented Salius
With an enormous African lionskin loaded
With the weight of its mane and its claws sheathed
　　in gold.
460　At this, Nisus complained, "If these are the prizes
You give the defeated—if you are so sympathetic
To those who fall—what prize will you give me
Equal to my deserts?—I deserved to win
And I would have won, had I not been embroiled
In the same accident as Salius!"—As he spoke
He displayed the mud and filth on his face and
　　limbs.
Aeneas, best of princes, smiled at him
And bade a shield be brought—the workmanship
Of Didymaon which the Greeks had wrenched

From Neptune's hallowed doorway once—and this   470
Munificent gift he gave to the noble youth.

So the race was over, the prizes duly awarded.
Then Aeneas said, "Let any man come forward
Of courage and quick wits, put on the gloves
And take his guard." He offered a pair of prizes.
A bullock garlanded, with gilded horns,
For the winner, for the loser as a sop
A sword and a splendid helmet. In an instant,
To a hum of admiration Dares heaved
The colossal strength of his mighty frame upright   480
And presented himself—it was he and he alone
Who used to pit himself in single combat
Against Paris—and beside great Hector's tomb,
It was this very man had smashed the all-
   conquering giant,
Butes who bore himself to the field of battle
With the blood of Bebrycian Amycus in his veins,
And stretched him dying on the saffron sand.
Such was the caliber of this Dares who
Now ranged his bulk in readiness for a bout,
Flexed his broad shoulders and indulged himself   490
In a burst of shadow-boxing. The only question
Was an opponent—but no one in all that crowd
Dared to confront him and put on the gloves.
Assuming therefore that nobody else intended to
   enter
Dares went strutting up to Aeneas and stood there
And brashly taking hold of the bullock's horn
In his left hand he said: "Son of a goddess
If no one dares to risk himself to a bout
How long do I have to stand here? How long is
   it right
To keep me waiting? Please give me the word   500
To take the prize away!" Then all the Trojans
Roared with one voice in favor of their champion
Being given the promised prize.
                              At this Acestes
Turned to Entellus who happened to be sitting
Beside him on a bank of lush green grass

And gave him the rough edge of his tongue, saying:
"Entellus, bravest of heroes—once! Does what
  you were
Mean nothing to you? Will you really sit there
  calmly
And let so great a prize be carried off
510 Without one blow, or thought for Eryx vaunted
  in vain
Your god and master? What of your fame become
A household word throughout all Sicily?
And the prizes hung in your own house?" He
  answered,
"It is not fear has quenched my love of fame,
Nor my ambition. No, but the chill of age
Has slowed my blood, and atrophied the sinews
Of all my body—if I still had in me
The sap of youth I had once—as that young lout
Boasts of with such loud-mouthed self-
  confidence—
520 No pretty bullock, nor bait of a reward
Need have been offered to tempt me into the
  ring—
I care nothing for prizes!" With these words
He hurled into the arena a pair of leathers
Of an immense weight which nimble Eryx used
To sheathe his arms in, when he came to combat.
Men's hearts stood still; so huge the seven oxen
These hides must have been from, now reinforced
With lead and iron stitched into them. More
  stunned
Than all the rest Dares just stood there gaping
530 And then backed well away; great-hearted Aeneas
Himself stood trying out their weight and turning
The massive bindings round and round in his
  hands.
Then from the depths of his heart the older
  contender
Entellus spoke: "Just think had anyone seen
The very leathers used by Hercules,
And the ghastly fight he fought on this very shore!
These arms were wielded once by our brother
  Eryx—

You can still see the bloodstains and the splayed
Fragments of brain—with these he stood his
    ground
Against great Alcides—when I was in my heyday   *540*
I used them regularly, before my rival—
Jealous old age—sprinkled upon my brows
His weakening snow. But if the Trojan Dares
Refuses to face me in this gear of mine,
If good Aeneas agrees and my sponsor Acestes
Approves my proposal—let us fight it out
On equal terms. I will spare you Eryx's gloves—
So calm your fears—and as for yourself put off
Your Trojan leathers." So saying, he flung from
    his shoulders
The double folds of his cloak and bared to view   *550*
The huge joints of his limbs, the mighty bones
Of arms and legs, and stationed his vast frame
In the center of the ring. The son of Anchises
Held up two equal pairs of gloves and, as part of
    his office,
Bound them about the hands of both contestants.
At once each took his guard, and without fear
Lifted his arms in the air, dancing on tiptoe.
They held their heads up and well out of range
And sparred for an opening, probing at each
    other—
Dares quicker on foot, reliant on youth,   *560*
Entellus the more powerful and the bigger,
But slow and weak in the knee, and out of
    condition,
Panting for every breath, his huge limbs heaving.
Many the blows they aimed at each other and
    missed.
Many the blows that hammered their hollow sides
Or thudded on ribs. Their fists kept lashing round
Forehead and ears, and uppercuts to the jaw
Rattled their teeth. Stolid Entellus stood
Rooted in one position—avoiding punishment
By his sheer vigilance and skill in balance.   *570*
Dares, it seemed, was like a general attacking
A high-walled city with siege-engines or
Investing a mountain fortress with his army

Who tries out every mode of approach in turn,
Exploring the whole position with all his skill,
And throws in every sort of assault—all to no
   purpose.
Entellus, then, gathered himself to strike
And lifting high his right hand shot it out,
But Dares, quick to anticipate, saw the blow
580 As it swept down and with a nimble sidestep
Slipped out of the way. And all Entellus' effort
Was wasted on the air, but the mighty impetus
Of his mighty blow caused the colossal fighter
To crash full-length to the earth, as a hollow pine
Torn up by its roots is sometimes seen to crash
On Erymanthus or on lofty Ida.
The Trojan and Sicilian youths sprang up
In their excitement; a shout rose to the sky.
Acestes was the first to run to his aid
590 And, though he was as old, he tenderly
Lifted his friend up from the ground. But the hero,
Neither dismayed nor shaken up by his fall,
Returned to the fight more fiercely still and anger
Charged him with new force—he began to blaze
In the fullness of his strength, pricked into action
By shame and the certain knowledge of his powers.
In a flame of fury he drove Dares headlong
Over the whole field showering blows upon him—
Now with his right, now with his left—allowing
600 Nor pause nor respite—thick as the hammering
   hailstones
A storm hurls on the roof, such was the storm
Of battering blows Entellus with both hands
Let fall on Dares and sent him staggering.
But finally chief Aeneas thought it fit
To put a term to this massacre—Entellus
Had glutted his savage spirit quite enough—
So he stopped the fight and rescued flagging Dares
And spoke these soothing words,—"Oh Luckless
   Dares,
What overwhelming madness has possessed you?
610 Do you not see this strength is supernatural?
That the gods have turned against you? Give way
   to the gods!"

Such were his words as he parted the two fighters—
There were faithful friends to help the wretched
 Dares
Whose knees were sagging, whose head hung
 loosely flopping
From side to side, as he kept spitting blood
And teeth with the blood as they led him to the
 ships.
Then summoned they received on his behalf
The sword and helmet—leaving to Entellus
The garland and the bullock. At this the victor
Bursting with pride in himself and in his trophy   *620*
Cried, "Son of a goddess, and you Trojans, now
You shall see the measure of what strength I had
In my body when I was young, and the sort of
 death
Dares escaped—who is now safe among you!"
Nearby the bullock stood, the prize for the fight,
And he took his stand directly in front of its
 muzzle;
He drew his right arm back and aiming the blow
Of his toughened leather exactly between the
 horns
Rose to his full height and crashed down his fist.
The bone was shattered, the brains were   *630*
 spattered out.
The bullock fell to the ground, quivering still, but
 dead.
Then spoke Entellus from the depths of his heart,
"This life I pay you Eryx, a better life,
In Dares' stead and here as a victor may
Lay down my gloves and the secrets of my skill."
Aeneas next invited competition
For any who liked the swift flight of the arrow.
He allotted prizes, and with his mighty hand
Himself set up the mast of Serestus' ship
And tied to the masthead on a cord bent round it   *640*
A fluttering dove, a mark for the iron-tipped
 shafts.
The archers gathered; and each dropped his lot
Into the waiting helmet and first to come out,
Before anyone else, and to everyone's delight,

Was Hippocoön's the son of Hyrtacus.
Next came Mnestheus only lately the winner
In the ship race, Mnestheus still with the green garland
Of olive on his head, and Eurytion third—
Your brother, Pandarus, you whose fame is immortal,
650 Who in those old days, bidden to break the truce,
Were first to hurl your weapons spinning into the thick
Of the Greek host. And last to fall from the helmet
Was Acestes' lot—an old man still prepared
To compete in a contest fitter for the young.
Now every man with all the strength he could muster
Was limbering up his bow, testing its powers
And drawing arrows from his quiver—the first
To slice the air came from the twanging bowstring
Of young Hippocoön and whizzing away it flew
660 Straight at the mast and struck and stuck in it.
The mast quivered, the dove in a flutter of terror
Wheeled whirling, amidst a thunder of applause.
Next was Mnestheus taut and keen, his bow
Drawn back and pointing up, his shaft and eye
Aligned in aim—but alas! he had no luck:
He failed to hit the bird with the iron tip of his arrow
But cut the knot of the string she was tethered to,
Tied by the foot to the masthead—and off she flashed
Into the murk blown up by the south wind!
670 Then quick as light, for he had had his bow
For long full drawn and an arrow nocked to the string,
Eurytion muttered a prayer to his brother and fixed
His eye on the dove as joyfully she winged
Her way in the waste of air and then transfixed her
As white she flew with a dark cloud behind.
Down, down she came and left her soul to inhabit
The starry stations of air, and her tumbling body
Brought home the embedded arrow to its owner.
With nothing to win there still remained Acestes:

And he discharged his arrow into the heights of   *680*
   the sky
To prove an old man still had skill and power
To wield the twanging bow. And all of a sudden
A portent fraught with hidden doom to be
Burst on their sight—the momentous aftermath
Was to disclose itself and prophets wise
After the event expound too late its meaning—
For as it flew in the formless clouds the shaft
Caught fire and flamed its way with diminishing
   fires
Until it vanished, burned out into the winds,
Like the shooting stars that sweep across the sky   *690*
Their burning tresses. With minds rapt in wonder
The Trojans and Sicilians rooted stood
And prayed. Nor was Aeneas one to deny
So great an omen—but he embraced Acestes,
Who was overjoyed himself and almost
   smothered him
Under a pile of costly gifts and addressed him:
"Take them, old father: for the mighty King of
   Olympus
Has willed it so. By these ineluctible omens
He has ordained you a prize for which no lot
   was cast.
The gift I will give you belonged to aged Anchises: *700*
It is a mixing bowl embossed with figures
Which long ago Cisseus of Thrace most generously
Gave to my father and bid him always keep it
As a remembrancer, an earnest of his love."
So saying he placed upon Acestes' brows
The wreath of bay and pronounced him the
   absolute winner.
Nor did Eurytion with his sense of fairness begrudge
The outstanding honor, although it was he indeed
And he alone who had brought down the dove.
Next after him Mnestheus got his prize   *710*
For severing the cord, and last Hippocoön
For fixing in the mast his speedy arrow.

Before they broke up after this event
Aeneas the chief had summoned Epytides

The tutor and companion of young Iulus
And whispered in his ear: "Now, off you go—
And if Ascanius has his squadron of boys
All mounted ready and drilled for his parade,
Tell him to lead them onto the field now
720 To pay their homage to his honored grandsire,
And show himself in arms." Then he himself
Ordered the crowd that had poured into the arena
To move well back and leave the whole space clear.
In rode the boys, the pride of their parents' eyes,
In shining lines upon their bridled horses,
And as they passed were met with admiring cheers
From the grown men of Sicily and Troy.
All had their hair bound, as the custom was,
With a chaplet of clipped leaves, and carried a pair
730 Of cornel-shafted javelins tipped with iron.
And some had polished quivers slung from their shoulders
And pliant chains of twisted gold were wound
Over their chests and twined about their necks.
They were in three groups of horses for their performance
And each group had its leader and twelve followers,
All divided alike, an equal glittering glory.
One band of the boys was led in its proud career
By a little Priam, whose name revived his grandsire's,
Your prince of a son, Polites, destined to found
740 A line of Italians—he rode a Thracian horse,
A piebald, the fetlocks of whose forefeet showed
All white as he pranced, with a white blaze on his forehead.
The second leader was Atys from whom the house
Of the Latin Atii spring—a little boy
And dear to Iulus as boys are dear to each other.
Then last of all, and exceeding all in beauty
Iulus rode on a Sidonian steed
Which lovely Dido had given him in remembrance,
And witness of her love for him. The rest
750 Rode on Sicilian horses provided for them

By Acestes their elder ally. The Trojans welcomed
The shy young lads with reassuring applause
And quizzed them with delight, remarking in them
Family and ancestral likenesses.
After the boys had joyfully paraded
The length of the whole gathering, under the gaze
Of their families, Epytides' voice of command
Rang out across the arena to where they were
    ready,
And he gave his whip a crack. They galloped away
In equal bands, then broke up into threes   760
As if for a figure of a dance, and then
At the next command they wheeled and charged
    each other
With lances couched. Then they engaged in a
    series
Of matching evolutions as the two
Companies faced each other, and then they rode
In interlocking circles left and right
And finally engaged in a mock battle,
Now with their backs exposed to flight, and now
Turning to the attack with lances poised,
Now making peace and riding side by side.   770
The story goes that once in the heights of Crete
There was a labyrinth with a tortuous path
Running between blind walls and treacherous
With a thousand twists and turns, whose baffling
    maze
Defied the following of any trail:
No man could solve it, no man retrace his step.
The course of these Trojan boys was not unlike it
As they wove in and out in mock attack
And mock retreat. They were like dolphins, too,
That sport their indolent way among the wavetops   780
Of the Carpathian or the Libyan sea.
When he was building the walls round Alba Longa
It was Ascanius who was first to revive
This kind of tourney and taught the early Latins
To celebrate it, as he had done in his boyhood
With all the Trojan boys. The Albans taught
Their sons, and from them Rome in the days of
    her greatness

Received and kept alive the old tradition.
So even now the boys are "Troy" and their troop
790   Is called "The Trojan Troop."
                                   This was the end
Of the games held in holy Anchises' honor.

Now for the first time Fortune turned against them.
For while the Trojans with their various games
Were paying their due obsequies at the tomb,
Saturnian Juno posted Iris down
To the Trojan fleet from heaven, wafting her
On the wings of a fair wind; pondering many
   things,
Her deep long-standing wrath as yet unsated.
Iris, speeding her passage along her bow
800   Of a myriad colors, and seen by no one, swiftly
Completed her journey. She marked the vast
   assembly
And made for the shore where she saw the
   harbor empty
And the fleet unmanned. But on a hidden beach,
Far off the Trojan women were keening for
   Anchises,
And weeping one and all cast wistful eyes
Out to the ocean deep and every heart
Was full of the same yearning cry: "Alas!
Such wastes of water for such weary souls,
So great a sea to cross!" They prayed for a city;
810   The toils of another voyage were too grim:
They could bear no more. So into their midst
   snapped Iris,
No tiro in the ways of making trouble,
And putting off the mien and garments of the
   goddess
She became Beroë, the aged wife of Doryclus
Of Tmarus, a woman whose name once was a name
To conjure with, who had borne sons—as Beroë
She joined the group of Trojan women and cried:
"O wretched women that you were not dragged
To death by the Greeks under the walls of the city!
820   Unhappy nation! What more disastrous death
Has Fate in store for you? It is now the end

Of the seventh summer since the sack of Troy
And all the time we are being harried onwards
From land to land, at the menace of every rock
In every sea, under every star in the sky,
And rolled from rolling wave to rolling wave
Seeking an ever-receding Italy.
And here is the country of our brother Eryx,
And Acestes is our host—who shall prevent us
From laying foundations here and giving our   830
   people
The city they crave? O fatherland, O gods
Snatched from the foe in vain—shall there *never* be
Walls we can call Troy walls? Shall we *never* see
Streams such as Hector loved? no Xanthus? no
   Simois?
Well, then! come follow me and set on fire
These accursed ships! For in my sleep I dreamed
The prophetess Cassandra handed me
Brands all ablaze and said, 'Seek here your Troy,
Here is your home!' Now is the time to act—
So great a portent admits of no delay.   840
See! Four of Neptune's altars! The god himself
Provides us fire and fires our courage too!"
So saying she sprang to the fire and fiercely
   snatched
A burning brand and drawing her right arm back
She whirled it round and sent it violently spinning.
The Trojan women stood appalled and dumbstruck.
Then Pyrgo, the oldest of their party, once
The royal nurse of Priam's many sons
Cried, "Ladies! I tell you, this is not Beroë
From Rhoeteum, the wife of Doryclus!   850
Do you but mark those signs of a heavenly beauty,
Those burning eyes: what presence, what pride of
   feature,
What tone of utterance, what dignity in her gait!
It was but a moment ago that I myself
Took leave of Beroë and she was sick and resentful
That she alone should fail to take her place
At such a ceremony and could not give to Anchises
His meed of honor." Such were her words and
   the women

Were in a quandary, balefully eying the ships
860   And torn between their pitiable yearning
To stay in the land they were in, and the call of
        the land
Promised by fate, when the goddess spread her
        wings
And soared up into the sky cleaving the clouds
With the huge arc of her bow as she flew away.
Then truly dazed and mazed with the apparition
And driven to frenzy they screamed and snatched
        up fire
From their household hearths—some of them
        sacked the altars,
And flung on the ships brushwood and brands
        and cuttings.
The Fire God raged unchecked along bench and
        oar
870   And sterns of painted pine.

       It was Eumelus
Who brought the news back to the tomb of
        Anchises
And the spectators sitting in the arena:
The fleet was on fire! And indeed from where
        they sat
They could see with their own eyes the sparks
        flying up
And the black smoke billowing.

       The first to respond
Was Ascanius who was still at the head of his troop
Gaily trotting along—then all of a sudden
Galloping off to the uproar by the fleet
Before his breathless aides had time to stop him.
880   "What new madness is this?" he cried, "you
        unhappy women,
What do you think you are doing? It is no Greek
        foe
Nor hostile camp you are burning—it is your own
Hopes for the future— See! It is I, your Ascanius!"
He took the helmet off which he had worn
In the mock battle and flung it down at his feet.
Up dashed Aeneas then and a host of Trojans
Hard on his heels. But the women scuttled away

In panic about the shore, making for cover
In every direction, seeking the woods or caves.
Already appalled at what they had done they   890
   dared
Not face the light of day: they had recovered
Their senses, knew who their friends were, and
   Juno's spell
Over their hearts was broken, but this return
To sanity had no power to extinguish
The fires which burned with an unquenchable
   violence;
For deep in the moistened timber the calking
   caught
And in slow coils the smoke came thickly up,
The creeping fires fastened upon the keels
And the danger threatened every part of the ships.
Though every hero slaved with all his might   900
And they poured in floods of water, they made
   no headway.
Then good Aeneas stripped the cloak from his
   shoulders
And stretching his hands to heaven invoked its aid:
"Almighty Jove, if you do not execrate
The Trojans to a man; and if your ancient
   compassion
Is yet aroused by human suffering, grant
Our fleet to escape from the flames, even now,
   O Father,
And save from extinction Troy's last slender
   hopes!
Or, if it is my desert, hurl down the wrath
Of your thunderbolt upon our remnant and   910
   destroy us,
Dash us to death now with your own right hand."
His prayer was scarcely prayed when a wild black
   storm
Boiled up, the rain poured in a torrent
And thunder shook the hills and shivered the
   plains.
The whole sky opened in a blinding cloudburst
Blown thick and black on the blast of the south
   wind.

The ships were filled, the smoldering timbers
    soaked
Till not a spark was left and all the vessels,
But for the loss of four, saved from disaster.

920   But Aeneas, reeling from the bitter blow,
Now set his mind, as leader of his people,
And conscious of the weight he had to bear,
To consider the question from every angle:
    should he
Forget the behest of fate and settle in Sicily,
Or should he still make for the Italian coast?
It was then that Nautes—an aged man and the one
The only pupil to whom Tritonian Pallas
Had taught the gift of prophecy and made him
Renowned for his powers—for schooled by her he
    was ready
930   To interpret the grim signs of the gods' anger,
Or what was the stern sequence of events
Ordained by destiny—it was then that Nautes
Addressed these words of comfort to Aeneas:
"O Goddess-born, we must follow the will of Fate
Foreward or backward—come what may, our
    fortunes
Can only be controlled by our own endurance.
You have Acestes here, a Dardan, divinely
    descended:
Make him your confidant—ask for the help
He is surely willing to offer you—hand over
940   To him the crews of our lost ships and all
Who have had enough of our great endeavor, more
Than they can bear—the older men and women
Are exhausted with seafaring—choose them out
And any more who are fragile or timorous.
Let the weary build the walls of their rest here,
And call their city Acesta, if leave be given."
The words of his old friend threw Aeneas' thoughts
Into a turmoil—never before had he suffered
Anxieties so complex and perplexing.
950   And now dark Night had driven her chariot
To the heights and held the canopy of heaven,
When down from that very sky a sudden semblance

Of his father Anchises seemed to materialize
Before his inward eye and spoke these words:
"My son, more dear to me than life itself
While life I had, my son whose burden is
The fate of Troy, I come at High Jove's command
Who saved your fleet from fire and at long last
Took pity upon you from his throne in heaven.
Obey the counsel wise old Nautes has given you,   960
None could be better. Take with you to Italy
An elect few, none but the bravest hearts.
In Latium there awaits for you to conquer
A people of tough fiber, of stubborn willpower.
Before you embark, though, you must make your
    way
To the Land of the Dead and, crossing deep
    Avernus,
Seek to meet me, my son. Do not imagine
That I am immured in ungodly Tartarus
Or some glum place of sorrows; no, I dwell
In Elysium in a concord of the blessèd.   970
A Holy Sibyl shall conduct you thither
After the sacrificial blood has flowed
From sable beasts. There you shall learn the tale
Of your posterity, every one, and the fortified city
That shall be granted you. But now, farewell!
For misty night has passed its turning point
And at my back I hear the panting breath
Of dawn's relentless team." Like smoke he
    vanished
Into the lapse of air. And Aeneas cried:
"Where are you rushing off in such a hurry?   980
Who are you flying from? What power denies you
To my embrace?" As he spoke he stirred the
    embers
Till their sleeping fires were roused, and in
    reverence
Prayed to the household gods of Pergamus
And the shrine of white-haired Vesta, dutifully
Offering holy meal and a full censer.

Immediately he called his comrades, calling
Acestes first and gave them an account

Of Jove's commands and his dear father's precepts
990 And the conclusions he himself had come to.
There was no argument: Acestes agreed
At once to these proposals. So they transferred
The elder women and all who wished to remain—
Ambitionless men without an itch for fame.
But the rest repaired the benches and replaced
Charred timbers in the hulls, refashioned oars
And renovated ropes, they were few in number
But each was a war-man of outstanding valor.

Meanwhile Aeneas took to the plough and cut
1000 The city bounds and allotted sites for the houses:
This district was to be "Ilium," that one "Troy."
Acestes, loyal Trojan, was delighted
With his new subjects, chose a suitable place
For public meetings and promulgated laws
To the assembled councilors. And next
On the heights of Eryx, neighborly to the stars,
They founded for Idalian Venus a temple
Within a glade of widespread holiness,
And with a priest to tend Anchises' tomb.

1010 And now the whole of this Trojan gathering
Had feasted for nine days and every altar
Had had its due of honor. Gentle winds
Had lulled the swell and the continual susurrus
Of the south wind enticed them towards the deep.
Then all along the winding shore there arose
A mighty weeping; in each other's arms
They lingered out the day and night—even those
    mothers,
Even those men, who had so lately quailed
At the sea's rough aspect and unbearable menace
1020 Craved now to go, and endure whatever hardships
The journey had in store. And to them Aeneas
In goodness of heart spoke words of consolation:
Commending them with tears to his kinsman
    Acestes.
Then he commanded the offering of three calves
To Eryx, and to the gods of Storm a lamb,
And gave the order to cast off—whilst he

With his head crowned in a wreath of close-
   trimmed olive
And a mixing bowl in his hand took his high place
On the prow and scattered the entrails into the
   waves,
And poured a shining river of pure wine.   1030
A following wind sprang up and speeded them,
And his crews in friendly rivalry struck the water
And swept the wavetops.

                         In the meanwhile Venus,
Frantic with cares, unburdened herself to Neptune
In a flood of heart-felt complaints: "I am
   compelled
By Juno's implacable anger, by Juno's insatiable
   spirit,
To resort to any and every sort of entreaty
However humble, Neptune; no length of time
Nor piety of men softens her heart;
She is neither curbed nor chastened by the Fates   1040
Nor by the command of Jove: it is not enough
To have torn Troy beating from the breast of
   Phrygia
In her monstrous hate, nor to have dragged the city
Through a gamut of vengeful torment—no! she
   pursues
The few survivors—even the bones and ashes!
Who knows but she the cause of rage so insensate?
But you yourself are my witness to the storm
She raised just lately in the Libyan sea,
The sudden mountainous waves that she reared up
To meet the lowering sky, daring to meddle   1050
In your domain when the winds of Aeolus
Had failed her purpose. And look at her latest
   deed:
She has even driven our Trojan women to crime,
She has wickedly burnt our ships compelling us
To leave the crews of the lost ships behind
In a strange land. As for these last poor few
I pray you—if my prayer be valid and if
The Fates allow them their walled city—let them
Sail safely over your seas and let them touch
Laurentine Tiber's mouth." Then Saturn's son,   1060

Lord of the ocean deeps, gave utterance:
"It is entirely right, Cytherean, to place your trust
In my realm of sea, from whence you arose
    yourself.
I too have earned your trust—I have often calmed
The rages, the ramping madness of sea and sky.
Nor less on earth—I call to witness the Xanthus
And the Simois—has been my guardianship
Of your Aeneas. For when Achilles was hunting
The breathless Trojan ranks and crushing them
1070 Against their walls, despatching them in thousands,
And choked with bodies the rivers moaned and
    the Xanthus
Could find no course to wind his way to sea,
Even then, as Aeneas confronted mighty Achilles,
Though not his equal in strength, nor in the help
He could hope from Heaven, I rustled him away
In a hollow cloud—though I myself craved
With my whole being to raze to their foundations
The walls of perjured Troy which I myself
Had built. Nor have my feelings changed one whit.
1080 Dispel your fears: Aeneas shall safely reach
The port of Avernus, just as you desire.
There shall be one and only one man lost—
Nor shall the sea restore him for all your asking.
One life, one life alone shall be given for many."

These soothing words rejoiced the heart of the
    goddess.
Then Father Neptune yoked his mettlesome horses
With a golden yoke and put the bits between
Their champing jaws and gave them a free rein.
The sea-blue chariot planed over the tops of the
    wavetops,
1090 And the waves fell, the swelling waste of waters
Subsided under the thunder of his wheels,
The storm-clouds fled from all the firmament.
Then there appeared his manifold retinue:
The vast sea-creatures, the ancient train of Glaucus,
Palaemon son of Ino, the speedy Tritons,
The whole parade of Phorcus and on the left

Thetis and Melitë, and Panopëa the virgin;
The Nereid Nesaeë, Cymodoce, Thalia and Spio.

And now through the anxious mind of father
   Aeneas
There was suffused a comfort of bliss abounding: *1100*
He bid every mast be raised and sail be broken
On every yardarm as speedily as possible.
Then all sprang to the ropes and now on the
   portside
Now on the starboard ran up sail and together
Swung on the yards and favorable winds
Bore the fleet on. At the helm of the leading ship
Sat Palinurus and he set the course
For the whole convoy. And now the dewy night
Had almost reached the zenith of its darkness
And the sailors lying stretched on the hard benches   *1110*
Beneath the oars relaxed their limbs in sleep,
When the Lord of Sleep slipped softly down from
   the stars,
Slid through the dusk and dispelled the shadows,
   alas,
Seeking you, Palinurus, bearing dreams
Of doom you had done nothing to deserve.
In the guise of Phorbas, the God took his place
On the high stern and so began: "Palinurus
Iasus' son, the seas bear on the fleet,
The winds blow square astern and steadily;
This is the hour for sleep! Lay down your head;   *1120*
Absent your weary eyes from working on!
Just for a while I will take your place at the helm!"
Hardly raising his eyes, Palinurus answered;
"What, me of all men, do you expect *me*
To misread a calm? Do you really expect *me*
To trust this devil sea? Do you think I'd trust
Aeneas to this cunning calm, this cheat
Of a fair wind?—me?—they've cheated me to my
   sorrow
Too often before!" And he hung on to the tiller
And never relaxed his grip and kept his eyes   *1130*
On the useful stars. But see! the god has taken

A branch dripping with Lethe's flood and drugged
With the properties of the Styx and made passes
Across his brows—and luckless Palinurus
Resist as he would could not resist and closed
His drooping eyes. And scarcely had this sleep
He had never asked begun to relax his limbs,
When the god bent over him and flung his body
Headlong into the sea and he ripped off
1140 Part of the stern and rudder which were still
Tight in his grip, but none heard him call
And call and call and call and call for help,
While the God of Sleep soared up into the air
On his light wings. And the fleet ran safely on
Over the sea in Neptune's promised surety.
And now it had sailed so far, it had reached the
  Rocks
Of the Sirens, hard to weather in days of old,
And white with sailors' bones, and the roar of
  the surf
Beat ceaselessly upon the ear from afar,
1150 When chief Aeneas felt his ship was yawing
And found her pilot lost and took the helm
Through the midnight sea with many a bitter sigh,
His spirit scored and scarred by his friend's loss.
"O Palinurus, did you trust too well
In a calm of sea and heaven? You will lie
A naked corpse cast on an unknown shore."

BOOK VI

So he spoke and wept, and bade his fleet full sail
And at last touched on the coast of Euboean
  Cumae.
They turned their prows to seaward and then
  each ship

Made fast with its anchor fluke and the shore
    was lined
With the curved sterns.
                        An eager band of youths
Leapt down to this Western shore and some of
    them searched
For the seeds of fire that lie deeply embedded
In veins of flint; others quartered the woods
Beating the tangled thickets for game, and marking
The streams' courses. But noble Aeneas sought   10
The height where great Apollo had his throne,
And the deep hidden abode of the dread Sibyl,
An enormous cave; for there the Delian prophet
Inspired in her the spiritual power
Of his own mighty mind, revealing things to be.
And now he neared the sacred groves of Diana
And the golden temple.
                        The story goes that Daedalus
Fleeing the rule of Minos dared to commit
His life to the air on speedy wings and sailed
To the cold north along a way unknown   20
And finally lightly landed on this Euboean hilltop,
And to you, Apollo,—for the land that first
    received him—
He dedicated his feathery gear and built
A majestic temple. On its doors was depicted
The murder of Androgeos and thereafter
The Athenians' dreadful penance—the yearly
    tribute
Of seven youths—O cruel expiation!
And there was the urn from which the lots were
    drawn.
Opposite this on the other half of the doors
To balance it, was Crete with the town of Knossos   30
Rising out of the sea, and the animal lust
Of the Bull, and Pasiphaë, and her stealth in love;
And there, as a horrible warning of such passions,
The dreadful offspring half-human and half-beast
The Minotaur; and there, too, was the palace
In all its grandeur, the maze none could escape
    from—
None, had not Daedalus taken pity on Ariadne

Because of her steadfast passion and himself
Guided the blind footsteps of her lover
40 With a thin clue of thread, and unraveled all
The treacherous windings of the labyrinth.
You, Icarus, too, in such a grand design
Would have had your place but for your father's
 grief:
Twice he tried to figure your fate in gold,
Twice the craft of his hands failed and he let
 them fall. . . .
They would have traced out every design in detail
Had not Achates, sent ahead, returned
That instant with Deiphobe, Glaucus' daughter,
The Priestess of Apollo and Diana.
50 "This is no time to gawk at pictures—come!
Separate seven bullocks never yoked
From the herd, for sacrifice and seven two-year
 sheep
Properly picked from the flock!" It was so she spoke
To Aeneas—(he made no delay, but obeyed her),
And so she summoned the Trojans, in her office
As priestess, to the temple on the hilltop.
One vast side of the Euboean hill had been
 hollowed
Into a cave—and a hundred broad tunnels
Led into it, and out of it a hundred
60 Voices poured out, the Sibyl's prophetic answers.
They came to the threshold and the priestess cried
"It is the time to make trial of the oracle!
Behold the god! Behold the god is here!"
As she stood at the door her mien was suddenly
 altered,
Her hair rose on her head, her color changed,
Her breasts heaved, she fell into a trance,
She seemed to grow, she spoke in no mortal voice,
And the spirit of the god, his very breath, came
 nearer, nearer . . .
"What are you doing, Aeneas man of Troy?
70 No offerings—no prayers—are you too lazy?
Unless you pray, the great doors of the cavern
Will never vibrate and open in holy marvel. . . ."
Then, not another word. A cold shudder

Ran through the Trojans' marrow, tough though
   they were,
And their Prince prayed then, with his full
   heart's fervor:
"Apollo, always you pitied the plight of Troy,
It was you who leveled Paris' bow and drew
His Trojan arrow straight to strike Achilles,
It was you who led me over so many oceans
That beat against great continents, and led me to   *80*
   probe
The remote Massylians, and coasts enclosed by
   quicksands.
Now, we have foothold in Italy at last
Let Troy's ill luck no longer dog our steps!
And all you other gods and goddesses,
Spare now the Trojan people though your eyes
Fell foul on Troy and our too glorious glory.
You, O most holy prophetess, foreseeing the
   outcome—
And I ask no powers outside the scope of my
   destiny—
Grant to my Trojans and their wandering gods,
Our travel-stained, our storm-tossed Trojan Gods,   *90*
A home in Latium. There will I build a temple
Of solid marble to Apollo and The Goddess,
The Triple One, and dedicate festal days
In Apollo's name, and we shall raise for you
A splendid shrine in our domains to house
The runes and secret oracles you shall speak
To my nation. And we shall consecrate
Priests for your pure service. Only one thing I beg.
Do not commit your prophecies to leaves,
Lest they become the mock and sport of the whirl   *100*
Of the wind. Speak with your mouth, I beg you!"
Amen to his prayer, he closed his lips in silence.
Meanwhile the prophetess, not yet resigned in
   willing
Submission to Apollo, mowed round the huge
   cavern
As if she hoped to shake off the god's grip on
   her being.
Yet all the tighter did he draw the bit

In her foaming mouth, breaking her wild heart
And crushing her spirit, molding it to his will.
And now of their own accord the hundred doors
110 Of the shrine swung open and the inspired answers
Were wafted through the air. "O you survivors
Of such mighty perils by sea—(yet there are
      mightier
In store on land), you sons of Dardanus
Shall come to Lavinia's realm—upon that score
You need have no fear—but there shall be no
      pleasure
In your arrival— War! I see savage War
And the Tiber seething blood! You shall not lack
Another Simois, nor Xanthus, nor a camp
Of Greeks. Another Achilles, and he, too, the son
120 Of a goddess breathes in Latium already!
Juno, your bane, will never be far away—
While you are suppliant—what city of Italy,
What nation will not have heard your beggar's
      knock?
And once again will a foreign bride be cause
Of calamity to the Trojans—a bride, too,
From the house of a host.
                          But still you must not yield
To affliction, but the bolder therefore go
To meet it, in so far as your Fate allows you,
*And the first way to safety lies where you least
      expect it—*
130 *From a Greek City."*
                          Such the oracular words
The Sibyl of Cumae spoke, awesome and strange,
As the cavern loudened her voice to a roaring
      boom
And the truth was wrapped in gnomic utterance.
Such was Apollo's power on the rein as she raved,
So deep was his spur driven into her heart.
But when the frenzy flagged and her mouth no
      more
Was possessed by madness Aeneas the hero
      answered:
"O Priestess no new aspect of suffering
Could take me by surprise—I have foreseen

Aeneas asking [illegible marginal note] to guide him

In my secret meditation every possible. 140
But one thing I pray: it is told that hereabouts
Is the gate to Pluto's realm and the dark pool
Of Acheron's overflow—may I be granted
Passage to within sight of my dear father
And meet him face to face. O tell me the way
And open the holy gates. It was on these shoulders
I rescued him from the ruck of our enemy,
Bore him through fire and the hail of a thousand
    javelins.
He was ill, he was old,—and old age should not
    suffer
Such ills as he endured as my companion— 150
Menaced by all that sea or sky could fling at us,
Yet he was my companion and he bade me—
The constant prayer he craved I should fulfill—
To visit you and kneel before your throne.
Pure one, I pray, take pity on father and son:
All things are in your power: how else had Hecate
Given you sway over the grove of Avernus?
If Orpheus had the power to beckon back
The ghost of his bride, by playing the Thracian lyre
With its resonant strings—if Pollux redeemed his 160
    brother
With his own death, in alternation passing
So often and repassing on death's road . . .
And what of Theseus? of Hercules? Need I go on?
I too am a true offspring of Jove's loins."
So he prayed, his hands fast on the altar,
And even while he prayed began her answer:
"O seed of divine blood, O Trojan son of
    Anchises,
The way down to Avernus is easy going—
Night and day the door of the Dark God
Is open wide—but to retrace your steps, 170
To re-climb to the upper air: what a task, what toil!
Some few whom Jove was right to love or whose
    innate
Virtues singled them out from the common run
    have done so.
The way is wholly a tangle of woods and Cocytus
Slides round in a black running noose of waters.

If any man has such a passionate yearning
As twice to float upon the mere of Styx,
As twice to see the dark of Tartarus,
If you are set upon this maniac venture,
180   Listen to what is imperative first to do.
There lies deep hidden in the shade of a tree
A Golden Bough—both leaf and limber stem—
Sacred to Juno of the Underworld,
Shrouded by all the forest, in the shadow
Of a shadowy valley. No man that has not gathered
That sprig of gold is given leave to penetrate
The hidden world beneath the mortal world—
Persephone has decreed it must be borne
To her as a proper tribute. Pluck one branch and
190   Another sprouts unfailingly, as pure
A golden twin. Keep a sharp eye, therefore,
To espy it, and when you do, be quick to pick it—
It will come easily, willingly, to your hand
If yours is the call of Fate—if not, no power
Of hand will wrench, nor blade will hack it off.
Meanwhile, though (alas you do not know it) the lifeless
Corpse of your friend lying unburied taints
The whole of your fleet with the odor of death, while you
Loiter here at my door in search of oracles.
200   Bear him to his due place, raise him a tomb.
Lead out black cattle. Let this expiation
Be as a first step—for so will you look on
The forests of Styx, regions where are no ways
For living men." She spoke. She closed her lips.

Leaving the cave Aeneas with face serious
And eye downcast turned over in his mind
The unforeseeable future, and steadfast Achates
Walked close beside him keeping careful step.
Their conversation ranged through many matters—
210   Whom did the prophetess mean—their dead comrade?
Whose body was to be buried? As they came—
Suddenly! there on the dry sand they saw it!
Misenus—son of Aeolus—Misenus

Whose sudden death was wholly undeserved:
No man excelled his skill on the brazen trumpet
To rouse men's hearts to battle by his calls;
Henchman of great Hector, at whose side
He faced the onset, famous for trumpet and spear.
And after Hector was conquered by Achilles
This most illustrious of heroes joined   220
Dardan Aeneas—no less a flag to follow.
But then by chance as he blew on a hollow shell
And his music rang across the seas, possessed
By mad conceit he challenged the Gods to outdo
    him.
And jealous Triton, if the story is true,
Trapped him and drowned him where the seas are
    a smother
Among the rocks. So all men stood there keening
With a great cry—Aeneas most of all.
Without delay they followed the Sibyl's orders.
Weeping still they gathered a funeral pyre,   230
Striving to pile the tree-trunks to the sky.
They went to the ancient forest, the lairs of the
    beasts,
And down crashed pine trees and the holm-oaks
    shuddered
At the thud of the ax, and beams of ash and oak
A wedge can split were split, and mighty rowans
Rolled down the hillside. And there, of course,
    was Aeneas,
Carrying tools like the rest, cheering them on.
But in his sad heart pondering his problem,
Surveying the vast forest, by chance arose this
    prayer:
"If only that Golden Bough would reveal itself   240
Somewhere in this huge welter of woods . . . for,
    alas,
In what she said of *you*, my poor Misenus,
The prophetess was right—she was all too true!"
He had hardly spoken when a pair of doves
Chanced to come gliding down out of the sky
Before Aeneas' very eyes and alighted
On the green turf. Then the great hero knew
These birds were his mother's, and prayed joyfully:

"Lead me, you two, if there be any way,
250 And through the air direct my steps to the grove
Where, in the fruitful earth, the precious Branch
Casts down its shadow. O my divine mother,
Forsake me not in this my hour of need!"
He spoke, and stopped still in his tracks to watch
What sign they would give and where they
   intended to fly to.
The doves flew on, then fed, then flew again
As far as any follower could keep them just in
   eyeshot,
Then when they came to the jaws and stench of
   Avernus
Swiftly they soared and gliding through clear air
260 Alit together on one chosen tree
Through whose dark branches shone a glint of gold.
As in the depth of winter-cold in the woods
The mistletoe is green with sprouting leaf,
The mistletoe that no tree seeds, that wreathes
Their trunks with its pale pearl-colored berries—so
In the evergreen-gloom of the dark ilex-tree
The leafy gold looked—so in the gentle winds
Jangled its metal foil. At once Aeneas
Eagerly pulled it down, though it withstood him,
270 And carried it to the prophetic Sibyl's home.

Meanwhile on the shore the Trojans bitterly
   weeping
Paid their last dues to Misenus—albeit it was
Beyond his powers to thank them. First they built
A pyre high-heaped with planks of oak and
   resinous
With pine, and wreathed its sides with gloomy
   leaves
And set in front a wreath of funeral cypresses,
And piled his glittering armor on the top.
Some warmed up water in caldrons simmering
Over their fires and washed the cold dead corpse
280 And anointed it. And then the keen was raised,
And they laid the body on the funeral litter
And cast upon it purple robes, as is meet.
Then some raised up the bier, a sad office,

Performed according to ancestral lore
And, heads averted, held a torch to it.
The heaped pile burst ablaze,—the offerings
Of food, incense, and oil from the votive bowls.
And when the flames died down and the ash
  caved in,
They drenched with wine the remains and the
  thirsty embers,
And Corynaeus gathered together the bones   290
And sealed them in an urn of bronze. It was he
Who purified his comrades encircling them
Three times and sprinkling from the fertile branch
Of an olive tree pure water; finally
He intoned the last valediction over the dead.
And good Aeneas raised a huge monument
Over the place and set up the hero's arms,
His trumpet, his spear, there at the mountain's foot
Which is named Misenus after him to this day
And keeps his memory green eternally.   300
This done he hastened to fulfill the commands of
  the Sibyl.
There was a vast cave with its jagged mouth
Gaping and guarded by a jet black mere—
So rank an exhalation reeked up to the sky
No bird could fly across its filthy jaws
And live,—*Aornus* the Greeks named it, "The
  Birdless."
Here as the first office of the sacrifice
The Sibyl stationed four black bullocks. Next
She poured wine on their foreheads and plucked
  out
The tufts of bristles growing between their horns 310
And laid them on the sacrificial flame,
As an outset of the rites, and cried aloud
To Hecate, mistress of Heaven and Hell.
Others applied the sacrificial knife
To the victims' throats and caught the still-warm
  blood
As it gushed in bowls. Aeneas drew his sword
And slaughtered a lamb of sable fleece in offering
To the mother of the Furies and to her mighty
  sister;

And, Proserpine, to you a barren cow.
320 Then he consecrated to the King of Styx
His altars for the Rites of Darkness piling
Whole carcasses of bulls on the flames and pouring
Rich oil on the glowing entrails. Then behold
Before the first glimmer of the rising sun
The ground beneath their feet began to bellow,
The woods heaved tossing to the mountain-tops,
And in the shadows the howling of spectral hounds
Proclaimed the goddess at hand.
                              "Keep off! keep off!
Whoever is unhallowed!" shrieked the priestess,
330 "Keep clear from the whole grove! You, Aeneas,
Step forth upon your way! Draw your sword from
     the scabbard!
Now is the time for courage, now for a steadfast
     heart!"
In very ecstasy she flung herself
Into the cavern's mouth. Without a falter
He followed in her footsteps pace for pace.
You gods whose sway is over the silent Shades,
You Souls, and Chaos, and you Phlegethon, river
Of rippling fire, and Night's broad still savannas,
Grant me the gift to speak without taint or flaw
340 *What I have heard, and with your divine favor*
Reveal things hidden deep in the dark of the earth!
On they went in the dark, their shadowy way,
The night aloof above them, through Pluto's void
Vacant dominion, through its lifeless homes—
It was like making way through a wood by the
     mean
Light of a fitful moon when almighty Jove
Has shrouded the sky with cloud, and black night
     sucked
All color out. And there was the very threshold,
The very mouth of Hell where Agony
350 And the Ache of Remorse had laid their beds:
     there—
O horrifying sights!—lay wan Diseases,
Unhappy Old Age, Fear, Hunger-that-goads-to-
     Evil,
Despicable Want, and Suffering and Death;

There Sleep, own-brother of Death, and Joy-in-
  Guilt,
And on the threshold of Death its herald War.
There were the iron cells of the Furies, there
Was Raving Revolution, her snake-locks
Bound with a bloodstained ribbon.
                              In the midst
There stood an elm, enormous in its shade,
Ancient and branchy, where, so the legend goes,   360
False dreams cling clutching under every leaf.
And there besides are many shapes of monsters,
Centaurs stabled, Scyllas half-beast half-man,
Briareus, hundred-handed, Lerna's Hydra
Hissing horribly, the Chimaera armed with flame,
Gorgons and Harpies, and the three-bodied ghost
Of Geryon. Suddenly seized with dread, Aeneas
Unsheathed his sword and poised the naked blade
To counter any attack—but his companion
Of her own deeper knowledge acquainted him   370
That these were bodiless forms that flitted empty
Of substance—or he would have run upon them
Lunging at mere shadows, thrusting to no purpose.
From here the road led to the Tartarean waters
Of Acheron. Here seethed the whirlpool in its deep
Abyss of filth disgorging all its waste
Into Cocytus. Here was the hideous Charon,
The keeper of this ford, revoltingly dirty,
A matted straggle of white beard on his chin,
His eyes glaring, a disgusting cloak   380
Knotted and dangling from his shoulder—as he
  poled
His ferry or trimmed the sails, and himself
  heaved over
The dead-weight of the dead in his dusky barge,
An old man—but a god with a god's evergreen
  age.
Towards him a whole multitude came flooding,
Pouring towards the bank—mothers, and heroes
Whose deeds of bodily prowess in life were done,
Boys and unwedded girls; and young men laid
On the funeral pyre before their parents' eyes,
As many as the leaves that droop and fall   390

When the first frost of autumn shivers the woods,
Or as the birds that flock in from the deep
And cluster upon the shore when the winter
   drives them
Over the sea to roost in more clement airs—
So they stood begging Charon to take them first,
But the glum ferryman picked now these, now
   those,
And fended others, barring them from the brink.
Aeneas indeed distressed and puzzled by this
   tumult
Cried to the virgin priestess, "Tell me the meaning
400 Of this gathering to the stream? What seek these
   spirits?
What choice decides who shall withdraw from the
   bank,
While some are rowed over these leaden waters?"
The ancient prophetess briefly made answer:
"Son of Anchises, scion assuredly
Of a God, you see the deep still pools of Cocytus,
And the Marsh of Styx, and if the gods swear
By this dread Power they dare not break their
   bond.
All this concourse are helpless because unburied:
Charon is Warden here—he only conveys the
   buried.
410 It is forbidden him to give any passage
From the dread shores and across the gurly
   swirling
Before their bones have found a resting place.
For a hundred years they are doomed to swither
   here
Hovering on this brink and then at last
They are let embark and see in truth these waters
They have longed so long to cross."
The son of Anchises halted in his tracks
And meditated deeply, his mind moved
To pity at the unequal fates of men.
420 For there he saw Leucaspis and Orontes
The captain of his Lycian ships—and both
Had sailed with him from Troy over the stormy
   waters,

But a gale from the south caught them, capsized
  their ship
And down to the bottom she went—lost with all
  hands.
And there was Palinurus one of his helmsmen.
It was not long since, on the voyage from Libya,
While he was plotting his course by observing the
  constellations
That he fell overboard from the tiller into the deep.
In such dark shadows to recognize anyone
Was hardly possible but Aeneas recognized   430
Palinurus, first of the two of them, and addressed
  him:
"Palinurus, what god was it snatched you from us
And drowned you in mid-ocean? Tell me. Apollo
Never deceived me, but this is the one time
It seems his oracle lied: Did he not promise
You would safely cross the sea and land in Italy?
Is this how he kept his promise?" Palinurus
Answered him then, "O Lord of Anchises' line,
Apollo's oracle never was false, no god
Drowned me—it was an accident; my fault.   440
I was at the helm, my proper place, and suddenly
I wrenched the stern post and the tiller with it
Clean out—we peeled off suddenly over the side,
And that was that—I was far more concerned
For the safety of your ship without a helm,
Without a helmsman, than with what rising seas
Could do to me, and the sea was rising steeply.
Three nights the gale blew southerly and I bobbed
On mountainous seas of storm; and then at dawn
On the fourth day I sighted Italy   450
From a wave crest, and little by little I paddled
In to the shore—I should have been safe then,
Sodden as I was, but a party of wreckers seized me
As I was scrabbling at the first cliff-edge,
Supposing I was something worth. And so
The sea has got my bones and the winds play
The shore for the flotsam and jetsam of me. Please,
By the light of happy heaven, by the air you
  breathe,
By all your hope for your son as he grows up

460 O unconquered one, rescue me from these evils—
(The gods are with you, or you could not now
Attempt to cross the Stygian Marsh, these breadths
Of mighty waters, I know it.) If there's a way,
If your divine mother can show you the way,
Give your poor comrade your right hand and
  conduct him
Across the stream and release him from his misery
And let him rest at last in death, in a calm repose."
These were his words and to him the prophetess
  answered—
"Palinurus! How dare you be so impertinent!
470 Why should you, you unburied as you are,
See the dread flow of the Styx, the Furies'
  forgiveless river?
Why should you come to the bank before your
  time?
The ordinances of Gods are not to be swayed by
  prayers,
But listen to me and comfort yourself with this:
Far and wide through the cities, divine revelations
Shall cause your bones to be revered as holy:
They shall build you a monument, they shall year
  by year
Perform rites in your honor for evermore,
And the place shall have the name of Palinurus."
480 These words brought balm to the grief of his heart,
The pain was assuaged in a little while—he
  delighted
In thinking a site would always bear his name.
So on they went and neared the river, and Charon
Who had seen them from afloat as they
  scrambled through
The silent grove and approached the river bank,
Challenged them sharply before they could utter
  a word:
"Whoever you are who come in arms to my river
Stay where you are, halt! and speak from there.
This is the place of Shadows, of sleep-inducing
  Night,
490 It is forbidden to ferry the living across the Styx.
I have no pleasant memories of conveying

Hercules over these waters, nor Theseus nor
  Pirithous,
Sons of gods though they were, unconquerably
  strong.
One came to kidnap from under the very throne
Of Pluto his watchdog Cerberus and drag him off
Trembling upon a chain; the other two
Tried to abduct Persephone from the very
Bridal bed of King Pluto!"—and the priestess
Of Apollo gave brief answer, "Have no fear;
We are not here to deceive you—nor do we bear   *500*
Our arms to attack a soul; the vast bulk
Of your gate-guard is safe—he can howl for ever
And make the slivers of shadowy ghosts shiver—
Faithful Persephone is safe—she need not
Bar any door of her homestead. Trojan Aeneas,
Famed for his feats of arms, as famed for his piety,
Has come to the deeps of the darkness of Erebus
To seek his father. If such great piety
Makes no impression upon you—let this branch—
(It was hidden under her robe—now, she   *510*
  produced it).
This you must recognize!" He said nothing more
But fixed his gaze in awe on the holy offering,
That fateful Bough before his eyes again
After so long a lapse of time. Stern first
He maneuvered his dark boat in towards the bank.
Then he shooed out those spirits who already
Were sitting upon the benches, cleared the
  gangways,
And straight away took the bulk of Aeneas on
  board.
Under his weight the seams gaped open, she
  sprang
A leak and shipped a deal of mud and water;   *520*
But in the end they crossed the river safely
And Charon disembarked the hero and the
  priestess
Safely upon the sludge and the gray rushes.
This was the region which huge Cerberus
Made echo with his three-fold howling throat
Slumping his vast length all across the cave-mouth.

Seeing the snakes on his neck beginning to rear,
The prophetess tossed him a scrap of food—doped
With honey and drugged corn. And the famished
    brute
530 Snapped it up slavering with his triple jaws
And settled his huge back and stretched his length
Along the floor of the cave. Aeneas seized
His chance as the monster lay unconscious and
    quickly carried
The entrance and put safe behind him the waters
Of no return. And immediately was heard
A crying—the vast wailing of infant souls
There in the very portal, snatched away
On a black death-day from their mother's breasts
Before they had tasted the sweet of life, doomed
540 To bitter death. And next to them the souls
Delivered to death on perjured evidence:
But here their place was not without appeal,
For Minos sits in judgment with a jury
Chosen by lot and bids the silent gathering
Listen to evidence of their lives and the charges
Preferred against them. Then next in their place
Were the grievous souls who committed suicide,
Though guiltless, in sheer hatred of the dayspring
Casting themselves away. How willingly now
550 They would bear every pain of poverty, every
Impost of toil in the bright air above!
Not far from here extending on every side
Were to be seen the Mourning Fields—for so
They were called, and here among secret paths and
Amid the seclusion of a wood of myrtles
Dwell those whom wasting love in its grim cruelty
Has brought to death—and even in death their
    sorrows
Do not loose their hold of them—and in this place,
Aeneas saw Phaedra, Procris, and grieving
    Eriphyle
560 Displaying still the wounds inflicted on her
By her brutal son; Evadne he saw, Pasiphaë,
And with them Laodamia, and there was
    Caeneus—

A young man for a while, but now a nymph
  restored
By the turn of fate to her original sex.
Among them wandering in the mighty wood
Was Dido the Phoenician her death-wound still
Livid upon her—and when the Trojan hero
Found he was near beside her and through dim
  shadows
Just recognized her (as a man might think
He sees or seems to see a young moon rising   570
Through banks of cloud), the tears rose to his eyes,
And in soft loving tones he said to her:
"O Dido, unhappy one, was the story true
That was brought to me? They told me you had
  bidden
A sword conduct you to journey's end—and I—
Was I the cause of that? I swear by the stars,
By the Gods above, by whatever there is true
In the earth beneath to its deepest depth, I swear
It was not of my own desire I left your land,
O Queen, it was the inexorable bidding of heaven   580
Which now has forced me to explore this wilderness
Of Darkness here, driving me through deep night
And dank decay—what could I do but obey?
How could I know my leaving you would cause
Such a paroxysm of grief? Oh stay your steps!
Do not withdraw yourself from my sight I beg you!
Whom do you fly from? I—these are the last
Words I shall ever speak to you; fate allows me
No more. . . ." Aeneas yearned to appease her
  inflexible fury,
And to induce her tears. But she, with her head   590
  averted,
And eyes fixed on the ground, was starkly adamant.
His pleading overtures moved her no more
Than had she been a flint or a block of marble.
At length she flung herself away and fled
Into the shadowy wood, implacable still,
And there, Sychaeus, her husband at the first,
Comforted her distress and gave her love for love.
Aeneas, none the less, shocked by her unjust fate

Followed her far, weeping, and pitied her as she
　　went.
600 Thereafter he bent his utmost to the journey.

Already they were approaching those farthest acres,
Those final fields where only the great war-heroes
Had their preserves. Here Tydeus ran to meet him,
Parthenopaeus famous in arms, and the pallid
Shade of Adrastus, here the Dardanids,
Fallen in battle and deeply mourned in the world,
And now as he saw them here in their long ranks
He grieved aloud—Glaucus, Thersilochus, Medon,
The three sons of Antenor, Polyphoetes
610 The priest of Ceres, and Idaeus still
Handfast to his armor and his chariot.
These spirits thronged around him, left and right,
Nor was one look enough for them; they delighted
To linger with him step by step and discover
The reason for his coming. But when the Greeks,
Agamemnon's chiefs, and their massed followers
Saw the great hero in his glittering armor
Stride through the shades, they were convulsed
　　with terror.
Some turned tail, as once towards their ships,
620 Some tried to raise a war-cry—but it died
Into a whimper, their mouths silently gawping.
And then he saw Deiphobus son of Priam,
His white body a mangled shambles; his face,
Both arms, his ears shorn from his head, his nostrils
Slit with a horrible wound—he scarcely knew him
As he cowered away to hide this ghastly
　　vengeance.
But Aeneas addressed him in the voice he knew:
"Deiphobus, great warrior, born of the blood of
　　Teucer,
Who was it craved to inflict so brutal a vengeance?
630 Who was allowed such a power over you?
On that last night the report of you I heard
Was that you sank down spent on a heap of bodies,
Worn out with slaughtering Greeks. Then I myself
Built on the Rhoetean shore an empty tomb,
And loudly called three times upon your spirit—

Your name and your arms are there to keep the
   place
In memory warm—but you yourself, my friend
I could not see nor lay your body to rest
In our native earth—the land I was forced to flee."
And the son of Priam answered, "You, my friend,   640
Left nothing undone—everything that was owed
To me or my shade, you have paid it in due order.
It was my own Destiny and the deadly
Wickedness of Helen that engulfed me
In this disaster— It is she that has left
These tokens of her love—you know yourself
How that last night was spent in false rejoicing:
One cannot but remember—with good reason—
When at one leap the Fateful Horse surmounted
The heights of our citadel, its womb heavy   650
With infantry full-armed, and she pretending
To lead a ritual dance ramped through the city
With a band of Trojan women in Bacchic frenzy
And, in their midst, held high a mighty firebrand
And from the top of the citadel summoned the
   Greeks.
But as for me, worn out with cares and sunk
In heavy sleep in our luckless bridal chamber
I lay and a sweet deep calm came over me
Most like the peace of death. But in the meanwhile
My splendid wife—she even had extracted   660
My trusty sword from under my own pillow—
Summoned Menelaus into the house and
Flung open the doors—hoping, I have no doubt,
That doing such a favor to her lover
Would soften his heart and erase the memory
Of all her evil misdeeds. But why should I
Drag out the story? Into the room they burst,
Ulysses with them instigator as ever
Of all things evil. O Gods, if the lips that pray
For retribution are pure, requite the Greeks   670
With equal barbarities!

                But tell me, Aeneas,
What chance has brought you living to this place?
Did you lose your bearing at sea? Or have you
   come

At the behest of heaven? Or what dire fortune
Has driven you to visit these sad sunless halls,
This place of confusion?"

               As they were thus engrossed,
The goddess of dawn in her rose-colored chariot
Had passed the zenith of her heavenly course,
And maybe in such talk they would have spent

680   The whole of their allotted time but the Sibyl
Upbraided her companion curtly and said:
"Night falls fast, Aeneas: yet we pass the time in
   weeping.
This is the spot where the road forks into two:
The right-hand path under the battlements
Of Mighty Pluto—there lies my own way to
   Elysium.
But the left-hand path leads evil men to Tartarus
And the exaction of due punishments."
Deiphobus answered: "Do not rage, great
   priestess,
I shall depart now and take my place again,

690   Back in the dark. But you Aeneas, go—
Our nation's glory—go on your way—go
And may Fate treat you better than I was treated."
Speaking these final words he turned and went.

Aeneas looked about and suddenly saw
At the foot of a crag to his left wide battlements
Enringed by a triple wall and round the wall
In cataracts of flame the Phlegethon,
River of Tartarus, roared and tumbled its
   rumbling boulders.
To the fore was a huge gate with columns of
   adamant

700   So strong no mortal force nor the embattled
Gods of heaven themselves could root them up.
Up in the air there rose one iron tower
And there Tisiphone sat, wrapped in a mantle
Sodden with blood, and sleepless guarded the
   courtyard
Day-and-night-long. And from within were heard
Deep groans and the savage crack of whips and
   the rattle

Of metal from dragging shackles. Aeneas stopped,
Horrified with this din, and asked: "O priestess
What manner of crimes have men committed, tell
    me,
And with what punishments are they expiated?   *710*
Why these appalling howls that rise to heaven?"
Then answered she: "Illustrious leader from Troy,
It is forbidden to an upright man
To cross that threshold, but when Hecate
Gave me authority over the groves of Avernus
She led me through all these regions and herself
Explained to me the punishments of Heaven.
Rhadamanthus of Knossos rules this place
With an iron hand: hearing each case of deceit
And fitly condemning it he compels each victim   *720*
To confess to the gods those crimes whose
    expiation
They had postponed in life—in their fatuous self-
    congratulation at having concealed them—and
    death came.
And it was too late. And in a flash Tisiphone
The torturer has pounced on the criminal
Whirling her scourge in her right and in her left
    hand
Brandishing a tangle of snakes and calling
The savage horde of her sisterhood . . . Look!
    Look!
(With a creak of hinges that struck terror to the
    soul
The sacred gates were swinging open.) Do you see
What manner of sentry guards the courtyard?   *730*
    What shape
Keeps safe the threshold? Inside there sits a
    Hydra,
A monster fiercer far with fifty throats
Hungrily gaping. Then there is the abyss
Of Tartarus itself falling sheer to the darkness
Twice as far as an upward-looking eye
Can see from earth to heaven.

                    And down there
In the uttermost depths flung down by a
    thunderbolt

Wallow that ancient race, the Titans, born of the
    earth.
And here I saw the twin sons of Aloeus,
740   Huge giants who with their own hands had tried
To pull down the vault of heaven and dispossess
Almighty Jove of his kingdom. And I saw
Salmoneus suffering cruel punishment:
He had counterfeited the thunder of Olympus:
Driving four horses, flourishing a torch,
He went through the tribes of the Greeks, he went
Through the midst of the city of Elis in a triumph
Demanding the homage only a god should have,—
Mad!—If he thought that he could counterfeit
750   With a rattle of brass and the beat of horny hooves
The storm-cloud, the inimitable bolt.
But the Almighty Father hurled his own
Bolt from the core of his clouds—it was no wispy,
No smoky brand, and hurled him headlong down
On the wings of a whirlwind.
                And there to be seen
Was Tityos, child of the all-fostering Earth
Whose body lies stretched over nine acres
And a great vulture with its hooked beak plucks
At his undying liver, and gripes his entrails,
760   Rich source of agony, mining its every meal
From his deep heart perpetually and giving
No respite to the ever-renewing sinew.
Why call to mind Ixion, Pirithous, or the Lapiths
Over whom towers a dark crag in the split
Second of ever-falling. Or tell of the banquets,
The luscious fare piled on the banqueting tables
With props of gold—but there at the head
    crouches
The chiefest of the Furies and bars their hands
From touching a crumb but leaps up clutching a
    torch
770   And shrieking with all her might.
                And here are those
Who in their lives detested their own brothers;
Who struck their parents; inveigled relatives
Into deceit; who grew rich and became
Misers and gloated alone, and never shared

A piece with their dependants—(these were the
  most),
Adulterers killed for their crimes, traitors in war
Betraying their masters without fear or shame:
All are penned here, to await their punishments.
Ask now what punishment, what form of doom,
Must overwhelm these men in their grim destiny.   780
Some roll huge stones, others spreadeagled hang
From the spokes of a wheel; Theseus sits in despair
And so will sit for ever. From the depth
Of his misery Phlegyas moans his message loudly
Through all the shades. 'Be warned! Learn to be
  righteous
And do not despise the gods.' And here is a man
Who sold his country for gold, and let in a dictator;
—This man could be bribed to make or unmake
  laws
—This one committed incest with his daughter—
All of them dared some hideous crime and did it.   790
Why, if I had a hundred tongues and mouths
And a voice of iron I could not complete the list
Of every crime, and name each punishment."
The ancient priestess ceased—and then she added,
"Come now, you must move on, you must fulfill
Your chosen duty—we must quicken our steps—
I see the ramparts forged in the Cyclops' furnace
And in that archway standing opposite
Is the spot divinely ordained for us to set
Our offering." Then step for step they traversed   800
The dim-lit way between, and came to the door.
Aeneas gained the entrance, sprinkled his body
With pure spring-water and fixed the Golden
  Bough
Upright upon the threshold.

                          So all was duly done,
Her rites performed for the Goddess, and at last
They reached the realms of Joy, the green delights
Of the Groves of Bliss, and the Halls of the
  Blessèd.
Here, a fuller air envelops the plains
In a glittering sheen—and the blessèd behold a sun
And stars which shine for ever for them alone.   810

Some of these spirits flex their immortal limbs
In the grassy wrestling-ring, for the sheer sport,
Or throw each other in the saffron sand;
Others chant songs or beat out with their feet
The rhythms of choric dance. And there is
   Orpheus,
The Priest of Thrace in his long robe, on the lyre
Tuning its seven notes in time to the measure,
Now with his fingers, now with an ivory plectrum.
Here is the ancient lineage of Teucer,
820   Most comely family, heroes of high courage
Born in happier times: Ilus, Assaracus,
And Dardanus founder of Troy. From afar Aeneas
Gazed in wonder at these heroes' armor
And idle chariots: their spears standing
Rooted in earth, and everywhere their horses
Loosed to graze in freedom over the plain.
All the delight they took, when living, in their
   armor,
Their chariots and their horses, their grooming
   and feeding—
All this delight went with them under the earth.
830   Then, lo, Aeneas looked to left and to right
Where other spirits feasted upon the grass
And sang in chorus hymns of joy. In a grove
Of scented bay they were, whence the full flood
Of the river Eridanus wound its forest way
To the upper world.
                      Here was the band of those
Who suffered wounds in war for the fatherland;
Of those who were chaste priests, in earthly life;
Of those who were faithful prophets, whose
   utterance
Was worthy Apollo's ear; there were those who
   had
840   Embellished life by the skill of their inventions;
Those called to mind by many for acts of grace;
And round their brows all wore a snow-white
   wreath
And as they crowded about her the Sibyl
   addressed
Musaeus, for he stood out in their midst,

Head and shoulders above the crowd, and seemed
Their spokesman. "Tell us dear spirits, tell us,
O best of poets, in what part, what place,
Does Anchises dwell? It is to visit him
That we have crossed the flood of Erebus."
Briefly the hero answered her: "No one here   850
Has one fixed dwelling—we consort in the shade
Of the groves, on the moss-soft river banks;
We live in the meadows sweetened by little streams,
But, if it be your pleasure, climb to this hill
And I can set you on an easy pathway."
So saying he went ahead and from the crest
Showed them a glistening land below, and down
From the crest they clambered.

                Now at this time Anchises,
Deep in a green valley, was surveying
With fatherly fond scrutiny the souls   860
Confined there with him, soon to make their way
To the light of day again—and as it so happened
Reviewing the whole strength of his own clan,
His dear posterity, their fates and fortunes,
Their bearing and their deeds. And when he saw
Aeneas coming towards him over the meadow
He opened his arms to him eagerly, the tears
Coursed down his cheeks and he cried out—"At last!
Have you come? Has your steadfast faith surmounted
The perils of the journey? I knew you would   870
Fulfill your father's hope, O my son, am I truly
Let look upon your face and hear your voice
And talk with you? Why, in my own mind
That was indeed what I reckoned—calculating
The passage of time, nor have I been deceived
For my pains—You are here, my son—after what perils
By land and sea! Oh sport of what terrible dangers!
How fearful I was the Libyan powers might harm you!"
Aeneas answered, "Father, it was you—
Your grief-engendering spirit time and again   880

Appeared to me and constrained me to make my
    way
To the edge of this world. My fleet rides safe at
    anchor
In the Etruscan sea. Oh father, your hand—
Give me, give me your hand to clasp in mine!
Do not draw back from my embrace!" The tears
Streamed down his face as he spoke. Three times
    he tried
To fling his arms round that dear neck, three times
The spirit melted from his hands
That clutched in vain, like the wind's breath it was
890 Or the swift dissolution of a dream.
And now Aeneas saw at the remote vale-head
A hidden grove and woodland-rustling spinneys,
And saw the River Lethe as it flowed
By these abodes of peace. And round about it
Hovered the souls of countless tribes and peoples
Like bees in the fields of a fine summertide
Flitting from flower to flower and everywhere
White lilies grow and the whole plain is humming.
Amazed at the sudden sight bemused Aeneas
900 Asked what it meant, what were those distant
    waters
And who the mass that clustered on the banks.
"They are the souls," answered his father
    Anchises,
"Whose destiny it is a second time
To live in the flesh and there by the waters of
    Lethe
They drink the draught that sets them free from
    care
And blots out memory.

                    For a long time
It has been my wish to tell you about these souls
And to parade them before your very eyes,
And number them, the inheritors of my blood,
910 And now that you have landed in Italy,
Rejoice with me the more."

                  —"But father, truly,
Am I to believe that any of these souls
Go hence to the upper air and again put on

The shackles of flesh? How could such an insane
Lust for the light delude these unhappy
  creatures?"
"Son, I will tell you and put your mind at rest."
Anchises then began his exposition:

"In the beginning know that heaven and earth,
The rivery plains, the glittering orb of the moon,
And the Titanic stars were animated   *920*
By a Spirit within, and a Mind interfused
Through every fiber of the universe
Gave vital impulse to its mighty form.
From these there spring the races of men and
  beasts,
The birds that fly, and all the strange shapes of
  creatures
The sea brings forth beneath its marbled surface.
Their life-force is drawn from fire, their creative
  seeds
Are of heavenly source, except as they are clogged
By the corrupting flesh, and dulled by their earthly
Habiliments, and limbs imbued with death.   *930*
From these derive our fears and our desires,
Our grief and joy, nor can we compass the whole
Aura of heaven shut as we are in the prison
Of the unseeing flesh. And furthermore,
When on the last day we are lost to the light,
We do not shed away all evil or all the ills
The body has bequeathed to us poor wretches,
For many flaws cannot but be ingrained
And must have grown hard through all our length
  of days.
Therefore we souls are trained with punishment   *940*
And pay with suffering for old felonies—
Some are hung up helpless to the winds;
The stain of sin is cleansed for others of us
In the trough of a huge whirlpool; or with fire
Burned out of us—each one of us we suffer
The afterworld we deserve: and from thence are
  sent
Through wide Elysium, and some few maintain
Ourselves in the Fields of Bliss, until length of days

When time has come full circle, cleanses us
950   To corruption's very core and leaves a pure
Element of perception, a spark of the primal fire.
After the cycle of a thousand years
God summons all these in a great procession
To the waters of Lethe, so that when they visit
The sky-encircled earth, being bereft
Of memory, they may begin to want
The body on again."

                              So spoke Anchises
And he led his son and the Sibyl both together
Into the midst of the chattering throng and took
960   His stand on a mound from which he could review
The whole of that long line and recognize
Each passing face.

"Come then, I shall show you the whole span
Of your destiny, I shall make manifest
What glory lies in store for the seed of Dardanus,
And what posterity, Italian-born,
Your blood shall fill, illustrious spirits all,
And heirs-to-be of our name. Do you see that
     youth
Leaning upon his yet unpointed spear?
970   Nearest he is to the light of day—so the lot
Has chosen—he will be the first to rise
To upper air with Italian blood in his veins—
His name is Silvius, an Alban name,
He is your son—to be born after your death—
Your wife Lavinia late in her life will rear him
Out in the woods, a king and father of kings:
Our ruling house in Alba Longa traces
Its origin from him. Then next is Procas
The pride of the Trojan people; then Capys;
     Numitor;
980   Then Silvius Aeneas, bringing your name
Back into use, and equally distinguished
In piety and warfare, if ever he shall sit
On Alba's throne— O look what splendid youths!
What strength of build—see how their brows are
     shaded
With cinctures of the civic oak-leaf? They

Shall build Nomentum for you and Gabii,
Fidenae's city and the mountain fortress
Of Collatia; they shall build you Pometii
And Inuus, Bola and Cora, with their camps.
These sites are nameless—they shall give them   *990*
   names.
And Romulus, too, the son of Mars shall come,
His grandfather at his side—that Romulus
Sprung from the blood of Assaracus, and his
   mother
Is to be Ilea, named from Troy and she
Is to bring him up—do you see the double plumes
That start from his helmet?—see how even now
He is marked out by his divine father,
With his own emblem, for the Upper World?
Behold, my son! Under his tutelage
Our glorious Rome shall rule the whole wide   *1000*
   world,
Her spirit shall match the spirit of the gods;
Round seven citadels shall she build her walls;
In her breed of heroes blest—as the goddess
   Cybele,
Charioted and wearing a towered crown,
Parades through the cities of Phrygia rejoicing
In all her brood of gods, her hundred grandsons
All heaven-dwellers, holders of the heights!
Now turn the gaze of your eyes this way—look!
Look at this people, your own Roman people.
Here is Caesar and all Iulus' line,   *1010*
Destined to pass beneath the great arch of the sky;
Here is the very man whom you have heard
So often promised you, Augustus Caesar,
Your child of the Divine who shall refound
A golden age for Latium—in those lands,
Those very lands where Saturn once was king,
Who shall extend the frontier of our rule
Beyond the Garamantians and the Indians
(A land that lies outside the track of stars,
Outside the course of the year and of the sun,   *1020*
Where Atlas the sky-bearer humps on his shoulder
The spinning pole of the world with its inlay
Of blazing constellations). And even now,

In expectation of his coming, the realm
Of Caspia quakes and the regions round Maeotis
Quiver in fear of the prophetess of the Gods,
And at the sevenfold mouth of the river Nile
A welter of confusion seethes.

　　　　　　　　　　　　　　Indeed,
Not even Hercules covered so much of the world
1030　Although he shot the brazen-footed deer
And brought peace to the Erymanthan forest
And intimidated Lerna with his bow.
No, nor Bacchus when in triumph he drove
His tigers in a harness of vine tendrils
Down from the heights of Nysa.

　　　　　　　　　　　　　　Then shall we
Still hesitate to prove our worth in deeds?
Shall fear prevent our setting a firm foot
On Italian soil? But who is that in the distance,
On his head a wreath of olive and in his hand
1040　The sacred vessels? I know by his white locks
And snowy beard he is that King of Rome
Who first shall base the city on firm foundations
Of Law—from little Cures called, from its barren
Fields, to supreme authority. And next
Tullus doomed to disrupt his country's peace
And rouse to battle warriors grown torpid
And columns lost to the habit of the triumphal
　　march.
Next follows the braggart Ancus—why even now
He is far too pleased at catching the popular
　　favor—
1050　But do you wish to see the line of the Tarquins?
Or the proud spirit of Brutus the avenger
And the fasces he won back? He shall be first
To assume a consul's power, the cruel axes,
And in the sweet name of liberty put to death
(Unhappy father) his own sons when they raised
The standard of new revolt: whatever is said
About these deeds in after times—that victory
Is love's—a patriot's love and a measureless
　　passion
For acclamation. But see, there in the distance,
1060　The Drusi and the Decii and Torquatus

Ruthless in wielding the ax and Camillus too
Who retrieved the standards. But those spirits,
   there,
Whom you see clad alike in glittering armor—
In harmony, now, and so long as this dark
   confines them—
But oh! if ever they come to live, alas,
How huge a war will they wage against each other,
What hosts of men! What heaps of dead! Caesar
Sallying from the ramparts of the Alps
And the fort of Monoecus, Pompey his son-in-law
With the whole force of the East disposed to   1070
   meet him.
Children, O children, never submit your minds
To become inured to such appalling wars,
Nor turn the sterling strength of your fatherland
To stab its very vitals—you be the first
In mercy, you who trace your line from Olympus
And have my blood in your veins—cast down
   your weapons!
—That man there, shall drive his chariot in
   triumph
To the high Capitol of defeated Corinth
After a memorable massacre of Greeks.
He, there, shall raze Argos and Agamemnon's   1080
Own city Mycenae, and kill that Aeacid
Whose blood is the blood of Achilles the mighty
   in battle,
Avenging his Trojan forbears and Minerva's
Polluted temple. And who would leave you, Cato,
Without an admiring word, or you Cossus?
Or the house of Gracchus? or those twin bolts of
   war
The Scipios, the scourge of Africa?
Or Fabricius powerful in poverty? Or Serranus
Sowing seed in his furrows. And where, you Fabii,
Do you force my weary way? You, Maximus,   1090
The one man with the power to save who saved
The State by your wise policy of delay.
And there are others, assuredly I believe,
Shall work in bronze more sensitively molding
Breathing images, or carving from the marble

More lifelike features; some shall plead more
    eloquently,
Or gauging with instruments the sky's motion
Forecast the rising of the constellations:
But yours, my Roman, is the gift of government,
1100 That is your bent—to impose upon the nations
The code of peace; to be clement to the conquered,
But utterly to crush the intransigent!"

So spoke father Anchises and while they wondered
    he addèd,
"See how Marcellus advances, wearing his
    General's trophies,
A conqueror towering over all his troops.
And when the state of Rome is rocked by rebellion
He shall restore order; his charger's hoof shall
Trample the Carthaginian, the risen Gaul,
And for the third time he shall dedicate
1110 The captured suit of armor to Quirinus."
—Here interjected Aeneas, for he saw
Beside Marcellus walked a beautiful youth
In gleaming armor, yet with downcast eyes
And little joy in his visage—"Tell me, father,
Who is his young companion—is it his son
Or one of the great line of his descendants?
What presence he has, how loud the hum of
    approval
Among his followers! Yet his head is veiled
In a drear cloud as black as night!" Anchises,
1120 His father, answered through a flood of tears:
"My son do not inquire of the great grief of your
    people,
The fates allow the world to catch but a glimpse
    of him
And then no more. Oh Powers of Heaven, the
    power
Of Rome would have seemed too strong had such
    a gift
Been theirs to keep. How the whole field of Mars
Shall ring to his own great city the weeping of
    warriors!
Tiber, what funeral rites what a tomb you will see

New-built as you glide by! No other boy
Of the Ilian breed shall raise so high the hopes
Of his Latin ancestors, never again   *1130*
Shall the Land of Romulus take such a pride
In any son she bears! Oh weep for his piety!
His faith like the faith of old! His invincible valor!
None could have brooked him in battle whether
  on foot
His onset, or driving the spur into his foaming
  charger.
Ah piteous boy! if there were any hope
Of bursting the bands of fate, you would be
  Marcellus. . . .
Bring lilies by the handful—let me strew
Bright wreaths of flowers and do his soul what
  honor
A grandsire may—an ineffectual office. . . ."   *1140*

And so they wandered far and wide on the plain
In the shining air and marked all that was there.
Sleep has two gates they say: one is of Horn
And spirits of Truth find easy exit there,
The other is perfectly wrought of glistening Ivory,
But from it the Shades send false dreams up to
  the world
And it is from this Ivory Gate that Anchises,
Now he had finished speaking, sped his son and
  the Sibyl.
Aeneas found a short way to his ships
And rejoined his comrades. Then he coasted to   *1150*
  Caieta.
Anchors were cast from prows; the ships were
  beached by the stern.

BOOK VII

For you, on your death, Caieta, O nurse of Aeneas,
Have given the headland and the harbor here
An everlasting repute—and to this day
You are honored here, and throughout the
    Western Land.
Your name is known by the resting place of your
    bones,
If that indeed be glory. So when good Aeneas
Had dutifully performed the final rites
And built a barrow, he watched for calm weather,
Then set sail from the port. A fair breeze
Blew nightward on, the white moon lit their way
And the sea sparkled in her quivering rays.
They coasted close in to the land of Circe,
The Daughter of the Sun, whose grove for ever
Thrills with the sound of singing in its fastness,
Whose splendid halls are lit against the night
With fragrant cedarwood, as through the delicate
    warp
She threads her rattling shuttle. They could hear
The angry snarl of lions chafed by their chains
And roaring into the midnight, the fume and fury
Of bristled boars and bears in cages, the howling
Of monstrous wolves—all these were human
    beings
Circe the cruel goddess had transformed
By her powerful drugs into the shapes and forms
Of wild beasts. But Neptune, so as to save
The pious Trojans from suffering such a fate
If once they put into harbor, or even neared
The magical shore, sent them a fair wind
That filled their sails and sped their passage past

178

The boiling shoals. The sea was already beginning
To glimmer with light-rays, and from the height   30
    of heaven
Aurora, saffron-clad, in her rose-colored chariot
Was showing clear, when suddenly the winds
Dropped to a dead calm and their oars struck
    heavily
Into an oily sea. And from his lookout,
Aeneas saw across the waters a towering forest
Through which the Tiber wound its delightful way
With swirls and rapids, and yellow with churned
    sand
Broke into the sea. Around and above,
Birds of the bank and stream made all the air
Mellow with song and fluttered from tree to tree.   40
He bade his comrades alter course and turn
Their prows to the land and joyfully he entered
The shady river-mouth.

                              Be with me, Erato!
And I shall unfold the names of the kings of
    Latium,
Her ancient state, the stages of her history
Until the time these strangers landed their army
On the shores of Italy; I shall recall and record
How the first blood was shed. Goddess, O guide
    me,
Goddess, O guide your poet! I shall tell
Of a grim war, of battle-lines, of kings   50
Whose courage drove them deathward; of Tuscan
    ranks;
Of the whole of Italy mustered under arms.
Grander the issues now before my mind,
To a grander task I turn.

                              The long reign of Latinus
Had brought to farm and city serene peace.
But the king was growing old, who we are told
Was son of Faunus and the nymph Marica—
A Laurentine nymph. And Picus was father to
    Faunus—
And you, it is said, O Saturn, begot him, you
Are the founder of his line—but King Latinus   60
By the will of the gods had no male heir, no son—

He had been cut off in the first flower of youth.
One daughter was all he had, his only hope
For the future of his royal house—a girl
Now woman grown, a flower for any man.
Many the man that sought her hand from the
    bounds of Latium
And from all Italy and by far the fairest
Was Turnus, favored both in his noble forbears
And by the queen who advanced his claims with
    eager devotion;
70 But sinister signs from heaven stood in the way.
There was a laurel-tree in the very heart
Of the inmost hall of the palace whose every leaf
Was sacrosanct—it had been held in awe
For many years and they say that father Latinus
Found it there when he came to build his citadel
And consecrating it to Phoebus called
His subjects after this laurel-tree, Laurentines.
And suddenly to the marvel of all who saw it
A swarm of bees whizzed buzzing through the air
80 And settled on the top, then interlinked
In a mill of legs the cluster hung from the leafy
Branch and at once a prophet interpreted:
"Lo, I perceive a stranger soon arriving
From that same quarter as the bees. He comes
Leading an army to their present lodging—
And so shall he hold sway over the citadel!"
And add to this, while the virgin Lavinia
Was standing beside her father as he kindled
The altar fires with holy brands, her hair—
90 O dreadful sight! her long hair caught afire
And all her headdress crackled in the flames—
Her royal tresses, her crown encrusted with
    jewels—
Till, wrapped in a livid pall of smoke, she scattered
The sparks of the fire god up and down the palace.
This was indeed a terrible sight, a miracle
Before their very eyes and the prophets said
That she was singled out indeed for a glorious
    destiny,
But for the nation it boded a terrible war.

Alarmed by these prodigies the king went
To the shrine of Faunus, his prophetic father,   *100*
To question at the glades beneath Albunea,
That greatest of the groves where a sacred spring
Comes bubbling up and from whose shadowy
     depths
Belches a noxious vapor. It is from there
That all the races of Italy and Oenotria
Seek answers to their deepest doubts; and there
The priest lays his gifts and in the silence of night,
Stretched on the skins of the sheep he has
     sacrificed,
He seeks for sleep and sees a host of phantoms
Flitting in marvelous forms, hears many voices,   *110*
Enjoys speech with the gods, or with the denizens
Of the Underworld to the last deeps of Avernus.
Here came father Latinus to seek an oracular
     answer.
He offered up, as was meet, a hundred two-year
     sheep
And stretched himself upon the pelt of their fleeces
When suddenly a voice rang from the depths of
     the forest:
"Seek not a Latin marriage for your daughter!
Put no faith, my son, in these present proposals!
Strangers shall come to commingle our blood and
     being our kindred
Shall bear our name to the stars, and our   *120*
     descendants
Rule all the peoples of the turning world
From sunrise to sunset!" Thus father Faunus
Answered out of the silence of the night.
But Latinus was not silent—the news spread
Like wildfire through the cities of Ausonia—
Even as by the grassy banks of the Tiber
The Youth of old Laomedon moored their fleet.

Aeneas, his chief captains and fair Iulus
Sat themselves down under a tall tree's branches
And set out a meal, and inspired by Almighty Jove   *130*
Put wheaten cakes on the grass to use as platters

And piled this meal of Ceres with wild fruit.
When everything else was eaten— (and since
  there was
So little to eat they were left feeling hungry)
They were compelled to turn to their thin platters
And boldly break them in their hands and crunch
These fateful rounds of crust nor spare the centers.
"Look here!" Iulus laughed, "we are eating our
  tables!"
That was all that he said, but his words spelled
An end of their toils to his hearers—and his father
Cut him off short as he spoke in awed amazement
At the divine revelation, and then said:
"Welcome, O promised land of my destiny!
And you my faithful Trojan Gods, all hail!
Here is my home, my country: For my father
Now I recall, Anchises, left me just
Such a secret of destiny—speaking thus to me,
*'My son when you have touched an unknown shore
And being bereft of food you are forced by hunger
To eat your tables—then remember, however
Exhausted you are—you can hope for a home
  there—
There lay your first foundation and rear a rampart!'*
This is that very hunger: the limit set
To our sufferings. Come therefore and joyfully
At the crack of dawn let us explore this country
And find out who are its inhabitants
And where their capital city—let us take
Different ways from our haven here. But now
Offer libations to Jove and remember Anchises
My father in your prayers and set more wine
Upon our tables!"

                         So he spoke and thereafter
Wreathing his forehead with a leafy branch
He invoked the Spirit of the place, and Earth
The first of the gods, and the Nymphs, and then
  the Rivers
Unknown to them yet—then Night and the
  Galaxies
Of stars appearing, and great Jove of Ida;
In her due place the Phrygian Mother, Cybele;

140

150

160

And his two parents, Above and Below as they
were.
Then the Almighty Father thundered thrice
High in the clear sky, and himself made manifest *170*
A cloud glowing with rays of golden light,
Quivering from his making-hand. The rumor
Ran rife through the Trojan lines that the day
had come
To found their destined city. Immediately
They set to the feast again and joyfully
To celebrate in wine the all-powerful omen
And wreathe their heads with vine leaves.

When dawn of the next day bathed the earth
with light,
Parties set out to seek for this people's city,
To trace their boundaries, to chart their coastline. *180*
And here was the glassy spring of the Numicus,
Here the river Tiber, here the dwellings
Of the brave Latins. Then the son of Anchises
Detailed an embassy of a hundred men,
Chosen from every class, to go to the capital
All wreathed with olive-sprays and bearing gifts
To the king and asking friendship for the Trojans.
Immediately they sprang to his commands
And hurried on their way while he himself
Marked out a plan of his walls with a slit-trench *190*
And leveled the site and built fortifications
In the style of a camp, there by the seashore.
By now the young Ambassadors had come
To the end of their journey and saw ahead of them
The towers and lofty mansions of the Latins;
Then they drew near the wall. In front of the city
Boys and young men in the first flower of manhood
Were riding or learning, in a cloud of dust,
To control chariots—or drawing springy bows,
Or practicing javelin-throwing, or challenging *200*
Each other to a race or a bout when a messenger,
Who had galloped ahead of them, brought to the
ears
Of the old king the news that a party of strangers,
Tall men in foreign dress, were approaching him.

The king bade them be summoned into the palace
And took his seat on his ancestral throne
Set in the midst of the hall. The palace was huge,
A noble building raised on a hundred columns
And set on the height of the city, the Palace of
    Picus,
210 A holy place within its screen of trees
Sacred for generations. Here, if his reign
Was to be blessed, a king must first receive
His scepter and the symbols of his office;
Here was their temple and their senate-house,
The hall of their holy banquets, where a ram
Was sacrificed and the elders, in one conclave,
Sat down to table. Here, too, stood in order
Statues of ancestors, carved out of ancient cedar,
Italus, father Sabinus the planter of vineyards,
220 Keeping his curved sickle secure as he did in life,
And aged Saturn and two-faced Janus—these
Stood in the entrance and all the other kings
From the beginning of time, and heroes wounded
In battle for the fatherland. And besides
There were many weapons slung from the sacred
    doorways,
And captured chariots and curving axheads,
Helmet-crests, and enormous bolts from gateways,
Spearheads, shields, and battering rams ripped off
From prows of ships. There too, portrayed sitting,
230 Quirinal staff and sacred shield in hand,
Clad in official toga was Picus the horse-tamer,
Whom goddess Circe his wife in a jealous frenzy
Struck with her wand and turned him by her
    simples
Into a bird and sprinkled his wings with speckles.
Such was the temple of his gods that Latinus
Was seated in, upon his ancestral throne.
He summoned the Trojans to him and when they
    came
Addressed these calm and measured words to them:
"Tell us, you sons of Dardanus, for indeed
240 We knew of what city and race you come, and had
    word of you setting
Your course across the sea towards our coast—

What do you seek? What reason or what lack
Has driven you onward over so many miles
Of the blue sea-breakers to the Italian shore?
Did you mistake your course? Were you storm-
  driven?
A sailor's life is open to so many
Trials and tribulations—whatever happened
You have entered our river-mouth, you have made
  fair haven,
So shrink not from our welcome, but recognize
The lineaments of Saturn's race in us—   *250*
We Latins peaceful without bonds or Law
But of our own free will in fealty
To the ancient God. Why, I myself remember
(Though it is too long ago to remember it clearly)
That Auruncan elders told of how Dardanus,
Who was born here, made an expedition as far
As the cities of Ida and Phrygia and to Thracian
Samos, the place they now call Samothrace.
Yes, he set out from his home in Etruscan
  Corythus,
And now a god he sits on a throne in the golden   *260*
Palace of star-sown heaven and has his altar
Numbered among the altars of all the gods."
He spoke and Ilioneus made answer to him as
  follows:

"King, famous son of Faunus, neither the heaving
  seas
Nor impulse of black storm forced us to land here,
Nor star nor seamark deceived us; it was our will,
Our common purpose, bore us to this city,
For we were driven from the greatest realm
The journeying sun surveyed in all his journeying.
From Jove we trace our house: and we descendants   *270*
Of Dardanus glory in our ancestor.
Our king himself, Trojan Aeneas, springs
From Jove's pure stock—it is he who has sent us
Here to your doors.

                        How terrible the storm was
That struck from fierce Mycenae and came pouring
Over the plains of Ida; how at the word of fate
Europe and Asia, two worlds clashed together:

—Is there a man that has not heard of it?—
    whether
He lives at the back of beyond where the Ocean
    coils
280 Back on itself or whether he lives in the central
Zone of the pitiless sun, cast off from human
    companions?
We fled from that cataclysm, we have tossed
Our way over leagues of ocean and now we beg
A narrow niche for our household gods, for
    ourselves;
A strip of harmless shore and the common freedom
Of air and water. We shall not shame your
    kingdom,
No man shall speak lightly of you—gratitude
Shall not grow old for the deed—nor shall the
    Italians
Rue the day they took Troy to their hearts.
290 I swear by the star of Aeneas, and by the strength
Of his right hand, proven in peaceful friendship,
    proven
In war. For many the peoples, many the nations
Have wished to ally or to unite themselves
With us—(do not despise us, then, because
Of our own free will we bear in our hands the
    wool-bound
Emblems of supplication, and prayers are on our
    lips).
It was the Gods' ukase, their inevitable decree
That drove us to seek your land and yours only.
For here was Dardanus born; and back we have
    come
300 At Apollo's bidding, at his express command,
To Etruscan Tiber and the holy fountainhead of
    Numicus.
Moreover Aeneas proffers these few and scanty
    presents,
Relics of past riches and saved from the sack of
    Troy:
—This was the golden cup Anchises used at the
    altar;
These were Priam's robes, when as custom was,

He promulgated laws to his assembled people;
Here is a scepter, here a sacred headdress,
And garments worked by the women of Troy."
                                        Latinus
Heard Ilioneus' words with gravity.
Dead-still he sat on his throne, his head bowed,   *310*
His eyes moving only in key with his deep
     meditations—
And these were not concerned with Priam's
     scepter
Nor purple finery so profoundly as
With his daughter's wedding and its
     consummation.
He turned in his heart the oracle of old Faunus:
This must be that man foretold of destiny
Who, coming from foreign lands, should wed his
     daughter
And rule with him in equal sovereignty;
Whose seed should be renowned for its superlative
Valor, and by their strength become masters of   *320*
     the world.
At last he cried, with joy: "May the gods favor
The designs we have begun, and thus fulfill
Their own presage! I grant your requests, O
     Trojans.
I accept your gifts. So long as I am king,
You shall not lack what fruitful earth can offer,
Nor shall you miss the prosperity of Troy!
Let but Aeneas come himself, if indeed his longing
Is such for us, if he yearns for the bond of
     hospitality,
To be treated as an ally. Let him not be afraid
To look on the face of his friends to be. For my   *330*
     part
Until I have taken your prince's hand in mine
Peace will not be complete. Now if you please
Carry my message back to your king. It is this.
I have a daughter. But I am forbidden
To wed her to anyone of my own people.
Every omen forbids it: there are the voices
From the shrine of my own father: there are
     countless

Heavenly portents. And all of these foretell
That her new kin shall come from foreign lands.
340 That is the future in store for Latium.
Our races shall intermarry, the new blood
Shall exalt our name to the stars. And if I have
Any powers of true prophecy I think
Aeneas is the elect of the fates. I believe it is he."
When he had spoken thus the king chose out
A number of horses from all the royal stables.
There were three hundred glossy-coated steeds
Standing in high stalls. Then he bade a horse
Be led to each Trojan in order of precedence,
350 A racer hung with purple-embroidered trappings,
And each with a golden poitrel at its chest;
Golden armor they had, and between their teeth
Bits of a matching gold. And for Aeneas,
Since he himself was not there, Latinus chose
A chariot and a pair of yoked horses
Of heavenly breeding, their nostrils snorting fire,
Of the bastard strain which cunning Circe had bred
By fraudulently crossing a mortal mare
With her father the Sun God's celestial stallions.
360 Such were the gifts and such the words of Latinus
Which Aeneas' embassy bore back, proud on
    their horses,
Bringing the news of peace.

But see, now! Juno the fierce Queen of Jove
On her way back from Argos, city of Inachus,
Was soaring through the sky and from high over
Sicilian Pachynus she looked down
And in the far distance she saw Aeneas
At last relaxed, content by the Dardan fleet—
Already she noted that building was in progress,
370 The ships deserted and the Trojans trusting
Themselves to the good earth. She stayed rigid
In a spasm of agonized fury—then tossed her head
As a torrent of words poured from her mouth.
"Detestable race! O loathsome Phrygian destiny
At odds with mine! Could they fall on the plains
    of Sigeum?

Escape the sprung trap? Be burned to death in
  Troy?
No! No! They found a way through the thick of
  the battle
And through the heart of the fire. Must I believe
My powers of godhead flagged, my hatred slaked?
Have I peace of mind? Why, when the Trojans   *380*
  were driven
Out from their country I deigned to follow the
  exiles
And harry them the length and breadth of the seas,
The uttermost strength of the sea and sky has
  been spent
Against the Trojans— What use to me were the
  Syrtes
Or Scylla or huge Charybdis?—here they are
In their longed-for haven, the Tiber mouth, safe
From ocean and from me! Yet Mars had power
To destroy the giant race of Lapiths— The Father
Of the Gods himself surrendered ancient Calydon
To Diana's malice— And what had the Lapiths   *390*
  done?
Did Calydon deserve such a dire fate?
But I, the wife of mighty Jove himself,
Determined to leave nothing untried, stooping
To any shift however degrading—I
Am vanquished by Aeneas. Very well!
Suppose the power of my godhead be too weak—
I would not shrink from seeking aid elsewhere,
Wherever I can find it— If I cannot
Prevail on Heaven I shall let loose Hell!
I cannot ban Aeneas from the throne—   *400*
Let that be so— Nor can I stop Lavinia
From marrying him, her fate is immutably fixed,
But it *is* in my power to put a spoke
In the wheel of these great affairs, to check and
  hinder
And rend in ruin the peoples of both these kings!
Your dowry shall be blood, my girl, the blood
Of Trojan and Rutulian—Bellona is waiting
To preside over your wedding. Not Hecuba only

Was delivered of a firebrand and bore the spark
of a blaze.
410   It is the same for Venus, and her child.
He is a second Paris, a brand to burn
Troy to a second death—even as she arises!"
When she had cursed her fill she dived headlong
Down to the earth, a ghastly apparition
And from the dark of hell, from the deep hall
Of the Goddesses of Dread she haled Allecto
To whom the taste of bitter wars, of hate,
Of treachery, and cruel crimes was sweet.
Even her father Pluto hated her, her Tartarean
420   Sisters detested the monster; so many the forms
She assumed, so savage her mien, so many the
serpents
That writhed and coiled black-clustered on her
head.
And Juno fueled her fury with these words!
"Maiden, born of night, do me a favor, I beg you,
A deed after your heart, to prevent my worship
And my renown from yielding place:—contrive
that neither
Can the Trojans entrap Latinus into this marriage
Nor threaten the frontiers of Italy. You have the
power
To set the lovingest of brothers fighting,
430   The happiest families at loggerheads.
You have the power to bring scourges and
funeral firebrands
Into a home, you have a thousand names
A thousand arts of hurting. Come, sharpen
Your teeming wits: shatter the peace treaty
Just now concluded, sow provocations to war!
Let all the young men in one same single moment
Desire, demand, and snatch up arms!"
                        Allecto
Loaded with Gorgon poison immediately flew
To the high palace of the Laurentine ruler
440   Of Latium, and there she hid and waited
By the still threshold of the Queen Amata—
She was already in a nervous frenzy

Over the Trojans' arrival and the thwarting of
  Turnus' marriage.
The fiend plucked one of the serpents from the
  blue-black
Coils of her coif and flung it at the queen,
Deep in her breast to worm its way to her heart
And cause her by its magic to set the house
In a wild uproar. It squirmed through the folds of
  her garments
Gliding about her soft breast though she felt
None of its cold coiling none of the viperous   450
  vapors
It hissed into her heart driving her mad.
Transformed to snake her golden necklet choked
  her
Transformed to snake the ties of her headdress
  writhed.
It threaded her hair, it slithered about her body
And while the poison in its first oozings
Was seeping through every pore and sense of her
  being,
Wreathing her bones with fire, but not as yet
In full spate flooding heart and soul, she spoke
Softly and as a mother will, with many tears
Bemoaning her daughter and the Phrygian   460
  marriage.
"O Father, is our Lavinia truly to be offered
In marriage to Trojans, exiles? Have you no pity
For her or for yourself? No pity for me her
  mother?
At the first breath of a north wind this pirate
Will take to the high seas with her, and carry her
  off.
—It was not like this when the Phrygian
  shepherd slunk
His way into Lacedaemon and abducted
Helen the daughter of Leda to Trojan cities!
Where is your pledged word? Where the concern
You have had so long for your people? The   470
  promise given
Again and again to Turnus? If this husband

We Latins seek must be a foreigner,
And Faunus's command is fixed immovably
I say that every land is foreign which is not ours
But is independent of our rule, and I believe
That is the gods' interpretation too.
And if you trace back Turnus' family tree,
His ancestors are Inachus and Acrisius,
And the heart of Mycenae, his home ground!"
    Latinus
480 Budged not an inch to her entreaties. She saw him
Inflexible against her and the sickening
Poison sank and thickened and diffused
Its madness through her system; then utterly
    fordone
And frenzied by the all-powerful drugs at once
She mopped and mowed the length and breadth
    of the city,
Like the gyrations of a whipping top
That boys have put their whole soul into lashing
About in an empty courtyard: and it reels in rings
As the whip drives and the boys crane over it
490 In puzzled amazement at the spinning boxwood
As it leaps to life at their strokes—even so the
    Queen
Was driven wild and whirling through the city
With its gantlet of sneering watchers. But that was
    not all.
For as if possessed by Bacchus she fled to the
    woods,
By greater frenzy driven to greater sin,
And hid her daughter among the mountain hangers
To scotch the marriage and keep the Trojans on
    tenterhooks.
"Evoe, Bacchus," she shrilled, "Oh none but you
Is worthy of this maiden: See!" she ranted,
500 "She takes the sacred Thyrsus in your honor,
She dances round you, she dedicates a lock
Of hair to grow for you!" Round flew the rumor
And soon the same hysterical frenzy fired
The hearts of other mothers with its wild
Compulsive urge to seek new homes—they
    deserted

Their own; they loosed their necks and hair to
    the winds.
Some dressed in fawn-skins, and bearing spears of
    vine-wood
Quavered their cries to heaven—the Queen in
    the midst
Brandished high a blazing firebrand, rolling
Her bloodshot eyes and chanting the wedding song   510
For Turnus and her daughter: then suddenly
She screeched like a savage: "Ay! mothers,
    mothers!
Listen, you mothers of Latinum, every one!
If you have any grain of kindness left
In your hearts for poor Amata, or any feeling
For a mother's rights, then loose your braided hair
And join the orgy with me!"

                      Thus Allecto spurred
The Queen, made maenad, now this way now that
About the woods and the remote lairs of beasts.
And having given impetus enough,   520
As it seemed to her, to the onset of madness
And overthrown Latinus' house and his purpose,
The grim goddess was born on her dusky wings
Far to the walls of spirited Turnus' city
Which, it is said, was founded by Danaë
For Argive settlers driven ashore by a gale there.
Our ancestors once called the city Ardea
—It keeps its great name still, but nothing else.
Here, in his high palace, Turnus lay
Deep in the sleep of midnight's dark. Allecto   530
Put off her bestial features, her Fury's limbs,
And took an old woman's face, her brow seared
With ugly wrinkles, her white hair bound with a
    fillet,
And wreathed with an olive branch. She appeared
To be Calybe the aged servant of Juno
And priestess of her temple and presented herself
To the young man, with these words.

                        "Turnus!
Will you stand by and see so much of your effort
    wasted?
And what is yours transferred to Trojan settlers?

540   The king is refusing to give you your bride, or
       the dowry
Won with your blood, and a stranger is being
       imported
To inherit the throne! Go on, expose yourself
To unmerited dangers! Be mocked! Go and mow
       down
The Etruscan ranks and shield the Latins with
       peace!
—These were the very words the almighty
       daughter of Saturn
Bade me to speak in your presence as you lay
Lapped in the calm of night. So up! and joyfully
       order
Your men to arms and march out through the
       gates!
As for the Phrygians who lie in our beautiful river,
550   Burn up their ships and their painted chieftains
       in them!
This is the inescapable command of Heaven.
Yes, let Latinus feel the embattled anger of Turnus
Unless he consents to give you your bride, and
       honors his promise!"
At this the young man opened his mouth to
       answer,
And mocked the priestess: "The news of a fleet
       arriving
In the mouth of the Tiber had not as you imagine
Escaped my ears. And do not conjure up
Such images of Terror to my eyes,
Nor think Queen Juno has forgotten me.
560   No, it is you, old crone, whom age has moldered
And sucked the truth from, and vexes to no
       purpose,
And mocks with false foreboding when you
       prophesy
Of kings at war. Stick to your statues and
       temples—
That is your sphere. Leave peace and war to
       men—
For that is theirs." At this Allecto's anger
Flared up, and a sudden trembling seized the youth

And his eyes set in a stare, so great the hissing
From all the Fury's serpents, so terrible
The visage that appeared. Then fixing him
With eyes of flame as he stammered and   570
   stumbled on,
She thrust him down and stiff from her head
   erected
Twin serpents in her hair and cracked her whip
And fulminated at him from her foaming lips.
"So! Look at me, old crone whom age has
   moldered
And sucked the truth from, and mocked with
   false foreboding
When I prophesy of kings at war. Look at this,
   now!
I come from the realms of the Dread Sisterhood;
It is War and Death I wield!"—with the words
   she hurled
A burning brand at Turnus and in his breast
She stabbed her torch which smoldered with   580
   black smoke.
He started up from sleep in a cold sweat
Of utter panic, shattered to the marrow.
Demented he yelled for his sword, rummaging
   under his pillow
And through the palace. A savage lust for steel
And all the filthy insanities of war
Took hold of him, and anger above all—
As when a noisy crackling fire of sticks
Is piled beneath the ribs of a bubbling pot
And the water seethes with the heat—
There inside is the water steaming and storming 590
Leaping and lipping the sides until no longer
Can it contain itself, but a dark scum rises
And frothing up it overboils and spills—
Just so it was with Turnus. He gave his captains
Orders to arm and march against Latinus,
Saying the king had broken the treaty and saying
He must save Italy and drive out the invader,
If need be he was a match for Latin and Trojan
   together.
When he had said these words he called on the gods

600 And the Rutulians eagerly rallied to arms;
    One fired by his leader's perfect grace and youth,
    Another by his royal line, another
    By the great deeds wrought his own right arm.

    While Turnus was instilling into his men
    A spirit of daring, Allecto whirled away
    Towards the Trojans on her Stygian wings.
    Choosing a new device she cast her eye
    On the coign of coastline where the fair Iulus
    Was hunting wild beasts with his nets and hounds,
610 And these the Hell Fiend suddenly drove rabid
    And filled their nostrils with a familiar scent—
    To set them in full cry after a stag. And this
    Was the first spark of trouble and the reason
    The country people turned their thoughts to war.
    The stag they hunted was a magnificent creature
    With splendid antlers—a stag that had been taken
    Before he was weaned from his mother and kept
        as a pet
    By Tyrrhus and his boys—(Tyrrhus was master
    Of the king's herds and keeper of all his pastures).
620 He was their sister Silvia's especial pet:
    She had trained him to obey her, entwined his
        horns
    With delicate flower-chains, groomed his coat
    And washed him in spring water, wild though he
        was.
    He would come to her hand, he would feed at his
        master's table,
    But he would wander wild through the woods and
        find his way
    However late at night back to the door he knew.
    Now as he strayed Iulus' maddened hounds
    Got on his scent as he drifted down the river
    Allaying the heat of the day under its green banks.
630 And Iulus fired with desire for this special trophy
    Bent his curved bow and shot an arrow—his aim
    (Some god guided it) was true—and the noisily
        whizzing
    Arrow ripped through the stag's belly and flanks.

Wounded, the beast dragged back to his known
   home
And lowing found his stable and bleeding filled
The whole house with his supplicating groans.
Silvia was first to act, clapping her hands on her
   arms,
Calling for help to the seasoned country people.
Amazingly quick they came (for ruthless Allecto
Lay doggo in the woods) one armed with a stake   640
   fire-tempered,
Another with a knoppy cudgel—whatever
Weapon came to each hand as his anger flared.
Tyrrhus marshaled his troop—he, as it happened,
Was splitting an oak into quarters and had just
Fixed in the wedges and he was breathing fire.
But from her lookout the savage goddess saw
The chance for further evil and flew to the roof
Of the stables and from its topmost peak blew
The Herdsman's Call, and on the curving horn
Sounded the full note of Hell which shook   650
The woods and made the furthest forest echo.
Far off it was heard beside the Lake of Diana;
The River Nar with its white sulfurous waters
And the springs of Lake Velinus heard it also,
And shivering mothers clutched their sons to
   their breasts.
Then quickly indeed to the sound of the grim bugle,
With weapons snatched up hastily, came running
From every quarter the dour country people.
Nor were the Trojan youths slower to sally
Out of the camp to come to Iulus' help.   660
They drew up their lines of battle—it was no
   longer
A rustic affray with cudgels and stakes fire-
   tempered,
But an issue to be tried with two-edged steel,
And far and wide a bristling crop of swords
Stood up like iron wheat, and the glare of bronze
Glanced back to the sun and gleamed to the
   underside
Of the high clouds— As when with a rising wind

The waves whiten, and little by little the sea
Steepens till from its lowest deeps it leaps to
   high heaven.
670 And now young Almo, eldest of Tyrrhus' sons,
Was killed by a whirring arrow as he stood
In a forward post ahead of the front rank,
For his throat was gashed with the wound
And the passage of his liquid voice was choked
With the rush of blood, and the vital windpipe
   blocked.
And many the heroes lying around him—among
   them
Galaesus an older man, killed as he interposed
His body between the forces to mediate.
He was a man of the uttermost probity,
680 None like him and no man so rich before
In Ausonian lands—he had five flocks of sheep,
Five herds of cattle and employed a hundred
   ploughs
To turn his soil.
               And thus on the plains the battle
Hung in the balance of the War God's favor:
The powerful goddess had performed her promise,
Bloody war was begun and the first blows
Of the grievous contest struck and so she left
The Western land and spanning the arch of the sky
Flew to the seat of Juno and spoke in arrogant
   triumph,
690 "See! Your thirst for discord slaked in war and
   its horrors!
Now bid them join in friendship and make peace!
I have already blooded the Trojans with
The blood of Italians—but if you give me leave,
I can do more than this—by spreading rumors
I can bring the neighboring cities into the war,
And craze their spirits till they burn with passion
For war, and come from every side to help.
I can disseminate war through the whole land!"
Then Juno answered: "There is enough terror
700 And treachery! the causes of the war
Are clear-cut now, there is hand-to-hand fighting
   already—

New blood is caked on the weapons chance first
   supplied.
Such be the bridal, such the wedding rites
That King Latinus and the famous son
Of Venus are to celebrate! But as for you,
It is not the Will of Jove, the Supreme Lord
Of high Olympus that such as you should wander
Too widely in the upper air: Give place!
If there be further chance for evil-doing
I shall deal with matters myself!" The daughter   *710*
   of Saturn
Put an end to this exchange. And then Allecto
With a hiss of serpents spread her wings and flew
To her home in Cocytus, and left the slopes of
   the sky.
There is a spot in the middle of Italy
At the foot of some high mountains, which is
   famous,
And talked of in many lands: it is called the Valley
Of Ampsanctus—a dark thickly wooded cleft
Down which a torrent roars and rolls its boulders.
Here you can see an awe-inspiring cavern,
The breathing-holes of pitiless Pluto, the huge   *720*
Gulf whence Acheron yawns its filthy jaws.
And into this the Fury dived, a hateful deity,
And lightened the earth and sky of the load of her.

Meanwhile the daughter of Saturn set her final
Seal on the war. There was a general rush
Of peasants into the city from the fighting
And they carried in the killed—the youthful Almo
And Galaesus with his mutilated face—
And prayed to their gods and supplicated Latinus.
Turnus was there among them busy, whilst   *730*
Hysterical reactions to the slaughter
Remained at fever pitch, whipping up terror:
"The Trojans have been invited to share the throne!
The Trojans are to mix their blood with ours,
And I am to be driven from the door."
Then came the relatives of the women bemused
   by Bacchus
Who went their orgiastic way through the trackless

Woods at the call of Amata (and hers was no name
   to bandy)
And *they* shouted for war till they were hoarse.
740 Then one and all, despite every omen and oracle,
But under the influence of an evil deity
Demanded an evil war, and in a body
Jostled and crowded round Latinus' palace.
He stayed immovable as a rock, as a sea-rock
The breakers ceaselessly batter yet it holds
Solid and stolid for all the snarl of the seas;
The reefs and foam-flecked bars roar round about
And the seaweed splits against it again and again.
—But seeing he had no powers to gainsay
750 Their blind decision, since events were shaping
As inexorable Juno chose, the old king raised
His hands to the heedless winds and to the Gods.
"Alas," he bewailed, "we are broken by our fate!
We are borne upon the whirlwind! O my people
My unhappy people, you shall pay for this
Sacrilege with your blood! You, Turnus, you—
The wickedness of your deed shall overtake you
And its dread punishment—too late will you offer
Vows to the gods, too late! I am too old myself,
760 I go to my rest; and all I am bereft of
On the threshold of death is a peaceful burial."
He spoke his last, immured himself in the palace
And let the reins of kingship fall from his hand.

There was a custom in Latium, the western
   country,
And all the Alban cities afterwards
Held it as sacred. (As now almighty Rome
When first we rouse the war god to join battle,
Whether it be to bring upon the Getae
The sorrows of war or the Arabs or the Hyrcanians
770 Or to march to the Indies towards the dawn,
Or force the Parthians to return our standards.)
There are Twin Gates of War, for so they are
   called,
By religion hallowed and held in awe for fear
Of pitiless Mars: and they are held by a hundred
Brazen bars and the everlasting strength

Of iron, and their guardian Janus never
Quits his post on the threshold. Now when the City
Fathers irrevocably vote for war,
The Consul in his Quirinal robe of State
And Gabine cincture unbolts the gates, and the   *780*
   hinges
Grind, and himself declares war; then every
   warrior
Takes up the cry and the brazen bugles blare
Their assent. It was by this ritual Latinus
Was bidden declare war upon Aeneas
And open the grievous gates. But the old king
Refused his hand and shrank from the filthy office,
And shrouded himself in the shadow of despair.
Then the Queen of Heaven herself descended
And with her own hand burst in the reluctant
   doors
And as the hinges turned, the Saturnian loosed   *790*
The iron-bound portals. Italy so calm
And pacific until then was in a ferment.
Some began to march over the plain,
Others in clouds of dust galloped high on their
   horses.
Arms! was the universal cry—some greased their
   shields
And javelins till they shone, or ground an ax on
   a whetstone;
All delighted to flourish their standards and hear
   the trumpets.
Five great cities set up new anvils to renew
Their stocks of arms—proud Tibur, powerful
   Atina,
Ardea, Crustumerium, and many-towered   *800*
   Antemnae.
They hollowed helmets to save their heads, they
   bent
Wicker frames of willow for shields; they
   hammered
Bronze corslets and beat out silver into greaves.
All their pride in the sickle and share, their love
Of the plough was over: they took their fathers'
   swords

And smelted them afresh in the furnace; the
    trumpets
Already were sounding for battle. The word went
    out for War!
And a trembling fellow snatched his helmet up
And dashed out of a house; and there was another
810 Yoking his snorting horses in a chariot,
Donning his shield and corslet of three-plied gold
And girding his sword on.

                    Now is the time, O Muses,
To grant me the freedom of Helicon and inspire
My verses to tell what kings came to the war;
Who followed whom and what was the battle-array
That filled the plains, who in those far-off days
Were the Flower of Italy's lush land, who blazed
    in arms.
For you are divine, you have the power to recall
Every event as it was but I am weak
820 *And but a whisper has come down to me.*

The first to march his men to the war was
    Mezentius,
A violent man who despised the gods and who
    came
From the shores of Etruria. And by him marched
    his son
Lausus a youth more handsome than any but
    Turnus.
Lausus, tamer of horses and scourge of the wild,
Who led a thousand men from the city Agylla
—Following all in vain—a boy deserving
More joy than being under his father's order—
Or, indeed, having Mezentius for father.
830 Flaunting his winning chariot over the grassland
After them came Aventinus as handsome a son
As his handsome father Hercules, his shield
Embossed with his father's crest of the Hydra's
    head
With its coil of a hundred snakes:—his mother
    Rhea,
A priestess, bore him into the light of day

Secretly in the woods of the Aventine mountain,
The offspring of her mortal body given
To the god Hercules when after killing Geryon
He came to the fields of Laurentum and there
    watered
His Spanish herds in the Etruscan river.   *840*
His soldiers were armed with javelins and
    pointed sticks
And fought, too, with sharp swords and Sabellian
    skewers.
He himself led the foot soldiers bristling
In a huge lion-skin, its mane uncombed
Its teeth bared in a snarl. He wore it flung
Over his shoulder, fierce as was his father, and thus
He came to the royal palace.

                                And after him
Came the twin brothers from the fortress of Tibur
Whose people take their name from another
    brother,
Tiburtus; these two were Catillus and eager Coras,   *850*
Argive youths, and ready to plunge ahead
Of the front rank into the ruck of weapons,
Like two Centaurs, born of the clouds, charging
Down from the top of a mountain at full gallop,
Down from Homole, down from snow-capped
    Othrys—
And the huge woods give them place and they
    smash their way
Through the undergrowth. The founder of
    Praeneste
Was with them, Caeculus whom after times
Have believed a son of Vulcan, of royal blood
Born among farm beasts and found by the hearth.   *860*
And with him were soldiers from high Praeneste
    itself
And from the pastures of Juno at Gabii,
And the chill Anio and the Hernican crags
That spring with streams; from Anagnia's rich
    lands;
From the Amasenus valley. Not all had arms
Nor rattled shields nor chariots—most of them

Would discharge pellets of gray lead; and some
Shook pairs of spears in their hands; and on their
     heads
They wore wolfskin caps; and they walked left
     foot naked
870   And right foot shod with rawhide.

                              But Messapus,
Tamer of horses, son of Neptune, a man
Whom it was forbidden for anyone to slay
With fire or sword, now suddenly called to arms
People long lost to the ways of war and happy
     in peace
And drew his sword again. These were the men
Of Fescennium, the Faliscans from the plain,
Men who abode below the peak of Soracte,
Men from the farms of Flavinium, and men
From the mountain of Ciminus with its lake
880   And the groves of Capena. Steadily they marched
Singing ballads about their king; even as snowy
Swans that fly among the wrack of clouds
As they return from feeding stretch their necks
And sing melodious measures, and the river
And the Asian Marshes echo far and wide.
—No one would think he saw an armored troop
In such a mighty rout, but a huge flock
Of noisy birds from the deep sea flying in
Towards the shore.

                         And look there! Clausus urging
890   A great company onward, Clausus sprung from
     the blood
Of Sabines of old, an army in himself,
From whom derive the Claudian family-tribe
Wide spread through Latium after the Sabines
     were given
Their share in Rome. With him came one huge
     body—
From Amiternum some, others the strict Quirites,
A band from Eretum, a band from olive-bearing
     Mutusca,
Some from Nomentum city, some from the
     countryside
Of Rosea by Velinus; some from the beetling

Crags of Tetrica, from Mount Severus, from
   Casperia,
From Foruli, and from the river Himella;   *900*
Men who drank the Tiber and Fabaris, men
Whom the cold Nursia sent, and there were
   companies
From Horta, and there were Latin peoples and
   others
Whose land is cut into two parts and watered
By the Alia, river of ill-starred name.
They were as many as waves on the Libyan sea
When savage Orion is hidden beneath its winter
   waters,
They were as close together as the ears of corn
Which ripen in the new strength of the sun
On the plain of Hermus or in Lycia's   *910*
Gold harvest-acres. Then shields clashed together
And the earth trembled at the beat of their feet.
Then next Halaesus, Agamemnon's henchman,
An enemy of Troy, hitched horse to chariot
And pressed a thousand warlike tribes to join
Turnus—some of them hoers of the soil,
The Massic soil so suitable for vineyards,
And some whom the Auruncan elders despatched
Down from the heights or from the neighboring
   seaboard
Of Sidicina, and some had left Cales;   *920*
Some dwelt by the shallow river of Volturnus;
And added to these there was a tough troop
From Saticula, and an Oscan section.
Their weapons were rounded javelins and their
   method
Was to attach them to elastic lines;
Arm-guards of leather protected their left arms
And for in-fighting they used falchions.
Nor from my song shall you be missing, Oebalus,
Begotten by Telon on Sebethys,
A nymph, in his old age when he was ruling   *930*
Over the Teleboae at Capreae.
But Oebalus was not content with his father's lands
And was already bringing under his sway
The Sarrastians and the plains, the Sarnus waters

And the men of Rufrae, Batulum and Celemna,
Or where the walls of Abella look down on the
  orchards,
And they were expert throwers of barbed spears
After the Teuton fashion, and their headgear
Was bark torn from the cork-tree and the bronze
940 Of their bucklers glinted and their bronze swords
  gleamed.

And Ufens, you were sent into battle from
  mountainous Nersae,
A warrior famed in song and a lucky fighter.
You from a clan especially outlandish,
Used to continual hunting and tilling the
  stubborn soil
Of Aequicula, carrying arms at their work,
And always prepared to plunder their neighbors
  and live
On the proceeds.
                    Then came a priest sent
From the Marruvian people and he wore
A favor of olive leaves above his helmet,
950 His name was Umbro, he was most courageous
And King Archippus sent him. He had powers
Of hand and incantation to charm to sleep
All kinds of vipers and poison-breathing hydras
And soften their anger and heal their bites with
  his art.
But he had no skill to counter and heal the blow
Of a Dardan spear, no soporific chant
Nor herbs culled in the Marsian mountains helped
With his own wounds: The grove of Angitia,
The smooth lake of Fucinus, the limpid pools
960 Mourn for you, Umbro!
                    Virbius came to the war,
Son of Hippolytus, a youth most beautiful
And noble, whom his mother Aricia
Sent from the groves of Egeria that lie
Round the marshy lake where she had brought
  him up—
There is Diana disposed to accept rich gifts at
  her altar.

Hippolytus, as the story goes, was killed
Through the arts of his stepmother, being split
   asunder
By bolting horses, so paying with his blood
His father's debt, but afterwards he was raised
To the air and the vault of the sky, called back   970
By Apollo's simples and the love of Diana.
But then the Almighty Father resenting a mortal
Being restored from the dark to the light of life
With his own hand struck Aesculapius,
The son of Apollo and the originator
Of healing powers so great, down to the Styx
With a thunderbolt. But kindly Diana hid
Hippolytus in a secret house apart,
Keeping him in the grove of the nymph Egeria
Where in Italian woods he must pass his life   980
Unknown and under the different name of Virbius.
This is the reason why horses with hoofs of horn
Are forbidden Diana's temple and sacred wood—
Because it was horses panicking at a sea-monster
That overturned the chariot on the shore
And killed the youth—but, none the less, now
His son was urging on his own highsteppers
Over the level plain as he drove full-tilt
In his chariot to the war.

                  Turnus himself
Went to and fro among his foremost warriors   990
Bearing his weapons, cutting a fine figure
A head taller than all. His helmet bore
A triple plume and a chimaera belching
The fires of Etna from its jaws, and in battle,
The harder the press the stronger the stream of
   blood,
So it roared louder and its flames burned hotter.
But it was Io who was embossed in gold
To grace his shield, already with upraised horn
And bristled hide, already a cow, a marvelous
   image—
And Argus guarding her virginity, and Father   1000
Inachus pouring his stream from a silver urn.
A horde of infantry followed Turnus, their shields
Swarmed over the whole plain, the youth of Argos,

Bands of Auruncans, Rutulians, Sicanian veterans,
And the striking force of Sacrania and Labicans
With painted shields; men from your banks, Tiber,
Who ploughed the sacred shores of Numicus, or
    worked
The Rutulian hills and the Port of Circeii
Where Jove of Anxur is the god who rules
1010 Over the farms, and Feronia delights in her
    green shade;
Men from the black marsh of Satura and the
    terrain
Whence shivering Ufens sneaks through the
    valley-bottoms
And hides at sea.
                  With these men came Camilla
Leading a troop of horses whose polished shields
Dazzled with bronze, a woman of war, not one
Whose hands were apt for the distaff of Minerva,
The wool-balls, but a maiden ready to take
The hard knocks of a battle, and to outpace
The winds in speed of foot. She might have raced
1020 Over the tops of the uncut corn without
Bruising their brittle ears, or made her course
Over the wavetops without wetting once
The sole of her swift foot. And as she passed
A crowd of mothers and all the youths who were
    rallying
From house and field gazed at her as she passed,
In gaping wonder at the purple cloak
On her smooth shoulder, at how a clasp of gold
Held all her hair; they gaped at her Lycian quiver
And at the shepherd's myrtle-crook she bore
1030 With a lance's point.

BOOK VIII

✤

As soon as Turnus had hoisted the ensign of battle
From the citadel top of Laurentum and the strident
Fanfare of trumpets had sounded, as soon as his
  fiery
Horses were roused and his armor clanged as he
  donned it,
War-fever seized on the minds of the people; at
  once
All Latium rose in an uproar, the young men
Lusted for blood. Their leaders Messapus and
  Ufens
And that contemner of gods Mezentius first
Mustered their men from all sides and unpeopled
  the fields
Of their tillers; and Venulus was despatched to   *10*
  the city
Of mighty Diomede to ask for help:
He was to brief him how the Trojans already
Had landed in Latium, how Aeneas had sailed
  there—
How he had introduced the vanquished gods
Of his own race and announced it his destiny
To claim the throne; that many peoples were
  joining
The Dardan hero, that his name and his fame
Were spreading widely through Latium. (What
  should befall
From these origins, what outcome of the contest
His heart relished, if fortune favored him,   *20*
Was plainer to Diomede than it ever was
To appear to Turnus or even to King Latinus.)
—Such was the state of affairs in Latium.

The noble scion of Laomedon seeing
The sum of events was tossed on a sea of anxiety—
Now to this point, now that, his quick mind moving
From facet to facet of the problem glancing,
Yet keeping the whole conspectus under review:
—Just as a flicker of light in water, quivering
30   In a brass bowl reflecting sun or moon ray,
Jinks hither and thither, and flicks up into the air
And dances on the ceiling of the roof.

It was night, and over all the earth, on cattle
On bird and beast, on all the world there had
   fallen
A profound sleep, when Aeneas, his people's
   guardian,
Distracted by his abhorrence of the war
Lay down on the river bank under the chill
Arch of the sky and at long last allowed
His limbs to relax.

                And then appeared to him
40   The very god of the place, old Tiber himself
Out of his pleasant currents, arising from the
   poplars,
Clad in a gray transparent linen cloak
And an abundant headdress of shady reeds,
Who spoke these words dissolving his cloud of
   care.
"Oh seed of the God's sowing, you who bring
Troy-city back to us from enemy hands—
Preserving Pergamus for ever —Oh long-looked-
   for
In Latian fields and on the sod of Laurentum,
Here is your haven, here is rest for your Gods.
50   Do not distrust me; do not be cast down
By threats of war; the Gods' festering fury
Has burst—it has died down. —And now, in case
You conceive this the vain figuring of a dream,
Under the ilex trees on the river banks you will
   find
A huge white sow just farrowed, with thirty
   piglings

All white as she is, lying on the ground,
And here the site of your city will be, sure rest
From toil, and in thirty years from now Ascanius
Founding a famous city here, shall call it 'Alba.'
I speak the firm truth, and now attend to me   *60*
And I will tell you briefly how to solve
Successfully the problems which confront you.
On this coast some Arcadians, a race deriving
From Pallas, comrades of King Evander, following
His standard, have picked a site and built a city
Up in these hills, called from their ancestor
Pallanteum. These folk incessantly
Wage war with the Latin nation. Make them allies!
Conclude a treaty with them! I myself
Will lead you along my banks and direct your   *70*
   course
So that your oars may overcome the currents.
Come, rise up, Goddess-born, and make your
   prayers
To Juno in due fashion as the stars
Begin to pale and set, and by your vows
And prayers prevail upon her wrath and threats.
Once you are victor you shall pay to me
Your meed of worship. For I am he the God
Tiber, the sky-blue-watered, whom you see
In full flow, scouring my brimming banks and
   winding
Through the rich harvest fields, the most belovèd   *80*
Of rivers in Heaven. Here is my palace-spring,
Life-fount of mighty cities!" The River God
Spoke and then plunged into his pool deep
Down to the bed—and night and sleep at once
Forsook Aeneas. He rose up and gazing
On the dawn-beams of the sun in the eastern sky
With reverence lifted in the palms of his hands
A libation of river-water and cried to heaven:
"O Nymphs, Nymphs of Laurentum, river-born,
And Father Tiber with your holy stream   *90*
Receive me, Aeneas, and at last be ward
Against my perils. Whatever spring now feeds
The pools where, pitying our long distress, you lie,

Whatever the soil you rise from in your beauty,
For ever shall I revere you with honor, with gifts
     for ever
Celebrate your name, O river crescent-horned,
Lord of all western waters. Only be at my side,
Confirm the heavenly tokens with your presence."
So he spoke and chose from his fleet two biremes
100 And manned them with rowers and at the same
     time
Called his companions to arms.
                              And then behold!
A sudden marvelous portent met their eyes.
There on the green bank lay in the undergrowth
A pure white sow, her pure white litter around her—
—To you Juno, Juno alone, almighty Juno
She must be sacrificed and Aeneas took
The sacred implements and set the sow
With all her young in station by the altar.
Then for that whole long night did Tiber rein
110 His thrusting stream and the water was silent-still
As peaceful standing waters, pool or marsh—
No current met the rowers, to contend with.
And so they made good speed, the journey
     propitious
With all Aeneas had told them; the polished hulls
Skimmed through the shallows; even the waves
     marveled
And the woods stared askance, strangers so long
To the gleaming shields of heroes, the bright colors
Of boats on the stream. They kept at the oars
By day and night as they covered the long reaches,
120 Shaded by many trees as they cut the still water
Among the green forests. The fiery sun
Had climbed to the zenith when they saw walls
And a citadel far off, and a straggle of dwellings
(Which now the Power of Rome has raised to
     heaven)
But you Evander lived there, poor in possessions.
At once they turned their prows towards the shore
And drew near to the city.
                              It so happened
That on that day the Arcadian King was engaged

In paying his annual honors to Hercules
And the other gods, in a grove before the city.   *130*
With him was Pallas his son and the cream of
    the youth,
And his Senate, men of meager substance all,
Were offering incense, and the new-shed blood
Reeked up from the altars. But when they saw
The swift ships between the darkling groves
And the oarsmen silently rowing, their hearts
    went cold
At the sudden apparition and all sprang up
In a body and left the tables. But Pallas boldly
Forbade them to break the sacrifice, and snatching
    a weapon
Sped off alone to meet them and from a distance   *140*
Standing upon a hillock he called out:
"Warriors, what has led you to explore
These ways unknown to you—where are you
    bound?
What race are you? Where is your home? Is it
    peace or war
You bring?" Then Aeneas the leader perched up
    high
On the stern with an olive branch stretched out in
    his hand,
In earnest of peace, replied. "You see before you
A people of Trojan birth: our weapons are drawn
Against the Latins only, who have driven us
Out of the land with tyrannous war though all   *150*
We asked was peace. And now we seek Evander.
Take him this message. Tell him that chosen
    leaders
Of Dardania are at hand to beg for an armed
    alliance."
At the sound of a name so celebrated Pallas
Stood rooted to the spot. "Whoever you are,
Come disembark," he said, "and speak with my
    father
And accept the hospitality of our hearth."
He gave his hand and grasped Aeneas' hand
Firmly and long. Under the shade of the grove
They left the river and came to King Evander,   *160*

Then in this friendly fashion Aeneas said:
"O best of the sons of Greece to whom at the
    bidding of fortune
I turned my prayers and proffered wreathed
    branches,
I never feared you for all that you were a leader
Of Greeks, an Arcadian, and allied by birth
To the two sons of Atreus. On the contrary,
My own nation, the hallowed oracles
Of Gods, the kinship of our father, your own
World-wide renown—all these have linked me
    with you,
170 Led here by destiny and desire at one.
Dardanus our first father—founder of Ilium—
So the Greeks say was born of Electra the
    daughter
Of Atlas and came to the Teucrians—mightiest
    Atlas
Who bears the constellations on his shoulders.
Mercury is your sire whom snow-white Maia
Conceived and bore on snowy Cyllene's summit;
But Maia, if we may credit the tradition,
Is daughter of Atlas, too, that very Atlas
Who bears the stars of heaven—so our two
180 Divergent families sprang from the same blood.
Trusting in this, my first approach to you
Was not through envoys nor diplomacy;
No, I myself in person have risked my life
And come a suppliant to your gates myself.
The Daunians, that same wicked race of people
That harry you with war, now harry us;
And if they drive us out nothing can stop them
Conquering all Hesperia and controlling
The seas that wash its either coast. Accept
190 Our friendship, give us yours! Our hearts are bold
In battle, we are brave spirits, our young manhood
Has proved itself by prowess in the field!"
Such were the words of Aeneas, and for long
Evander had been gazing on his face
And in his eyes, and raking his whole frame,
And briefly he answered: "O bravest of the
    Trojans

With joy I recognize and receive you here!
How well I recall Anchises, that great man,
And his face and his words! For I remember how Priam
Son of Laomedon passed here on a visit   *200*
To the realms of Hesione his sister, making for Salamis,
And thence to cross Arcadia's cold frontiers.
The first flush of my youth was on my cheeks
And I hero-worshiped all the Trojan leaders—
Priam himself, but especially Anchises
Who strode out a head taller than them all.
My young heart burned with yearning to speak to the hero
And shake him by the hand. And so I did.
Then to my joy I squired him to the walls
Of Pheneus. And as he took leave of me   *210*
He gave me a marvelous quiver of Lycian arrows
And a cloak wrought with golden thread and a pair
Of golden bits which my Pallas has to this day.
Therefore the pact and all you seek lies here
In the right hand I pledge you with, and when
Tomorrow's dawn lightens up the world
And I speed you on your way you will rejoice
In the armed force and in the stores I furnish.
Meanwhile, since you have come as friends, join with us
And celebrate these annual rites of ours   *220*
(Sin it would be to postpone them) and accustom
Yourselves to the hospitality of your allies!"
When he had said these words he bid the banquet
Which had been removed be set on once again
And placed his warrior-guests on seats of turf.
But for Aeneas he had a special welcome,
Seating him on a throne of maple-wood
Draped with a shaggy lion-skin. Then the priest of the altar
And his chosen youths with nimble skill brought on
The roast bulls' meat and, piled in baskets, the gifts   *230*
Of the corn goddess and poured the wine of Bacchus.
Aeneas and all the warriors of Troy

Fed on a whole chine and the sacrificial entrails.
When hunger was appeased and appetite
Surfeited, King Evander said, "This ceremony,
This ritual feast, this altar set up to honor
So great a deity—this is not done lightly
Nor in forgetfulness of the ancient gods.
No, Trojan guest, it is due honor we pay
240   In evergreen thanksgiving for deliverance
From bitter dangers. Now, first, look up there
At that hanging crag on the rock face and see,
     beyond it,
There is a mountain lair now desolate and
     shattered
With enormous slabs of rock and a trail of havoc
Left by an avalanche. It was once a cave
Cleft to a vast depth, beyond the reach
Of the sun's rays, and there a terrible monster
Half-beast, half-man, Cacus, made his dwelling.
And always the ground was reeking with new
     blood
250   And nailed to the huge doorway human heads
Hung grisly-pale in grim decay. The monster's
Father was Vulcan—from Vulcan derived the fires
That smokily belched from his own mouth as he
     heaved
His colossal bulk along.

                                        But in the end
Our prayers for help were answered and a god
     came.
For Hercules that greatest of all avengers,
In high fettle having despoiled and killed
Geryon the three-headed, he marched our way
Driving before him the mighty bulls he had won;
260   And the cattle filled the valley and the river.
But Cacus, his mind a ferment of mad frenzy,
Determined not to leave a trick or crime
Undared or unattempted, stole four bulls
In especially prime condition from the stables,
And four of the finest heifers, and lest they
     should leave
Their natural trail of hoof marks he seized their
     tails

And dragged them backwards into his cave and
   hid them
Behind a wall of rock and not a clue
Led to the cave if anyone gave search.
But meanwhile Hercules, now they were fed,   *270*
Prepared to drive his herd out of their stable
And leave the country, and the cattle lowed
As they departed and filled all the woodland
With plaintive mooings and left the hills ringing—
And from the depths of the enormous cave
One beast made answer cheating Cacus' hopes
Of keeping them in thrall. Then truly an anger
Blacker than ever before blazed up in Hercules!
He seized up arms, his heavy knotted club,
And rushed for the precipitous heights of the   *280*
   mountain.
We, for the first time, saw Cacus blanch
And terror in his eyes. And he made for the cave
Faster than east wind and fear gave wings to his
   feet.
He was just in time to immure himself by breaking
The fastening of a huge suspended rock
Hung by his father's art from an iron clamp,
And had jammed his doorway up with this obstacle,
When lo! the son of Tiryns appeared in a spate
   of fury
And sought to force an entry, now here, now there,
Grinding his teeth. Three times in seething anger   *290*
He circled the mountain, three times to no purpose
He tried the rocky doorway and three times
Sank back exhausted to the valley bottom.
There was a sharp spur that stood up sheer,
As if the surrounding rock had been cut away,
Rising above the back of the cave, the highest
Point for the eye to catch, a perfect place
For the nests of birds of prey—it sloped away
To the river on the left and Hercules
Heaving upon the right worried and loosened it   *300*
Until he tore it up and suddenly
He sent it crashing down—and all the sky
Throbbed as with thunder, the banks of the river
   gaped,

And the stream ran back in terror! Then the cave
And the huge den of Cacus was clear to view
And all its dark recesses open wide.
It was as if the earth should quake and split
To disclose the world below, the pale kingdom
The gods detest, and the appalling abyss
310 Was to be seen from above and the ghosts
   shuddering
At the onset of light. So in this unwonted
Glare suddenly caught, pinned in his own cave,
Cacus lay yelling as Hercules rained on him
Every conceivable weapon, pulping him
With branches of trees and enormous lumps of
   rock.
And he, seeing he could not escape from his
   perilous plight,
Belched from his jaws a billow of thick smoke
And plunged the cave into pitchy darkness blotting
Out sight and in the depths of the hollow he
   massed
320 A fuming night of darkness blent with fire,
An amazing sight to see. But Hercules
Would not brook this but with a headlong spring
Plunged through the fire into the heart of the
   smokewaves
Where they wreathed thickest in the enormous
   cave.
Here in the shadows he seized on Cacus, vainly
Vomiting useless fire, and twisted his limbs
Into a knot and kept a stranglehold
Till his eyeballs started out and his throat was
   bloodless.
Then were the doors burst down and the vile house
330 Laid open, and the stolen cattle Cacus
Had been compelled to disgorge, loosed to the
   light.
The hideous corpse was dragged out by the heels.
The onlookers could not look long enough
On the dreadful eyes, the ghastly face, and the
   chest
Of the monster matted with hairs, and his mouth
   snuffed

Of its flames.
                        From that time on, we have held
A celebration in his honor from generation
To generation worshiping the god.
And foremost among us is Potitius who founded
The rite, and then the Pinarian house, the   *340*
    guardians
Of the worship of Hercules, set up this altar
Which always is named by us our greatest altar
And always shall be greatest. Therefore come,
O warriors, and wreathe your hair with leaves;
Hold out your cups in your right hands in honor
Of so worthy and great a deed and invoke the god,
Both yours and ours, and willingly pour the
    libations!"
These were his words and as he spoke he took
A spray of poplar, Hercules' own tree,
With its gray-green leaves, and twined a wreath in   *350*
    his hair.
He held the sacred cup in his right hand.
Then swiftly, happily, all poured their due libations
Upon the tables and offered prayers to the gods.
Meanwhile the evening crept up the lower slopes
    of Olympus
And now there came the priests led by Potitius
Garbed in their ritual skins and carrying torches.
The feast began again and the tables were heaped
With new provisions, brought for a second session,
And the altars groaned with high-piled dishes
    again.
The Salii appeared with wreaths of poplar   *360*
Upon their brows to sing by the kindled altars—
One was a chorus of youths, the other of old
    men—
And they sang paeans in praise of the glorious
    deeds
Of Hercules: how in his cradle he strangled
With his own baby hands the messengers
Sent by his stepmother—two monstrous serpents;
How he destroyed in war two famous cities,
Troy and Oechalia; how for King Eurystheus
He did a thousand chores imposed upon him

370   By Juno's enmity. "O unconquerable!
        Slayer of those two-formed and cloud-born
          creations
        Hylaeus and Pholus, of the Cretan abortion,
        And of the huge lion beneath the Nemean rock,
        You, that set the Stygian pool ashudder
        And Cerberus where with his paws on bloody
          bones
        He lay at his lair's mouth, that never blanched
        At any bodily shape not even Typhoeus
        Looming in arms; (nor did your reason quail
        When the snake of Lerna coiled itself around you,)
380   Hail! true son of Jove, new luster to heaven,
        Approach and grace our rites with your very
          guidance!"
        Thus in their songs they celebrated, and above all
        Sang of the Cave of Cacus and the fire-breath of
          him,
        And the whole wood rang with the sound and the
          hills re-echoed it.
        Then when the sacrifice was over the company
        All returned to the city. The King moved slowly
        Stiff with age and Aeneas and young Pallas
        Accompanied his steps and he lightened the
          journey
        With various talk. Aeneas' quick eyes
390   Took everything in with wonder and delight
        And putting questions about the ancient records
        Of ancient men Evander answered him,
        Founder of Rome's citadel. "These groves
        Were the native haunts of the Nymphs and
          Fauns once,
        And a race of men born from the trunks of oak
          trees
        Who had no laws or culture, they did not know
        How to yoke oxen nor to produce food
        Nor conserve stores, but they lived off branches
        And whatever the struggle of hunting could
          provide.
400   Then Saturn came, expelled from the heights of
          Olympus
        An exile, kingdomless, in full retreat

From the weapons of Jove. And he reformed this
   people:
From being wildly scattered about the mountains
He molded them into one and gave them laws
And chose the name of 'Latium' for the place,
From its lying safely hidden within its bounds.
Under his rule there passed the centuries
We call the Golden Age, so calm and peaceful
His reign, until little by little the race
Coarsened and worsened and were mad for war   *410*
And the lust of possession. Next an Ausonian tribe
And a race of Sicanians came and again and again
The land of Saturn changed its name, and then
There were Kings, for instance Thybris with his
   vast
Body from whom in after times we Italians
Have named the river Tiber, and it lost
Its true and ancient name of Albula.
I myself was driven from my country
And sailed to the edge of the world till I was
   forced
By all-powerful fortune and inescapable fate   *420*
To choose this place, led here by the dread
   warnings
Of my mother the Nymph Carmentis and the
   sanction
Of Apollo the divine." He had scarcely finished
When he moved forward to point out the altar
And then the gate the Romans call the Carmental
In memory of the ancient honors paid
To the Nymph Carmentis, prophetess of fate,
Who first sang of the future greatness promised
The sons of Aeneas and Pallanteum's glory.
—Next, the huge grove which doughty Romulus   *430*
Was to reserve as his "Asylum" later,
And under its dank rock the Lupercal
That by Arcadian custom bears the name
Of Lycaean Pan. And added to that he showed
   him
The grove of sacred Argiletum, calling
The place to witness as he recounted the death
Of his guest Argus. Then he conducted Aeneas

To the Tarpeian temple, the Capitol,
All gold-inlaid today but shaggy then
440 With tangled undergrowth. And even then
It was a place of terror to the rustic,
A sacred awesome spot, and even then
They trembled at the woodland and the rocks.
"This grove," he said, "this hill with its wooded crest,
Is the abode of a god, which god we know not.
The Arcadians say they have seen great Jove himself here
Shaking his darkling Aegis time and again
In his right hand, raising storm. And see there also
Two towers with shattered walls, the memorial
450 Relics of ancient men—that built by Janus,
And this by Saturn—hence they have long been named
The Janiculum and the Saturnia."
Speaking of things like these they came to the dwelling
Of needy Evander and everywhere cattle lowed
In what is now the Forum and the rich
Quarter Carinae, and when they were seated Evander
Said, "Hercules stooped down to enter here.
This royal dwelling sufficed him—so, my friend,
Be bold to despise wealth and make yourself
460 Worthy to talk with gods, do not despise
The welcome of poverty." He led mighty Aeneas
Under the sloping roof of his narrow dwelling
And showed him a bed of strewn leaves covered
With the pelt of a Libyan bear.

                                        Night fell
And folded the earth within her dusky wings,
But Venus, Aeneas' mother, deeply perturbed
By the Laurentine threats and the general commotion
Spoke to her husband Vulcan in their golden
Bridal room and breathed a breath of her godlike
470 Love into what she spoke. "While the Argive princes
Were laying Troy waste and its doomed citadel

Condemned to destruction in the fires of hate,
I never once asked help for my pitiable people
Nor arms nor the resources of your craft.
No, dearest husband, I never wished to force you
To exert yourself in labors, although I owed
So much to the sons of Priam and often wept
Over the bitter fortunes of Aeneas.
But now by Jove's imperial command
He has found a foothold in Rutulian country.   480
I have come to you as a suppliant and a mother
And beg of your godhead arms for my own son.
The tears of Heaven's daughter, the tears of the
    bride
Of Tithonus were potent to prevail upon you—
See what peoples are gathering, what walled-cities
Have shut their gates and sharpened up their
    weapons
To kill my people!" And having spoken thus
The goddess twined her snow-white arms about
    him
Enfolding, wheedling him with her embrace.
Then suddenly he felt the fires of love,   490
As strong as ever, coursing through his bones
Right to the marrow, like a lightning-streak
That flashes gleaming bright through a thunder-
    cloud
And his wife, conscious of her powers, happily
Knew that her wiles had worked. Then the old
    man
Caught in the toils of his undying love
Said, "Why do you seek a plea from the long past?
Can you have lost your faith in me, my goddess?
If in the past your anxiety had been
So great, there was no ban upon my arming   500
The Trojans, nor did Jove the All-Powerful
Nor Fate forbid that Troy should stand and Priam
Survive for ten years more—but now if truly
You are preparing for war and that is your will,
Whatever by my art I can provide,
Whatever can be made of iron or molten
Electrum, whatever powers my forge
And my bellows possess—come, stop this begging

And doubting your own powers": even as he spoke
510 He took her in his arms as she had desired
And on the breast of his wife he took his pleasure
And fell asleep, his body gratified.

Now when it was after midnight and the first
    deep rest
Of night was passed, the time a housewife rises
Whose living depends on her spinning and the
    slender
Aid of Minerva, and she revives the fire
That sleeps in the embers and adds nightwork to
    day—
And in the lamplight keeps her servants hard
At their long grind so she may keep unsullied
520 Her marriage ties and bring her children up,
So at this small hour the Master of Fire,
As busy as she, got up from his bed of down
And set himself to work at his own craft.
Just near the Sicanian coast and Aeolian rocks—
    Lipare
Juts up an island, steep with smoking crags—
Beneath it roars a cavern hollowed out
By Cyclopes' forges, the very bowels of Etna,
And you can hear the anvils ring with blows
Re-echoing round and Chalybean smeltings
530 Hiss in the rocks and the furnaces pant with fire,
And this is Vulcan's home and called Vulcania.
Here then the Master of Fire descended from
    high heaven.
In the huge cave Cyclopes were working iron—
Brontes and Steropes and naked Pyracmon:
They held in their hands a rough-cast thunderbolt
Such as the Almighty Father showers in dozens
From every quarter of heaven onto earth,
Part of it polished for use and part half-finished.
Three spokes of twisted rain they had assembled
540 And three of watery cloud, three of red fire
And three of winged south wind, and at the
    moment
They were amalgamating with their workings
Terrible flashes, all the noise and the panic

And the furies of hounding fires.
Others were building Mars a chariot
With flying wheels, with which he rouses warriors
And whole cities; and, vying with each other,
Some were making the awe-inspiring aegis
To arm Athene in anger, making it glitter
With golden serpent scales, with serpents twining;   *550*
And for the centerpiece, for the Goddess's breast,
The Gorgon's head itself, with severed neck
And eyes rolling and— "Stop all this!" cried
   Vulcan,
"And put aside whatever you have begun!
You Cyclopes of Aetna attend to me!
We are to make arms for a doughty warrior.
Now exert your fullest powers, now exercise
The deftness of your speedy hands, now use
The utmost of your craft! Begin this instant!"
He said no more and quickly, altogether,   *560*
They allotted each his task and set to work.
Bronze and gold ore poured out along the channels
And steel, with its power to wound, was melted
   down
In the large furnace. Then they roughly molded
A mighty shield that could withstand by itself
All the weapons of Latium, and welded it
Circle by circle in seven layers. Some
Worked at the bellows puffing in and out,
Others tempered the hissing metal in water,
The cave reverberated with its weight of anvils.   *570*
They raised their arms in time with all their force
And with their tongs kept turning the masses of
   metal.
Now while the father god of Lemnos sped
This work on Aeolian shores, the gentle light
And the morning songs of birds under the eaves
Roused King Evander from his humble bed.
The old man struggled up and put on a tunic
And bound Tyrrhenian sandals round his feet,
Then slung a Tegean sword from his right shoulder
To hang at his side, and over his left he flung   *580*
A panther's skin. And with his two watchdogs
Running before him, roused up from his doorstep,

He went to seek Aeneas in the guest-house
Having in mind their talk and the help promised,
Fine hero that he was. Aeneas was up too.
Pallas walked with Evander and Achates
Was by Aeneas' side, and so they met
And took each other's hands and settled down
In the center of the court and seized the chance
590   Of mutual talk. The King was first to speak:
"Greatest of Trojan leaders, while you are alive
I cannot think of Troy nor her realm as fallen,
And we, alas, have only slender resources
With which to aid so great a name. We are
      bounded
On one side by the Tuscan stream, on the other
The Rutulians press upon us and round our walls
Their weapons ring—but I have a mighty nation,
A powerful army I can ally with you
And this hope of safety we owe to a slice of luck,
600   And Destiny's hand it is that brings you here.
Not far off from here is Agylla a city
Founded on ancient rock where once the Lydians,
A people famous for war, settled themselves
In the Etruscan hills and for many years
The city flourished until Mezentius
Tyrannized over it with a reign of terror.
Why call to mind his hideous holocausts?
His unspeakable misdeeds?—may all the gods
Serve him and his family likewise—why he would
      even
610   Bind living men to the dead, lashed hand to hand
And face to face—could one conceive such
      torture?—
And in the corruption and running filth of this
Appalling embrace do them to lingering death.
At last the citizens, weary of tyranny,
Rose in revolt and besieged the infamous brute
In his own palace and cut down his retainers
And spattered the roof with firebrands. But he
      himself
In the midst of the melee escaped across the
      border

Into Rutulian country and took refuge
With Turnus who was friendly. All Etruria   *620*
Then rose in righteous fury and demanded
The surrender of their king for instant death.
Aeneas, this is the army I shall offer you
Leadership of: a mass of ships lies chafing
Along the entire seaboard—bidding the trumpet
Sound for battle, and only an ancient prophet
Holds them in check with his fateful prophecy.
'You chosen youth of Maeonia, the flower,
The soul of an ancient people, whom resentment
Justly spurs into action against the foeman,   *630*
Mezentius, upon whose head the weight
Of your kindled anger falls deservedly—
It is not meet for any Italian born
To take so proud a people under his sway.
You must take a foreign leader.' So the Etruscans
Repitched their camp there on the plain in awe
Of the divine warning. Tarchon himself
Has sent me ambassadors here with the royal
  crown
And scepter, wishing me to accept the insignia
If I would join his camp and mount the Etruscan   *640*
  throne;
But I am cold and slow in my old age,
The lapse of time has sapped away my strength,
My fighting days are done and I am not fit
For high command. I should have encouraged my
  son
Save for his mother's Sabine blood which makes
  him
A half Italian. But you, the favored
Of fate in age and race, the elect of heaven,
On to your destiny, most gallant leader
Of Trojans and Italians! And I shall give you
My Pallas, my one hope and consolation.   *650*
Under your guidance let him learn to bear
The sweat of war, the grim works of the war god,
Let him mark your deeds and from the very
  beginning
Model himself on you. I shall allot him

Two hundred Arcadian knights, the chosen
Strength of our youth; and Pallas, as his gift,
In his own name shall give you as many more."

Scarce had he spoken, and with downcast eyes
The son of Anchises and loyal Achates stood
660 In gloom of heart pondering many perils,
When the Cytherean out of the clear blue
Gave them a sign. For unforeseen from the
    heavens
Lightning flashed and a crash of thunder rolled
And suddenly the whole sky seemed asunder
And through the ether seemed to ring the sound
Of an Etruscan trumpet. They looked up
And again and again the tremendous din crashed
    out.
Then in a calm reach of the firmament
They saw arms, wrapped in cloud, all glowing red
670 In the sun's rays and ringing as if clashed,
And all were stunned with amazement save
    Aeneas
Who recognized in the sound the promise made
    him
By his divine mother. Then he cried out:
"Truly, my host, ask not what this portends!
It is the Gods and it is me they call for!
This is the sign my goddess mother foretold me
That she would send if there were threats of war:
And she would bring me through the air, to help
    me,
Armor forged by Vulcan—alas, what carnage
680 The miserable Laurentines have in store!
What vengeance, Turnus, shall I wreak upon you!
O Father Tiber, how many shields and helmets
And how many bodies of brave warriors
Shall you roll beneath your waves! Yes, let them
    call
For battle now and let them break their pledges!"

When he had spoken thus, he raised himself
From his high seat and first of all stirred up
The smoldering fires sacred to Hercules

Upon their altars and joyfully approached
Yesterday's hearth and its small indwelling gods.   690
Evander then for his part, and for theirs
The Trojan youth, made a due sacrifice
Of chosen two-year sheep and when this was done
Aeneas strode to the ships to revisit his comrades
And from their number chose an elite few
To accompany him on his embassy of war.
The rest went coasting easily down stream
With the following current to bring Ascanius
News of his father and of all that had happened.
The Trojan party bound for Etruscan fields   700
Were furnished with horses and an especial one
Was singled out for Aeneas, its whole body
Decked with a tawny lion-skin, its claws
Gilded and gleaming.

             Suddenly rumor took wing
And spread like wildfire through the little town:
The horsemen were to muster to the palace
Of the Etruscan king. And cold with fear
Mothers redoubled their prayers, and the danger
   grew
To twin the dread, and the shadow of war
   loomed larger.
Then did Evander, the father, cling to his son   710
Clasping his right hand, for he was going,
And wept the tears no weeping will assuage,
And cried out, "Jove!—could He but bring me
   back
My bygone years and make me again as once
I was when under the walls of Praeneste
I razed the front rank of the foe and victoriously
Set fire to piles of shields and with this hand
Despatched King Erulus to his doom, whose
   mother
Feronia had given him three lives—
A fearful thing to recount—and the bodily powers   720
To bear arms thrice and therefore thrice must he be
Sent down to death— And yet this hand of mine
Took all three lives that day and stripped him bare
Of all three suits of arms! O, if I were now
As once I was, my son, I should never be torn

From your dear embrace! Never Mezentius
Had put so many to the savage sword
Or so widely widowed his city, with a disdainful
Shrug at his feeble neighbor!—Oh you Gods,
730   Take pity, I beseech you, on this King
Of Arcadia and hear a father's prayer!
If your divine desire it is to keep
My Pallas safe, if it is destined thus,
If truly in life I am to see him again
And we are to be together, I pray to live:
There is no suffering I could not endure
For this. But, Fortune, if you are threatening him
With some unspeakable calamity—
Let me be rid at once, now, of a life
740   Too cruel to bear, while there is still a doubt
Among my apprehensions, while a ray
Of hope still lights the cloudy future, while
I hold you in my arms, my darling boy,
My late, my own delight—before my ears
Are pained by news more terrible!" So a father
Poured from his heart these words on the brink
    of parting,
Then fainted; and his servants bore him within.

And now the cavalry had passed through the
    open gates,
Aeneas and faithful Achates among the first,
750   Then the rest of the Trojan nobles; and Pallas
    himself
In the column-center sparkled in his cloak
With its gay colors and his colored armor
Like the morning star fresh from the waves of
    ocean
Whose light above all others Venus loves,
When it has lifted its sacred countenance
Into the sky and melted the darkness. Mothers
Stood trembling on the walls and followed the
    dust-cloud
And caught with their eyes the glint of brass from
    the riders
As on they pressed through the scrub, taking the
    quickest

Way to their goal. Listen! A shout went up.   760
They formed a column; their hooves' fourfooted
   beat
With rumble of thunder drummed on the
   crumbling plain.

There is a vast grove by the cool stream of Caere
For generations widely held in awe;
On all sides it is enclosed by a coil of hills
Which guard the dark pine-glade. The old
   Pelasgians
Who long ago were the first inhabitants
Of the Latin land had consecrated the grove,
So goes the story, to Silvanus the god
Of the flocks and fields, and it had its festival.   770
And not far off from here Tarchon and the
   Etruscans
Had pitched their camp on a safe natural site,
And from the hilltop could be seen the whole
Of their array as they bivouacked at large
Over the plain. And hither the lord Aeneas
Came with his chosen party of young warriors,
Weary they were, and set about the refreshment
Both of themselves and their horses.
                                But the Goddess
Venus, her beauty shining out from among the
   clouds
Had come with her gifts; and when she saw her son   780
Withdrawn far off across the cooling water
In a secret valley, she went directly to him
And spoke these words, "Behold, the promised
   gifts
Fruits of my husband's skill are now completed!
Now, son, you need not hesitate to challenge
Any haughty Laurentine or even fiery Turnus."
The Cytherean sought her son's embrace
Even as she spoke; and she laid the glittering gear
Under an oak-tree. He for his part rejoiced
In the gifts of the goddess, and such honor done   790
   him.
From point to point his eyes roved in delight
Nor could he ever gaze his fill, he marveled

As in his arms and hands he turned them over:
The fearsome helmet, belching crests of flame,
The sword, the death-dealing, the corslet of stiff
    bronze
Blood red and vast as a dark cloud caught by the
    rays
Of the sun that glows and gleams afar; then next
The polished greaves of refined gold and electrum,
The spear, and last the shield whose design was far
800 Beyond the powers of language to describe.
For there the Master of Fire, being familiar
With all the seers, and versed in the times to come
Had graven Italy's story and the triumph of the
    Romans.
There was the royal lineage, all, from Ascanius
    onward,
And there the succession of battles to be fought.
There he had graven the mother wolf stretched out
In the green cave of Mars whilst at her teats
The twin boys fearless tugged and played and
    sucked,
And she meanwhile, her lissom neck bent round,
810 Caressing them in turn licked their limbs into
    shape.
Close by, he had put in Rome and the lawless rape
Of the Sabine women from among the crowd
At the Circus while the Great Games were in
    progress,
And the sudden outbreak of new war between
The tribe of Romulus and aged Tatius
And his stern men of Cures; but after that
The two kings were depicted, their quarrels
    mended,
Standing beside the altar of Jove-in-arms,
Their sacred cups in hand to pledge a treaty
820 Confirmed by the sacrifice of a sow. Nearby
Mettus was shown already torn apart
By the four swift horses of his chariot—
(You should have kept your word, O man of
    Alba)—
And Tullus dragging the liar's flesh through the
    woodland

And the blood bedewing the briars. And Porsenna
Insisting Rome take back the exiled Tarquin
And vesting the city in a dreadful siege.
And there were heroes of Aeneas' blood
Dashing themselves to death for freedom's sake.
And again you could see Porsenna, in the posture 830
of fury
And in the posture of menace because Horatius
Dared to cut down the bridge and because Cloelia
Broke from her chains and swam the river Tiber.
Manlius guardian of the Tarpeian Rock
Stood at his post in front of the Temple, holding
The heights of the Capitol, while the palace
Of Romulus stood out with its stiff new thatch.
And there was a silver goose flapping its wings
In the golden cloister cackling that the Gauls
Were on the threshold—and there were the Gauls 840
Who under cover of night in the grace of darkness
Had wormed their way through scrub and reached
the summit;
Golden their hair was and golden were their
garments,
They gleamed in stripy cloaks and torques of gold
Were round their milk-white necks: each warrior
Brandished two Alpine javelins in his hand,
His body guarded by a full-length shield.
Then he had graven the Salii at their dances
And naked Luperci; and there were the tufted caps
And the shields that fell from heaven; and there 850
were
Chaste mothers in soft carriages conveying
Sacred vessels of worship through the city.
Some way from these Vulcan had introduced
The halls of Tartarus and the high looming
Portals of Pluto; the punishments of the wicked—
You, Catiline, dangling from a louring rock
And blenching at the faces of the Furies;
And the Good set apart and Cato their Lawgiver.
Between these scenes on a broad swathe there
swept
A golden semblance of the swelling sea, 860
Its blue billows flecked with whitening wave-crests,

And all about it dolphins silver-bright
Threaded, and thrashed the surface with their tails.
Then you could see as centerpiece the battle
Of Actium and the brazen-armored fleets,
All Leucate was clear as it throbbed with warwork,
And the waves gleamed with gold. There was
    Augustus
Leading the Italians into battle, the whole Senate
And people behind him, and the small household
    Gods,
870 And the Great of Heaven—he stood on the high
    stern:
Twin flames played round his joyous brow, the Star
Of his Fathers dawned above his head. Elsewhere
Agrippa, with the aid of winds and gods,
Towering led his line and on his brows,
A proud war-emblem, gleamed the naval crown
Embellished with its replicas of ships' rams.
Opposing them was Antony backed by the riches
Of all the East and various nations' arms,
A conqueror from the far East and the shores
880 Of the Red Sea, enlisting with him Egypt
And the strength of the Orient and the farthest
    limits
Of Bactria and—shame!—his Egyptian spouse.
The navies closed at speed and the whole sea
Boiled with the oar-strokes and the three-
    pronged rams.
They sought the open sea and you would think
The Cyclades uprooted were afloat,
Or that high mountains crashed against high
    mountains
So bulked the embattled poops on which the
    warriors mustered;
Wads of blazing tow and a whirl of steel
890 From every hand came hurling and Neptune's
    fields
Were newly incarnadined. In the midst the Queen
Rallied her forces with her native timbrel
Nor did she give us yet a glance at the pair
Of asps in wait for her. Here were her gods,

Monsters of every kind, to the baying dogheaded
  Anubis,
With weapons poised against Neptune, against
  Venus,
Against Minerva. In the thick of the fray
Raged Mars, picked out in iron, and from the sky
Loomed the grim Furies; Discord swept along
Rejoicing, her mantle rent, and Bellona followed   *900*
  her
With a bloody knout. Apollo of Actium
Seeing all this from above, was drawing his bow
In dread of which every Egyptian,
Indian, and Arab, every Sabean there
Was turning his back for flight. The Queen herself
Was shown as she whistled for the wind of flight
And setting sail she was shaking loose the sheets.
The Master of Fire had printed upon her the pallor
Of her approaching death, as she forged ahead
Cleaving the slaughter, with following wind and   *910*
  tide.
Before her was the Nile, his mighty length
One throe of grief, opening all his breast
And with his whole raiment summoning the
  defeated
To the lap of his blue stream, his harboring waters.
But there was Caesar in a threefold triumph
As he entered the walls of Rome and vowed to
  the Gods
Of Italy a deathless vow to build
Three hundred mighty altars throughout the city.
The streets all hummed with jollity and delight;
In every temple danced a band of mothers;   *920*
In every temple the altars blazed and before them
The floors were strewn with slaughtered bullocks.
  Caesar
On the snow-white porch of shining Apollo sat
Conning the gifts of the nations and setting them
  up
On the proud Temple gates, and conquered races
Filed past in a long line, as various
In dress and form of weapon as in speech.

Here Vulcan had portrayed a tribe of Numidians
And mincing Africans, here Lelegeians and
    Carians,
930   And Gelonians with their quivers; the river
    Euphrates
Already flowed more quietly—the Morini
Remotest of men were seen, and the two-horned
    Rhine,
The unconquered Scythians and the river Araxes
Chafing at its bridge.
                    Such were the scenes
Deployed on Vulcan's shield, his mother's gift,
At which Aeneas stared in wonder and delight
In the depiction of events beyond
His scope of knowledge, and hoisted to his
    shoulder
The destinies and the fame of his descendants.

BOOK IX

✠

While this was happening in a far part of the
    country
Juno the daughter of Saturn sent down Iris
From heaven to bold Turnus. He it chanced
Was sitting in a grove in a holy valley,
A grove reserved for his ancestor Pilumnus,
And from her rosy mouth the daughter of
    Thaumas
Addressed him thus: "Turnus, mere lapse of time
Has brought you of itself a thing no god
Would dare have promised you for all your
    prayers.
10   Aeneas has quit his fleet his comrades and his
    camp
And gone to seek Evander in his capital

On the Palatine hill—nor is that all—he has
  pushed
Right to the furthest cities of Corythus
And enlisting the country folk is forming a band
  of Lydians.
Why hesitate? Now is the time to call
For horse and chariot—brook no delay, catch
The camp unaware and capture it!" She spoke
And soared into the sky on her poised wings
And cut a great rainbow, shining against the
  clouds,
As she fled away. And Turnus recognized her   20
And lifted his two hands to the sky and called
After her, "Iris, glory of heaven who sent you
Down from the clouds to earth, to me, here?
Whence comes this sudden supernatural weather?
I see the firmament split, the stars loosed
About the height. I follow so great a sign
Whoever you are who summon me to arms."
So saying he went to the stream-side and drew up
A handful of water from a swirling eddy
And prayed a prayer and piled heaven high with   30
  vows.

Now the whole army with its wealth of horses,
Its wealth of embroidered cloaks and gold began
To move across the open plain. (Messapus
Marshaled the vanguard, Tyrrhus' sons the rear
With Turnus himself, as general, in the center.)
Their column seemed like Ganges silently rising
Through all its seven calm channels deepening,
Or Nile when it withdraws its fertilizing
Flood from the plains and settles in its bed.
And suddenly the Trojans sighted a gathering   40
Cloud of black dust and a shadow creep over the
  plain.
From the rampart top it was Caicus who first
  yelled—
"What is this mass of black gloom rolling
  towards us,
My countrymen? Come quick with sword and
  weapon

And man the walls! Ho, there! The foe is upon
   us."
Shouting loudly the Trojans scurried in
Through every gate, and stationed themselves on
   the ramparts.
For when he set out Aeneas, that best of generals,
Had warned them if in the meanwhile some
   sudden
50 Emergency should arise, they were not to risk
A formal battle in the open field
But from the safety of the camp defense-works
Hold their position. So though shame and anger
Goaded them on to engage, they obeyed his
   orders,
Kept the gates closed, and waited for the enemy,
Armed in their watchtowers.
                    Turnus had galloped
Ahead of the slower column and suddenly
With a chosen troop of twenty horses surprised
The Trojans by appearing at the gateway.
60 (His mount was a Thracian piebald and he wore
A golden helmet with a scarlet crest.)
"My warriors! who will be first of you
To attack the foe with me?" he cried. "Now,
   look!"
And spun his javelin hurtling through the air
As overture to battle, and himself
Cavorted over the plain. His comrades seconded
His challenge with a yell and, following him,
Uttered blood-curdling cries. They were astonished
At the Trojans' lack of spirit—were they warriors
70 And dared not face them in the open field
Nor meet them man to man but skulked in camp?
Round and round the walls, seething with rage
Rode Turnus probing for an opening
But there was none.
                As a wolf lying in wait
By a fold full of sheep comes snarling up
To the very hurdles, at midnight, undeterred
By wind or rain, and the lambs bleat and bleat
Snug by their mothers, and he in a bateless fury
Grinds his teeth at the prey out of his reach,

While a long and increasing hunger nags his dry   80
And bloodless jaws—so it was with Turnus.
His anger blazed as he eyed the walls and the
   camp,
Frustration burned him to his iron marrow
As he wondered by what means to force an entry
And how to winkle the Trojans from their rampart
And spill them into the open.

          Close by the camp,
Concealed by an earthwork and the river's
   channels
The fleet lay: something Turnus could attack.
He bid his exulting friends bring fire, in a gust
Of passion he clutched a flaming brand himself   90
And every one fell to with a will, urged
By his powerful presence—every one of his band
Somehow equipped himself with a smoking torch,
Hearths were stripped and fuming pine-brands
   threw
A resinous glare, and Vulcan wafts to the stars
A cloud of sparky smoke.

          What God averted
So dire a conflagration from the Trojans?
Who kept off from the fleet so vast a blaze?
Tell me: O Muses. That the tale is true
Is a very old tradition—true or not,   100
It is ever new in the telling.

          At the time
When first Aeneas began to build his fleet
On Phrygian Ida and was making ready
To sail the deeps of the sea, the Berecyntian
Mother and Queen of the gods, so the story goes,
Addressed these words to Jove, "My son, great
   Lord
Of Olympus now give heed to your mother's
   prayer
And grant her what she asks. I had a forest
Of pine trees which I loved for many years.
It was a grove on the heights of my demesne   110
Where worshipers brought offerings, and dark
With pitch-trees and the trunks of maple: but when
The Dardan youth had need of a fleet it pleased me

To give him them: but now I am wracked with fear.
Now, set my fears at rest and let the prayers of
   a mother
Avail this much at least: that never never
By any shattering voyage or battering gale
May these ships be overmastered: let them have
The fortune of their origin on my mountain."
120 Answered her Son who rules the wheeling stars:
"O mother, what are you asking the fates to
   perform?
What do you seek for your ships—are hulls built
By mortal hands to have immortal license?
Would you have Aeneas journey scathelessly,
Impervious to peril? To what god
Are powers so great permitted? No, but when
Their journey done they reach an Ausonian haven,
Then from each ship that has escaped the waves
And brought the Dardan chief safe to the soil of
   Laurentum
130 I shall slough off its man-made shape and bid
Each be a goddess of the mighty sea,
Like Doto and Galatea, Nereids
That cleave the foaming wavetops with their
   breasts."
So he spoke and by the stream of his Stygian
   brother,
By the pitch-black banks that yawn on the pitchy
   torrent
He ratified his words with a nod of his head
That made Olympus shudder through and through.
So now the promised day had come and the Fates
Had fulfilled the appointed time and Turnus'
   threats
140 Warned the Great Mother to ward off the brands
From her holy ships. So now, all in a moment,
A strange new light flashed before every eye
And a huge cloud, gathering from the East,
Came streaming across the sky and in its wake
Mount Ida's troupes of dancers: then through the
   air,
Rang out an awesome voice that filled the lines
Of Trojan and Rutulian: "Be not alarmed

O Trojans!—nor is there any need to rush
To the defense of my ships, nor arm yourselves.
Sooner shall Turnus be let burn the ocean   *150*
Than burn my sacred pines—you, ships of mine,
Go free! Go, my sea goddesses—your mother
Bids you go free!"

                      Immediately each ship
Snapped her stern hawsers and, like a dolphin,
   dipped
Her prow and dived to the bottom—and re-
   emerging,
O marvelous sight! came forms of maidens, as
   many
As a moment ago were ships with their bronze
   prows
Laid up on the shore, and now they swam in the
   sea.
The Rutulians stood paralyzed, Messapus
Was panic-stricken as his horses, and the river—   *160*
Tiber himself—with a grating roar checked
His seaward flow and drew his waters back.
But Turnus never blanched, and confidently
Inspired his men and even upbraided them.
"It is the Trojans this miracle singles out
For Jove himself has robbed them of their ships,
Main source of their safety, even before we
Rutulians with fire and sword could so do!
The seas are now impassable for the Trojans—
No hope of escape there—they have lost half   *170*
   their world,
But the land is in our hands—the peoples of Italy
Thousand on thousand march with us in arms.
Let the Phrygian boast of divine oracles—
Whatever they are, I have no fear of them!
Enough for the Fates and Venus that the Trojans
Have landed on our fertile Ausonian fields.
But I have a Destiny too!—with my own sword
To hew to pieces the vile people who
Have stolen away my bride: such a disaster
Is not exclusive to the sons of Atreus,   *180*
Nor to take arms the sole right of Mycenae,
And if they say, "To have perished once is enough"

I answer, was not that one crime enough?
Must they then loathe the entire sex of women?—
These men who draw their courage from their trust
In the wall and ditch, death's narrow distance
    from them,
Did they not see the walls of Troy sink
Into the flames, though built by Neptune's hand?
But you, my comrades, which of you is ready
190 To raze the rampart and join me in the assault
On the cowering camp? I need no arms from
    Vulcan,
No thousand ships to launch against these Trojans.
—Let all the Etruscans come and join their
    alliance!
Nor need they fear the cowardly theft by night
Of their sacred image after the massacre
Of their sentries in the citadel— Nor shall we
Crouch in the belly of a horse unseen.
No! By the light of day, in the sight of all
My purpose stands—to ring their walls with fire.
200 They shall soon realize (I shall see to that)
They are not dealing with the youth of Greece
Whom Hector kept at bay for ten long years.
But now, men, the better part of the day
Is spent—in what remains look to your comfort,
Content with your achievements, and trust me
There's fighting in the wind."
                      Meanwhile Messapus
Was ordered to oversee the posting of watchers
To guard the gates; and to set a chain of watch-
    fires
Along the walls.
                 Fourteen Rutulian chiefs
210 Were picked to keep the walls under observation,
And each led a company of a hundred soldiers,
With scarlet crests and glittering with gold.
They buckled to, relieving each other by turn—
Then sprawled on the grass and gave the wine its
    turn—
Tilting their brazen bowls. The watch-fires burned;
And the guards gamed their way through the
    sleepless night.

From the rampart tops the Trojans surveyed the
   scene
Armed on their height; and anxiously, fearfully,
They tested their gates and, weapon in hand,
   linked
With bridges their strong-points. And in the fore,   *220*
Commanding them were Mnestheus and keen
   Serestus—
Whom wise Aeneas had appointed, if
Danger should threaten, to conduct affairs
And direct the warriors; and now their total force
Was mustered along the wall. They drew lots
For the dangerous positions, and relieved
Each other at the posts assigned to them.
The guard of the gate was Nisus son of Hyrtacus
An intrepid soldier sent to attend Aeneas
From Ida, home of hunting; a man swift   *230*
With javelin and light arrow: close beside him
Stood his companion Euryalus—
There was no man of all the men of Aeneas,
None wearing Trojan armor, fairer than he was—
Boy as he was his beardless cheeks declaring
His tender youth. And these two were united
In mutual love and side by side they charged
Into the ruck of battle—and there indeed
They were keeping guard together at the gate.
And Nisus said, "Euryalus, is it the Gods   *240*
That put into our minds this zest for battle?
Or do we impute to a god what is indeed
An ungovernable craving of our own?
For my part a craving for some positive action—
Any high deed, keeps churning in my mind.
I am sick of this peaceful lull. Just you look there;
Their confidence has made the Rutulians
   careless—
Half their watch-fires are out—look at them
   splayed
In drunken sleep—the whole camp is silent.
Perhaps you can guess what I have in mind, what   *250*
   thoughts
Are uppermost there—for everyone insists,
Elders and common people as one man,

Aeneas must be sent for, men must be sent
To tell him how things stand. If they will grant you
What I propose to ask—for the honor and glory
Is all I want for myself—I think that round
By the base of that mound, there, I could find a
    way
To the walls and the ramparts of Pallanteum."
Euryalus was stunned; and stimulated
260 By ambitions of his own he gave this answer
To his chafing comrade: "Nisus, are you chary
Of having me with you on so bold a venture?
Am I to send you out to face such peril alone?
It was in no such code that my father Opheltes
Instructed me as he brought me up amid
The toils and terrors of Troy; nor have you had
Such usage from me since with you I followed
Great-souled Aeneas and his direst fate."
Nisus answered: "Believe me, I never feared
270 Any such thing with you. That would have been
Against nature, No! But would that Almighty Jove
Or whoso looks on us with impartial eyes
May bring me back, in triumph to your side—
But if anything goes awry (and in a venture
Such as this is there are a thousand ifs),
By chance or by God's will, my wish would be
For you to live—at your age you have a truer
Claim upon life. Let me indeed have a champion
To rescue me in fight or ransom me
280 And finally to bury me—or if Fate forbid
(For it can happen) to pay me the due rights
And deck a sepulcher in my absent honor;
Nor let me cause such utter grief to a mother,
The only one of many mothers to quit
Without a pang the ramparts of Acesta
And follow after her son!" Then he replied,
"You are weaving idle pretexts, with no point.
My purpose holds—nor will you find me waver!
Let us make haste!" At once he called the reliefs
290 To replace them at their post and he in step
At Nisus' side withdrew, and together they went
To seek their prince.
                              Throughout the entire world

All nature else was sleeping freed from care,
Their hearts forgetful of their toils, but the
  Trojan leaders,
The flower of her manhood, were debating
Upon the gravest issues of the state,
Discussing what to do and whom to despatch
With news to Aeneas. So they stood leaning
On their long spear-shafts, with their shields
Still in their hands in the middle of the camp.   *300*
Then Nisus and Euryalus arrived
In eager haste and begged to be admitted:
The matter was important and well worth
The interruption—Iulus was the first
To welcome them and calm their agitation,
Then he bid Nisus speak.
Then said the son of Hyrtacus, "O men of Aeneas,
Listen to us with your minds and judge not
Our proposition by our youth. The Rutulians
Lie slumped asleep in drunken stupor. We   *310*
Have spotted for ourselves an ideal place
For a surprise attack—where two ways meet
By the gate nearest the sea; their fires are out
  there—
Only black smoke is coiling up to the stars.
If you will let us take our chance to go
To the walls of Pallanteum to seek Aeneas
You will soon see us back here with our spoils,
A mighty slaughter done. Nor shall we lose
Our way as we go— We have glimpsed the city
Already from the cover of the valleys   *320*
Where we are always hunting and we know
The whole course of the river." Aletes answered,
A man whose judgment matched his many years,
"Gods of our fatherland, under whose tutelage
Troy lives for aye, not yet is it your purpose
To destroy us Trojans utterly, when you breed
Youth of such spirit and such steadfast heart!"
And as he spoke he clapped them on the shoulder
And wrung them both by the hand in a flood of
  tears.
"What possible reward can I conceive   *330*
Fit for the heroes of a deed beyond

The scope of mortal praise—the gods and the glow
Of your own hearts will give the first and sweetest;
Then good Aeneas will grant you all your due
And young Ascanius, who will never forget
So great a service"—Ascanius here burst in
Crying, "Let me speak! for my one hope and
    safety
Lies in my father's return: I adjure you, Nisus,
By our great Household Gods and the Deity
340 To Assaracus dear and the shrine of white-haired
    Vesta;
And into your hands I deliver all my trust
And all my fortune—summon home my father
And restore him to my sight—for once restored
I have nothing left to fear. And I will give you
Two cups of solid silver wrought with relief—
My father won them when he conquered Arisba—
And a pair of tripods and two great talents of gold
And an ancient mixing bowl Sidonian Dido gave
    him.
But if it be our fortune to conquer Italy
350 And seize the scepter of power and be arbiters
Of the division of spoils—well, you have seen
The charger Turnus rode and the golden armor
In which he is caparisoned—I shall single
That very steed out from the rest of the booty
And his shield too and his scarlet-crested helmet
And you shall have them, Nisus, for your reward!
My father shall also allot you twelve of their
    women
All hand-picked, and captive warriors too
Each with their arms, and in addition to these
360 The regions that Latinus now is king of.
But you, revered youth, you who are not
So very much older than I am, with my whole
Heart I embrace you and take you as my comrade
In every enterprise, whatever befalls.
Never shall I seek glory on my own
Apart from you, whether in peace or war
And I shall trust your judgment above all others
In what I do and say!" Then Euryalus answered,
"The day will never come that finds me false

To my present bold designs if only fortune   *370*
Favors and not thwarts us. But I beg
One further boon to add to all your gifts.
I have a mother, of Priam's ancient lineage,
Nor could the land of Troy nor the ramparts of
   King Acestes
Withhold her, wretched soul, from coming with me.
And now I am leaving her and she knows nothing
Of all our danger, whatever it chance to be,
I leave her without a greeting—may the night
And your right hand be witness—for I know
I could not brook a parent's tears. Oh I beg you,   *380*
Console her in her need and help her if she be
   helpless.
Let me be certain-sure you will not fail me
And I shall go to meet whatever befalls
In bolder spirits." Touched to the heart the
   Trojans
Gave themselves up to tears—and more than any
The fair Iulus—as upon his mind there flashed
A vision of his own love for his father:
So then he said: "You may rest assured of this:
All shall be done as your mighty deed deserves.
Your mother shall be as my own mother wanting   *390*
Only the name Creüsa—for such a son
No little gratitude is owed her. And now I swear,
Whatever happens, I swear by my own head
As by *my* head my father used to swear,
That all I promise to you if all goes well
And you return, that the very same reward
If things go ill, shall be in all its fullness
Retained for her and for your family."
So weeping at his need to speak such words
He unslung from his shoulder a golden sword   *400*
Fashioned with wonderful skill by Lycaon of
   Cnossus
And fitted for easy port in an ivory scabbard.
Mnestheus gave to Nisus a shaggy lion-skin,
And faithful Aletes exchanged his helmet with
   him.
So armed they started out, and as they went to
   the gates

They were escorted by the entire body
Of Nobles young and old, and godsped with their
   prayers.
And there was fair Iulus, in mind and manly poise
Far older than his years, to give them many
410   A message to be carried to his father.
—But the winds would scatter every one of them
And sow them on the deaf ears of the clouds.

They crossed the fosse and were out making
   their way
Towards the enemy camp, the destined ground
Of many an enemy death now—everywhere
They saw splayed on the grass in drunken sleep
The bodies of men, and chariots tipped over
Upon the shore, and among the wheels and the
   harness
Their drivers lying slumped among piles of armor
420   And pools of wine. Then hissed the son of
   Hyrtacus,
"Euryalus, this is our moment; here is our way;
We must brace our arms for the utmost action.
   You
Must keep our rear with close and wary cunning,
While I do devastation among these files
And hew a high road for you." He was silent
And took to the sword, attacking proud Rhamnes
Who lay exposed on a high pile of rugs,
Blowing with all his lungs fanfares of sleep.
He was a king indeed and indeed the prophet
   most pleasing
430   To Turnus the King but powers of prophecy
Availed him not to avoid his own death.
Three of his servants next, slumped down among
   their weapons,
He did to death, and Remus' armor-bearer
And his charioteer close under his horses' flanks—
He slit their lolling throats with his sword, then
   lopped
Their master's head off leaving the trunk to spout
With bubbling blood and saturate the earth
And the bedding too, in its black gory flood.

Then he made an end of Lamyrus and Lamus
And Serranus, the young and beautiful,   440
Who most of the night had gambled and now lay
In a full-drunken stupor—luckier he,
Had his play lasted nightlong, had he kept
Going until the day. Like a famishing lion
Starvation spurs to run amok through a fold
Teeming with sheep and he mangles and drags
    them out,
The soft beasts dumb with terror, and roars from
    slavering jaws—
So Nisus slew, and Euryalus no whit less—
In his flare of steady fury he despatched
A host unknown to fame—Fadus, Herbesus,   450
Rhoetus and Abaris—all unaware save Rhoetus
And he was awake and he saw everything,
But in his terror he only could cringe behind
A wine-jar and then, as he rose to engage,
Euryalus drove the whole length of his sword
Into his breast and drawing it out again
Let loose the flood of death. The dying man
Retched his spirit away in a bloody flux
Still mixed with the wine he drank. Euryalus
Went pressing upon his silent murderous way.   460
And now he was nearing the pitch of Messapus
And his henchmen, where the last campfire lay
    dying,
And he saw the tethered horses cropping the grass
When Nisus, perceiving he was being carried away
By the sheer lust for a holocaust, rapped out,
"We must stop now! dangerous dawn is near.
We have had vengeance enough. Our way through
    the foe is open."
Many the warrior's weapons of solid silver
They had to leave behind and mixing-bowls
And beautiful coverlets. But Euryalus   470
Seized on the trappings of Rhamnes and his
    sword-belt
With golden studs, that once in times long past
The wealthy Caedicus had sent as a present
To Remulus of Tibur in earnest of offering
    friendship.

He, when he died, bequeathed them to his
  grandson
After whose death the Rutulians won them in
  battle,
And these Euryalus now slung on his strong
  shoulders,
Though all to no purpose: then fitted Messapus'
  helmet
With its gay crest on his own head and wore it.
480 They left the camp then, heading for safe regions.

Meanwhile a band of horse sent on from the city
  of Latium
(While their main forces waited in the plain
In battle order) was on the move bringing
An answer to King Turnus—three hundred men,
All bearing shields, and Volscens was their leader.
They were just nearing camp, they were almost
  under
The walls when in the distance they caught sight
Of the two warriors veering to the left—
And it was the helmet, glinting in the night-shade
490 And glittering as the moonlight fell full on it,
Betrayed Euryalus, unwitting as he was.
The significance of the sight was not mistaken.
Volscens roared from his place in the column,
  "Halt,
You warriors! What's your business? Why are
  you armed?
Who are you? Where are you going?" They made
  no move
To answer but fled full-tilt into the woods,
Trusting the darkness to save them. But the
  horsemen
Stationed themselves at every familiar track-way
And left and right blocked every possible egress.
500 The wood stretched widely away in a tangled
  blackness
Of thicket and ilex and on every side
Was choked with briars—but vestiges of a path
Just glimmered through the shock of undergrowth.

The darkness cast by the boughs and his weight
  of body
Hampered Euryalus and panic mazed him
To miss his path. But Nisus got clean away
And, forgetting his friend, he had escaped the foe
And reached the spot that later was called Alban
From the name of Alba; (but then King Latinus
Had a corral there:) then he halted and in vain   510
Looked back for his friend: he was nowhere to
  be seen.
"My poor Euryalus! Where did I leave you?
Where shall I begin to search for you,
Unwinding all the twists and turns of the way
Through this deceiving wood?" Even as he spoke
He began to trace his backward tracks and
  wandered
Through the still thickets. Suddenly he heard
Horses, halloos, and signals of pursuit.
Then, in a moment, a shout came to his ears
And he saw Euryalus, overcome at last   520
By the wiles of darkness and the treacherous
  terrain
And the sudden bewildering clamor, seized,
In the hands of the whole melee, and hustled off
Despite the utmost of his futile struggles.
What should he do? What force, what feat of arms,
Dispose to save his friend? Should he dash to a
  certain
Death in the bristling thicket of sword-points
And speed to a glorious end in a welter of
  wounds?
Firmly he braced his arm and flexing his spear-
  shaft
He looked to the moon on high and made this   530
  prayer:
"Thou, goddess, glory of stars and guardian of
  the woods,
Latona's daughter be near and help these my
  endeavors,
If ever my father Hyrtacus brought gifts on my
  behalf

To deck your altars, if ever by my hunting
I added my share and hung my offerings from
   your dome
Or fastened them upon your holy rooftree,
Let me confound this band, O guide my weapons
Straight through the air." He spoke and with the
   whole
Coiled might of his body he despatched the spear:
540 The flying steel seared through the shades of night
And struck right home into the back of Sulmo,
Snapped short and pierced his heart with splaying
   splinters!
Over he rolled, the warm stream of his life
Upgushing from his breast and his sides shuddered
With long and choking gasps and he went cold.
The others looked round everywhere. While he,
The fiercer for this blow, leveled another
Spear and, see! he held it ready poised by his ear
And while confusion reigned the spear went
   whizzing,
550 Bored through both temples of Tagus and bit
   there,
Warm clenched in the brain. But wild with fury
   Volscens
Could nowhere see the discharger of the weapon,
Nor anyone to vent his rage upon.
So turning on Euryalus he swore:
"But you, meanwhile, shall pay the debt for both
With your warm heart's blood and give me my
   due vengeance!"
With his sword drawn he turned upon Euryalus.
Then truly out of his mind, in a frenzy of horror,
Nisus cried out for he could no longer bear
560 To hide in the shadows with such weight of grief,
"It is I who did it, I! and here I stand!
Rutulians turn your swords on me, the blame
Is wholly mine—the boy had not the resource
Nor power to do you harm. I appeal to the sky and
To all the stars above to be my witness;
He simply loved his luckless friend too well!"
But even as he pleaded the sword was driven

With all its power and pierced the ribs and rent
The snow-white breast, and shuddering down to
 death
Euryalus fell and the blood spread out   570
Over his beautiful limbs and his head went limp
And sank upon his shoulders: just as when
A shining flower is severed by the plough
And wilts to death, or poppies droop their heads
On feeble necks, weighed down by a sudden
 shower.
But Nisus charged into the thick of the foe,
His sole aim Volscens, seeking him alone—
He had no other object and though hemmed round
By a mass of hostile bodies he forced his way
Whirling his lightning sword until he plunged it   580
Deep in the shrieking face of Volscens, and dying
Took the life of his foe and flung himself,
Pierced through and through, upon his breathless
 friend
And there at last found calm in peaceful death.
O happy pair! If there is any power
In poetry of mine no day shall ever dim
Your memory in Time, while the royal house of
 Aeneas
Dwells in the Capitol's immovable rock,
And a Roman father holds the rule of the world!
The Rutulian victors, having gained new spoils   590
And regained what was lost, with weeping bore
The lifeless body of Volscens back to camp.
Nor was the lamentation less in the camp.
The murdered body of Rhamnes had been found
And all those chiefs despatched in that one great
 slaughter,
And Serranus and Numa. A large crowd
Gathered about the dead and the near-dead
Where the ground still reeked with the slaughter
And streams of blood were fully foaming still.
They passed the spoils from hand to hand, they   600
 noted
The glistening helmet of Messapus the trappings
It had cost such sweat to recover.

But now the Goddess of dawn was already arising
From Tithonus' saffron couch and sprinkling the
     light
Of a new day; and sunlight streaming out
Revealed all things afresh. Now, fully armed
Turnus aroused his warriors to arms,
And each commander mustered his own men
In their brazen armor, and used every sort
610 Of anti-Trojan speech to whip up their fury.
Nay more—and a pitiful sight it was—they impaled
The heads of Nisus and Euryalus
On spear-points, and then followed them,
     shouting madly.
Aeneas' doughty men took up position
On the left flank (for the river guarded the right)
Holding the great moats, and standing-to
In the high towers, grieving, for at once
They saw the brandished visages of their friends,
Known all too well, and dripping with dark blood.

620 Meanwhile through the fearful camp winged
     rumor rushed
Her message straight to the ears of Euryalus'
     mother
And suddenly she went cold to the marrow, the
     shuttle
Leapt from her hands and the skein unwound from
     its spool.
With a woman's wail of anguish, tearing her hair,
She rushed out in her grief and madly sought
The front ranks on the wall oblivious
Of warriors or the dangers of flying weapons
And there she filled the heavens with her keening.
"Euryalus, is it you that I see? How could you
     leave me?
630 You that have been the one last solace of my age—
O cruel one! O wretched me, could you not
Even allow me to speak my last farewell
As you set out upon such a perilous venture?
Alas you lie in an unknown place abandoned
To the curs and carrion crows of Latium
And I, your mother, have not walked in mourning

Beside your bier nor closed your eyes nor laved
Your wounds nor wrapped you in the shroud I
    struggled
By night and day to finish for you; a task
To solace an old woman such as I.   *640*
Where shall I seek you? In what land are lying
Your severed limbs and mutilated body?
O son of mine is this all of yourself
You can bring back to me? And is this all
I followed by land and sea?
                          If you have any pity
Transfix me, O Rutulians, shower on me
The weight of all your weapons, let your steel
Sup first on me. . . .
                          Or, Father of the Gods,
Do you have mercy and strike down to Tartarus
This hated existence, if in no other way   *650*
I may cut short this torture of a life!"
All hearts were moved to tears and a groan of
    sorrow
Rose from the ranks; their zest for battle flagged,
Their strength was broken. Then as the pyre of
    her grief
Burned fiercer Idaeus and Actor bidden
By Ilioneus and by Iulus wracked with sobs,
Supported her between them and took her off
Back to her own dwelling.
                          But now, from afar,
The trumpet from its brazen throat blared out
Its terrible call. A shout rang out and the sky   *660*
Volleyed the echo back. The Volscians swiftly
    advancing
Under a level carapace of shields
Meant to contain the moat and from there rip down
The palisade. One party sought directly
To scale the walls with ladders where it seemed
The line was thinly manned and the light showed
Through gaps in the defense. Against them the
    Trojans
Poured every sort of weapon and prodded them
    back
With heavy poles, being experienced,

670   After their long siege, in the defense of walls;
      And they kept rolling down stones of a killing
         weight
      In hopes of breaking through the enemy armor
      Although it seemed the carapace of shields
      Could happily withstand whatever it had to.
      But not for ever: for where a solid wedge
      Threatened the rampart the Trojans heaved into
         place
      And let fly a colossal boulder that crashed through
      The Rutulian shields and crushed a mass of men.
      And after that the Rutulians had less fancy
680   For close fighting under cover but attempted
      To drive them from the ramparts at long range.
      In another sector, a terrifying sight,
      Mezentius brandished an Etruscan pine-brand
      Bringing fire and smoke to bear. But Messapus,
      The tamer of horses, the begotten of Neptune,
      Tore at the palisade and called for ladders
      To scale the ramparts.

                              O Calliope!
      Bring all your muses to assist my song,
      As I tell what a holocaust the sword of Turnus
690   *Wrought in that place, what deaths he dealt, what*
         foes
      Each warrior despatched to the land of death!
      Help me unfold in its entirety
      The pattern of this war for you, O Goddess,
      Have power to paint the scenes you know full well.

      There was a tower, a vast sight from below,
      On a point of vantage, with high companion-ways,
      And this the entire Italian force was trying
      With every means in its power to take by storm
      Or overturn, and on their side the Trojans
700   Were defending it with stones and, concentrating
      In its apertures, hurled weapons through at their
         foes
      Whom Turnus led. He flung a blazing torch
      And set fire to the tower-side; fanned by the wind
      The flames licked through the planks and catching
         the uprights

Took firm control. Its inmates were panic-stricken
And vainly they craved to escape their terrible
  plight.
They bunched together and cringed back to a part
  of the platform
As yet unscathed and under their weight the tower
Suddenly fell, and with its mighty fall
The sky reverberated. Down to earth   *710*
Pierced by their own spears, their breasts impaled
By the hard splinters half-dead the victims crashed
And the huge structure crumbled on top of them.
Helenor alone and Lycus with him
Barely escaped. In the prime of his youth
Helenor was the man the slave Licymnia
Had borne in secret to the King of Maeonia
And she had sent him to Troy in arms, though
  forbidden,
Bearing simply a naked sword and a plain
Unblazoned shield. And when he found himself   *720*
In the midst of Turnus' thousands, the embattled
Ranks of the Latins closely surrounding him,
Like a wild animal close hemmed in a ring of
  hunters
That fronts their darts with fury and then
  deliberately
Leaps to its death full onto the hunting spears,
So into the heart of the foe rushed Helenor
And made for the place where he saw their
  weapons thickest.
But Lycus was a better runner by far
And snaked his way through his enemies and
  their weapons.
He gained the wall and tried to clutch its top   *730*
And got a hand to the outstretched hands of his
  friends
But Turnus had followed him up, casting his spear,
And mocked him in triumph. "Fool, did you
  really hope
You could escape me?" And as he hung there
  seized him
And tore a great part of the wall down with him.
—Just as that bird, the armor-bearer of Jove

When clenched in his hooky talons he has a hare
Or a snow-white swan and soars up into the sky;
Or as from the fold a wolf, the War God's brute,
740   Snatches a·lamb whose mother bleats and bleats
As she seeks it. From all sides a shout arose
And Turnus' men rushed up to fill the moat
With broken earth while others tossed up
    firebrands
Onto the tower-roofs. And Ilioneus
Destroyed Lucetius with a rock as huge
As a mountain spur just as he reached a gate,
His torch in hand. Emathion fell to Liger:
Corynaeus finished Asilas; Liger was sure with
    the javelin,
Corynaeus with the arrow shot from a distance
750   And flying unseen. Then Caeneus killed Ortygius
And Turnus slaughtered Caeneus as he did so,
And Itys also, Clonius, Dioxippus,
Promolus, Sagaris and Idas as he stood
On the top of a turret. Capys shot Privernus;
He had just been grazed by a light spear of
    Themillas'
And the poor fool had dropped his shield and put
His hand to the wound, and so the speeding arrow
Pinned his hand to his left side and burst
The inmost source of breath with a mortal wound.
760   There stood the son of Arcens in splendid armor
And an embroidered mantle a brilliant purple
With Spanish dye—a man of magnificent mien,
His father Arcens had sent him to war, who had
    reared him
In his mother's groves beside the river Symaethus
Where stands Palicus' altar, rich with gifts.
Mezentius put his spears down, loaded his sling
And whirled it whistling three times round his
    head
And with the leaden missile now grown hot
He split his enemy's temples clean in two
770   And laid him low full-length upon the sand!
And then it was, they say, that Ascanius
Who up till then had only used his arrows

To flush wild beasts and send them scattering,
Used a swift shaft in warfare and overthrew
With his own hand the brave Numanus. Remulus
(His second name) was a man who had lately
    married
A younger sister of Turnus. This Numanus
Went strutting in front of the front of the front
    rank
Blatantly blurting words both meet and unmeet
For me to tell, blown out with his self-conceit   780
In his new relations with royalty, making himself
Mighty in his own eyes by the noise he made:
"Twice-captured Phrygians are you not ashamed
To be besieged and pent a second time
Behind a barricade, to put your walls
Between you and death? And behold the very men
Who demand our wives from us at the point of
    the sword!
What god drove you to Italy, or what madness?
There are no Atridae here; no forger's lips like
    Ulysses'—
We are a tough people, we temper our newborn   790
    sons
In the ice-cold of relentless river-water!
Our boys hunt on, without sleep; they exhaust
    the woods;
Their play is the breaking of horses, and archery
    practice.
Our youths are trained in the school of want and
    hardship,
Either subduing the soil with the rake or shaking
A city with warfare; at every stage of life
We are close to iron: to goad our bullocks we use
The butt of a spear; old age may slow us down
But does not impair the force of our spirit or
Diminish our vigor: we thrust our whitening hair   800
Into a helmet and ever it is our pleasure
To bring home booty and live on what we plunder.
But you, you are cluttered with clothes, tricked out
    in saffron
And flaring purple, you relish a life of sloth,

You delight to indulge in dancing, your very tunics
Have sleeves and your headgear tie-strings.
  Phrygian women,
Not Phrygian men, —go run to the heights of
  Dindyma
Where you will hear the two-stopped pipes you
  know;
The Berecyntian drum and the flute of Ida's -
  mother
810 Summon you—leave arms to *men*, let be the
  sword!"
Ascanius could no longer brook such boasting
Ill-omened words and drawing his horsehair
  bowstring
He stood with arms apart his arrow nocked,
But first he prayed in humble supplication
This prayer to Jove: "I shall set before your altar
A snow-white bullock, his horns gilt, his head
Up to his mother's in height already ripe
To butt and paw the sand up with his hoofs."
The All-Father heard and thundered on the left
820 Out of a clear blue sky, and in unison
The fatal bowstring twanged. The arrow flew
Whizzing horribly from the back-drawn string.
It clove the head of Remulus clean through
And the tip pierced to his brain and Ascanius cried,
"Go, then, make mock of valor with your boasts!
This is the answer we twice-captured Phrygians
Make the Rutulians!" That was all he said
And the Trojans backed him with a joyful roar
And their spirits leapt heaven-high.
                      Now it so happened
830 That from a county of heaven long-haired Apollo,
Throned on a cloud, was looking down upon
The Italian forces and the Trojan camp
And thus he addressed victorious Iulus:
"Rejoice in your new powers, brave boy begotten
Of gods, and father of gods to be—it is so
Men starward fare! Justly has Fate decreed
That every war-to-be shall find its peace
Under the sway of the house of Assaracus.
The limit of your prowess is not Troy!"

He spoke these words and as he did he dived 840
From the heights of heaven, cleaving the swirling
   air
Straight for Ascanius. And he changed his features
To a semblance of old Butes who had been
Anchises' armor-bearer and faithful keeper
Of the gate at Troy, and afterwards Aeneas
Had made him his son's guardian—as he went
Apollo seemed his ancient image in every
   particular:
His voice, his color, his white hair and the savage
Clank of his armor, and at once he spoke
To Iulus who was blazing with excitement. 850
"Enough, O Son of Aeneas, that unavenged
Numanus lies the victim of your bow.
Mighty Apollo grants you this first feat
Of glory, nor is envious of arms
That are not unlike his own. But for the rest,
Brave boy, abstain from the war, as befits your
   youth!"
Even as he spoke he faded from men's eyes
Into thin air and vanished far from sight,
But the Trojan chieftains recognized the god
For they knew his weapons and heard his quiver 860
   rustle
As he flew off. And therefore at Apollo's
Express injunction they restrained Ascanius
From further battle, keen though he was to fight.
But they advanced again into battle and hazarded
Their lives to utmost danger. Along the walls
From point to strong point rose a shout, and
   keenly
They bent their bows and whirled their tautened
   slings.
Everywhere the ground was piled with weapons;
Now shield and hollow helmet rang as they
   clashed;
The fight grew fiercer; as when a storm breaks 870
Out of the west at the setting of the rain-fraught
Stars of the Kid and lashes the earth, or as heavy
As hail hurled into the sea when Jove unleashes
The bleakness of his blasting southerly tempest

And bursts the cloudy hollows of the sky.
Then Pandarus and Bitias the sons of Idaean
    Alcanor
Reared in Jove's holy glade by Iaera the
    woodnymph,
Young warriors tall as the pines and the mountains
    of their birthplace,
Threw open the gate their commander had put
    them in charge of
880 And wholly upon their own initiative
And trusting their own prowess invited the enemy
Into the fortress: they themselves stood sentry
In front of the gate-towers to the left and right
Armed to the teeth, the plumes tossing upon
    their helmets
Even as high in the air beside flowing rivers—
Perhaps on the banks of the Po or by pleasant
    Athesis—
As twin oak-trees raise to the sky their unshorn
    foliage
And nod their lofty heads.
                      In rushed the Rutulians
Seeing a way open. But immediately Quercens
890 And fair Aquicolus and headstrong Tmarus
And Haemon, scion of Mars, and all their
    henchmen
Either turned tail and fled or lost their lives
On the very threshold. Then the fury of all
Seethed even stronger and the Trojans massed
To the spot and took to fighting hand to hand
And even dared to sally out into the plain.
A message was brought to Turnus the leader-in-
    chief
As he raged and havocked in another quarter
That the enemy had got new heart from his recent
900 Successful slaughter and was even daring
To open the gates and offer entrance. Turnus
Broke off his present engagement and rushed
    headlong
With a giant's fury towards the Trojan gate
And these arrogant brothers. Antiphates was first
To stand in his way so he was first to die,

The bastard son of Sarpedon born of a Theban
   woman,
Killed by a javelin—the shaft of Italian cornel
Winged through the yielding air and biting deep
Into his belly gouged its way up into his chest.
The cavernous black wound gushed out its flood   910
And the iron lodged in the lung grew warm with it.
Then Meropes and Erymas and Aphidnus
Felt the force of his hand and then Bitias—
With his blazing eye and the torrent of his valor—
But not with a javelin, he would never surrender
His life to a javelin wound—but now there flew,
Fired from its sling with the force of a thunderbolt,
A hurtling burning plummet and not two layers
Of bullhide nor his trusty corslet doubly
Inforced with golden scales could stay its impact.   920
The vast limbs wilted and sank; and the earth
   groaned;
The massive shield rang thunderously down
On top of the body. So it is, sometimes,
At Baiae, on the Euboean coast, where men
Heap up a huge pile of rocks and then
Lever away and let it go with a crash
To fall into the sea and it plunges down
With a long wake of wreckage, cleaves the shallows
And settles on the seabed and the sea
Is all churned up and aswirl with murky sand.   930
Then high Prochyta trembles with the noise
And the island of Inarime that pins down
Typhoeus, at Jove's command, to his painful bed.

And now Mars, Lord of Arms, inspired the Latins
With added strength and courage and screwed
   their hearts
To even more, and implanted in the Trojans
A spirit of flight and terror. From all sides
The Latins gathered and the Warrior God
Entered their souls as scope for battle grew.
When Pandarus saw the body of his brother   940
And saw how the day went, and the turn of
   fortune,
With a great heave he swung the gate on its hinges

Putting his mighty shoulder to the effort
And cutting many of his comrades off
To face their fortunes in the field outside,
But many others in full flight he secured:
Yet the poor fool never discerned that Turnus,
King Turnus, was included in the rabble
Pent in the fortress by this act of his—
950   A monstrous tiger pent with a herd of helpless
          cattle!
Immediately new fire flashed from his eyes,
His armor rang with a grisly resonance,
His crest quivered blood-red upon his helmet,
And he made lightning flashes leap from his shield.
Then suddenly the men of Aeneas blenched
To recognize that hated face and the huge
Frame of the man. But mighty Pandarus
Sprang out and burning with his brother's death
He cried: "This place is anything but the palace
          of Amata,
960   Your dowry-dwelling—nor is the city of Ardea
Embracing you now with its friendly walls of home.
You see your enemies' camp. There is no chance
          of escape!"
But confidently Turnus answered smiling
With quiet assurance, "Very well, begin,
If you have the courage, come, begin the fight!
You will soon be telling Priam that here also
You have found an Achilles." He said nothing
          more.
Then Pandarus flung a rough-hewn spear at him
Still with its green bark and knobbed with knots,
970   But the air stalled it and Saturnian Juno
Glanced off the wound to be and the spear stuck
Hard on the gate.
                    "You shall not escape *my* steel!"
Cried Turnus, "and the full force of my blow
Or I am not the source of wound and weapon!"
And so he spoke and lifted up his sword
And rose to the stroke and dealt a terrible blow;
He cleft in two the temples and cut through
To the young beardless chin. There was a crash
And the earth trembled with the mighty weight.

Pandarus fell at the point of death, his limbs   *980*
Splayed out, his arms brain-spattered and blood-
  spattered
And his divided head flopped equally
Upon each shoulder. The Trojans turned and fled
Crazy with fear and if at that moment of victory
Turnus had thought of smashing with his fist
The bolts of the gate and letting in his comrades
That day would have been the last of the war and
  the Trojan Nation.
But rage and an insensate lust for slaughter
Impelled him on, and first he surprised Phaleris,
Then hamstrung Gyges; then seized their spears   *990*
  and hurled them
At the backs of the fleeing Trojans. Juno imparted
The strength and courage to him. He added Halys
And Phegeus to his toll, stabbed through his shield;
Then he surprised at their zealous sentry-go on
  the turrets
Alcander, Halius, Noemon and Prytanis.
Then Lynceus made for him, calling for support,
And he with a sweep from the rampart on the right
Beheaded him with a single close-struck sword-
  stroke
And his head, with its helmet on, lay far away.
Next fell Amycus, the bane of the wild, and no   *1000*
  man
Was more expert than he at using poisons
To tip the dart and reinforce the sword;
Then Clytius, Aeolus' son, and Cretheus friend of
  the Muses,
The Muses' own companion to whom songs
And verses set to the lyre were heart's delight,
For ever he sang of warriors and of charges
And all their arms and battles.

                Now at last
The Trojan leaders, Mnestheus and fierce Serestus
Heard of the scourge among their men and saw
Their friends in flight and the enemy in the camp.   *1010*
Mnestheus shouted "Where are you fleeing, men?
What other wall, what further fortress have you?
My friends, shall it be said that a single man

Surrounded on every side by your own
    fortifications
Has spread such devastation through the camp
And survives unavenged—a man who has sent
So many of the best of your warriors to their
    deaths?
O cowards, do you feel no shame? Do you feel
No pity for the ancient gods of your country,
1020 Nor for your great Aeneas?" Kindled thus
They rallied and formed up into close array.
Little by little Turnus backed from the fight
And made for the river and that region where
The water flowed. The Trojans pressed more hotly,
Shouting and bunched together. It was like
Hunters advancing on a savage lion,
Their weapons poised and he afraid yet furious
Gives ground with glaring eyes, for wrath and
    valor
Forbid him to turn tail, nor dare he charge,
1030 For all he wants to, through the spears and
    hunters.
Just so did Turnus doubtfully draw back
Unhurriedly, his heart boiling with rage.
And even so he twice charged into the thick
Of his foes and twice put them to ragged flight
Around the walls—but now from the camp all
    the warriors
Hurried together and formed into close order
Nor dared Saturnian Juno to supply
Renewed strength to oppose them, for Jove had
    sent
Iris from heaven down to his sister's ears
1040 Bearing a stern ukase should Turnus not
Retire from the high ramparts of the Trojans.
So the young lord no longer had the strength
To hold his own with shield or sword, and weapons
Showered upon him hurled from every side.
Around his hollow brow his helmet rang
With ceaseless dinting and his armor's plates
Yawned from the showers of stones; from off his
    head

The plumes were razed, his shield boss could not
    bear
The weight of blows. And all the more the Trojans,
Mnestheus the foremost, redoubled the rain of   *1050*
    spears.
Then he broke out in sweat all over his body
And poured in streams (he had no chance to
    breathe)
And his trembling limbs were racked with feeble
    gasping.
So then, at the end of his tether, he dived headlong
Into the river with all his armor on
And the river took him to its yellow breast,
Buoyed him on kindly waves and washed his blood,
And bore him back to his comrades, full of joy.

BOOK X

Meanwhile the doors of the palace of powerful
    Olympus
Were flung wide open and the Father of Gods
And King of men summoned a council to sit
In the starry dwelling, whence he could gaze down
On the whole world and on the camp of the
    Dardans
And on the people of Latium. The gods
Took up their seats in the twin-entranced chamber.
Then he himself opened the meeting. "Oh mighty
Sky-inhabiting gods, what is the reason
To reverse your judgment and so to engage   *10*
In such a violent clash of opposing interests?
I had forbade that Italy war with the Trojans.
Why has my veto been flouted in this flagrant
    manner?

What fears have prompted one side or the other
To take up arms and to unsheathe the sword now?
In its due course shall come the time for battle—
Hasten it not—the time when violent Carthage
Shall force the passes of the Alps and wreak
Appalling havoc among the Roman strongholds.
20 Then may your hatreds be permitted, then
May you plunder as you please—but now, let be!
And ratify in good faith the peace that is my
    pleasure."
Brief was the speech of Jove but not the answer
Of golden Venus. "O Father, O everlasting
Lord over men and all things on the earth,
—For where else can we turn, to whom else
    implore?
Do you not see how the Rutulians insult us,
How haughty Turnus drives his charging steeds
Right through our ranks, puffed up with the favors
    of Mars?
30 No longer do their walls keep safe the Trojans—
The enemy is within their gates and fighting
Among the very earthworks of the defenses
And filling the dikes with blood. And all this time
Aeneas is away and he knows nothing.
Will you never never grant them rest from siege?
Once more an enemy threatens the walls of a Troy
Just striving for new birth, once more an army,
Once more a Diomede rises against the Trojans,
This time from Aetolian Arpi. And, as I think,
40 My wounds are still to come and I, your daughter,
Hold in suspense some mortal encounter in battle.
If it was truly without your leave and against
Your divine ordinance that the Trojans made
Landfall in Italy—let them atone
For their offenses, and let you withdraw
Your aid from them. But if indeed they followed
So many oracles both from the Gods above
And from the Gods below, then how can anyone
Have power now to reverse your ordinance
50 And plot for them a quite new course of fate?
Must I remind you how their fleet was burned
To ruins on Eryx shore? Or how the King

Of Tempest roused his raving hurricanes
Out of Aeolia? Remind you of Iris sent
Posting down from the clouds? Now, what is more,
Juno has routed out the Underworld to her aid
(A part of nature never before exploited)
And suddenly, launched on the upper world
Allecto lurching rampant through the cities
Of Italy. No longer have I any   60
Desire for sway—while fortune favored us
I had such hopes: now let win whom you will.
But if there is no place anywhere in the world
Your implacable consort will concede to the
     Trojans
I adjure you, Father, by Troy's smoking shambles
Let me despatch Ascanius my grandson
Safe from the war; let him survive. Let Aeneas
Indeed be tossed on unknown seas and follow
Wherever fortune lead him—but Ascanius—
May I have power to shield him and withdraw him   70
From the horrors of battle. But the city of Amathus
Belongs to me, as do the heights of Paphos,
Cythera and the temple of Idalium—
Let him lay down his arms in one of my holdings
And eke his life out reputationless.
Then be your command that Carthage crush Italy
Under her iron heel: The Tyrian cities
Need fear no hindrance from Ascanius.
Of what advantage has it been to him
To escape the scourge of war, to have fled   80
     unscathed
Through the heart of burning Troy, to have had
     his fill
Of every danger the sea and the broad land offer
While the Trojans seek in Latium Troy restored?
Had he not better have settled on the last
Shards of his home, the cinders where Troy stood?
Give Xanthus back, I beg, give back Simois
To that wretched race, O Father, let the Trojans
Once more enact the tragedy of Troy."

Then Queenly Juno flared in a passion of
     absolute fury,

90   "Why do you force me to break silence, to make
         known
     To all, the secret springs of my bitterness?
     What man, what god, I should like to know
         compelled
     Your Aeneas to make war, and impose his enmity
     Upon the king of Latium? And you say
     The Fates constrained him to seek Italy—
     (Or was he not gulled to go by Cassandra's
         frothings?)
     Let it be what it may! Did I exhort him
     To leave his camp and trust his life to the winds?
     —To hand over the supreme command of the war
100 And the defense of his fortress to a boy?
     —To pother Etruscan loyalties and trouble
     A nation's quiet? What god, what brookless power
     Led him to do this ill? Can you detect
     The hand of Juno or of Iris posted
     Down from the clouds in any of these events?
     So it is monstrous that the Italians ring
     This nascent Troy with fire? Monstrous that Turnus
     Whose grandsire was Pilumnus and whose mother
     The goddess Venilia, should take his stand
110 On his own country's soil?—Then what do you say
     When the Trojans with their pitchy brands assail
     The Latin people, and crush them, farm and field,
     Under an alien yoke and plunder them—
     Choose, at their whim, what girls to wed, and rape
     The betrothed from their lovers' arms?—And
         these are they
     Who stretch their hands out suppliant for peace,
     But bristle their ships with arms!
                                   And you have powers
     To wile away Aeneas out of the clutch of the
         Greeks,
     And substitute for your champion wreaths and
         currents of vapors,
120 And you can transform his navy into a bevy of
         nymphs—
     Is it so shocking, then, that I succor the Rutulians?
     "Aeneas is away and he knows nothing."
     Let him remain away and knowing nothing!

You have, you say, your Paphos and Idalium,
You have Cythera's heights—why do you meddle
With a city ripe for wars and fierce in spirit?
Do you think it is I who have tried to overturn
From their foundations your fading Phrygian
    fortunes?
Is it I or the mortal who dragooned luckless
Trojans to fight Greeks? What was the reason   *130*
Europe and Asia rose against each other,
Their pact of peace broken by treachery?
Was I the guide of that adulterous Dardan
When he stormed Sparta? Did I supply him
    weapons,
Or foment war with his lust? Then, indeed,
Fears for your people had befitted you—
But now it is far too late to raise objections:
Your objections are ill founded and the abuse
You hurl at my head mere baseless rhetoric."

So Juno spoke and all the immortals murmured   *140*
Assent to one or other party, a sound
Like the first rustles deep down in the forest,
Strange and invisible, that warn the sailor
Of an oncoming gale, though all seems still.

Then the Almighty Father, the primal Power
In all the universe began to speak.
The high hall of the gods with his first utterance
To silence fell, earth shuddered to its core,
The sky to its utmost height was still, and the
    winds
Lulled into rest and the sea calmed all its waves.   *150*
"Take my words to your hearts; engrave them
    there.
Since it is not permitted that the Ausonians
And Trojans sink their differences in a treaty,
Nor can your wranglings come to a conclusion,
Let each man's fortune be as it stands today;
Let him plough whatever furrow of hope he may!
I will show favor to no man, neither Rutulian
Nor Trojan, whether it be through destiny
That the Italians encompass the Trojan camp

160 Or whether it spring from the doom of errant Troy
And malevolent oracles. Nor do I absolve
The Rutulians. Let every man work out
By his own exertions his own destiny
For good or evil. I, Jove, am king of all;
To all alike. The Fates shall find a way."
And swearing by the streams of his Stygian brother
And their banks of boiling pitch and the abyss
Yawning in murk between them, with his nod
He made Olympus quake to its foundations.
170 This was the end of the debate. Jove rose
From his golden throne and the sky-inhabiting
gods
Conducted him in their midst towards the
threshold.

Meanwhile the Rutulians surged around at the
gates
Eager to slaughter the foe and ring the defenses
With a ring of fire. But the whole force of Aeneas
Was cooped and cribbed within their fortifications
With no hope of escape. In wretched plight
They stood on their high towers or formed
A tenuous line of defense along the walls.
180 Asius son of Imbrasus, Thymoetes
Hicetaeon's child, and the two Assaraci,
And aging Thymbris, Castor at his side—
All these were to the fore—and by their side
Sarpedon's two brothers, Clarus and Thaemon,
From noble Lycia. Acmon of Lyrnessus,
No lesser hero than his father Clytius
Or his brother Mnestheus, bent all the strength of
his body
To carrying a colossal rock, a sizable
Piece of a mountain. So they struggled on
190 With javelins some, others with stones—some
With fire, and others arrows shot from the bow.

And see, in their midst stood the young Prince
himself,
(Truly for Venus' attentions the fittingest object)
His beautiful head bare and like a jewel

In a gold setting—an ornament designed
To be worn on the neck or head, just so he
   sparkled,
Or as a skillful inlay of ivory gleams
In boxwood or Orician terebinth.
His hair below its clasp of malleable gold
Flowed down his snow-white neck. You, too,   200
The noble-hearted tribes could see you, Ismarus,
Tipping your bolts with poison and dealing
   wounds,
Scion of noble Lydian stock from the land
Men till for its rich harvest, a land watered
By Pactolus' golden stream. There stood
   Mnestheus
In the full flush of his triumph of yesterday
When he had driven Turnus from the ramparts;
And there was Capys from whom Capua
Derives its name.
So the two armies lay locked close in combat   210
Of bitter war. And now at midnight Aeneas
Was cleaving the ocean. For after he left Evander
He broached the Etruscan camp and approached
   their king,
Told him his name and his race, what he had to
   offer
And what he needed, explained to him what forces
Mezentius had caused to muster and why,
Expatiated on Turnus' violent nature
And on the mutability of fortune,
And seconded reason with entreaty—Tarchon,
Without a moment's pause, joined forces with him 220
And made alliance. So the people of Lydia
Fulfilled their fated destiny and embarked
According to the ordinance of heaven
Committing themselves to the care of a "foreign
   leader."
Aeneas led the line, his vessel embellished
With Phrygian lions harnessed on the prow,
Mount Ida towering above them, a truly enspiring
Sight for the exiled eyes of the Trojans. Great
   Aeneas
Sat in the bows brooding upon the war

230 And all the doubts concerning its outcome, Pallas
     At his left side stood guard and questioned him
     About the stars by which their course was plotted
     Through the dark night, or about all the toils
     Aeneas had endured by land and sea.

     Now, Goddesses of Song, fling Helicon wide.
     Inspire my muse to tell of the force that followed
     Aeneas from the Etruscan shore, that manned
     The warships—sailing over the sea.
                                              Massicus
     Led the flotilla in his ship the *Tigress*,
240 A bronze-bound vessel with a bone in her teeth.
     A body of a thousand warrior-youths
     From Cosae and the walls of Clusium
     Was under his command, whose arms consisted
     Of lethal bows and arrows carried in quivers
     Light on the shoulder; with him fiery Abas,
     Whose complement was clad in splendid armor,
     The stern of whose ship gleamed with a gilded
          Apollo.
     Populonia was the mother-city that sent him
     Six hundred of her sons, all skilled in warfare;
250 Three hundred came from Ilva an island rich
     In inexhaustible mines of iron ore.
     Third came Asilas the great mediator
     Between men and the gods, a magus wise in the
          lore
     Of sacrificial entrails, whom the stars
     Of the sky obeyed and the tongues of holy birds
     And the flashes of prophetic thunderbolts.
     He urged on a thousand close-packed troops,
     A bristle of spears,—the Etruscan city Pisae
     Sprung from its sister on Alphaeus banks
260 Had set him over them. There followed Astur,
     Most fair of all men Astur, trusting his charger
     And many-colored armor. Three hundred men,
     All of one mind in following his service,
     Were rallied from the inhabitants of Caere,
     And the farms by the Minio, from ancient Pyrgi,
     And the foul airs of Gravisca.
                                        And Cynirus, you—

Shall I omit you, bravest Ligurian leader?
Or you Cupavo with your little handful
And your swan-feather crest?—Symbol of love,
Symbol of guilty love, and your father's change.   270
For, so the story goes, Cycnus in grief
For his beloved Phaethon, assuaged
His broken heart by singing in the shade
Among the poplars, Phaethon's sisters once,
And as he sadly sang he softly drew
An old age of white feathers over him
And left the earth, singing towards the stars,
His son, now, with a great press of his peers
Drove on his ship with oars, the mighty *Centaur*:
She, with a great stone for figurehead,   280
Threatening the wavetops, ploughing through the
    ocean
With the long colter of her keel.

                                   See Ocnus,
Another who had raised a native troop,
Son of the prophetess Manto and the river
Of Tuscany, who gave to Mantua
Her walls, her name, O Mantua so rich
In diverse glories of diverse ancestry!
—Three separate strains she has, and every strain
Is parceled into four aboriginal peoples,
Yet she is their capital city and her strength   290
Drawn from Etruscan blood. From this same
    district
Mezentius had roused against himself
Five hundred men, whom Mincius clad in gray
Vestments of reed, own son of Benacus Lake,
Led in their pine-built ships to the high seas.
Sluggish and slow Aulestes struck the sea
With a hundred oars as ponderous as trees,
And the wavetops whitened with the churn of
    water.
His ship was the *Triton* an enormous ship
Whose figurehead with its conch appalled the   300
    waves—
Its hairy torso down to the hips was human
But there the belly merged into a monster's,
A sea-monster's, and underneath this

The water frothed and muttered.
Such was the tally of the chosen chiefs
Sailing in thirty ships to the help of Troy,
Their brazen prows cleaving the briny plains.

And now the day had faded from the sky
And Phoebe the benign in her nightwandering
　　chariot
310　Was trampling the midheaven. But Aeneas,
Whose anxious thoughts would give his limbs no
　　rest,
Was himself seated at the tiller, his hand
On the main sheet, piloting the ship.
But suddenly behold! full on his course
A band of friends appeared to him—the Nymphs
Gracious Cybele caused to be transformed
From ships into sea-goddesses—and now
They swam abreast of the ship and cut the waves,
As many nymphs as there had been brazen keels
320　Beached on the shore. They gamboled round
　　their king
Whom they had recognized from far away.
Cymodoce, most skillful in speech among them,
Swam in his wake, and holding onto the stern
With her right hand she heaved her body half
Out of the water paddling with her left
And thus to Aeneas, still bemused, she spoke:
"Aeneas, son of the gods, are you awake?
Awake! Slack off the sheet! You see in us your
　　fleet—
Once pines from Ida's sacred summit—now
330　Nymphs of the sea. For when the treachery
Of Turnus menaced us with fire and sword
Against our will we slipped our mooring chains
And sought you through the deep. And Cybele,
　　in pity,
Remolded us, our mother, in this fashion
And granted us to be sea goddesses,
And live our lives beneath the ocean swell.
But young Ascanius meanwhile is contained
Within his walls and dikes and the Latins abristle
　　with battle

Swamp him with weapons. Already Arcadian
  cavalry
And a body of brave Etruscans are in position   *340*
And poised for action and it is Turnus' intention
To interpose the weight of his own forces
And cut them off from joining the Trojan camp.
Come, then, rise up and at the first hint of dawn,
Order your comrades to stand to, under arms,
And take your shield which the Master of Fire
  made
To be invincible, rimmed with red gold,
And gave to you himself. Tomorrow's sun
Will see great heaps of slain Rutulians
If you will but believe my words are true."   *350*
She spoke and as she left she gave a thrust
Against the high stern with her hand well knowing
What power of onward impulse to impart.
Then swifter than a javelin sped the ship,
Swifter than arrow, swift as the very wind.
The rest of the fleet came speeding equally after
  her.
Not knowing what to think, the Trojan the son
  of Anchises
Sat stunned, but spurred his spirit with the omen.
Then looking up to the vault of heaven he prayed:
"Gracious Mother of Gods, mistress of Ida,   *360*
Who hold dear to your heart the height of
  Dindyma
And towery cities, and lions yoked in pairs,
Be now my leader in the fight, fulfill
This prophecy aright, be at the side
Of the Phrygians, goddess with your favoring
  footfall."
Such was his prayer. And now the dawn was up
The full light quickened and the night had fled.
So first he gave the order to his comrades
To rally to their standards and steel themselves
For combat and prepare for a pitched battle.   *370*
And now from his lookout on the lofty stern
Aeneas could already see the camp
And his fellow Trojans—immediately he raised
His sunbright shield on high in his left hand.

And from their walls the Dardans raised a cheer
That rang to heaven. In a new flush of hope
Their martial fury quickened and they hurled
A flight of weapons, like a flight of cranes
From Strymon, silhouetted against black clouds
380 Blown helter-skelter before a southerly gale
Crying their cries and haunting the after-air
With the clamor of their passing.

                  To King Turnus
And his Ausonian leaders it seemed unbelievable
Until they looked and saw the fleet already
Making inshore and the whole sea a sliding
Pattern of warships.

                  Aeneas' helmet blazed,
A stream of fire poured from his plumy crest,
A golden fount gushed from the great shield-boss,
—As on a clear night comets glow with a grim
390 And blood-red gleam, or as the glare of Sirius,
The star that brings to frail mortality
Disease and thirst and rises sickling heaven
With boding light.

             But Turnus never wavered
Entirely confident that he could seize the shore
And drive the invaders off.

              "Your prayers are answered!"
He cried to his men, "to break through at the
   swordpoint—
The heart of Mars lies in a brave man's hand!
Let every one of you think of his wife and children
And recollect the imperishable deeds
400 That keep your forbears' memory green. Forward!
And meet them at the water's edge, before
They have got firm foothold, while the first
To disembark are hesitant and unsure.
The bold are favored by Fortune."
So he spoke, and debated in his mind
Whom he should lead to the assault and whom
Entrust with the continuance of the siege.
But even while he spoke Aeneas was landing
His men from the high sterns. Many leapt
410 Into the breakers as they withdrew and trusted

Their luck to the shallows, some used the oars as
    gangways.
Tarchon examined the shore and chose a place
Where no waves broke, where burst no battering
    backwash
But gently the sea surged with the rising tide,
And suddenly there he steered his ships and
    invoked his comrades,
"Now, my chosen band, strike with your doughty
    oars!
Lift us, carry us home! Let us plough up
The enemy's homeland with our prows, each keel
Cutting its own furrow! To land here,
To get ashore, I would not shrink from shipwreck!"   *420*
So Tarchon spoke and his comrades stretched to
    the stroke
And charged their ships, all bow-wave, on Latin
    land
And every ship was safely beached—alas!
Save Tarchon's, yours, which ran onto a shoal
And rocked on a reef, in trouble, to and fro
Until the waves had had their way and it broke up
And into the breakers went its crew in a bungle
Of broken oars and floating gear and the ebb
At the same time swept their feet from under
    them.

No idle sloth had Turnus in its grip,   *430*
But quickly he deployed his whole attack
Against the Trojans fronting them on the shore.
The trumpets sounded. Aeneas was in the fore,
A good omen, to charge the country levies,
The first to get to grips, and he killed Theron,
The giant who first pitted his strength against
    him—
Thrust through his mail of bronze and his tunic
    armored
With gold and opened a gaping wound in his flank.
Then he killed Lichas, cut out from the womb
Of his dead mother and, Phoebus, dedicated   *440*
To you because he had been let escape

The knife in infancy. And not long after,
As brawny Cisseus and the enormous Gyas
Were felling his ranks with clubs, he crashed
   them down
To death—the arms that Hercules affected
Availed them nothing nor that their sire Melampus
Had been the stalwart henchman of Hercules
So long as he had labors to perform.
See Pharus, idly boasting and doing nothing!
450   Aeneas scored a bullseye in the braggart's mouth
With a well-cast javelin! And you, unhappy Cydon,
Trailing your newest light-of-love young Clytius,
His cheeks blooming with their first golden down,
You might have fallen, at the Dardan's hand,
Free from the loves of boys that so beset you,
You might have lain pitiably low,
If the tight knot of your brothers, sons of Phorcus,
Your seven brothers had not barred the way
And thrown their seven spears: and some
   rebounded
460   Harmlessly from his shield and helmet, some
His guardian Venus deflected as they grazed him.
Aeneas spoke to loyal Achates and said:
"Bring me a pile of weapons—every weapon
That found its mark in a Greek on the plain of
   Troy—
None, you will see, shall miss a Rutulian now."
With that he snatched a mighty spear and threw it
And, flying, it pierced the bronze of Maeon's shield
And burst in one instant his breastplate and his
   breast.
His brother Alcanor rushed up to support
470   The falling man with his arm—another javelin
Shattered his arm in passing on its flight,
Now dripping blood, and the arm hung by its
   tendons
As good as dead from the shoulder. Numitor
Snatching a javelin from his brother's body
Made at Aeneas—but it failed to strike
Full on the body of supporting Achates
But merely grazed his thigh. Then up came Clausus
   of Cures

In the self-confidence of his youth and struck
Dryops under the chin with a long lunge
Of his unbending spear and pierced his throat   480
And robbed him of his life and breath in the
   middle
Of a word, and he struck the earth with his
   forehead and vomited
Clotted blood from his mouth. Aeneas also
Despatched three Thracians of the most noble line
Of Boreas, and another three, whose father
Idas had sent to war from their country Ismara,
By various means he killed. Then next Halaesus
With a group of Auruncan men closely engaged
   him;
Then Messapus, far-famed for his horses, the son
Of Neptune. All in turn strained to the utmost   490
To drive out the invader: the very threshold
Of Italy became the field of battle.
Just as the winds run counter in the firmament
And clash together with equal strength and
   purpose
And neither yields, nor do the sea or the storm-
   clouds,
But the battle hangs in the balance for long and
   they strive
In total deadlock; so the Trojan army
And the army of Italy were locked in battle
Foot to foot, man to man, milling together.

But in another part of the field a torrent   500
Had scored and scoured its course over a wide
Tract of the plain with trundled boulders and trees
Uprooted from its banks. And Pallas saw
That his Arcadians who were unaccustomed
To fight on foot and who had been compelled
To discard their horses because of the rough going
Had turned their backs on the pursuing Latins.
In such straits there was only one course left,
And now with prayers and now with bitter jibes
He tried to rouse their ardor: "Comrades! where   510
Are you flying to? By your own brave deeds, I
   implore you,

By the name of your chief Evander and the
    victories
Won under his command, by my own passion
To be my father's rival in renown
Upon this field, trust not your feet in flight.
Your way lies through the enemy ranks, a way
To be hewn with steel! There where, the press is
    thickest,
There lies the way your noble fatherland
Demands of you, and me your leader Pallas!
520   It is no gods that harry us—but men.
We are harried by men as mortal as *we* are—
We have as many lives, as many hands!
Look! with its whole great barrier the sea
Is hemming us in—and where is there land open
For our retreat? There is none. Troy or the sea?
Which shall we seek, my friends?" He cried and
    charged
Headlong into the ruck. It was Lagus first
Whom some unlucky fate put in his way,
And he was pierced with a javelin through the spot
530   Where the spine divides the ribs, in the very act
Of trying to heave up a weighty stone.
And Pallas retrieved his spear from where it lay
Jammed in the bones. Alas for the hopes of Hisbo
Whose plan was to surprise him in the act!—
For as he charged in a blind fury wild
With the bitter death of his companion, Pallas
Was ready for him and took him with a sword-
    thrust
Home to his swelling lung. Then he attacked
Sthenelus and Anchemolus, a man
540   Of the ancient house of Rhoeteus who had once
Dared to defile his own stepmother's bed.
And you, twin brothers, you Larides and Thymber,
The sons of Daucus so entirely alike
Not even your parents in loving perplexity
Could tell apart—you fell in Rutulian fields,
But Pallas marked you with a brutal difference:
For, Thymber, you he beheaded with the
    broadsword of Evander;
Your hand, Larides, hacked from its right arm

Now sought in vain its master, the half-dead fingers
Still twitching as they tried to clutch the steel.   *550*
Then the Arcadians stung by the rebuke
Of their heroic leader and seeing his marvelous
    feats
In mingled shame and rage turned on the enemy.
Then Pallas struck through Rhoeteus as he fled
Past in his two-horse chariot. And by this chance
He gained just so much breathing space, for his
    stalwart
Spear, flung from afar, was aimed at Ilus,
And Rhoeteus it intercepted in mid-flight
As he fled from noblest Teuthras and his brother
Tyres; and toppling from his chariot rolled   *560*
And drummed with nerveless heels the Rutulian
    soil.
—And as a shepherd has his will and the winds
Obey his want and he touches here and there
The summer woods with fire and suddenly
They merge and grow into a single front
And Vulcan's sparky hordes are on the march
Across the width of plain, and the shepherd squats
Hugging his relish of the triumphant flames:
So, Pallas, all your comrades linked their sparks
Of courage to a single blaze to aid you.   *570*
But swift Halaesus dashed into the fray
And primed himself with arms to attack the
    Arcadians.
Ladon he slew, and Pheres and Demodocus,
And with his flashing sword flicked off the hand
Strymonius had put up to his throat,
Then smashed the skull of Thoas with a stone
And laced the ground-in bones with brains and
    blood.
His father, foreseeing Fate, had hidden him
In the woods but when white-haired he came
To easeful death, Fate seized on his victim son   *580*
And offered him up to the javelins of Evander—
So Pallas, now, drew a bead on him and prayed:
"Grant, O Father Tiber, to the weapon
I am now poised to throw a prosperous highway
Through the resistant breast of hard Halaesus,

And then your sacred oak shall have his arms
And the warrior's spoils." The god gave ear to this.
So as Halaesus strove to shield Imaon,
Leaving himself exposed, the unlucky man
590 Defenseless fell to the Arcadian thrust.
But Lausus, a staunch warrior in the war,
Refused to let his troops be thrown in panic
By such a mort of slaughter: and despatched
Abas, the first man in his path, the ban
And bar to a battle whose red harvest reaps
Sons of Arcadia, sons of Etruria, sons
Of Troy whose lives the Greeks had failed to take.
The hosts were clinched in combat, both in
     strength
And leaders equally matched. The rear pressed up
600 Till neither side had elbow-room to maneuver.
On one side Pallas cheered and urged his men on,
On the other Lausus, almost one in age,
And both a nonpareil of manhood—yet
Fate had forbidden to both ever to see
Their native land again—but He who reigns
On high Olympus suffered them not to meet
In single combat—each had his doom ordained
At the hand of a mightier foe.
                              Meanwhile Turnus,
At the fond prompting of his gracious guardian,
610 Was warned to come to Lausus' help and carved
His way through the host in his swift chariot.
As soon as he saw his comrades he said to them:
"Stop fighting now! Pallas is my preserve:
He is mine alone to attack—I wish his father
Were here to see!" He spoke and at his order
His friends withdrew.
                    And Pallas was amazed
At their withdrawal and these arrogant words.
Sizing Turnus up he let his eyes
Travel the length and breadth of the monstrous
     frame
620 Conning each feature with an implacable glare
Across the space between. And into the teeth
Of the prince he threw this challenge of his own.
"A fig for your threats! Soon I shall have my fame

Either by seizing spoils from a king or gaining
Glory in death—in either event my father
Can bear the outcome!"

              So he spoke and marched
Into the ring of challenge—Arcadian hearts
Went cold, their blood froze. Turnus vaulted
Down from his chariot and disposed himself
To the assault on foot, just as a lion   630
When he sees from some high lookout a bull
   pawing
The plain and rehearsing fight, leaps down to
   answer,
Such was the vision of Turnus' answering onset.
When Pallas judged him within scope of a spear-
   throw
He edged forward, his purpose to compensate
The difference of their strengths by sheer daring,
And he trusted to luck; and offered this prayer
   to heaven:
"O Hercules, by your friendship with my father
And the bond you shared, though you came as
   a stranger,
Stand by me in my great design, I pray you.   640
Let Turnus see me strip his bloodstained armor
From his body as he dies and his glazing eyes
Endure the sight of his conqueror." Hercules
Heard the young Pallas and stifled a heavy sigh
Deep in his heart and shed unavailing tears.
Then the Great Father spoke these well-meant
   words
To soothe his son. "For every man is ordained
His appointed day; for every man the sum
Of his days is short and none can have them again.
But to prolong your fame by mighty deeds—   650
That is the office of valor. So many sons
Of the Gods lie fallen under the high walls
Of Troy—even Sarpedon my own son.
And Turnus, too, is summoned to his fate;
He has reached the end of his allotted years."
He spoke and turned his eyes away from the
   Rutulian pastures.
But Pallas hurled his spear with all his might,

Then drew his gleaming sword from its hollow
    sheath.
The spear in its flight forced through the edge of
    the shield
660 And struck the topmost part of the shoulder-armor
And finally scored a scratch on the mighty body
    of Turnus—
Who then discharged the spear he had long held
    poised,
A shaft of oak shod with an iron point,
Shouting these words: "See if my weapon now
Is not the sharper!" And the spearhead plunged
With quivering penetration through his shield
Despite its plates of iron and bronze, despite
The thickness of its bullhide bindings, and smashed
Clean through his corslet home to his mighty
    breast.
670 In vain he plucked the weapon warm from its
    wound,
For after it from that very rent poured out
His blood his lifeblood and he toppled over
Onto his wound and his arms clanged above him.
In his death-throes he bit at the enemy earth
With bloody mouth, and Turnus straddling over
    him
Cried out, "Arcadians! See that you remember
My words and take them back to King Evander:
I send him back the Pallas he deserves!
Whatever honor there may be in a tomb
680 Whatever comfort in a burial
I grant him gladly. Yet he will find the welcome
He gave Aeneas not a little costly!"
And with these words he trod with his left foot
On the dead body and ripped off the huge belt
Which was engraved with a picture to strike terror:
—A band of young men on their wedding night
Brutally murdered and the bridal chambers
Bespattered with blood, which Clonus son of
    Eurytus
Had chased on the wealth of gold. And Turnus
    now
690 Gloated over the spoil and exulted in his trophy.

But the minds of men are blind to fate and the
    future
Nor do they know how to control themselves
And keep their balance when the luck is with
    them.
A time will come for Turnus when he would
Willingly pay a fortune to have Pallas
Safe and unharmed, when he will hate the spoils
And the day he won them.

                          But now Pallas' comrades
Crowded around with many a groan, and tear,
And placed him on a shield and bore him off!
Alas, the grief that your return to your father   700
Will bring and the high glory! This first day
Gave you to war, this very same first day
Reaves you away, albeit you leave behind
A mighty heap of the Rutulian dead.
And now there flew to Aeneas no mere idle rumor
But intelligence impossible to question.
The message warned him that his army stood
A hairsbreadth from destruction; that it was vital
To help the routed Trojans immediately.
Laying about with his sword on every side   710
He hacked a wide path through the enemy line
Seeking for Turnus proud of his new conquest.
In his mind's eye Aeneas saw Evander,
Pallas, and the board where first as a stranger
He tasted hospitality and shook
The hand of friendship.

                          Now he took alive
Four stripling sons of Sulmo and four others
Brought there by Ufens, having it in mind
To sacrifice them to the ghost of Pallas
And lace with captive blood the flames of the pyre.   720
Next he leveled his spear for a long cast
At Magus who ducked adroitly, and the spear
Whizzed quivering overhead and, coming close,
He cringed and clutched Aeneas' knees and
    whined:
"By your dead father's spirit, by your hopes
For Iulus as he grows, Oh spare my life,
For *my* father and *my* own son. I have

A lofty palace and buried in its vaults
Are talents of chased silver and gold ingots
730 Both worked and unworked. The victory of the
    Trojans
Does not depend on *me*. One single life
Will not make so much difference. . . ." So he
    prayed.
Aeneas answered, "Spare for your sons the many
Talents of gold and silver you tell me of.
When Turnus slaughtered Pallas he put an end
To such negotiations as are possible
In a chivalrous campaign. Anchises' spirit
And young Iulus speak their thoughts through
    me."
And as he spoke he gripped the suppliant's helmet
740 In his left hand and even as he pleaded
Bent back his neck and thrust his sword blade in
Up to the hilt. Nearby was Haemonides
His temples wound with the sacred ribands, the
    priest
Of Phoebes and Trivia, and dressed from head to
    foot
In brilliant white with shining insignia.
The Trojan met him and drove him over the field,
And when he stumbled Aeneas towered above
    him,
Slaughtered his victim and whelmed him in vast
    darkness.
Serestus took off his arms and bore them away
750 Over his shoulders—a trophy, Mars, for you.
But Caeculus, of Vulcan's lineage,
And Umbro, he who haled from the Volscian Hills,
Rallied the ranks. And opposite them fumed
The Dardan chief. He had just sliced off with his
    sword
Anxur's left arm and the whole round of his
    shield—
That man had uttered, maybe, some great boast
Believing he could bolster word with deed
And, puffed up to the sky, had promised himself
Gray hairs and a long life. And now Tarquitus
760 Leapt out against him in his glittering armor,

Whom the nymph Dryope had borne to Faunus
God of the woods. He barred his fiery progress:
Aeneas drew his spear back and then skewered
The boy to his breastplate and the cumbrous
  weight
Of his own shield—and as a stream of prayers
Poured from his lips and even as he thought
Of many more his head was swept to the ground.
Aeneas spurned the warm trunk with his foot
And rolled it over and over, muttering
In the fury of his heart as he stood above him.   770
"So we must fear you, must we? Then, lie there!
And never shall your loving mother bury you
Nor lay your limbs to rest in your father's tomb.
You shall be left to the wild birds of prey
Or, tossed and swallowed in the swirl of waters,
The hungry fish will mumble at your wounds!"
—Then next Aeneas hunted down Antaeus
And Luca, front-rank warriors of Turnus,
And bold Numa, and Camers the yellow-haired,
Son of the noble-minded Volscens wealthiest   780
In land of all the Italians, and he reigned
In still Amyclae.

                    And like Aegaeon
Of whom the legend tells, who had a hundred
Arms and a hundred hands and belched out fire
From fifty mouths and fifty breasts, and brandished
Fifty identical shields and fifty swords
As he faced Jove's thunderbolts—so seemed
  Aeneas
As over the whole battlefield he ranged
In an orgy of slaughter once his blade was warm
With blood.   790
                Now see him threateningly advance
Against the four-horse chariot of Niphaeus.
But when the horses saw his menacing mien
And his loping strides they turned and, terrified,
Ran away at the gallop tipping out their master
And whirled the chariot away to the seashore.
But Lucagus meanwhile was moving up
Into the fray, he and his brother Liger
Who held the reins of the two white chariot-horses

While lusty Lucagus swept his naked sword
800   In swingeing circles. Aeneas could not brook
The fiery impulse of their charge—he rushed
Against them looming large his spear upraised:
Then Liger cried, "These horses you see here—
They are not Diomede's, nor is this chariot
The chariot of Achilles nor these plains
The plains of Troy! This is our land, and here
And now the war shall end—and your life with it!"
Such were the words that in his madness Liger
Scattered broadcast. But it was not a word
810   The Trojan here flung back at him in answer—
It was a spear. As Lucagus leant forward
To goad his horses onward with his sword,
His left foot forward ready for instant action,
The spear ripped through the very bottom edge
Of his glinting shield and entered his left groin.
Pitched from the chariot he rolled in his dying
   agony
Over the earth and good Aeneas mocked him
With bitter words: "No Lucagus, it was
No panic-flight upon your horses' part
820   Betrayed your chariot, no shying at empty shadows
Turned them away for the enemy—it was you,
You who deserted them and jumped down from
   the wheels!"
So saying he took hold of the horses' harness
While wretched Liger slid down from his seat
And stretched his hands in helpless supplication:
"O man of Troy by your own self I beg you,
And by the parents who begot your greatness,
Take pity on my pleas and spare my life."
He had more to say but Aeneas cut him short.
830   "Just now you spoke a different tune. Now die!—
It is not brotherly to forsake a brother!"
He took his sword and striking through the breast
Laid bare his very vitals.
                              —Such were the deaths
The Dardan leader dealt about the plain.
His fury seemed the fury of a torrent
Or a black whirlwind. And at last the Trojans

Broke out and quitted the camp—the young
　　Ascanius
And all the flower of youth. The siege was over.

And Jove meanwhile addressed himself to Juno,
"My sister and my well-beloved queen,   *840*
You were not deceived in your opinion. Venus,
As you supposed, upholds the Powers of Troy:
It is not the prowess of their own right arms,
Keen though they be, it is not their dauntless spirit
That braves all danger. It is indeed Venus."
And Juno meekly answered, "Fairest lord,
Why do you vex me? I am sick and afraid
Of your ruthless bidding. Oh, but if there were
That influence in my love which once there was,
And it is right there should be still, All-Powerful,   *850*
You would not have denied me this at least—
The power to extricate Turnus from the battle
And keep him safely for his father Daunus.
As it is, let him perish. Let him give
His sinless blood to slake the Trojan vengeance.
Yet he derives his name from our own lineage,
Pilumnus was the grandsire of his grandsire,
And often he has piled your temple-threshold
With gifts from his own generous hand."
　　　　　　　　　　　　　　　　The King
Of skyey Olympus answered Juno shortly: *860*
"If your entreaty for the youth concerns
No more than a reprieve from present death
And breathing space—for he is doomed to die—
And you accept that this is my decree,
Then see to his escape and snatch him off
From his approaching destiny. So far
It is permitted to indulge your prayers.
But if some deeper hope of remission lie
Hidden under these prayers, if you imagine
The course of the whole war can be changed or   *870*
　　altered
You nurse a foolish hope." Then Juno wept
And said: "Only suppose your heart might grant
What your words grudge and Turnus be given grace

To live a longer span? For as things stand,
A ghastly end awaits him though he is guiltless—
Or I am void of the truth and all astray?
If only I were mocked by unfounded fears
And you—for you alone have power to do so—
Would lead your counsels back to better
    courses . . . ?"

880   When she had spoken thus, cloaked in a cloud
And driving a storm before her Juno launched
From the heaven's height and sought the Trojan
    host
And the Laurentine camp.

                    Then, being divine,
She molded in her hands a tenuous strengthless
Wreathing of hollow cloud into the shape
Of Aeneas, a miraculous sight, and equipped it
With Dardan weapons and with counterfeits
Of the shield and helmet-crest of the goddess-born.
She gave it words that were insubstantial, sounds

890   That had no governing mind behind them,
    rendered
His gait and carriage to the life; the wraith
Was such as flit when death is past, they say,
Or such as mock our senses deep in dream.
So now the phantom strutted gaily to the fore
And goaded Turnus with its show of arms
And words of challenge. Turnus made a sally
And from afar despatched a whizzing spear:
It wheeled in its tracks and fled. Then truly Turnus,
Believing he had Aeneas on the run,

900   Let a vain hope take hold of his turbid heart:
"Where are you fleeing, Aeneas?" he shouted out,
"Do not desert your promised bridal bed:
The soil you came to seek across the ocean
This hand shall give you—this right hand of mine!"
So bellowing and waving his drawn sword
He followed, nor had he the wit to see
That the source of his joy was a mere wind-born
    wraith.
It happened that a ship was lying moored
To the edge of a high rock, its ladder down,

910   Its gangway in position—the ship on which

Kingly Osinius had been borne from the borders
  of Clusium.
Hither the wraith of flying Aeneas hastened
And shrank into hiding. Turnus was on its heels,
Full-tilt over every snag and he bounded across
The high-raised gangway. Scarcely had he touched
The prow when Saturn's daughter loosed the
  moorings
And swept the drifting ship out on the ebb.
Aeneas meanwhile hunted for his enemy
Demanding combat, and sending down to death
Many a valiant man who crossed his path.   920
But now the airy phantom sought no longer
For hiding place, but soaring into the sky
Dissolved in a dark cloud. But as for Turnus
He was drifting at the mercy of the wind
Out into mid-ocean. He looked around him.
He could neither apprehend nor comprehend
The course of events but he was far from pleased
At his escape and lifted up his hands
And voice to heaven and cried, "Almighty Father,
Have you indeed considered that I have done   930
So great a wrong? Do you wish me truly to suffer
So great a punishment? Where am I going?
Where have I come from? Why am I in flight?
What am I? Shall I ever see the camp
Again? or Laurentum's walls? What of my men
Who followed me and my cause to war? Oh
  horror!
And it is these men that I have abandoned
To deaths unspeakable—I see them scattered,
I hear the groans of the fallen. What can I do?
What deepest gulf of earth will swallow me?   940
No, winds, *you* pity me! drive the ship
On reef or rock (I Turnus freely implore you).
Dash me on quicksand or cruel sucking shoal
Where none that know my fame, where no
  Rutulian
May ever follow me!"
                    Swithering in his mind,
Now one way now the other, beside himself,
He wondered if for such a foul disgrace

He should impale himself upon his sword
And force the merciless iron through his ribs,
950 Or throw himself into the sea and swim
For the curving shore and offer himself again
To Trojan arms. And thrice he tried each course:
And thrice the powers of Juno held him back
And, struck to the soul with pity, she restrained
    him.
So cleaving through the deep, with tide and current
Setting his way, he drifted and was borne
To the ancient city of his father Daunus.
But in the meanwhile, warned by Jove, Mezentius
Took up the fight with burning ardor and charged
960 The triumphant Trojans. The Etruscan forces
Closed in, and on this man, on this one man,
They concentrated all their fire and fury.
He stood like a rock that juts into the welter
Of open water, exposed to the lash of the wind
And the smash of breakers and withstands the
    onset
Of every sea and sky however threatening
And yet remains unmoved.
                                            First he laid low
Hebrus the son of Dolichaon, with him
Went Latagus and lily-livered Palmus.
970 Anticipating Latagus he struck him
Full in the mouth with an enormous boulder,
Palmus he hamstrung and left him to lie there
    helplessly twitching.
He handed over their armor for Lausus to wear
On his shoulders, and fixed their plumes in his
    own helmet.
He slew Evanthes, the Phrygian, he slew
Mimas the friend of Paris and coeval—
For on the selfsame night as his mother Theano
Bore him into the world to his father Amycus,
Cisseus' queenly daughter, great with a firebrand,
980 Bore Paris—and he lies dead in his father's city,
But Mimas lies in Laurentum's foreign fields.
Mezentius was like a fierce wild boar
That after many years of living safely
In the pinewoods of Vesulus or the Laurentine

Marshes, browsing among the tangle of reeds,
Is flushed from mountain-heights by the fangs of
    the hounds
And stands at bay now, in a ring of nets,
Roaring defiance, all his bristles up:
And no one has, in his anger, quite enough
Courage to come to closer quarters—but   *990*
Keeps a safe distance, throwing his weapons and
    shouting—
Even so, among those who hated Mezentius
With justifiable hatred not one man
Had courage enough to draw his sword and close—
But shouting and yelling they harried him at long
    range:
He faced them every way with dauntless heart
And grinding his teeth he shook the hail of
    weapons
Off from his shield.

                Now Acron was a warrior,
A Greek from Corythus, that ancient region,
Who had been expelled when on the point of   *1000*
    marriage:
And when Mezentius saw him, he saw him proud
In the crimson of his plumes and the purple robe
His bride-to-be had given him—and he
Was creating havoc in the center of the battle:
And just as, often, a famished lion goes prowling
Through high-fenced cattle pens, frantic with
    hunger
And if he happens to glimpse a fleeing goat
Or a stag with branching antlers licks his chops
With certain relish, his jaws agape, and later
With ruffed-up mane lies crouched over the   *1010*
    entrails
While the blood drips grimly from the murderous
    jaws:
Just so it was that swift Mezentius sprang
Into the heart of the foe. Unlucky Acron
Was felled and with his dying gasp he drummed
The blackened earth with his heels and bloodied
    all
His broken arms. Then as Orodes fled

Mezentius did not deign to strike him down
With an unseen stab in the back, but overtook him
And met him face to face; he meant to show
1020 He was the better in fair fight, not guile;
Then with his foot on the body and lunging
      down on
His spear, he cried: "Here lies Orodes the mighty,
A man we dared not despise, a man who was
A linchpin in the war—and here he lies!"
His followers roared triumphant affirmation.
Then, as he died, Orodes answered him:
"Whoever you are, my victor, your rejoicing
Shall not last long: I shall not lie for long
Before vengeance comes: as dire a fate as mine
1030 Is on the watch for you and soon you will lie
On this same field." Mezentius answered smiling
With an undertone of anger: "Die, now! As for
      me—
That . . . Begetter of Gods and King of men can
      cope!"
So saying he plucked his spear from Orodes' body:
Grim quiet of iron sleep clamped on his eyes,
Their light was quenched by darkness without end.

Caedicus slew Alcathous, and Sacrator
Slaughtered Hydaspes, Rapo finished off
Parthenius and Orses, toughest of men:
1040 Messapus cut up Clonius, killed Erichaetes
Son of Lycaon—Clonius as he cringed
On the ground unhorsed, the other foot to foot.
Agis the Lycian trotted feinting forward
But Valerus, not less valorous than his grandsire,
Hurled him to earth; and Thronius was felled
By Salius, Salius by Nealces, expert
In javelin-throw and arrow unforeseen
Fired at long range.
                    And the God of War dealt
An equal dole and death to either side:
1050 Alike they slew and were slain, victors and
      vanquished,
And neither side harbored a thought of flight.
The gods in the halls of Jove looked down in pity

On the pointless strife, the needless sufferings
Of mortal men inevitably doomed.
On one side Venus watched and on the other
Saturnian Juno; the ghoul Tisiphone
Among the thousands of warriors on the field
Swilled more blood than her due. . . .

                      But now Mezentius
Shaking his massive spear strode furiously
Into the vortex. He seemed like huge Orion   *1060*
As he ploughs his way on foot, on the ocean bed,
Through Nereus' deepest deeps, but head and
    shoulders
Above the surface; or as he carries home
An aged rowan-tree from the mountain tops,
His foot on the valley-bottom, his head in the
    clouds—
So seemed Mezentius in his mammoth armor.
Aeneas saw him from afar as he
Surveyed the long line of battle and disposed
    himself
To meet him in combat. Still Mezentius
Was undismayed and steadfast and solidly   *1070*
Stood waiting his great-spirited enemy.
Then shrewdly judging with his eye the range of a
    spear-throw
He prayed: "Oh my right hand, the only god of
    my worship,
Oh weapon poised to strike, be with me now.
I vow to my son, Lausus, as trophy of Aeneas,
The spoils that I shall strip from his robber's
    carcass!"
Such were his words and from long range he cast
The whirling spear: it glanced from Aeneas' shield
And traveled on to strike the fair Antores,
Who was standing near, between his thigh and   *1080*
    groin,
Antores, friend of Hercules, who was exiled
From Argos, and had tagged on to Evander
And settled in an Italian city. Ill fated,
He fell to a stroke intended for another
And stared at the sky, and saw in his dying eye
A vision of his beloved Argos. Then

The good Aeneas threw his spear. It pierced
The hollow disk of triple-plated bronze,
The threefold thickness of bulls'-hide and linen,
1090 And made a flesh-wound low down on the groin,
But nothing more. Aeneas whipped out his sword,
Delighted at the spurt of Etruscan blood,
And darted towards his unnerved enemy.
When Lausus saw this he groaned in agony
For love of his father, and tears gushed down his
     cheeks.
And here, O gallant boy, if deeds of old
Can win their way to glory in our hearts
I shall not let the bitter chance of your death
Go by untold nor your supreme valor,
1100 *For you are truly memorable and should be.*

Mezentius was retreating, scotched and disabled,
Dragging his enemy's spear back, stuck in his
     shield,
When out his son sprang and took up the fight—
Just as Aeneas wound himself up to strike
The death blow with his sword he parried it
And held him off. His comrades rallied cheering
And kept the foe at distance with a shower
Of whirling weapons, while Mezentius
Covered by Lausus' shield withdrew from the fray.
1110 Aeneas glowered but kept himself covered too.
And as it happens when a flurry of hail
Hurls down and every ploughman and laborer
Breaks from the open fields and every traveler
Shrinks into some safe niche of shelter—the bank
Of a river, or an overhanging rock—
While the rain pelts down, and hopes the storm
     will pass
And the sun will shine again and give the chance
To carry on with the day's work: even so,
Aeneas braved the storm of weapons pouring
1120 From every side until its force was spent,
But kept on girding at Lausus, threatening Lausus:
"What are you doing—throwing your life away
In a deed beyond your strength? Your love for
     your father

Has made you reckless." None the less the boy
Madly persisted: and a savage anger
Swelled in the Trojan leader's heart and the Fates
Gathered the final threads of Lausus' life:
Aeneas plunged full-force with his great sword,
Sheer through the midriff, right up to the hilt.
The sword-point traveled searing through his   *1130*
  buckler,
Too light defense for his defiant temper,
And through the tunic his mother had
  embroidered
With golden thread, and the blood gushed into
  its folds.
Then sadly Lausus bequeathed his life to the
  breezes
And his body to the Shades. But when he saw
That pallid face and the mysterious
And changing hues of the approach of death,
The son of Anchises heaved a sigh of pity,
And stretched a hand out, seeing in his heart
An image of his own love for his father: *1140*
"O hapless boy, what gift shall good Aeneas
Bestow on you? What gift can be in keeping
With such a glorious feat, with such a spirit?
Retain the arms you so delighted in!
And I myself shall restore you to the Shades
And Ashes of your fathers—if that be
Anything to you—but this at least should solace
The misery of your disastrous death:
You fall at the right hand of great Aeneas!"
Then, on the instant, he upbraided the slackness   *1150*
Of Lausus' comrades, and was the first to lift him
From where he lay defiling his neat hair
With his own blood.
                    Meanwhile, by the river Tiber,
Mezentius lingered stanching his wounds with
  water
Leaning against a tree, to relieve his body.
His golden helmet hung from a distant branch,
His heavy armor lay slumped on the grass.
Around him stood his chosen bodyguard
While gasping with the pain he flexed his neck

1160 And his combed beard flowed down to cover his
          breast.
      He kept enquiring for Lausus, he kept despatching
      Messengers with orders to recall him—
      The orders of a grieving father. Alas,
      His weeping comrades even then were bearing
      The lifeless body of Lausus on his shield,
      A mighty hero felled by a mighty wound.
      His heart full of foreboding Mezentius knew
      The sounds of grief far off for what they were.
      He heaped his hoary hairs with dust, he raised
1170 Both hands to heaven, then clung to the body.
      "My son, has such a lust for life possessed me
      That I could let you, my own begotten son,
      Take up the challenge in my place and meet
      The foeman's hand? And is it through your wounds
      That I am preserved, your father? through your
          death
      That I am alive? Alas I am in despair,
      Oh, now I know the uttermost of exile,
      The wound is driven deep! It is I, my son,
      Who have fouled your name with guilt—my guilt—
          It is I
1180 Was driven hated from the throne and realm
      Of my own fathers—a hatred justly incurred
      By my own acts— And retribution was due
      To my country and my people's hatred: I should
          have given
      My forfeit soul to every sort of death,
      And willingly given—but still I am alive
      And still I am slow to leave the light of day,
      And the world of men. But leave them I will!"
          So saying
      He raised himself on his wounded thigh, and
          though
      The deep wound sapped his strength, he resolutely
1190 Ordered his horse to be brought—his pride it was,
      And solace—it had borne him home victorious
      From many a war. And now, as it seemed to
          grieve,
      He spoke to it, beginning with these words:
      "Rhaebus, we two have lived long lives, if anything

May be called 'long' to mortals bound to die,
Today you shall either bear victoriously
The head of Aeneas back and the spoil bedewed
With his own blood and join me in avenging
The sufferings of my Lausus, or if our force
Is not enough to open up a way   *1200*
We will lie together, you and I, for I know,
My bravest one, that you will never deign
To obey a foreign spur or a Trojan master!"
He spoke and levered his body into the saddle
And settled himself into his usual position
Cramming both hands with sheaves of pointed
    javelins.
His helmet glittered upon his head with its tufts
Of horsehair plume. So into the fray he charged,
And in his heart there seethed a terrible shame
Mixed with a mad agony of grief   *1210*
And love driven to frenzy and an awareness
Of bravery unsullied. And three times
At the top of his voice three times he called on
    Aeneas
And Aeneas heard and joyfully prayed this prayer:
"May the All-Father of Gods, may noble Apollo,
Grant you to come to the issue with me now!"
So saying he advanced upon his enemy
With his spear poised to strike. Then said
    Mezentius,
"O cruelest of men, now you have killed
My son, do you suppose you have any power   *1220*
To terrify me? You have already found
The one means of destroying me and used it.
Death holds no horror for me! nor have I any
Respect for any god! Enough then, I have come
To die; but first here are the gifts I bring you!"
Saying these words he hurled a javelin at him,
Then came another and another after it,
As he galloped in a great ring round Aeneas.
But the gold shield-boss withstood every shock.
Three times Mezentius rode left-handed circles   *1230*
Around him as he faced him in the center
Hurling his javelins. And three times Aeneas,
Turning to front him, bore a porcupine

Of spears in his bronze shield. Then, at last,
Irked by the long delay and the plucking out
Of endless weapons and the strain of fighting
On such unequal terms beginning to tell,
He considered many courses and finally
Jumped in, and saw his well-aimed spear strike
   home
1240 Into the hollow temples of the war-horse.
It reared upright and pawed the air with its
   forefeet
Throwing Mezentius and then crushing him
Under it as it fell headfirst to earth,
And lay with its shoulder broken.

                    The sky rang
With the wild shouts of Trojan and Latin warriors.
Aeneas darted in and drawing his sword
Stood over him. "Where now is fierce Mezentius?
Where is that raging impetuousness of spirit?"
When the Etruscan opened his eyes again
1250 And recovered his senses he replied, "Implacable
Enemy, why do you mock me, why make menace
Of death?—You commit no crime in killing me—
Such thoughts were never in my mind as I came
To give you battle nor did my Lausus make
Any such pact with you on my behalf—
But this one thing I ask, if a conquered foe
Has any mercy owed him; grant my body
Its covering of earth. I am surrounded—
(And well I know it) by the bitter hatred
1260 Of all my people—protect me from their fury,
I beg, and grant me a share of my son's tomb."
He spoke these words. Then, knowing all, he
   received
The sword-guest to his throat, and let the lifeblood
Gush over all his arms and drain away.

BOOK XI

Meanwhile the Goddess of dawn had left the ocean
  and risen,
And the thoughts of death preyed on Aeneas'
  mind
And he wished for leisure to bury his companions.
The first rays of the dawn lit on him paying
Vows to the gods, as befits a conqueror.
He lopped its branches from an enormous oak
And set it up on a mound and hung upon it
The spoils of Mezentius the chief, the bulk of his
  shining armor—
A trophy, God of War, to your majesty.
He fixed the crests still dripping blood and the   10
  broken
Weapons, the dinted cuirass twelve times pierced,
He bound the brazen shield to the left-hand side
  of the trophy
And hung from its neck the ivory-hilted sword.
Then he began to exhort his cheering friends,
For his whole band of captains was close around
  him,
"My friends, we have won a resounding victory!
Put from your minds all fear of future trials,
These are the spoils of a proud king, the first
  fruits—
See what my hands have made of Mezentius!
Now we must march to the very walls of Latium   20
And King Latinus. Be ready in fighting trim,
Look to the coming clash with hope in your hearts,
Let there be no delays through lack of forethought,
No dilatory halfheartedness when the Gods
Give us the sign to pluck our standards up,

303

Strike camp, and march. But meanwhile let us
    consign
The unburied bodies of our friends to earth—
The only honor that avails them now
In the deep pit of Acheron. Go!" he cried,
"Pay your last tributes to these glorious souls
Who have bought us our new country with their
    blood.
And first let Pallas be borne to Evander's
    sorrowing city,
A warrior carried off by an evil day
And drowned before his time in the dark of death,
Though he had no lack of valor." He spoke
    weeping,
And turned to his tent door again where the body
Of lifeless Pallas was laid out, watched over
By the veteran Acoetes, who in the old days
Was Evander's armor-bearer in Arcadia
And later, under less auspicious stars,
Had been appointed guardian of his beloved
Young protégé. Around the bier was gathered
The whole of Aeneas' retinue and a crowd
Of Trojans and with their hair unbound
In mourning mode women of Ilium.
But when Aeneas entered the tall doors
They beat their breasts and raised the keen to
    the stars
And the royal dwelling echoed the bitter woe.
Aeneas gazed on the pillowed head of Pallas
And his snow-white countenance; and the gaping
    wound
Cleft in his marble breast by the Ausonian spear.
Tears started to his eyes and he began,
"Did Fortune envy you, poor luckless boy,
That she bereft me of you when she came
To me and smiled her favors, forbidding you
To see my kingdom or ride home in triumph
To your father's home? Not such were the
    promises
I gave on your behalf when I left Evander
And he embraced me, speeding me on my way
To a great empire, and warned me anxiously

That we should find our enemies fierce, and fight
Grim battles with an obdurate race. And now
In the grip of hopeless hopes perhaps even now he
  is offering
Vows to the gods, heaping the altars with gifts,
While we with the vain office of our griefs
Dead-march with the dead boy who owes
No debt to heaven's powers; now or henceforward.
O wretched father to see with your own eyes
The agonizing funeral of your son!
Is this the promised, this the returning triumph?   70
This, all my pledge was worth? Ah yet, Evander,
It is no coward you shall look upon
With despicable wounds—you shall not be
A father craving death for the dishonor
A living son has brought so safely home.
Italy, cry alas for the great defender
Lost to you now, and lost to you, Iulus!"

When he had wept his fill Aeneas ordered
The poor corpse to be lifted up, and picking
A thousand mourners from his whole array   80
He sent them to attend the final rites,
And with their presence soothe a father's tears—
Scant solace for such weight of grief, but the due
Of the wretched parent. Others with quick fingers
Plaited the pliant framework for a litter
From shoots of strawberry-tree and twigs of oak
Shading the raised-up bed with sprays of leaves.
High on the rustic bier, they laid the boy
And he lay there like a flower plucked by the
  fingers
Of a young girl, a delicate violet   90
Or a wilting fleur-de-lis before their hue
And living form are lost to them, though the earth
No longer gives them strength and sustenance.
Aeneas next brought forth two garments stiff
With gold and purple which in a day gone by
Had been a labor of love to Sidonian Dido
As she made them for him, working the thin
  threads
Of gold along the hems with her own hands.

As a last act of homage sadly Aeneas
100   Wound the young warrior's body in one of these
And with the other muffled up his head
So soon to be consumed on the funeral pyre.
Also he piled the many spoils of battle
Pallas had won in Laurentum, and commanded
The long train of his loot to be led forth.
He added also the horses and the weapons
Stripped from the foe. There stood the victims too,
Hands bound behind their backs, whose doom it
      was
To appease in death the spirit of the dead
110   And with the blood of sacrifice imbue
The holy flames. Then next he ordered the leaders
To carry tree trunks hung with enemy arms
Each labeled with its owner's hated name.
Acoetes was led tottering along
Worn out with age and grief, beating his breast,
Clawing his cheeks till he collapsed and lay
Full length on the ground. They also pulled along
Chariots soaking in Rutulian blood,
Then came his charger Aethon, stripped of his
      trappings,
120   Tears pouring down his face. Then other bearers
Carried his spear and helmet—his conqueror
      Turnus
Had kept the rest of his arms. Then came the
      whole
Host of the Trojan mourners, all the Etruscans,
And the Arcadians, arms reversed, and finally
When the whole cavalcade had passed in its long
      procession
Aeneas paused and said with a heavy sigh,
"The Fates call me away to other tears,
The same implacable destinies of war.
I bid you hail for ever, heroic Pallas,
130   For ever farewell!" There was no more to say.
He turned back to his own high ramparts, he
      strode
Back into camp.
                              And now from the city of Latium
Ambassadors arrived, with olive branches,

Begging a favor from Aeneas: *would he return*
The dead who lay about the plain as the sword
Had strewn them, and allow their burial
In proper graves? Nobody may sustain
A quarrel with the dead and lost-to-light.
Let him show mercy to his onetime hosts
And kinsmen of the bride betrothed to him!   140
This was no prayer to merit a rebuke
And generously Aeneas granted it
Adding these words: "What utter ill luck led you
So undeservedly to become embroiled
In a war so terrible, men of Latium—you—
And forced you to abjure your friendship with us?
Is it you that ask for peace for the dead, for the
  losers
In the grim hazard of war? For my part I
Had rather grant it to the living! Indeed
I would never have come here had not destiny   150
Allotted me this land to be my home.
It is not on your nation I make war.
It was the King abused our proffered friendship
Preferring to rely on Turnus' army—
Fairer if Turnus himself had faced the death
That these have suffered; if he means to end
The war by force of arms and expel the Trojans
It would become him better to meet me
In single combat—and let that man survive
Whose life was earned from Heaven or by his   160
  prowess!
But now depart and kindle the funeral fires
Under your wretched fellow citizens!"
He ended there and they, eying each other,
Stood in dumfounded silence. Finally Drances,
An older man who never forewent a chance
To smirch young Turnus with taunts and
  objurgations,
Opened his mouth and answered, "Man of Troy!
By repute so mighty, mightier in the deeds
We have known you do, what words of praise shall
  I use
To exalt you to heaven? Shall I admire first   170
Your love of justice or your exertions in war?

On our side we are delighted to be the bearers
Of such an answer to our native city
And, if we light on an auspicious moment,
To ally you to our King Latinus—Indeed,
Let Turnus try to make peace for himself!
We would be proud to help raise up those fated
    walls
To their full height and hump on our own
    shoulders
The stones of your new Troy!" These sentiments
180 Drew from the rest a murmur of assent.
Twelve days were set for truce, and under the
    warrant
Of peace the Trojans and the Latins wandered,
Mutually harmless, mingling in the woods
Or on the mountain slopes. The tall ash trees
Rang to the stroke of the two-edged ax, and pines
With tops among the stars came crashing down.
Incessantly they drove their wedges in
To oak and resinous cedar tree and hauled
The trunks of rowans on their groaning wagons.

190 Now flying Rumor, but a moment ago
Proclaiming Pallas Latium's conqueror,
Was harbinger of grief unbearable
And now the news came to Evander's ears,
Then to his household, then to all the city.
The Arcadians rushed to the gates and as they
    went
They snatched up funeral torches in accordance
    with ancient custom,
The highway glowed with the long lines of flame
That clove the countryside in two. To meet them
Came the cortege of Trojans and they mingled
200 Into a single mourning throng. And as soon
As the elder women saw them approach the houses
They kindled the whole city with their keening.
There was no power could hold Evander back.
He rushed into their midst and directly the bier
Was set upon the earth he hurled himself
On Pallas and clung to him, weeping, groaning,
Till, at long last, he forced out through his grief:

"O Pallas, Pallas, this was not the promise
You gave me once. You swore you would take
　care,
Nor blindly fling yourself into the arms　　　　210
Of the savage God of War! But well I know
That yearning for the first day of glory in action,
The ineffable taste of honor won in a first
　engagement!
Alas the ill-starred first fruits of your youth!
The bitter lesson of a war so near!
And not one god of all the gods gave heed
To my vows and prayers! O my most blessed wife,
Lucky the death that spared you of these sorrows!
An opposite fate is mine; by living on
I have defeated my destiny, only to be　　　　220
A father left in solitariness.
Had I but followed the friendly flag of Troy
And fallen to a hail of Rutulian weapons!
If only it had been my life in forfeit,
My body borne in this procession home,
Not Pallas. But I lay no blame on you
My Trojan friends, nor on our mutual treaty,
Nor in the hands we joined to seal it with.
This was the lot inevitably destined
To fall on my old age. But if my son　　　　230
Was doomed to an early death what better death
Could I wish for him than falling as he led
His Trojans against Latium, having killed
The Volscians in their thousands?
I could not ask for a nobler funeral
Than good Aeneas and the Phrygian nobles
And the whole Etruscan army and their leaders
Have accorded to you. They have brought mighty
　trophies,
Those whom your strong right arm despatched to
　Death.
And you too, Turnus, would have found your　　240
　place there,
Yes, as a mighty tree-trunk hung with your
　armor—
Had Pallas been your equal in age and strength.
And let no grief of mine delay you Trojans

From waging the war. Go now, and bear this
    message
Back to your King: If I prolong a life
That is hateful to me now that Pallas is dead,
It is because of your sword-arm which, you admit
Owes us, father and son, the death of Turnus.
This is the one, the only, deed undone—
250   The key to your success and my deserts.
I seek no joy in life (nor rightly should I);
But to my son, down there among the shades,
I would be glad to bear some joyful news."

Meanwhile the dawn had raised her tonic light
For suffering mortals, bringing back the round
Of task and toil. And now Aeneas the leader
And Tarchon built their funeral pyres along
The winding shores: and here the living brought
Each man the bodies of his dead according
260   To the custom of his ancestors. Thickly smoking
The torches were applied and the whole sky
Became one pall of smoke, black and opaque.
Three times they circled round the blazing pyres
Their armor glittering; three times they rode
Their horses round the grievous funeral fires
Uttering lamentations. The earth was wet
With tears, their weapons dripping with their tears.
Their cries and trumpet-peals rose to the sky.
Some tossed on the fires spoils stripped from the
    Latin dead,
270   Helmets and elegant swords, bridles and chariot
    wheels:
Others brought offerings of personal gear,
Things dear to the dead, their helmets and the
    weapons
That had not saved them. Many the carcasses
Of oxen immolated there to Death:
They slit the throats of bristly boars and cattle
Seized out of every field, and gouts of blood
Were poured onto the flames. And now along
The whole length of the shore they stood and
    watched
The burning of their comrades and kept guard

Over half-burnt pyres and nothing could tear   *280*
   them away
Till dewy night fell and the sky was studded
With the cold fires of the stars.
                    The unhappy Latins
In a different quarter were no less engaged
In building countless pyres. Of the many bodies
Of their warriors some they buried in earth, some
They carried away to fields nearby to send them
Home to their cities; the rest, an enormous heap
Of entangled corpses, they then and there
   cremated
Uncounted and unhonored. Everywhere
For miles the countryside gleamed with the flare   *290*
Of more and yet more fires.
                And now the third
Daybreak had lifted from the sky its chilling
   shadows.
And the mourners came to level the piles of ashes
And muddle of bones from the beds of the
   funeral fires
And heap upon them mounds of earth which
   their heat
Still had the power to warm.
               But within the walls
Of rich Latinus' palace, within the city—
Here grief could dive no deeper nor lamentation
Touch greater heights. Here were stricken mothers
And their sons' wretched brides, here breaking   *300*
   hearts
Of loving sisters, here were children orphaned,
All cursing the insufferable war
And Turnus' purposed wedding. They demanded
That he and he alone should put the issue
To the test with his own sword since it was he
Who claimed the throne of Italy and the position
Of highest honor. The bitter tongue of Drances
Was loud in their support and he added weight
By swearing that Aeneas challenged only
Turnus in single combat: Turnus only.   *310*
But Turnus had supporters who put forward
Many an argument too; and added to that

Was the protection of Her Majesty
And his own great reputation evidenced
In the trophies he had won.

                    In the middle of this uproar,
As the quarrel reached white heat, the
   ambassadors
To the mighty city of Diomede returned.
Their gloom was plain to see: a crowning blow.
From all their efforts nothing had resulted;
320   The gifts, the gold, the earnest prayers had gone
For exactly nothing. They must seek alliance
In arms from somewhere else or sue for peace
From the Trojan King. It was the last straw
And left them—even King Latinus—crushed.
The anger of the gods, so manifest
In the new-made gravemounds there before their
   eyes
Prompted a new awareness that Aeneas
Was by the will of the gods a man of destiny.
Therefore Latinus, under royal decree,
330   Convened a council of his foremost citizens
To meet within his high walls. They poured in
Through the crowds on the streets and assembled
   in the palace.
Latinus by reason of his age and his supreme
   position
Sat gravely in the midst with serious mien.
Immediately he bade the ambassadors
Sent back from the city of Diomede to report
And answer in fullest detail his every question.
Then silence was proclaimed and Venulus
Obeying his command began to speak.
340   "Citizens, we have seen Diomede, we have seen
His camp of Argives. We survived the journey,
Surmounted every hazard and touched the hand
Of the man who brought down Troy. This
   conqueror
Was busy building this city called Argyripa,
After his ancestors, by Garganus
In Iapygian country. Then as soon
As we were admitted and given leave to speak

We proffered our gifts, we stated our name and
   country,
We informed him who was our invader, we
Made clear the reasons for our coming to Arpi.   *350*
He heard us out, and tranquilly answered us:
'O happy people, subjects of Saturn, Ausonians
Of an ancient race, what strange caprice of chance
Disturbs you in your peace and goads you on
To provoke war—when you know nothing of war?
Why, all of us who ravished with our swords
The land of Ilium have paid and paid to the full
In unutterable torments everywhere
In the whole world (of the hardships we endured
Warring under those lofty walls, of the heroes   *360*
Simois clamps down to his watery bed
I will say nothing). We are a band of men
Whom even Priam might find pity for—
As may the blighting star of Minerva witness
And that Euboean reef, Caphereus the avenger.
Disbanded from that nation we were driven
To the ends of the earth. Menelaus the son of
   Atreus
In exile to the pillars of Hercules—
Ulysses to see the Cyclops tribes of Aetna—
Need I recall how Neoptolemus found   *370*
His kingdom? How Idomeneus' home
Was shattered? How the Locrians now lodge
On the Libyan coast? Even the King of Mycenae
The grand commander of the mighty Greeks
Met death at his own doorway by the hand
Of his evil queen— He who had vanquished Asia
Vanquished by the adultery in his home!
Oh jealousy of the gods! debarring me
From my ancestral home, never to see
The wife I craved nor Calydon my fair city!   *380*
But worse was yet to come—terrible portents
Pursued me—I was reft of all my comrades:
They took to the air on wings, and as water-birds
Haunted the streams (alas for the ghastly fate
Of my own folk!) and made the rocks resound
With their dismal cries. Yes, from that very day

When, out of my mind, I drew my sword and
   assailed
The fleshly forms of the gods inflicting a wound
On the right hand of Venus—from that day
390 I had no other lot to look for. No, no, friends,
Do not induce me towards wars like these.
Since Pergamus was razed, I have had no quarrel
With any Trojan—nor does the memory
Of those old evils give me any pleasure!
Far better offer Aeneas the gifts you have brought
From your fatherland and meant to offer me!
We have clashed spear to cruel spear, we have
   clinched
In combat hand to hand: trust me, I know
How great his towering might behind his shield,
400 And with what whirlwind force he hurls his spear!
Had Ida's land but borne another two
Such heroes, Dardanus could have sallied out
To attack the cities of Inachus in his turn,
And, fate reversed, it would be Greece to mourn.
In all that time of fret before the walls
Of obdurate Troy it was Hector and Aeneas
Whose hands alone denied the Greeks their victory
And kept it out of reach till the tenth year.
Both men a model of courage, masterly
410 In their exercise of arms; but Aeneas the nobler
By reason of his piety.

                 Whatever the terms,
Clasp your right hands in treaty; but beware
Of a clash of arms with him.'

                        So you have heard,
O noblest majesty, both his princely answers
And his opinion of this mighty war."
Scarce had Venulus ceased when a mouth-to-
   mouth
Muttering of various comment arose
Among the Ausonians, like the sound of the water
When boulders block the swift course of a river
420 And caught in swirls and eddies it clucks and
   gurgles
And the nearby banks echo the burbling babble.

But as soon as their minds were at ease and their
   anxious mouths
Silent once more the King from his high throne
Invoked the gods and then began:

                        "My wish
Would have been (and better it would have been)
To have come to a decision on this matter
Affecting the whole state some time ago,
And not to summon a council at such a moment
When the enemy is camped before our walls.
My friends, we are engaged in a grievous war   *430*
With progeny of gods, unconquered heroes
No battles tire, nor in defeat even
Can they lay down the sword. If you had hopes
Of an Aetolian alliance put them away.
Let each hope as he may but you see how slender
Hope has become. As for the rest, the wreck
And ruin lies there obvious to the eye
And for the hand to touch. I blame no one.
What the utmost bravery *could* do has been done;
We have thrown the resources of the entire realm   *440*
Into this conflict. But now let me express—
Though tentatively—what is in my mind.
I will be brief, so give me your attention.
I own an ancient territory close
To the Tuscan river, the length of it extending
Westward as far as the Sicanian frontier
And beyond that. The Auruncans and Rutulians
Have sown it and reclaimed the stony hillsides
With the plough, and pasture sheep on the
   roughest slopes.
Let us give all this acreage to the Trojans,   *450*
And the pine forest in the mountain heights
As a gift of friendship: let us propose a treaty
With mutual obligations and let us invite them
To share our realm as allies. Let them settle
And build a walled city—if indeed this be
Their brookless passion—but if they have in mind
To canvas another nation for other space
(They are free to quit our country if they choose to)
Let us build them twenty ships of Italian oak,

460   Or more if they can man them: there are planks
      All ready stacked down by the river—they
        themselves
      Can decide the design and number of ships they
        want—
      Let us provide them bronze, shipwrights, and
        fittings.
      In addition it is my desire that an embassy
      Of a hundred men of noble Latin blood
      Should go with olive-branches in their hands
      Carrying also gifts—talents of gold and ivory,
      A chair of state and a robe that are the symbols
      Of this our majesty. Debate the matter
470   How we can best restore our failing fortunes!"
      Then up sprang Drances, hostile as before.
      The fame of Turnus tortured him—he was wracked
      With bitterness, he was warped with envy. Drances
      Was rich, and readier to use his tongue
      Than his sword in battle, but had the reputation
      Of being a sound adviser in debate
      And powerful in intrigue (on his mother's side
      He was of noble lineage but none knew
      His father's antecedents) and now he rose
480   And spoke with a measured spiteful emphasis.
      "O gracious majesty, what you put forward
      Is a matter clear to every one of us:
      I need not enlarge upon it. Everyone
      Knows in his heart what state the state is in,
      But mutters under his breath and will not speak out.
      Let him stop threatening us, let him allow us
      Freedom of speech—and I speak of that man
      Whose ill-starred leadership, whose crooked temper,
      (Yes, speak I will, and let him threaten me
490   With a duel or death)—has led to the destruction
      Of so many of the finest of our leaders.
      We have seen this happen, seen the entire city
      Deep in its desolation—and all the while
      He makes his sorties against the Trojan camp,
      Whirling his arms enough to make heaven cringe—
      Because he knows he can safely turn to flight.
      Most gracious Majesty, do but add one more
      To all those many gifts you have bidden be sent

Or promised to the Trojans—nor let the violence
Of any man constrain you: give your daughter   *500*
In marriage to this most estimable man,
As it is your right as a father, and seal this peace
With a bond that will abide for evermore.
But if our hearts and minds are possessed wholly
By terrors so absolute, let us present
Ourselves to Aeneas in person and appeal
For clemency from him, and beg him to yield
And grant their sovereign rights to king and
    country.
Why do you hurl your wretched citizens
Time and again into the open arms   *510*
Of danger—you, the very source and spring
Of the evils come upon us Latins? War
Offers no hope: it is peace we all demand.
Yes, Turnus, and the one inviolable
Guarantee of that peace. And I am the first
I—whom you seem to imagine your enemy,
And indeed I may be—see! I kneel before you.
Pity your own people, abate your pride
And accept defeat. We have had our fill of defeat,
We have seen deaths enough and the broad acres   *520*
Bereft and bare of people.

                              Or if it is glory
That spurs you, if your spirit is adamant
In its resolve, if your whole heart is fixed
Upon a palace and a dowry— Dare!
Go out and meet your enemy breast to breast!
Must we then strew the plains in herds unwept
    and unburied,
We worthless creatures, simply so that Turnus
May make a royal marriage? As for you,
If you have any spunk, if your warlike father
Bequeathed you any blood: Go, face your   *530*
    challenger!"

Turnus was stung to fury at this speech,
He gave a growl and then a flood of words
Burst from the depths of his heart,

                              "As usual, Drances,
You have plenty enough to say—just at a time

When it is swords we want not words. When it is
   a council
You are the first to come. But while our
   earthworks
Keep off the foe and the moats are not overflowing
With blood, it is not the moment to fill the
   council chamber
With your mighty mouthings—spoken in absolute
   safety.
540   Accuse me of cowardice, Drances, yes, let fly
In your usual vein—when your right hand has piled
As many heaps of Trojan slain as mine has,
And studded all the fields with splendid trophies!
Nothing prevents your trying for yourself
What shining valor can do. And the enemy
Is hardly far to seek—they are everywhere
All round the walls. Shall we march out to meet
   them?
What are you waiting for? Is your martial ardor
In the hot air of your windy tongue alone?
550   And the speed of your feet as you flee? So I am
   beaten?
Vilest of liars! who dares brand me beaten,
Seeing the Tiber swollen and swelling with
   Trojan blood
And the whole house of Evander, Pallas and all,
Brought down to the dust and the Arcadians
Stripped of their arms. Was I beaten?—ask Bitias
And mighty Pandarus—ask the thousand heroes
I conquered and despatched on a single day,
Though I was shut within their walls and penned
Within their ramparts. *"War offers no hope"*
560   You are out of your mind! Apply your words of
   sooth
To the Trojan state and to your own—! Continue
To spread panic and extol the strength of a people
Already conquered twice, at the same time
As you belittle the arms of King Latinus.
It seems the chiefs of the Myrmidons now tremble
At the Trojans' feats, that Diomede is aghast
And Larissaean Achilles—and the Aufidus
Flows backwards from the advancing Adriatic!

See how the cursing crook pretends to cringe
And uses his fear of facing me to barb   570
His accusations with! You can stop all that.
This hand of mine would never demean itself
To take a life like yours—you are welcome to it!
Your breast is the right and proper place for it.
But now, Sire, let me return to you and the
   serious matter
Under discussion. If it be true that you place
No hope whatever in any further engagements,
If we are so completely cowed and forlorn,
And after one defeat, and only one
We have collapsed never to rise again,   580
And our star is set for ever, then let us wave
Our strengthless beggars' hands and whine for
   peace.
But oh! if a grain was left of our old valor—
Lucky the man, I hold, above all others
Blessed in his acts and noblest in his spirit
Who rather than see such a day as this, would fall
And dying bite the dust once and for ever!
But if we still have a reserve, if still
Some source of our young manhood is unsullied,
If still there are cities and nations of Italy   590
Left to come to our help—and if the Trojans
Have won their glory not without loss of blood
(The storm of war swept over us all alike)
Why do we tamely wilt on the mere threshold?
Why do our knees begin to knock even
Before the sound of the trumpet? Days go by
And in their whirligig bring the unlucky
To better times and turn and turn about
The throws of Fortune set us up or down
And then establish us on solid rock.   600
We will get no help from Arpi, from the Aetolians,
But Messapus is for us and Tolumnius
The fortunate, and so are other chieftains
These many peoples have sent. No little glory
Will be the lot of those, the chosen flower,
Of Latium and Laurentum and that noble lady
Camilla with her troops of Volscian horsemen,
Her squadrons bright with bronze.

                                        But if indeed
        The Trojans demand me and me alone
610   In single combat—and if that is your pleasure
        And I am the stumbling-block to the common
            good,
        Victory has not so far recoiled from me in loathing
        That I should refuse to venture for hope so fine.
        I shall go boldly out to meet him though his might
        Is greater than Achilles and he wears armor
        Of a like nature and forged by Vulcan too.
        Turnus am I, and I yield place to none
        Of the heroes of old times, and I am dedicated
        To you and Latinus father of my betrothed!
620   'For me Aeneas' challenge and me only?'
        I crave his challenge! And the gods' displeasure
        Becomes apparent at the core of this.
        I do not care for Drances to pay forfeit,
        His death for mine, and, if it be but a question
        Of honor and glory, to filch what is mine by right."

        So they crossed swords—in bitter debate—but
            Aeneas
        Was moving out of camp into position
        And see! a messenger came bursting in
        Cramming the palace from end to end with his
            news—
630   Uproar prevailed, panic straddled the city:
        The Trojan forces in full array and the Tuscan
        Supports were sweeping from the river Tiber
        And brimming all the plain! Immediately
        With shattered minds and shaken hearts the people
        Were shocked into unbalanced belligerence.
        They snatched up arms in haste, the cry went up
        "To arms!" The young men yelled for arms,
            arms, arms,
        Their elders sadly whispered to each other.
        From everywhere a tangled dissonance
640   A hurly-burly arose to heaven like
        The mingled murmurations of flocks of birds
        Settled by chance in a high wood, or like
        Harsh honkings of swans about the fishy pools
        Of the river Padusa. Seizing his moment Turnus

Mocked, "Citizens! It is time to convene your
  council!
Sit yourselves down and commend us peace—the
  invaders
Are at our gates!" Without another word
He started up and hustled from the palace.
"You Volusus" he ordered "go bid the Volscians
Fall in their companies! Lead the Rutulians out!   *650*
Messapus, you, Coras with his brother,
Deploy the cavalry in breadth over the plain.
Let a squad guard the approaches to the city
And man the towers; as for the rest of you,
You will attack where I direct and lead you."
They mustered to the walls from every part of
  the city
And King Latinus abandoned the debate
With all its deepest decisions undecided.
He was moithered by the ill turn of events
And bitterly self-reproachful for refusing   *660*
Freely to welcome Dardan Aeneas and make him
His son-in-law and ally to the city.
Meanwhile they were digging dikes in front of
  the gates
And hoisting stones and stakes into position.
The trumpet blared the bloody call to war.
Then a conglomerate crowd of boys and old
  warriors
Stood to the walls. For now the supreme effort
Was asked of everyone. The queen herself
Was drawn to the temple on the heights of Pallas
Attended by a great throng of older women.   *670*
She brought with her gifts, and at her side the
  maiden
Lavinia cause of the whole disaster glided
With her beautiful eyes downcast. The women
  pressed
Into the temple and soon the incense billowed
And the sound of their sorrow poured from the
  high doors.
"Lady of arms, Tritonian maiden, mistress of war,
Shatter the spear of the Trojan plunderer
With your own hand, and hurl him to the ground

And stretch him splayed under your own high
    gates."

680 Charged with his fury Turnus prepared for battle.
He was already accoutered in his corslet
Glowering stiffly with its red-bronze scales;
His golden greaves were on, his head was bare,
He had girded on his sword and it shone golden
As he bounded down from the height of the citadel
To launch himself upon the enemy,
His heart and hope as high as they could be.
He seemed like a stallion that has burst his tether,
Escaped his stall, and free at last to gallop
690 Has all the plain to choose and either he makes
For the mares' crowded pastures or goes to bathe
In a long-loved river pool and coming out
Cavorts and whinnies, tossing his head, his mane
Shivering over his shoulders in his joy.
And as he went Camilla rode to meet him,
Her Volscian fighters with her, and with the grace
Of the queen she was dismounted under the
    shadow
Of the very gates. And following her lead
Her whole band slipped from their horses. Then
    she addressed him,
700 "O Turnus, if the brave may fitly feel
Confident of themselves I am confident.
I offer therefore boldly to oppose
The Trojan cavalry forces and I myself
Will ride alone against the Etruscan horsemen.
Let my hand strike the first blow of the perilous
    battle;
Do you dismount and stand-to by the walls
And guard the ramparts." Turnus fixed his gaze
On the awe-inspiring maid and answered her:
"Glory of Italy! maiden, what can I say
710 To express my thanks, or make fit recompense?
But since your spirit soars beyond all compare,
Then share the toil with me. The rumor goes,
And the scouts that I sent out confirm as fact,
That Aeneas has shrewdly sent his light-armed
    cavalry

Forward to engage the plains while he himself
Comes by the steep and undefended path
Over the mountain and straight down on the city.
I have in mind a stratagem of war.
There is a wooded gorge up there—my plan is
To post an ambush at each end and block it.   720
Your role is to be set ready to receive
The onslaught of the Etruscan cavalry:
Messapus will be with you in keen support
And the Latian squadron and Tiburtus' troop.
You are to be in joint command with me!"
Such were his words and with similar exhortations
He screwed up Messapus and his allied leaders
To battle-pitch, then moved to meet the foe.
There is a tortuous narrow glen ideal
For ambush and the sleights of war, both sides   730
Shelve steeply down in a dark tangle of foliage,
And the path is scarcely visible into it,
Its jaws are narrow, its entrance fraught with
     menace.
Above it, among the tops and vantage-points,
There lies a hidden level, safe out of sight,
The perfect spot from which to mount an attack
Either from left or right, or holding it,
To roll great boulders down. And hither Turnus
Hastened along the paths he knew so well
And occupied the place and settled down   740
In the cramped confines of the woods.

                                   Meanwhile,
Latona's daughter in the Halls of Heaven
Was having speech with one of the maiden
     members
Of her sacred retinue, swift Opis. Her words
Were full of dole: "O maiden mine, Camilla
Is off to a brutal war. Beyond all others
She is dear to me and now in vain she is girding
Our weapons on—oh, it is no new thing,
This love that I, Diana, bear for her,
No sudden tenderness that has stirred my soul.   750
When Metabus was driven from his throne
Because of the hatred his tyranny had aroused,
When he was forced to flee from his ancient city

Privernum, he bore his baby daughter with him.
Clean through the heart of the insurrection he
     bore her
To share his exile, and after her mother Casmilla,
Changing one letter, he called the child Camilla.
He clasped her to his breast as struggling onwards
He made for the high mountain ridges clothed
760 In their solitude of forest, while from all sides
The hostile weapons hailed as the Volscians threw
A cordon of troops around him. And suddenly
There was the Amasenus barring the way,
Pouring in flood above its broken banks,
So great a cloudburst had come battering down.
He was prepared to swim for it, but his love
For his baby checked him, he was wracked with
     fear
For his precious burden, and in his mind he
     rehearsed
Every conceivable angle of action and suddenly
770 Made his decision though he doubted its wisdom.
He chanced to have in his strong hand a war-spear
Knotty and tempered tough, and swathing his
     daughter
In a sheath of cork-tree bark he bound her to it
Just in the middle to balance, and poised the spear
In his giant hand and spoke to heaven this prayer:
'Diana, maiden goddess, kindly dweller
In the woods, I vow my daughter, I her father,
To be your handmaid—yours is the first weapon
She has ever held as, whirling through the air,
780 She flies from her enemies your suppliant.
Take her, O goddess, I beg you, for your own—
As I entrust her now to the trustless wind.'
He spoke and drew back his arm and hurled the
     spear.
Loud roared the flood and over the racing river
Whirled poor Camilla strapped to the whizzing
     spear.
And Metabus, as the main body of his enemies
Pressed ever closer, took to the flood himself,
Won his way over, and plucked from the grassy
     bank

The spear with his daughter, Diana's novice now.
No city would admit him to its houses 790
Nor even within its walls, nor would the wildness
Of his nature ever bow to discipline.
He lived his life at the solitudinous heights
Of mountain shepherds. And there among the
  thick
Of savage thickets gave his daughter suck
At the teats of a wild mare, kneading its udders
Into her tiny lips. And when she tottered
Her first few steps on her own he thrust a javelin
Into her hand and hung from her infant shoulder
A bow and arrows. Instead of a golden hair-clasp, 800
Instead of a mantle falling to her feet,
A tiger-skin was flung around her neck
And huddled down her back; with her tiny hand
She threw her miniature weapons; she could whirl
A sling around her head on its leather thong
And bring a crane from Strymon down to earth
Or a white swan. Indeed there were many mothers
In every Etruscan town who yearned to bring her
To their son's marriage-bed—in vain. She was
  utterly
Content to dedicate her being to Diana 810
And cherish for ever her chastity and her weapons
Inviolate. How I wish she had never been
Dragged into such a war—had never tried
To challenge the Trojans: she might still have been
My votaress, my beloved intimate.
But come, Opis my nymph, since destiny
Dives crushing down upon her, glide from heaven
To the bounds of Latium, where even now
The bitter battle is joined in a cloud of doom.
Take these: and from this quiver draw the arrow 820
Of my vengeance and extract the penalty
Of blood for blood from any man, Italian
Or Trojan, it matters not, if he inflict
A deathly wound upon her sacred flesh.
Afterwards I will bear her body off—
The body I must mourn so piteously—
In a hollow cloud, all undespoiled her body,
And lay her down for burial in her homeland."

She spoke; and swiftly Opis plummeted,
830   Through the light airs of heaven her body wound
In a dark whirlwind.
                              Meanwhile the Trojans
Drew near the walls and the Etruscan leaders
With all their cavalry disposed in squadrons
Of equal numbers. Over the whole expanse
The horses jockeyed and pulled against the bit,
Neighing and prancing now this way now that.
The whole field far and wide was ripe with an
      iron harvest.
The plains were a blaze of weapons uplifted high.
Against them Messapus and the speedy Latians
840   And Coras with his brother, and the force of the
      maiden Camilla
Advanced to meet them over the plains, their
      spears
At the ready with quivering points, as they drew
      back
Their strong right hands as far as they could go.
The armies closed; the horses neighed; the tension
Began to grow and now they came to a halt
Facing each other within the range of a spear-
      throw.
Then with a sudden shout they dug their spurs
Into their horses and set them to the charge.
And as they charged they poured a shower of
      weapons
850   As thick as snowflakes and the sky was darkened
With the shadow of them. Immediately Tyrrhenus
And fierce Aconteus, leveled spears in hand,
Charged at each other—and first they were to fall
With a terrible crash as the breasts of their
      horses burst
In the shock of collision. Aconteus, shot far
Like a thunderbolt or a stone from a siege-engine,
Fell headlong, scattering his life to air.
At once the line was broken, the Latins turned
Slinging their shields behind them and rode for
      the city.
860   The Trojans gave them chase, Asilas leading

His own men in the van. But as the Latins
Drew near their gates they raised a rallying-cry
And turned the pliant necks of their horses round.
The Trojans in their turn gave their horses rein
And fled far off: they ebbed and flowed like the
    sea
That now comes flooding in towards the land
And bursting over the rocks with clouds of spray
And sopping all the sand to the last inch,
Then swiftly turns to ebb and rolls the shingle
Back with its sucking undertow, and the waves   *870*
Withdraw in sliding series from the shore.
Twice the Etruscans routed the Rutulians
And drove them to their walls; twice in their turn
They were repulsed and looking over their
    shoulders
Covered their backs with shields. But the third
    time
The whole of the line engaged and was locked in
    battle,
And each man picked his adversary—then indeed
The groans of the dying rose; bodies and weapons
Lay sodden in pools of blood and half-dead horses
Were churned around in the welter of human   *880*
    carnage.
The battle rose to a new pitch of violence.
Orsilochus flung his spear at Remulus' horse—
He was afraid of its rider at close quarters—
And he left the spearhead lodged under its ear.
The charger was maddened by the blow and reared
Heaving his breast up sawing the air with his
    forelegs
In uncontrollable agony at the wound.
Remulus unseated rolled on the ground.
Catillus unhorsed Iollas and Herminius
A man of mighty courage and mighty frame.   *890*
His hair shone yellow-gold on his bare head,
His shoulders were bare, wounds held no terrors
    for him
So potent were his powers in battle—yet now
A spear was thrust between his mighty shoulders

And stuck there quivering and made the hero
Bend double in agony. Blood streamed
   everywhere;
The combatants dealt out death with the steel,
   and sought
To die in the glory of their many wounds.
But through the midst of the slaughter ramped
   Camilla
900 Her quiver on her back like an Amazon,
One breast laid bare for ease in the fight—now
   see her
Volleying showers of javelins with all her strength
Or wielding a heavy two-edged ax in a hand
Nothing could weary; and vibrant on her shoulder
A golden bow, the armament of Diana.
And even, as sometimes happened, if she were
   forced
To retreat she turned in flight and loosed from
   her bow
A stream of arrows. Her chosen intimates
Were round her—Larina, Tulla and Tarpeia
910 Who flourished a brazen ax, Italy's daughters,
All chosen by Camilla devotee of Diana,
To be her pride and joy, her attendant spirits
In peace or war—they were like Amazons
Of Thrace who make the banks of the Thermodon
Ring with their hoofbeats as they ride to battle
With their painted arms, following it may be
Hippolyta, or warlike Penthesilea
When she drives back in her chariot surrounded
By leaping yelling crowds of women warriors
920 Exulting as they shake their crescent shields.
O maiden fierce as fire, who was the first
Your dart unhorsed and who the last? How many
The bodies you made measure their last length?
Eunius son of Clytius was the first.
As he shaped up to her she gouged her way
Through his unguarded breast with her pinewood
   spear.
Vomiting streams of blood he fell and clenched
   his teeth

In the bloodstained earth as he writhed on his
  wound
And died. Then it was Liris' turn and down
On top of him went Pagasus—the former   930
Had been unhorsed when his mount was stabbed
  in the belly
And he was gathering his reins, and Pagasus
As he ran to help and stretched his unarmed hand
To his falling comrade: but both alike went
  headlong.
To these she added Amastrus, son of Hippotas,
Then at long range and bending to the effort
She cast at Tereus and Harpalycus
Demophoön and Chromis. For every spear
She spun from her maiden hand, a Phrygian fell.
In the distance on an Iapygian horse   940
There rode Ornytus: Ornytus was a hunter
And quite unused to war—but now turned warrior
He wore on his broad shoulders a bullock-skin
And on his head for helmet a huge wolf-mask
With gaping jaws and a snarl of snowy fangs;
His only weapon was a rustic hunting spear.
As he moved through the midst of his fellow
  horsemen
He was taller by a head than any of them.
She singled him out, nor was it hard to do so
When all were in full flight, and ran him through.   950
Then standing over him hissed these words of
  hatred:
"Etruscan, did you suppose you were still in the
  woods
Hunting wild beasts? The day has come to prove
To you and your friends the folly of your thoughts—
A woman's weapons are proof: yet you shall bear
Down to the spirits of your ancestors
No name to trifle with—for you were killed
By Camilla's spear."

                  Next she despatched Orsilochus
And Butes, two of the toughest of the Trojans.
Butes she speared from behind between his corslet   960
And helmet where a rider's neck shows white

And his shield hangs from his left arm—as for
    Butes
She fled from him at first, in a wide circuit,
Then narrowing inward tricked him and the hunted
Became the hunter; and rising in her stirrups
She took her heavy battle-ax and hacked
Time and again cleaving his armor and cleaving
Clean through his bones, for all his prayers for
    mercy:
Her butchery splayed his face with brains still
    warm.

970 Next met her and stood rooted to the spot
In terror of her mien the warrior son
Of Aunus, who lived in the Appenines,
Not least of the Ligurians while fate
Allowed him scope for deceit. But when he saw
He had no chance to wriggle out of a fight
However fast he fled, nor turn aside
The onset of the queen, he had it in mind
To insure his line of escape by a trick, and began,
"What is so wonderful in a woman fighting
980 If she merely relies on the mettle of her horse?
Now set aside your means of flight and brace
    yourself
For a hand-to-hand fight on an equal footing.
You will soon see to whom such windy vanity
Brings its deserts." But she blazed up in fury
At the bitter insult and handing her horse to a
    comrade,
Stood her ground fearlessly equipped as she was
With naked sword and a bare shield—but the
    youth,
Thinking his trick had succeeded, on an instant
Reined round his horse and galloped away in flight
990 Goading his wretched charger with his spurs.
"Ligurian fool! It is you that have vaunted in vain
Your arrogance, and conceit, you slippery fool!
Trying your father's tricks has been no use,
No wiles will bring you safely back to Aunus
Your wily father!" So shouted the maiden
And quick as a flash she whipped to the horse's
    head

And seized the reins and turned to the encounter
And slaked her vengeance with his hated blood—
As easily as a falcon the bird of augury
Flies up from a lofty rock and stoops on a dove   *1000*
High in the clouds and clamps it in its grip
And disembowels it with its hooky talons,
And blood and plucked feathers falter down from
   the sky.

Meanwhile the Father of Gods and men enthroned
On high Olympus was no blind observer
Of all these deeds, and He it was who roused
Etruscan Tarchon into the ruthless battle
And goaded his anger with no gentle goads.
Thus, Tarchon spurred his war-horse into the thick
   of the slaughter
Where the ranks were in retreat and rallied them   *1010*
Using every means he had to appeal to them,
Calling each man by name, and rousing the routed
To return to the fight: "What do you fear,
   Etruscans?
Oh my Etruscans, will nothing *ever* shame you?
Will nothing *ever* spur you into action?
What new despond of cowardice are you sunk in?
So a woman can put you all in a panic of flight?
What are your swords for? Why are these
   weapons lying
Unproven in your hands—you are not so slow
When love enlists you in her midnight sorties   *1020*
Or the curved pipes call you to Bacchic revelries:
Or when there is a feast and plenty of wine in view
(For there's your bent and your true passion) and
The priest has prosperous omens to report
And the meaty victim summons you to the stately
Trees of the sacred grove!" With these hard words
He spurred his horse into the fray prepared
To do or die, and madly charged at Venulus
And grabbed him off his horse and grappled him
To his chest with an iron right arm and galloped   *1030*
   off.
A shout rose to the sky and all Latin eyes
Were riveted on the deed as Tarchon flashed

Over the plain bearing the armored hero.
Then snapping off the point from his own spear
He probed for a vulnerable place to plant
A mortal wound; and his foe wrestled with him
Striving to keep his right hand off his throat
And countering force with force. As a golden eagle
Soars in the air with a snake secure in the clutch
1040 Of his clenching talons and the wounded snake
Writhes in its coils and ruffs its stiffening coils
And hisses from its mouth, wriggling and threshing
And none the less the eagle strikes at its struggles
With his hooked beak and his wing-beats pulse on
    the air—
So in his triumph Tarchon carried off his prey
From the Tibertine lines. And emulous
Of their leader's splendid lead the Etruscans
    charged.
Then Arruns, a man already pledged to fate,
Went circling round Camilla, for all her swiftness
1050 And her javelin poised, forestalling her every move
And sparring for the easiest opening.
Wherever the maiden threaded her fury through
The tangle of battle he silently drew nearer
And dogged her steps. And whether she turned
    in triumph
Or whether she had to flee, the young man
    stealthily
Kept edging his horse towards her, sidling up.
He tried from the left, he tried from the right, he
    tried
Every approach—he still went circling round her
His unwavering hatred poised in his quivering
    spearhead.
1060 It chanced that Chloreus, sacred to Cybele
And once her priest, a cynosure from afar
In his Phrygian armor, was eagerly spurring on
His lathering horse: and this had a covering
Where a pattern of bronze scales in the shape of
    a plume
Was knitted together with gold. And he himself
Conspicuous in his red and his foreign purple
Was firing Cretan shafts from his Lycian bow—

A bow embossed with gold that twanged at his
  shoulder,
And gold was his prophet's helmet, and gold the
  brooch
That gathered the rustling folds of his saffron   *1070*
  mantle,
His tunic was golden-threaded, his legs gaudy
In barbaric gaiters. He it was that the maiden,
With the blind concentration of the hunter,
Picked out from the whole ruck of battle (whether
To adorn the temple with a Trojan trophy
Or wishing to flaunt herself in captured gold)
And recklessly she tracked him through the ranks,
Her woman's heart aglow for possession and
  plunder.
At last the moment came, and Arruns sniped her
With a spear she never saw, praying aloud: *1080*
"Highest of gods, Apollo, guardian of holy Soracte
You know us to be your foremost worshipers:
For you the pine is fed to the holy pile:
For you we devotees, firm in our faith,
Pass through the heart of the fire and traverse the
  living embers,
O grant all-powerful Father that my arms
May rid us of this disgrace. I seek no spoils,
No trophy if the maiden falls to me,
Nor any plunder, let my other deeds
Bring me what fame they may—but only grant   *1090*
This pestilent woman vanquished by my wound
And I shall return to the cities of my homeland
In happy obscurity."

                      Apollo heard him
And in his heart decided to vouchsafe
A part of his prayer—the other part he left
To the will of the wandering winds—he granted
To shock Camilla down in sudden death:
But did not grant his noble land to see
The day of his return—and the gusts dispersed
His prayers into the breezes of the south.   *1100*
And so, when his hand had done its work and
  the spear
Went whistling through the air the Volscians all

To a man had eyes for no one but their queen
And all their thoughts were on her.
But she was utterly unaware of the whirr
Of the spear as it whirled towards her through
    the air
Until it struck her just below that breast
She had bared for battle and there lay fast
    embedded
Drinking her maiden blood. Her anxious comrades
1110 Rushed to support their mistress as she staggered.
Arruns bolted away: he was more appalled than
    any,
Joy and horror conflicting in his heart.
No longer did he dare to trust his spear
Or face the darts of the maiden, as when a wolf
Has killed a shepherd or fat bullock and beats
A speedy retreat to the trackless tops of the
    mountains
Before any weapons can be thrown to stop him,
And well aware of the boldness of his deed
He lets his tail droop and then claps it quaking
1120 Between his legs and onto his belly and makes
Straight for the wood—so Arruns his mind in a
    turmoil
Was glad enough to escape and hide himself
In the thick of the battle. Camilla plucked at the
    spear
With dying fingers, but the iron point was fast
In the deep wound between the bones of the ribs.
Drained of her blood she sank to the ground and
    her eyes
Glazed with the chill of death; and all the bloom
Fled from her cheeks. Then with her dying breath
She murmured to Acca, one of her companions,
1130 Who beyond all the rest was near to her
And shared her inmost thoughts: "Acca my sister
Thus far have I wrought: but a bitter wound
Has overcome me and all the world around me
Grows shadowy and dark. Escape from here,
Go straight to Turnus and take him my last
    message.

Let him take my place in the battle and fend the
   Trojans
From the town. And now, farewell." Even as she
   spoke
She let slip the reins and could not help but slump
Down to the ground: and gradually she was loosed
From her body as the cold crept through her limbs,   *1140*
Her neck lolled limp and in the grip of death,
Dropping her armor, she laid down her head.
And griding bitterly and loath to go
Her soul fled to the shades. Then truly the roar
That struck to the golden stars as it arose
Was measureless. And with Camilla fallen
The battle grew yet fiercer: the whole force
Of Trojans and Etruscans, and the Arcadian
Cavalry of Evander charged in a body.

Diana's sentinel Opis had for long   *1150*
Been at her lookout high among the peaks
Calmly watching the battle. And when far off,
Among the mill of frenzied warriors
She saw Camilla amerced by cruel death,
She sighed and from the depths of her heart she
   mourned:
"Alas, poor maiden, too heavy and too bitter
The penalty you have paid for trying to challenge
The Trojans in war. And nothing have you gained
From lonely worship of the woodland goddess
Nor from the quiver of our cult you wore   *1160*
Slung from your shoulder. But, even in death's
   extremity,
Your Queen has left you not unhonored, your end
Shall not be without fame throughout the world,
Nor shall you suffer the taint of the unavenged."
At the high mountain's foot was a huge mound
Of heaped earth—the tomb of Dercennus king
Of Laurentum in days gone by and ilex-trees
Shaded the place, and here the goddess halted
Most beautiful in her grace of speed, and standing
Upon the top of the mound marked Arruns   *1170*
   coming.

And as she saw him gleaming in his armor
And swelling with vanity she accosted him:
"Why do you turn? Come, guide your steps this
    way,
Come here and die and take requital fit
· For Camilla! O, it demeans Diana's weapons
To taste such blood as yours, but die you shall!"
The Thracian goddess drew a speedy arrow
From her gilded quiver and with deadly aim
She bent her bow drawing the bowstring back
1180 Till the curving bow-ends almost touched, and
    applied
Her hands with equal power till the iron barb
Of the arrow touched her left, and her right had
    drawn
The bowstring back to touch her breast. And
In the same instant he heard the whizz of the arrow
And felt the barb strike home into his flesh.
Forgotten by his comrades he lay dying
Gasping his life out and left groveling
In the dust of a hidden coign of the battlefield.
Opis took wing and was wafted up to Olympus.

1190 Their mistress lost, Camilla's light-armed
    squadrons
Were the first to fly; the Rutulians panicking
    followed;
And tough Atinas quitted the field—captains
Cut off from their men and men cut off from
    their captains,
All sought the safety of the walls and galloped
Full-tilt for the ramparts. Nobody could withstand
The Trojan assault or hold their deadly onset
With any counter-fire but slack bows slung
From their bowed shoulders fled: their hooves'
    four-footed flight
With rumble of thunder drummed on the
    crumbling plain.
1200 Dust rolled towards the walls in a blanketing
    darkness
And from their lookout posts the women raised

The women's wail to the stars and beat their
    breasts.
The first of the rout to pour through the open gates
Had the enemy horde so close upon their heels
That on the very threshold, with the walls
Of their native city about them, as the open doors
Of their very houses signaled "safety"—no escape
From a wretched death was offered them. Run
    through,
They breathed their last. Then it appeared
    essential
To bar the gates, nor did they dare admit   *1210*
Their friends for all their begging, and there
    ensued
A most tragic internecine strife between
The guardians of the gate and their routed friends
Who fought for entry. Before the very eyes
Of their sobbing parents some were bundled
    headlong
Into the moat by the press of the retreat,
Some blindly frenziedly spurred on their horses
To charge the posts of the gates that barred their
    way.
O love of country burning bright! On the walls
Some women in the utmost throes of the struggle, *1220*
Themselves hurled weapons from their trembling
    hands,
Emulous of Camilla, improvising stakes
Of oak, fire-pointed, to do the work of steel,
Burning to be the first to die in defense of the city.

Meanwhile in his forest ambush the shattering
    news
Was brought to Turnus: Acca informed the prince
Of the scope of the disaster; the utter wreck
Of the Volscian ranks, the downfall of Camilla;
The irresistible all-conquering advance
Of the enemy, striking panic to the city . . .   *1230*
In a fever Turnus quitted his ambush in the
    mountain
(For Jove's demands are brookless and inexorable)

And left the woodland wilderness—and scarcely
Had he withdrawn from his position and moved
Down to the plain, when lord Aeneas entered
The unguarded glen, traversed the watershed
And came out of the darkness of the forest.
So both pressed on towards the city walls
With all their forces, and not far apart.

1240 At one and the same moment Aeneas peering
Across the plain aswirl with dust saw Turnus
With his Laurentine column and Turnus saw
Aeneas rampant with his full array
And heard the tramp of feet and snort of horses.
And then and there they would have closed in
    combat
And the arbitrament of battle, had not the sun
The reddening sun, begun to bathe his team
His weary team, in the western seas of Spain
And brought the night back on the heels of day.

1250 So they encamped before the city walls
And reinforced their ramparts of defense.

BOOK XII

Mars was against them: Turnus could see the Latins
Beginning to back down and everyone looking
    his way:
It was his to make good his promise. *Now* said
    their eyes.
A natural fiery fury burst from his breast
Implacable as an African lion's frenzy
Hunters have hurt to the heart, but he is fortified
In his last foray by the feel of death—
He ruffs up his mane in delight from his stricken
    neck,
Snaps off the hunter's spear flush with his wound,

And roars defiance from his bloody mouth.   *10*
So it was with Turnus boiling over with bile,
And so he spluttered his fury to the king:
"I am Turnus. I-I-I am not waiting— Those cowards
Aeneas' crew can withdraw their challenge, they
Can go back on their words—but as for me—I
    fight!
Well, father, fetch the fitting sacrifice,
Draw up your treaty— You may sit and watch,
You Latins, I with my right arm shall rout
This rat from Asia and despatch him headlong
To Tartarus and with my single sword   *20*
Expunge our nation's shame—or if I am beaten
Let us acknowledge our lord and let Lavinia
Mate with our master!" And Latinus answered
With all the self-control he had, "Turnus!
Nobody doubts your daring, but as it waxes
The more I must take note and weigh my foresight
In the cold scales against your impetuous valor.
Your father Daunus left you a kingdom, you
Have added cities to it by your sword,
And I have a fortune, and I uphold your cause.   *30*
There are other girls—girls of good lineage
In Latium and Laurentum. Let me speak
My mind straight, though you may not like what
    I say.
But take it to heart, please. I could not engage
    my daughter
To any one of her earlier suitors—every
Warning of God and man was against it— But I
    did so.
My love for you, our being kin, the tears
Of the queen, made me throw all to the winds.
I broke my word to the man she was betrothed to,
I embarked on an unjust war. O Turnus, do you   *40*
    not see,
You most of all, what disasters we have suffered,
What this war has brought us? Utterly defeated
In two great battles, what hope have we left
Of holding our city, the key to Italy?
The Tiber steams with our blood, the plains are
    snowed with our bones:

Must I go on harping on this? What madness moils
  my mind?
If you were dead, Turnus . . . would not I welcome
  these Trojans
As allies? I would. Then why not end this struggle
While you are still alive? What is the point of it?
50   What will your kinsfolk say, the Rutulians, if I
  send you
To death (God grant I do not) simply as one
  seeking
To be allied by marriage. Think of the chances
  of war.
Pity your aged father, so far away,
Sad in his house in Ardea, mourning your long
  absence!"
But Turnus' frenzy could not be budged by words,
Not by a hairsbreadth. In fact the voice of reason
Only enraged him the more (since he saw its
  point).
As soon as he could utter he snarled out:
"Thank you for your kind solicitude,
60   My dearest friend, but you can count that out!
I am grateful for the fine anxiety
You feel on my behalf but still I will thank you,
My dearest friend, to leave me alone to pledge
My life for Honor! Look, I can cast a javelin,
I can stab with the best of them, the wounds I
  inflict
Bleed to the death. Aeneas' mother-goddess
Will not be there to shroud her son's retreat
In mist—a typical woman's trick—or hide
  themselves
In empty shadows."
70   But the queen was appalled at the new risk of
  battle
And clutched the raving boy, her daughter's lover,
As if she were at the point of death and sobbed,
"Oh Turnus, if my tears move you, if you have
  a spark
Of love left for Amata—you are the only hope,
The balm of my wretched old age—you hold in
  your hands

Our Power and Glory, the whole house of Latinus
Relies on you, you are the only prop!
One thing I beg you: Do not cross swords with
  the Trojans,
For whatever the outcome of this fight my fortune
Will be the same as yours—if you die, Turnus,   *80*
I shall die too. I could not bear to see,
With captive eyes, my daughter wed to Aeneas."
At her mother's words Lavinia burst into tears,
Her cheeks suffused with a scarlet fever-flush—
As when a worker of Indian ivory
Has stained it with scarlet dye or where pale lilies
Are mingled with roses and glow with reflected
  color,
So did the colors come and go in her face.
Wild with passion Turnus gazed in her eyes
But all the more was he absolute for arms.   *90*
He answered Amata curtly, "No tears, please.
No such glum harbingers shall be my escort
Onto the grisly field, my dearest mother!
I am not free, I Turnus, to put off death!
Here, Idmon! Go and take to the tyrant Aeneas
This message which will not please him. Tell him
  this:
As soon as dawn tomorrow lights the sky
With her glowing wheels, let him make this
  command:
No Trojan may go into action against Rutulian.
Let Trojan and Rutulian rest suspended in truce.   *100*
And let us two alone decide this war
With our own blood. The hand of Lavinia
Upon that field alone must be sought and won!"

He spoke these words, then rushed into the palace,
Called for his horses, and reveled in their restive
And lively mettle—these were the horses given
By Orithyia herself to Pilumnus, they were his
  pride—
They were whiter than snow and speedier than
  the wind.
Around them bustled the busy charioteers
Patting their chests with the hollows of their hands *110*

And grooming their long manes. Now Turnus
    fitted
Onto his shoulders a hauberk stiff with scales
Of gold and golden-bronze, and got his sword,
His shield, and his helmet with its red-plumed
    horns
Adjusted comfortably,—the very sword
The Fire God forged for his father Daunus and
    held
White-hot, to anneal it in the waters of Styx.
Next he snatched his sturdy spear which was
    leaning
On a tall column in the palace-hall,
120   Spoil from Auruncan Actor, and brandished it
Till the shaft quivered; and he cried out, "Now!
My good spear that has never failed me yet—
The time has come! The famous Actor once
Wielded you, now in his right hand it is Turnus
Who wields you! —Oh grant me to lay him low—
This softy Phrygian and strip him of his armor,
And rub his crimped and oily hair in the dirt!"
And so he fulminated, his eyes flashing,
His whole face blazing in a passion of fury
130   Just as a bull bellows before a fight
And makes a passing pass at a tree with his horns,
And tosses the wind and scatters the sand, sparring
Before the fight for life begins in earnest.

Not a whit the less did Aeneas indulge his fury
And edge for battle, rampant in the armor
His mother had given him, delighted at this truce,
And the chance of ending the war. Then he
    soothed the fears
Of his comrades, and of nervous Iulus, expounding
The workings of fate and bid an answer be taken
140   To King Latinus stating his terms of peace.
Scarce had the day begun to spangle the
    mountain peaks
With glittering light, and the horses of the sun
Arisen from the deep, the breath from their
    nostrils bursting
In fiery steam, when the Trojans and Rutulians

Set out the grand Lists in a measured space
Beneath the walls of the mighty city; with hearths
And altars of turf set in the middle to gods
They honored in common. Some brought fire,
  some water,—
Priests these, in their ritual robes and wreathed
  with vervain.
The Italian host poured out in a flood from the   *150*
  gates,
Their javelins ready. From the other camp the
  whole
Of the Trojan and Tuscan force came headlong
  out,
With their varying weapons, no less fully armed
Than if the War God summoned them to battle.
Their commanders proudly flaunting their gold
  and purple
Streaked through the ranks of their thousand
  warriors—
Mnestheus, seed of Assaracus, brave Asilas,
Messapus tamer of horses, son of Neptune . . .
Then at a given signal each side turned back
To a sphere allotted. They drove their spears in   *160*
  the earth
And leant their shields against them. Then in a
  mob
Came the mothers, the unarmed crowd, the feeble
  old men,
And squatted on the towers and rooftops and took
  their stand
By the tall gates.
               But Juno from the heights—
(The hill is called the Alban hill today
But then it had no name nor honor nor glory)
Let her eyes range the plain and saw both armies,
Laurentine, Trojan; and saw Latinus' city.
Immediately she addressed herself to Juturna,
The sister of Turnus a goddess like herself   *170*
Whose sway was over the pools and the sounding
  rivers.
(The high King Almighty Jove had given her
This office as a sop for the maidenhead

He took from her.)
                    "Dear Nymph, grace of all rivers,
And very close to my heart—you are the dearest
Of all the nymphs of Latium whom the lust
Of Jove has forced to pleasure pleasureless,
Freely I gave you your due place in the Heavens—
Now learn from me the sorrows you must bear—
180 They are none of my making: lay no blame on me.
When fortune seemed to favor the Latian cause
And the Fates allowed it, I defended Turnus
And your city's walls—but now I see the boy
Involved in affairs beyond his power to control.
The day of doom and his enemy's triumph are
     near.
I cannot look on this combat or this treaty
With my own eyes—but you indeed may go
If you have the courage and bring your brother
     help
Greater than I can—and it is your sister's duty.
190 Juturna burst into tears and beat her beautiful
     breast.
"This is no time to weep!" cried Saturnian Juno—
"Hurry, and snatch your brother from death if
You can find any way, or break this treaty
And rouse the hosts to general war once more.
I am behind you to bolster your resolution!"
So saying she left her, wretched and perplexed.

Meanwhile the Kings came out. Latinus driving
A heavy four-horse chariot—his brows ablaze
With a circlet of twelve golden rays in token
200 Of the Sun his avatar. And Turnus rode
Behind a pair of white war-horses, and grasping
A pair of wide-bladed and iron-pointed spears.
Then lord Aeneas, root of the Roman race,
Refulgent with his starry shield and arms
Of heaven's making and after him Ascanius
Great Rome's next hope, came riding from the
     camp.
A priest in a snow-white robe drove in the young
Of a bristled sow, and an unshorn two-year sheep
And drove them to the altar already afire.

The heroes turned their eyes to the rising sun   *210*
And offered the salted grains and marked the
  animals'
Brows with their swords and poured the due
  libations.
Then reverent Aeneas prayed on his drawn sword,
"Let now the sun be witness and this very land
For whose sake I have endured so many trials,
Eternal Father and your Saturnian Consort,
O Goddess kindlier to us now, I pray;
Incomparable Mars, whose nod decides the battle;
On springs and rivers I call and every Power
Of the blue sky above, and of the blue sea below,   *220*
If the chance fall on Turnus the Italian
It is agreed the defeated shall depart
To Evander's city, Iulus shall resign
His claims upon this land and never again
Shall children of Aeneas come in arms
Or threaten this land with war. But, if (as I
Am disposed to believe, and may the gods
  confirm it)
Victory prove the favor of Mars to be mine—
I shall not bid Italian truckle to Trojan,
Nor seek a crown for myself—let our two peoples   *230*
Unconquered and on equal terms combine
Confederate for ever. I tender my own
Gods and their rituals; Latinus, as lord of both
  nations,
Shall have all Power civil and military;
My Trojans shall build and fortify me a city:
And Lavinia shall give her name to it."
First spoke Aeneas and then Latinus followed,
His eyes on heaven, his right hand stretched to
  the stars,
"I, too, Aeneas, swear by land and sea,
By the heavens above and by the twins of Latona,   *240*
By two-faced Janus, by the Infernal powers,
And by the shrines of that implacable Pluto;
Let our Great Parent hear whose thunderbolt
Confirms all treaties; I lay my hand on the altar,
I call to witness the gods and these fires between
  us—

Never shall come the day, I speak for all Italians,
That breaks this Treaty of Peace, whatever befall.
No Power on earth shall turn aside my purpose
Not though it plunge the world in a flood of waters
250 And shiver the heavens and crush them down to
　　hell!
—Even as this scepter (for it happened he held
A scepter in his hand) even as this scepter never
Could break into new leaf nor offer shade
From the moment it was cut from the living wood
And the ax lopped its foliage and its limbs,
And a craftsman worked it, sheathing it with bronze
And gave it for the Latin leaders to wield!"
With words like these they ratified the treaty
In the sight of all the nobles. Then performed
260 The ritual slaughter of the hallowed beasts,
Tore out their entrails, throbbing yet, and piled
　　them
In sacred dishes and laid them on the altar.

But in fact the Rutulians had for a long time
Felt dubious about this fight and now the more so
As they saw how unequally matched the
　　combatants were.
Turnus confirmed their fears as he softly stepped
Up to the altar and prayed with downcast eyes
And they saw his wasted cheeks and the color
　　drained
From all his youthful body—and Juturna
270 Immediately she saw the drift of their talk
As it spread from mouth to mouth among the
　　ranks,
And everyone uneasy and uncertain,
Put on the form of Camers—he was a hero
Of famous ancestry (the fabulous valor
Of his father no less evident in himself)—
As Camers, she threaded her way through the
　　army,
Knowing exactly what her purpose was,
Sowing the seeds of various rumors, saying:
"Do you feel no shame, Rutulians, to sacrifice
280 This single life for all of yours? Are we not

Of equal strength and number? Look, there at
  the Trojans,
The Arcadians too, and that infamous band of
  Etruscans,
The foes of Turnus; why, if but half of our army
Went into action we would scarcely have foes
  enough!
Turnus indeed will go to the gods at whose altars
He kneels, and his fame is sure; he will live on
  the lips
Of all men—we who now sit on, so inert and
  passive
On the very fields we may lose, our country lost—
We shall be forced to obey these insolent masters!"
With words like these she roused the young   *290*
  soldiers' hearts
To a fever pitch and more and more the murmur
Pervaded the ranks—both Latin and Laurentine
Were utterly changed. And men whose only
  thought
Was rest from battle and hope for peaceful times
Now called for arms and wished the treaty undone
And had sympathy for the unfair fate of Turnus.
And now Juturna added the final touch—
A sign from heaven, a sign which could not more
Completely confuse the minds of the Italians
And make them dupes of its supernatural meaning, *300*
For the Bird of Jove, an eagle red-gold on the wing
In the glowing sky was harrying the shore-birds
And the whole screaming flock of birds in the air,
When suddenly he stooped to the wave-level
And snatched a magnificent swan in his cruel
  talons.
The Italians watched intently and saw a marvel,
For all the birds with a cry turned flight into
  attack!
They darkened the air with their wings and like
  a cloud
Mobbed him so fiercely he could not sustain their
  insistent pressure
And the swan's weight, and let it fall from his   *310*
  claws

Into a stream and fled into the clouds.
The Rutulians greeted the augury with a roar
And made ready for action. Tolumnius the prophet
Was first to put his feelings into words:
"This O this is what I have often prayed for!
I embrace it, I see in it the hand of heaven!
I will lead you, even I! Take up your arms
O my unhappy people whom an invader
Cruelly menaces with the threat of war
320 And holds your shores by force—as if you were
A feeble flock of birds—but it is *he*
Who shall hoist his sails and seek escape far
Over the deep sea! Be single-hearted!
Close up your ranks and rally to the prince
This fight would rob you of!" And rushing forward
He hurled a spear into the heart of the foe.
The cherry-wood shaft whistled as it clove the air
And as it flew a colossal shout arose.
In all the ranks was uproar and hearts beat wildly.
330 The spear whirled on and directly in its path
There stood by chance nine brothers, splendid sons
Whom one devoted Tuscan mother bore
To Gylippus the Arcadian. One of these
It was whom the spear struck at the waist
Just where the braided belt chafes and the buckle
Presses the sides—he was a fine pattern
Of young manhood in his glittering armor,
But now transfixed through the ribs he fell, stricken
Full length on the yellow sand. And now his brothers
340 In a single body of grief and fury charged
Blindly with swords and iron weapons: against them
Advanced the Laurentines—then all the melee:
Trojans, Etruscans, Arcadians in painted armor
Poured like a flood, obsessed by one single passion—
To settle the issue with steel. The altars were stripped—
(A shower of weapons blackened all the sky)
They took the hearths and votive cups away—

(A storm of deadly metal came lashing down).
Latinus now the truce was broken fled
With his discomfited gods: some of his men   *350*
Harnessed war-chariots, others leaping on
   horseback
Paraded with drawn swords and fiery Messapus
   craving
To break the truce spurred his war-horses on
Against the king Aulestes a Tuscan king
In full regalia, and the wretched fellow
Retreating tripped on the altars set behind him,
And fell flat down on his head and shoulders,
   Messapus
Rearing above him brandishing his spear,
Thrust home as he prayed for mercy, shouting out:
"He has his answer! This is a better offering   *360*
To the almighty gods!" The Italians rushed
To despoil his body still warm as it lay.
Corynaeus snatched a firebrand from an altar
Anticipating Ebysus as he closed,
And set his beard afire—and his heavy beard
Flared up and smelt of its singeing hair and flesh,
And Corynaeus followed his first thrust up,
And grasping his dazed enemy by the hair
With his left hand and digging his knees in his back
With all his weight pinned him down to the ground   *370*
And knifed him. Podalirius overran
Alsus the shepherd as he threaded through
The maze of front-line weapons and stood over
   him
With naked sword: but he drew back his ax
And split him neck and chine and the blood
   spurted
All over all his arms; and a grim repose
Crushed out the light and eternal darkness pressed
Down on his eyes, a heavy iron sleep.
But good Aeneas, his head bare, stretched out
His hand unarmed and shouted to his men: *380*
"Where are you rushing off? Why this sudden
   uproar?
Oh, curb your wrath: the treaty is made already
And all its terms agreed! It is my right

And mine alone to fight—I will ratify
This treaty with my strong arm—then please
   allow me
My right and have no fears—Turnus is mine
In accordance with the sacrifice, he is mine alone!"
But even in the midst of those adjurations
See, where an arrow came whistling through the air
390   Straight for the hero—none knew who was the
   archer,
Or on what airs let loose, nor who should win
Such renown for the Rutulians—was it a god?
Was it sheer chance? The author of the glory
Remained unknown or hidden—none ever boasted
Of wounding Aeneas.
                              Turnus saw Aeneas
Leaving the field, his captains in dismay,
And a sudden spark of hope flared in his heart.
Exulting he called for horses, arms, with a leap
He was in his chariot, ready, and grasped the reins.
400   Many a hero fell to his whirlwind onset,
Many were bowled over to live or die as the
   chariot
Mowed through the ranks, or as he gathered up
New spears to hurl at the backs of fleeing men.
He seemed like bloodstained Mars as he churns
   along
By the icy Hebrus, clanging on his shield,
Giving his horses rein as they scent a battle;
(Faster than southern or western wind they course
Over the plains, Thrace shudders at the pulse
Of the hoofbeats and around him loom the figures
410   Of Fear, black visaged, and Wrath, and Treachery,
His henchmen). So through the thick of battle
   Turnus
Flashed at full tilt, lashing his sweating horses,
Trampling his wretched foes, and the flying hoofs
Showered a bloody dew till the sand was caked
With Trojan blood—
                              The blood of Sthenelus,
Thamyrus, Pholus—these two in close combat—
All done to death. And from afar, like Sthenelus,
Glaucus and Lades, Imbrasus' two sons.

He had brought them up in Lycia and trained them
  for battle
Both in close combat and in horseback tactics,   *420*
To outstrip the wind in speed and he had
  equipped them.
—And now Turnus had killed them. On another
Front of the battle Eumedes rode out,
The famous warrior-son of ancient Dolon,
Taking after his grandfather in his name;
In his courage and bodily skill after his father
Who once had dared to demand Achilles' chariot
As his reward for going out to spy
On the Greek camp—but Diomede saw that he got
A reward far other—he had no pretentions now   *430*
For Achilles' chariot. . . . And so Turnus
Saw him, from far away across the plain,
Took a long shot with a javelin and closed in,
Jumped from his twin-horsed chariot, stood over
  him,
Put his foot on his half-dead neck and wrenched
The sword from his enemy's flaccid hand and
  plunged it
Flashing into his throat and mocked him crying:
"Trojan! this is a bed of western land you lie on,
This is the measure of your conquest—you who try
To try *me* with the sword! Your bones are your   *440*
  city's foundations!"
And his next spear-thrust sent Asbytes to join him.
And Chloreus and Sybaris, Dares and Thersilochus
And Thymoetes thrown from his bucking horse.
And just as the blast of the north wind from
  Edonia
Ruffles the Aegean, and blows back the breaking
  wave,
So, wherever he cuts his path, the waves of
  warriors
Yield and turn back and his impetus bears him
  onward,
The winds blowing his plume back in his chariot
  wake.
But Phegeus would not budge in his obstinate
  enmity;

450   He hurled himself at the foaming horses' heads
     And with his strong right hand he turned them
       aside,
     Then he hung on, was dragged as he clung to the
       harness,
     And Turnus speared him through his twin-plated
       mail,
     And gave him a flesh-wound: but he had his shield
       at guard,
     Hung on and tried to bring his sword to bear
     When the chariot wheel in its headlong revolution
     Struck him and laid him flat, and Turnus
       following up
     With a sword sweep, exactly between breastplate
       and helmet,
     Cut off his head and let his trunk rot in the sand.
460   But now while Turnus ramped death-dealing about
       the plain,
     Mnestheus, Ascanius and loyal Achates
     Supported Aeneas bleeding and lurching back
     To camp, his limping weight leant on a long spear.
     In a frenzy he tugged at the broken arrow-shaft
     Then bid them enlarge the wound with a broad
       sword
     Down to the hidden barb as the readiest method
     Of easing the pain and getting him back to the
       fight.
     Iapyx, now, Iasus' son came to his side,
     Whom Apollo adored—to whom, so infatuated,
470   The god would willingly have given the bent of
       his being,
     And his arts: the lyre, his powers of prophecy,
     His speed as an archer. —But Iapyx was set
     On keeping his dying father from the grave,
     And he preferred to know the properties
     Of herbs and the technique of healing and quietly
     To ply his quiet art. Aeneas, propped
     On his long spear, cursed and swore indifferent
     To the crowd of anxious warriors around him,
     Deaf to Iulus' grief. And the old doctor,
480   His garments taut about him in the manner
     Of Paeon the God of doctors, tried his skill,

Tried everything he knew, every single one
Of Apollo's potent herbs—but nothing worked.
He tried to ease the arrowhead with his fingers
And then with his forceps—neither worked at all.
Nor Fortune favored him, nor his patron Apollo.
And all the time nearer and louder, louder
And nearer grew the louring threat of arms
Over the plain. The sky thickened with dust,
The horsemen closed at the gallop: their darts   *490*
    rained down
Into the midst of the camp. The sour cry
Of young men battling, of young men fallen
In the throes of battle rose and filled the sky.
But Venus, seeing her son's unmerited woes
Picked from Mount Ida in Crete the plant
    Dictamnus—
Its stalk stands high with leaves, its flower is
    purple,
And the wounded wild goats eat it when they
    have arrows
Stuck in their backs—and, cloaked in a cloud of
    mist,
She carried this plant down and infused with it
The waters they had poured into an urn,   *500*
And added tonic ambrosia, a scented panacea,
And nobody knew it. Old Iapyx knew nothing,
As he bathed the wound with the water ignorant
Of its powers—but suddenly all the pain Aeneas
Had felt vanished, and the wound's bleeding
    stanched.
Then of itself, without anyone freeing it,
The arrowhead fell out into his hand
And Aeneas was restored to his full strength.
"Quickly!" Iapyx shouted, "bring the hero his
    arms!
Can nobody move?" (and he was the first to rouse   *510*
Their spirits to fight the foe). "This was not done
By human agency nor medical skill,
Nor was it my right hand healed you, Aeneas;
Some greater power, some god it was and he
Is sending you back to even greater deeds!"
Eager for battle, he donned his golden greaves

And shook his glittering spear chafing
At these delays, and as soon as his shield was
    adjusted
And his cuirass on his back he embraced Ascanius
520 And kissed him through his vizor and said to him:
"Learn from me what is valor and true endeavor.
Learn luck from others! Today it is my right hand
That shall keep you safe in battle—and it shall
    lead you
To great rewards—now see to it, my son,
When you have grown to manhood that you keep
The example of your kinsman clear in mind—
I am Aeneas, I am your father, Hector
Your uncle—let us be your inspiration!"
So saying, out through the gates of the camp he
    bore
530 His mighty frame shaking his huge spear.
At the same time Antheus and Mnestheus,
Their companies in close order, hurtled out.
The camp was emptied, the whole force streamed
    to the field,
The plain was blind with dust, the earth quivered
And quaked with the beat of their feet. And
    Turnus saw them
From his rampart opposite, his Ausonians saw
    them
And a chill shudder shook them to the marrow.
And first, of all the Latins, Juturna heard
And understood the sound, and shrank back
    trembling.
540 Over the plain sped Aeneas urging his
    threatening forces,
Like a storm-cloud he came that bursts from
    heaven,
Bred in the mid-sea sweeping towards the land,
And far inland the wretched farmers' hearts
Beat in foreboding—it will uproot and wreck
Their fruit-trees, it will dash everything flat
And the winds are its harbingers—bearing its
    sound to the shore.
—Even so, as he urged his forces against the foe,

Was the Trojan leader and his men massed
  together
To form a single body. And Thymbraeus
Put vast Osiris to the sword. Mnestheus   *550*
Accounted for Archetius, Achates
Cut Epulo to pieces, Gyas Ufens,
Tolumnius the prophet who had been
The first to throw his dart against the Trojans
Himself fell, and a shout was raised to heaven
And now it was the Rutulians' turn to break
And flee across the plain in whirls of dust.
Aeneas would not stoop to kill these flyers
Nor to engage any that offered combat
Foot to foot with weapons poised—through the   *560*
  thick murk
He was on the track of Turnus, none but Turnus,
No other foe did he claim to fight but Turnus,
Demanding him for combat and none else.
Appalled with fear at thought of such a battle
Juturna brave as a man, pitched out Metiscus,
Turnus' charioteer, as he stood with the reins
  gathered,
And left him far behind in the chariot's wake.
Taking his place she gripped the flexing reins
And drove the chariot in Metiscus' guise—
Voice, body, armor—as a coal-black swallow   *570*
Flits through the wide rooms of some wealthy
  squire
Picking up tiny scraps for her clamoring nestlings,
Now twittering in the empty barns, now round the
  farm-ponds,
Just so Juturna jinked her way through the enemy
And traversed the whole plain at full tilt.
Sometimes she let them see her glorying brother
But never enough for a blow: she whirled over
  the plain.
No less Aeneas tracked his twisting path
And clamored for Turnus through the general
  welter.
Often he sighted him, and on foot strove   *580*
To pace the horses, as often Juturna wrenched

The chariot aside. What could Aeneas do?
Hither and thither he lunged, all to no purpose,
His mind distracted with conflicting aims.
Then suddenly Messapus, running lightly,
With a couple of tough spears in his left hand
Aimed at Aeneas and shot a spinning throw
That seemed sure to strike him, but Aeneas ducked
Onto one knee shrugging close his armor
590 And the spear lopped the top off the crest of his
    helmet:
His anger boiled. He felt riled by the enemy
    treachery
As he saw the chariot and its horses whirl away.
Long he invoked Jove and the altars of the
    broken treaty,
Then flung himself into the thick of things
And with the help of Mars began to inflict
A ruthless wholesale slaughter, giving free rein
To all his fury.

What god shall sing of the bitter strife, of the
    different
Ways to their doom of the slaughtered chiefs as
    now
600 Aeneas here and Turnus there quartered the
    battlefield?
O Jove, was it indeed your will that nations
Who were to live together in peace for ever
Should meet in such a clash? Aeneas confronted
    Sucro
The first Rutulian to stem the Trojan onrush—
But not for long—the hero drove his sword
Death's swiftest way to the heart through its fence
    of ribs.
Thrown from his horse Amycus fell foul of Turnus,
And fought on foot, and so did his brother
    Diores—
The one was slain with a long spear, the other
610 With the sword-blade, then Turnus cut their
    heads off
And hung them from his chariot, and bore them
    off

Dripping their bloody dew. Aeneas despatched
  Talo
Tanais and brave Cethegus, the three together,
And sad Onites too he sent to his death,
A son of the house of Echion, Peridia's son.
Some brothers from Lycia, from Apollo's lands,
Were killed by Turnus and so was poor Menoetes
A youth who hated war—in vain—an Arcadian
Whose craft it had been to fish the well-stocked
  waters
Of Lerna, who lived in poverty and knew nothing   *620*
Of power and place, whose father rented ground
  there
And sowed his crops. But now like fires let loose
From different sides to consume a bone-dry forest
Where the bay-bushes spit and crackle; or like
  two streams
Roaring in foaming cataracts from the peaks
That rush to the sea, each scouring its own
  channel—
So no less swiftly did Turnus and Aeneas
Tear through the battle, their fury in full spate,
Now, now, as never before—their invincible hearts
Swollen to bursting, the sum of all their strength   *630*
In every blow. Aeneas felled Murranus
With the whirling hurl of a large chunk of rock—
Murranus, chanting ever the ancient names
Of sire and grandsire, all his lineage traced
Through the line of Latium's kings, stretched now
With the reins and the yoke of his chariot above
  him—
And the wheels rolled him forward to be trampled
Under his horses' hoofs all heedless of their
  master.
Turnus disposed of Hyllus as he charged
In wild overweening fury, his dart struck home   *640*
On the golden forehead-guard of his helmet,
  pierced it,
And stayed fixed in his brain. And you, Cretheus,
Bravest of Greeks, not even your strong right arm
Could save you from Turnus; nor could
  Cupencus' gods

Protect him from the onset of Aeneas.
Poor wretch, his brazen shield afforded him
No check to the thrusting steel and he took the
　　blow
Full in the breast. You too, O Aeolus,
The Laurentine plains saw fall and lie spreadeagled
650　Upon their floors. You fell, whom the ranks of
　　Greeks
Could never overthrow, no, nor Achilles
The wrecker of Priam's empire—and here was
　　your end:
Your halls were at Ida's foot, the great estates
Of Lyrnesus: your tomb is here, on Laurentine soil.
But now in their full strength the two armies
　　clashed,
All the clans of Latins, all the Dardanids,
Mnestheus, and fierce Serestus, Messapus tamer
　　of horses,
Valiant Asilas, the whole contingent of Tuscans,
Evander's Arcadian horsemen, and every man
660　Strained to the uttermost, the uttermost peak
Of his resources, without rest or respite,
Were locked in the throes of all-embracing battle.

Then Venus, most beautiful mother of Aeneas,
Put in his mind this thought: to march to the walls,
To switch his forces suddenly onto the city
And stun the Latians in a surprise attack.
And he, as he tracked Turnus through the battle
Hither and thither, cast his hunting eye
On the safe city basking in its immunity
670　From the turmoil of the battle, aloof and quiet.
The vision of a more telling feat of arms
Immediately gripped his mind: he summoned his
　　captains
Mnestheus, and Sergestus, and bold Serestus,
And standing on a mound to which the rest
Of the Trojan forces rallied in close order
Their weapons at the ready, standing there
On the top of the mound he spoke these words
　　to them.
"These are my orders: to be obeyed at once:

Jove is with us. Let nobody be the slower
Because this change of plan is a sudden one: *680*
Today I propose to raze this city, the cause
Of the war, Latinus' capital. —Unless
They acknowledge defeat and willingly submit
I will level its smoking turrets with the ground.
Am I going to wait for Turnus till he is pleased
To fight me?—and, beaten, ask for a second chance?
O Countrymen, here is the root and branch
Of this evil war! Fetch faggots! Exact with fire
The restoration of the broken treaty!"
Such were his words, and all his troops massed   *690*
Into a wedge and advanced to the city walls.
Suddenly, in a flash, scaling ladders and torches
Appeared and some of his men surprised the
    gateposts killing
The sentries, others discharged their spinning darts
And blackened the sky with weapons. Among
    the first,
Aeneas shook his fist beneath the ramparts
And calling the gods to witness cursed Latinus
For forcing him a second time to battle
And breaking the new treaty like the old.
The dithering citizens gave way to panic: *700*
Some bade the city and its gates be opened
To the Trojan invaders, and dragged the king
    himself
Onto the walls; but others seized up arms
Obdurate in defense—as when a shepherd
Has traced a swarm of bees to their hidden hive
In a hollow of volcanic rock and fills it
With acrid smoke and the desperate bees inside
Whirl round their waxen citadel and whet their
    wrath
With violent buzzings and the black smoke winds
Through every cell and the whole rock hums   *710*
With the pent noise within, and the smoke rises
Into the empty air.
                          —Then another blow
Fell on the weary Latins and shook the city
To its foundations. For when the Queen from
    her palace

Saw the enemy advance, the walls assailed,
Fire leap to the rooftops, and nowhere any counter,
No Rutulian stand, no sign of Turnus' troops,
The unhappy woman assumed her son had been
Killed in the battle, and her mind gave way.
720 In an access of sudden agony she shrieked
That she was the cause and fountainhead of
    these evils
And wildly pouring words in her frenzy of grief
She tore her purple robes with desperate fingers
And, fixed on a horrible death, knotted a noose
From a high beam. And when the unhappy women
Of Latium became aware of this tragedy,
Lavinia her daughter was the first
To rend her yellow hair and her rosy cheek
With her own hand and everyone about her
730 Went wild with grief and the palace rang with
    lament.
And soon the ghastly story spread outside
Through all the town, hearts sank, Latinus rent
His robes in shreds, numbed with his wife's end
And the ruin of his city, matting his white hairs
With a thick scurf of dust and cursing himself
For not receiving Aeneas from the first,
And freely fostering his daughter's marriage.

Meanwhile right at the far end of the plain
Fire-eating Turnus was chasing a few stragglers,
740 But his ardor was waning fast; and his zest and
    relish
In the onrush of his horses lessened and lessened,
Borne on the breeze he heard a confused clamor,
Foreboding unknown terrors, the joyless swell
Of the city's wailing—"Alas for me!" he cried,
"What grief is this so great that it shakes the walls?
What is that cry that strains here for the city?"
He tugged the reins and halted, torn in mind.
And then his sister, still rigged as Metiscus
Guiding the chariot, at the reins made answer:
750 "Let us hunt these Trojans here, where our success
Shows us it is our way—there are many others
Perfectly able to defend our homes:

Aeneas attacks the Italians, and gives battle:
Then let us deal as ruthless death to the Trojans—
Shall you take second place in number of slain,
In prowess and in honor?" And Turnus answered,
"Sister, I knew you from the very moment
Your cunning wrecked the treaty and you launched
Yourself to war, and now it is in vain
That you disguise your godhead— But what God   760
Upon Olympus willed that you should come
And bear such heavy toil? Was it to see
The cruel death-throes of your wretched brother?
For what can I do? What turn of luck can offer
Me safety? I have seen before my eyes
Murranus die calling upon my name—
My dearest friend, nor could there be a dearer,
His mighty body felled with as mighty a wound.
Poor Ufens is dead too—at least to be spared
The sight of my disgrace— The Trojans hold   770
His body and arms, and must I suffer our homes
To be razed—the one disaster lacking yet—
And not avenge with my sword the taunts of
    Drances?
Shall I turn tail, shall this country see me fleeing?
Is death so bitter then? O, you Powers of Death
Be gracious to me, since the Gods above
Have left me, I shall come down to you
A stainless soul and guiltless of cowardice
Worthy in all my deeds of my famous forbears!"
He hardly had time to finish when, behold!   780
Through the midst of the enemy ranks, his horse
    lathered,
Saces came tearing, an arrow fixed in his face,
Imploring Turnus— "Turnus, our last hope
Is in you! Have pity on your people! Aeneas
Lours with thunderous arms and threatens to raze
Our citadel to the ground, our tall Italian
    stronghold!
Already the firebrands fly roof-high and every
    Latin—
Head, heart, and eye is turned towards you—
    Latinus,
Our very king, but mumbles wondering whom

790   To call his daughter's lord, and with whom is his
           alliance.
       The Queen too, your most trustworthy ally,
       Has died by her own hand in terror of the times:
       It is only Messapus and fierce Atinas
       Who have kept our line together before the gates
       And they are ringed with a thick hedge of steel,
       While you range in your chariot wide about
       A plain the war has ebbed from!"
       Turnus stood dumfounded in a silent moil of
           thoughts,
       A deep shame seared his heart but mingled with it
800   Was grief and madness, passion fanned to frenzy
       And consciousness of Right. And when his
           thoughts
       Returned to the actual present his burning gaze
       Focused upon the city walls and anxiously
       He surveyed the mighty city from his chariot . . .
       Oh, and a plume of flame reared up over the roofs
       And leapt sky-high and licked the top of a tower,
       A tower which he himself had built up high,
       Founded on wheels with reinforcing beams
       And a drawbridge at each story. And he said,
810   "O sister, now is the moment, now the triumph
           of Fate,
       Do not attempt to delay me. Wherever the Gods
       And cruel fortune bid, there must we follow.
       I am set upon meeting Aeneas, face to face.
       I am set upon bearing whatever bitter form
       Of death I must, but never more, my sister,
       Shall you see me disgraced. But first, I beg you,
       Let me indulge my frenzy before I die
       In one last deed!" So saying he leapt down
       From his chariot and rushed through the rain of
           enemy weapons,
820   Leaving his sister grievous, and burst full-tilt
       On the enemy lines. He came like a rock
       That from a mountain peak comes suddenly
           . headlong
       Nudged by the winds, or washed out by a storm
       Or by the long loosening of time. Sheer down
       The grim rock borne by its own huge impetus

Plunges and rolls men, trees, and beasts in its track.
—So Turnus shattered the ranks and tore his way
To the city walls where all the earth was deepest
In bloody slush and the air was shrill with spears.
He made a sign with his hand and shouted loud,   *830*
"Rutulians, cease! Latins put up your weapons!
Whatever fortune brings, the lot is mine—
Juster it is that I alone should expiate
The truce for all of you, and settle this with the
     sword!"
Then all his men drew back, and left a space in
     the middle.

But hearing Turnus' name Aeneas the leader
Quit the high citadel, quit the walls, brushed off
All hindrance, broke off his whole assault,
Shouted for joy, struck thunder from his armor,
As huge as Athos or Eryx or Father Appenine   *840*
When he throbs loud with his quivering holm-oaks
And lifts his snowy head with joy to the sky.
At this fell moment Rutulians and Trojans
And all the Italians fixed their eyes upon him,
Those who were holding the high towers, those
With battering rams beating at the foundations—
All took their armor off. Even Latinus
Stared in amazement at the two great heroes
Born in such different quarters of the world,
Now met together to contest the issue   *850*
At the point of the sword. As soon as a space
     was cleared
The two advanced throwing their spears from a
     distance,
Then closing with a brazen clang of shields.
Earth groaned; their swords clashed faster and
     faster clashed,
Each had his mingled share of luck and skill.
As when on mighty Sila or Taburnus heights
Two bulls in bitter rivalry charge at each other
With lowered horns and their terrified herdsmen
     shrink
And the whole herd stands dumb with fear while
     the heifers

860 Await in silence who will be the leader
Whom all the herds are to follow: and they clash
In violent onslaught themselves with lowered
    horns,
And neck and shoulder stream with gouts of blood
While the whole grove resounds with their
    bellowing—
So did Aeneas of Troy and Daunian Turnus
Clash with their shields, and the colossal din
Filled all the firmament. Almighty Jove
Balanced the two heroes in his scales
To see which would be doomed and sink to death.
870 Thinking the time propitious Turnus led
And put his whole weight behind a single sword-
    thrust.
The Trojans and anxious Latins yelled, both armies
Tensed with excitement. But the treacherous sword
Shivered to bits in mid-stroke and his doom was
    sealed
If he could not flee for respite. Faster than east
    wind
He fled, as he saw the hilt of a strange sword
In his helpless hand. Was it his charioteer's
Metiscus' sword he had snatched up in his haste
As headlong for the battle he boarded his chariot
880 Leaving his father's sword behind? So went the
    story.
At least for a long time it had sufficed to drub
Retreating Trojans—but faced with a sword forged
By Vulcan himself the mortal blade splintered
Like brittle ice at the first blow, and now
Its fragments glittered from the yellow sand.
And Turnus panicked at the sight and tried
To escape into open country, now here, now there,
Weaving a fruitless course, for all around him
The encircling Trojans stood in a ring unbroken,
890 And one way lay a wide marsh and the other
The city's ramparts frowning barred his way.
Although the arrow-wound slowed him at times,
Aeneas pressed in pursuit of his frightened foe
—He was like a hound that has its stag penned
By a river or shied by a line of scarlet feathers,

And closes up in full cry and the poor beast
Caught between riverbank and snare, in terror
Doubles a thousand ways and the Umbrian hound
Keen for the kill snaps empty jaws in the air
By a hairsbreadth missing his hold.   *900*

                And then the shouting
Grew to a roar and the river banks and pools
Re-echoed round about and the heavens rang.
And Turnus as he fled chid all the Rutulians,
Calling on each by name and clamoring
For his own sword; but Aeneas threatened death
And total destruction of the city if anyone
Dared to produce it, so none dared for terror.
And on he thrust despite the wound. Five times
They circled, to and fro five bitter times,
This was no exhibition match for a prize,   *910*
They were fighting for Turnus' life, for his
   lifeblood.
It happened a bitter-leaved wild olive tree
Sacred to Faunus once had flourished here;
Now it was just a stump revered by sailors
Who, saved from the sea, were used to fasten to it
Their votive offerings to their Laurentine God,
Their dedicated robes, but the gross Trojans
Having no reverence for this god had felled it
To level the Lists for the fight—and in this trunk
Aeneas' spear stuck fast, as it had flown   *920*
Of its own momentum; now it was stuck fast.
And Aeneas stood over it and heaved and
   wrenched,
Needing to throw it after a foe too fleet
For him to close with. Turnus mad with fear
Prayed to the god, "O Faunus, pity me;
And you, dear native soil, hold fast the spear,
If I have kept you in reverence when these Trojans
Impiously have defiled you by this invasion."
His prayers were not in vain, the god came to his
   aid.
Nothing Aeneas could do with all his might   *930*
Could budge the spear from the vise of the holy
   wood.
And while he wrenched and heaved at it, Juturna

Once more in the guise of Metiscus darted up
And gave her brother his proper sword again.
Venus, furious at the license given
This minor goddess, loosed the spear from the bole
And the two heroes, refreshed in body, rearmed,
Turnus wielding his sword, Aeneas his long spear,
Bristled opposed again under the sway of Mars.

940 In the meanwhile the all-powerful King of Olympus
Addressed Juno as she watched the battle
Wrapped in a cold cloud, "My wife, my Queen,
What is the end of this to be? What coup de grâce
Have you in mind? —You know, and admit you
      know,
That Aeneas has his niche as a god in heaven—
What is your place in that cold cloud, what are
      you plotting?
Was it right a mortal should mar a god with a
      wound?
(And saving Juturna's aid would he have his
      sword back?)
Should beaten Turnus have a new lease of life?
950 Now at the last gasp, listen to my entreaties,
Do not, I beg you, bite your lips and swallow
Resentment down so often in silence. Now
Is the moment of decision. You have had power
To harry the Trojans, land and sea, to induce
This loathsome war, to smirch a house and taint
A wedding with pain. More I forbid completely!"
So Jove pronounced, and Juno with downcast eyes,
"Indeed, great lord, because I know it to be
Your will I unwillingly withdraw my favor
960 From Turnus—or you would not see me aloof
Aloft alone, enduring whatever I must,
Deservedly or no; but girt with flame
I would take my stand in the very battle line
And force the Trojans into their enemies' hands!
As for Juturna, I confess I urged her
To go to the help of her hapless brother approving
Deeds even greater if she could save his life,
But never that she should wield a bow or spear.
And now I swear by the source of the river Styx,

That unappeasable spring, the one sanction   *970*
That binds us gods above. I, for my part, withdraw
And quit this detestable battle. But I beg
One boon forbidden by no laws of Fate.
I sue for Latium and the dignity
Of a race that is your own, when peace at last
Is ratified by a happy marriage, and a treaty
Of mutual alliance made, so be it. —Then, my lord,
Let it not be your will to force the Latins
To change their ancient name in their own land,
Let them not be Trojans. Let them not change   *980*
Their language or their way of dress. Let Latium
Still stand, let Alban kings in endless dynasties
Reign there, and sturdy from Italian stock
A breed of Romans arise. But Troy has fallen.
So let her lie fallen, her name with her!"
Smiling, the Father of Mankind and the World
Made answer, "Own true sister of Jove indeed,
And child of Saturn also, so high the seas
Of passion surging in your breast! But come,
Quell this frenzy that you have indulged in vain.   *990*
I grant your petition, you have gained your way,
And willingly I obey you. The Ausonians
Shall keep the speech and customs of their
    forefathers,
Their name shall be as it is. As for the Trojans
They shall but blend and mingle with Latin blood.
I shall direct them in their modes of worship
And sacred rites, I shall see they are all Latins
And speak one tongue. The race that shall arise
From this infusion of Ausonian blood
In piety shall transcend all men on earth   *1000*
And even the gods; no nation, you will see,
Shall worship you more reverently than they."
Juno nodded assent and her sullen mood
Was turned to joy, and in that very instant
Quitting her cloud she departed from the sky.

This done the Father communed with himself
Weighing in mind a plan to wean Juturna
Away from her fighting brother.
                   There are twin fiends

Known as the Furies born of the blackest midnight,
1010 Megaera of Tartarus with them, at one birth,
And their dam enwound them in serpents and gave
    them wings
With the speed of the wind. And these two lie by
    the throne
To wait on His royal wrath and twist the knife-
    point
Of fear into weak mortality whenever the King of
    the Gods
Wreaks pestilence or death, or terrorizes
Cities deserving his censure with threats of war.
One of these it was that the God despatched
From the height of heaven and bade her confront
    Juturna
As earnest of his will. And down like a whirlwind
1020 She stooped to earth, like an arrow shot through
    a cloud
By a Parthian or Cydonian—an arrow tipped
With poison for which no antidote exists—
Whirring through wreathing mist, impossible to
    foresee,
Yet suddenly striking home—and even so
This daughter of Night dived headlong to the earth.
Soon as she saw the Trojans, and Turnus' army,
She suddenly shrank into the shape of the bird
That sits by night on tombs and deserted roofs
Croaking late song amid the gathering gloom.
1030 Again and again in this disguise the fiend
Flutters in Turnus' face, flapping aside his shield
With her wing-beats.

                              Turnus was paralyzed
With a strange terror: his hair stood on end
And his voice stuck in his throat.
But when Juturna recognized from afar
The pulse of the Furies' wings the wretched nymph
In a sister's throes scored her cheeks with her nails,
Beat her breast, and plucked at her loosened hair:
"What help can your sister bring you now, Turnus?
1040 And what is to be my fate, after such long
    endurance?
What art have I to prolong your life? Can I range

My powers against such a monster? Now, now,
I must quit the field. You disgusting birds of ill
    omen
Do not appall me more; I am afraid already.
I know the beat of your wings with its sound of
    death—
It is the overmastering will of Jove,
I cannot fail to see it. Is this the reward
For my lost virginity? Why did he give me the gift
Of eternal life? O why was the law of death
Annulled for me? Else I could put an end   1050
To this tale of anguish, now at this very instant,
And hand in hand with my wretched brother go
To Death's dark house! Is this my immortality?
Will there be any joy in life bereft
Of you my brother? O that a gulf might open
Deep enough in the earth to swallow me,
For all I am a goddess, down to the Shades!"
Such were her words. And then she swathed her
    head
In a gray veil and shaken with heavy sobs
Plunged to the depths of her stream and hid her   1060
    godhead.

As for Aeneas he was closing in
Brandishing his spear huge as a tree-trunk,
And from his iron resolve he roared out: "Turnus!
What new delay can you make? Do you still
    retreat?
This is no foot race, is it?
This is a hand-to-hand fight—a fight to the death.
Take any disguise you may, summon whatever
Reserves of strength or cunning you possess,
Take wings to the starry heights, if you like, or
    hide
In the cavernous depth of the earth!" And   1070
    Turnus answered
With a toss of his head: "Fierce man, I am not
    afraid
Of your violent words—it is the gods I fear,
And my enemy Jove." He said not a word more,
But suddenly catching sight of a huge stone,

Ancient and huge, that lay by chance on the plain,
(An old mere-stone to mark a boundary
And save disputes) and scarcely could a dozen
Men of our own day have raised it to their
    shoulder
So puny are the frames our world produces—
1080 Yet he, great hero, snatched it up in his hand,
Drew himself up and taking a run to do it
Hurled it against his foe—but had no feeling
Of heaving or hurling, running, or moving the
    missile.
His knees gave, his blood froze. And the stone
Lobbed through the empty air and fell short
Doing no damage.
                Just as it is in dreams
At the time of night when we are deepest asleep,
We seem to want to exert our utmost efforts
But cannot move and in the very midst
1090 Of our greatest striving helplessly sink down,
Our tongues cleave, we cannot move a muscle
Though knowing our bodies' powers, we cannot
    utter
A word or a sound—just so it was with Turnus.
Whatever outlet of his powers he sought
The baleful Fury banned. Then through his mind
Passed a succession of changing images.
He looked to his Rutulians and to his city;
Faltered in fear, shrank from the immanent spear,
Found no escape, could summon no strength to
    attack,
1100 Nor could he see the chariot with his sister.

Aeneas, as Turnus shrank, stood poised to strike
With the fatal spear; judged the range with his eye,
And then with all his strength behind it, hurled!
Never did block of stone shot from a siege-engine
So loudly whirr, never did thunder-peal
So loudly crash after the lightning-stroke;
Like a black whirlwind on whistled the spear
With its load of dreadful death and penetrating
The edge of the sevenfold shield, then the cuirass,
1110 Skewered the hero's thigh, and down he sank

His knee doubled under him. The Rutulians rose
With a groan that the hills and groves re-echoed
Far and wide. Stretched on the ground Turnus
Looked up at Aeneas and raised an entreating
   hand,
"This is my due," he said, "I make no appeal.
Use what your fortune proffers. Only this.
If you can feel for a father's misery
(Anchises was a father such as mine)
Pity my father Daunus, he is old,
Restore me alive, or dead if death you choose,   *1120*
To my own kin. You are the conqueror.
The Ausonians have seen my conquered hand
Upstretched. Lavinia is your bride to wed.
Let your hate reach no further."

                        Aeneas stood
Vital and still and fierce in his array.
His eyes darted about, his right hand stayed
   suspended.
And now it was, yes now, that Turnus' plea
Working upon him might have wheedled him.
But suddenly a glitter caught his eye:
Turnus was flaunting on his conqueror's shoulder   *1130*
The belt of his friend Pallas—with those shiny
   fastenings
He knew so well, before the boy was killed
By Turnus—this Turnus! wearing upon his
   shoulder
Spoils fatal now to himself. Aeneas' eyes
Drank in the sight—emblem of bitter grief.
His fury overflowed and in a terrible voice,
"Do you think to slink from my grasp—you, you
Clad in the spoils of my friend? It is Pallas, Pallas
Who with this blow makes you his sacrifice!
It is he who exacts his vengeance with your blood,   *1140*
You accursed fiend!" As he spoke he plunged his
   sword
In fury deep into his enemy's heart.
But as for him his limbs lay slumped and chill
And his soul flew, resentful of its fate,
Down to the Shades, with many a sigh and groan.

THE WANDERINGS

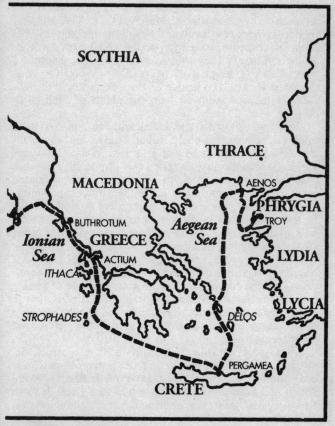

SCYTHIA

THRACE

MACEDONIA   AENOS

                             PHRYGIA

• BUTHROTUM   • TROY

Ionian   GREECE   *Aegean*
Sea   *Sea*
                                    LYDIA
        • ACTIUM

ITHACA

                                   LYCIA

STROPHADES   *DELOS*

                        PERGAMEA

                CRETE

OF AENEAS

AFTERWORD:
VIRGIL AND *THE AENEID*

Publius Virgilius Maro died almost two thousand years ago, in 19 B.C. He was born in 70 B.C. Julius Caesar was assassinated on the Ides of March, 44 B.C. This moment in Roman history is known, through the medium of William Shakespeare, to many people who know no other Roman history. They will know then what happened after Caesar's death; how Mark Antony and Octavius defeated Brutus, the leader of the conspiracy, "the noblest Roman of them all," on the plains of Philippi in 42 B.C.

Octavian, or Octavius as I shall still call him, had been adopted by his great-uncle, Julius Caesar, and made his heir. He was born in 63 B.C. and died in A.D. 14. Virgil was his contemporary. Octavius was physically a delicate man, as Virgil was, and his opponents underestimated his strength of purpose and his brilliant political acumen. After Philippi he succeeded in persuading Antony, his ally in the destruction of Brutus, into accepting the wrong half of the Roman world and into marrying his sister Octavia. Octavius retained the western half, including the central government. Antony went East, and what happened next can be found in another of Shakespeare's plays—*Antony and Cleopatra*. It is an example of Shakespeare's instinctive genius and feeling for history that in each play it is Octavius who speaks the concluding lines and that in each case these are objective, civil, and compassionate.

After the sea battle of Actium in 31 B.C., which destroyed Antony, Cleopatra, and the power of the Eastern Empire, Octavius was master of a Roman world which had known no peace for a hundred years. He was to be a good master, a great and pacific administrator. But unlike his great-uncle—perhaps he had learned from Caesar's career—he was subtle enough not to make his mastery blatantly apparent. Finally, it seemed almost against his will that he was made Emperor and called "Augustus," a word which derives from the verb *augeo* ("I increase, I strengthen") and moves into its adjectival form as meaning somebody or something "worthy of honor" for these reasons. The Romans named their month of fruition after him. To many people, still, who do not know the history of Octavius, an "Augustan age" symbolizes an age of peace and order.

Virgil's life spans the culminations of civil strife and the beginnings of a new order. It was the supreme moment to write of Rome's glory. Shakespeare got his background material for *Julius Caesar* and *Antony and Cleopatra* from North's translation of Plutarch's *Lives*. It would seem likely that he read all the lives, and that he saw in this period of Roman history some kinship with his own times. A hundred years of civil strife in England had culminated in a new dynasty and the defeat of a foreign invader.

And peace proclaims olives of endless age.

This is a truly Virgilian line, as are the opening lines of this famous, yet enigmatic sonnet (cvii)

Not mine own fears, nor the prophetic soul
Of the wide world dreaming on things to come . . .

What better description of Virgil can one find than "the prophetic soul of the wide world dreaming on things to come"? The answer is simple: he did not only dream on things to come but on things past, and things present, and, like Shakespeare, he meant by "dream" the *imaginative reality* of things, affairs, people as they were, are, and will be.

The Roman world in which Virgil lived was, in fact, not unlike the world in which Shakespeare lived. In each case a people emerging from a past of violent strife, dominated by a dogged purpose to be themselves, suddenly found they *were* themselves, in a world of which they were masters. Each had for ruler a benevolent despot whom they could respect, wielding absolute powers from behind a cloak of democratic institutions. The mixture of intrigue, political brilliance, and luck which set Queen Elizabeth I on the throne is not unlike that which transformed Octavius into Augustus. I do not propose to draw these parallels too far. Virgil and Augustus mutually approved of each other and never fell out, whereas the Elizabethan Court gave little back to its poets. Edmund Spenser, the most persistent toady, was grimly surfeited with his reward of government in Ireland, for example. The point about parallels is that they do *not* meet. Too often one tries to draw them where one line is aesthetics and the other politics.

The important point is that Shakespeare and Virgil, both supremely great artists, lived in times where there was the same sort of unusual situation to deal with: a prolonged period of strife seeming to produce the ruler, in his just hour, who was for peace.

The greatest artists—Aristophanes and Thomas Hardy are two others—know the illusion and futility of the idea that war is a success. "Most great poems are concerned with wickedness, violence, and horror. But often, at least among civilized people, the whole tendency of the same poems is really towards peaceful goodness, humanity and reconciliation." So writes the greatest living Virgilian scholar, Professor W. Jackson Knight. His words are abundantly true of the *Aeneid*; and the progress of epic poetry in the Western world adds confirmation to them.

It is essential to understand that the *Aeneid* has been the greatest book of the Western world for two thousand years: older, indeed, than the Bible as we know it. It is a secular book, but still a magic book. The "Sortes Virgilianae," practiced within living memory, meant opening Virgil at random, finding a line or so at random on this random page, and making life-binding decisions from so doing.

The *Aeneid* is, superficially, a narrative of the wanderings of Aeneas, the mythical founder of the Roman people: a hero of Trojan stock, half-god, half-man, who escaped from the sack of Troy and—after appalling hardship, suffering, violence, and disaster—gained for the remnant of his people their foothold in Italy. I am not going to recount the story—the poem will do so—but it is not merely narrative, not simply a course of natural (and supernatural) events. It is a moral and spiritual journey.

What, in essence, is Virgil's philosophy, so manifest despite "wickedness, violence and horror"? It is that violence cannot be justified, that men must come to terms with violence, whether it is called malevolence of gods or malevolence of men; that good men do not give in to this malevolence but conduct themselves morally. "Morally" means acting well, with a knowledge of good and evil in this world, uncluttered with superstition. Living as Virgil did so soon before the Christian era, it is not surprising that Christians soon read into the beautiful fourth *Eclogue*, which foretells "the birth of a boy who shall at last bring the race of iron to an end, and bid the golden race spring up all the world over" (Conington's translation), an inspired prophecy of the birth of Christ.

But Virgil would not have been held in such absolute veneration, I think, had not the morality of all his work been so clear. There is little doubt that his ideas of good and evil derive from Platonic philosophy, and Professor Jackson Knight most fascinatingly interprets the golden bough wherewith Aeneas gains entrance to the "Spiritual World beyond death" as a symbolic reference to Plato. As embodied in Virgil's poetry, the moral ideas are of profound value to Christian and pagan alike: there are the strongest grounds for saying that Virgil is the greatest creative genius of Western civilization.

It is for this reason that it is necessary to put him into however slight an historical frame. He was Augustus' friend. He was, indeed, subsidized by him. It is said that Aeneas was Augustus glorified, as it is said that Tennyson's King Arthur was Albert the Prince Consort. There is no question that Virgil was influenced by the times he lived in. How can a great artist not be so influenced? But it is a silly simplification to say that Virgil wrote his *Georgics*—his "versified treatise on farming"—because there were repeated attempts in his lifetime to settle and resettle soldiers on the land. (He is said to have been himself dispossessed in this process!)

It is difficult to segregate politics from morals. Virgil was not an active politician nor a propagandist. He was a creative artist. When you ask of Shakespeare's historical plays, "Whose side was Shakespeare on?" you get dusty enough academic answers. The same thing applies if you ask if Virgil was on Aeneas's side. We are not inclined to dispute that the Emperor Augustus was a great statesman. We are inclined to dispute, rather pointlessly, whether or not Virgil prostituted his gifts to serve Augustus. We cannot know, in the sense that we only have what Virgil *did* write and not what he might have written or ought to have written. What is necessary is to emphasize that he wrote what he did write in a certain period of history about which a great deal is known and can be discovered by anyone; that it is likely he wrote what he wrote because he lived when he did. If you belong to a set which includes Augustus, Maecenas, Pollio, and to which you introduce Horace, you are not living *in vacuo*. Poets don't. The greatest of them are more of their time and less of their time than any other of their contemporaries. Virgil fulfills this condition supremely. So does his masterpiece. The *Aeneid* was the work of his maturity. It was begun when he was forty—the year after the battle of Actium, the first year of Augustus' power—and eleven years later, though the poem was totally in being, he asked on his deathbed for its destruction: at least another three years of further revision would be required before it would be ready. Luckily, Augustus forbade his literary executors to destroy it.

Epic poetry in the West seems likely to appear after prolonged periods of strife. One might say, then, why not all the time? But there are moments in which the majority of human beings are led to believe that the ruling minority is not working for the *next* period of strife, but consolidating on the last. This is called peace.

I hope it will not therefore seem too paradoxical to write of Milton, the writing of whose masterpiece *Paradise Lost* took place mainly during the English Civil War. But as a young man Milton inherited the Elizabethan concept of peace and greatness and it was always his intention to write an epic. He first considered the subject of King Arthur, our English mythical Augustus. Why did he abandon the idea? Some of the answer I believe can be found in the *Aeneid*. Milton had no real allegiance to a living Arthur: he did not believe in Cromwell as a man, as Virgil did in Augustus, nor could he fuse the actual with the historical past or the mythical past into an epic. Shakespeare could—and did—fuse the affairs of his time with the immediate past and the long past, in a dramatic way, that is, an ephemeral way which awaits time's ratification of permanence.

An epic which is truly to be a national epic, as Virgil meant his to be, must so to speak be permanent from the start. So steeped in Virgil was Milton and such a brilliant scholar that he even had thoughts of writing his epic in Latin, since Latin was still the *lingua franca* of educated Europe. The *Aeneid* is a masterpiece about how men live and behave on this earth—a psychological masterpiece as one would say now, if one allows Virgil to believe his beneficent and malevolent deities to be both extraneous to human life and also projections of it. I cannot see why one should not. Thomas Hardy's philosophy of life in the nineteenth century is little different save that the deities do not become personally embodied. But Milton believed in one God, and could not dare to become involved in multiple deities. Arthur was hardly a subject for a country which had just beheaded its monarch, so he abandoned Arthur for God and the Devil and wrote in English an equivalent of the *Aeneid*. The two poems, *Paradise Lost* and the *Aeneid*, have much in common: the nobility of purpose, of language, and of architecture. Yet there is a difference. *Paradise Lost* is a tract. It is to "justify God's ways to men." Virgil's purpose is to present men in their environment, bedeviled by gods as they always will be, and simply say, "This is what life *is*. These are the kind of things which happen." So Aeneas in an hour of extremity in a strange land sees a pictured portrayal of the siege of Troy, sees his father and himself portrayed, and knows that human sympathies exist.

En Priamus: sunt hic etiam sua praemia laudi;
Sunt lacrimae rerum et mentem mortalia tangunt.
                    Aeneid I: 461–462.
("See there Priam. Here, too, worth finds its due reward; here too there are tears for human fortune and hearts that are touched by mortality."
                    —Conington, trans.

"Look; there is Priam. Even here high merit has its due; there is pity for a world's distress and a sympathy for short-lived humanity."—W. Jackson Knight, trans.

Such lines stop the hearts of those who know what

the words say. They are, truly, untranslatable. Try to translate into French such easy lines as:

> We are such stuff
> As dreams are made on, and our little life
> Is rounded by a sleep. (Shakespeare: *The Tempest*)

But the epic has moved on a pace with Milton to a further exploration of human being. Though this is a specifically Christian poem, in a sense that the *Aeneid* is not specifically pagan, nobody appears in it who could not really have appeared in the *Aeneid* as a moral, amoral, or immoral character. Mezentius certainly takes his place in both! That is why William Blake divined that Milton was of the devil's party without knowing it. Let me define the difference very simply between these two poems. Virgil begins

> Arma virumque cano . . .

This is personal. I am going to tell you a story of a man, a hero, and his battles. Milton begins

> Of man's first disobedience . . .

Man is abstract before he is Adam. What follows in *Paradise Lost* is a superb poem which, though it has had its ups and downs in critical opinion, is truly an epic. The overtones of the narrative transcend the story of the fall of Lucifer. But it is a poem in which the beings, human or elemental, take second place to the system of thought Milton wanted to impress on his readers. This is the opposite of Virgil; yet in the end it is the human beings who win. It is Adam and Eve about whom we care:

> The world was all before them, where to choose
> Their place of rest, and Providence their guide:
> They, hand in hand, with wand'ring steps and slow,
> Through Eden took their solitary way.

I am not unaware of Dante or of the actual part Virgil plays in his poem, but I am naturally more concerned with our own language. In certain respects, one might say that Wordsworth's *Prelude* was the logical successor to *Paradise Lost*, though it would be difficult to claim it as an epic. His poem is purely autobiographical—it is subtitled "The Growth of a Poet's Mind"—but it has the essential Virgilian power of transcending the immediate meaning of its words and of offering to the sensitive reader phrases which are keys to the universal experience of man.

Tennyson, of all English poets perhaps, read Virgil with the greatest and fullest awareness. His ear was supremely sensitive to the sounds of words, his mind closely attuned to Virgil's. It may be that this was one of the reasons that he found himself incapable of, or perhaps not desirous of, writing an epic. He chose the subject Milton had rejected, the mythical King Arthur, and there is no doubt that he wanted in some measure to do for his country what Virgil had done for Rome. But the *Idylls of the King* are what he intended—Idylls. Often they are technically as brilliant as the *Aeneid*. Instead of upbraiding Tennyson for not writing an epic after the style of Virgil, it is far better to praise him for writing a work of great originality which has its roots in his love for the Roman poet.

> Thou that seest Universal
>   Nature moved by Universal Mind:
> Thou majestic in thy sadness
>   At the doubtful doom of human kind . . .
>
> I salute thee, Mantovano,
>   I that loved thee since my days began,
> Wielder of the stateliest measure
>   Ever moulded by the lips of man.

"Mantovano," because Virgil was born near Mantua in northern Italy, in the valley of the River Po.

Virgil was given the best possible education his parents could afford, ending in Rome where he may first have met Octavius. But he did not care for the life of the capital. He was a country person. He was very shy, and soon he moved near Naples to live a retired life dedicated to reading and writing. He was a scholarly man, intensely well and widely read. Many people nowadays seem to regard T. S. Eliot as the inventor of the poetic technique of introducing quotation, allusion, and the borrowings and reshapings of other poets' work into the body of their own. But Virgil did this with the greatest subtlety and skill. It is not possible to say how far this was a conscious technique. With pretty well all the poetry of his world stored in his mind, lines and phrases may have bubbled up without having been summoned. However it was, all became transmuted and molded into Virgil's personal style. This is a style of great complexity and artifice. He was a supreme craftsman

> . . . who would write ten lines, they say,
> At dawn, and lavish all the golden day
> To make them wealthier in his readers' eyes.

His range was immense. As Jackson Knight says, "He normally wrote with dignity and a certain formality. But he used informality also: occasionally there is an effective colloquialism and even here and there something like slang. Virgil had some of the caprice which is usually found in very great men. He also had that masterful impatience with conventional and accepted speech which seems to be typical of the greatest poets."

Tennyson called Virgil, "Wielder of the stateliest measure/Ever moulded by the lips of man." This measure, or "meter" as we are likely to call it, is the hexameter, the same used by Homer for the *Iliad* and the *Odyssey*. Both Greek and Latin are syllabic languages. English relies on stress or emphasis. A syllabic language has clear rules for the measurement of its syllables. They are long or short according to these rules, and this longness or shortness of a syllable scholars have called "quantity." Of course, there are exceptions: the general rule is for a vowel to be long if it is followed by two consonants, but in the line *Sūnt lăcrĭ|māe rērum| ēt mēn|tēm mōr|tālīa tāngūnt*, the first *a* is short.

The reader will see this line has six divisions—that is why it is called a hexameter. These divisions are of two sorts. One is called a dactyl because δακτνλος, Daktulos, is the Greek for a "finger," and a finger has one long and two shorter joints. The other division is called a spondee.

Let us look at the English blank verse line, the vehicle of our own greatest poetry. It is a line which has five stresses based on the even beats, but this pattern allows of great variation:

And peace proclaims olives of endless age . . .

Thick as autumnal leaves that strow the brooks . . .
(Milton)

Fair seed-time had my soul, and I grew up . . .
(Wordsworth)

The old order changeth, yielding place to new . . .
(Tennyson)

So deeply was the learning of Latin and Greek ingrained in our language and our educational system that you will often see the blank verse line described as an "iambic pentameter." This means precisely what I have said: "A line which has five stresses based on the even beats," but somehow "iambic pentameter" has a more classic ring. And what has been written about prosody, the science of versification, has been mostly written on the *a priori* that English can be treated like Latin or Greek. It cannot.

Some remarks of this kind are essential and will help to put a translator of Latin in his place. It is to further this end that I have tried to set the *Aeneid* beside some other great English poems. Never let us lose sight of the fact that it is a *poem*—an integrated work of art. *Paradise Lost*, the *Prelude*, the *Idylls of the King* only serve to emphasize what a great and indivisible work of art it is.

A translator stands before the *Aeneid* in awe and in love and with the certain knowledge that he is doomed to failure. "Poetry, indeed, cannot be translated," says Samuel Johnson, "and therefore it is the poets who preserve language." So it is a question merely of what sort of failure one is doomed to. That the *Aeneid* is written in a "dead" language provides a further twist of the knife. The problem is even more complex than that which faces a translator of Dante. This Virgilian Latin language is preserved forever. It does not stand in relation to modern Italian as Shakespeare does to modern English. But it is a translator's justification if he can make a great work of art live for the people *he* lives with and the age *he* lives in, without doing too much violence to his original. My own starting point, therefore, is that the *Aeneid* is a poem to be enjoyed. The nearer one can come to what Virgil wrote, the more chance one's reader will be entranced and moved by the awareness that he is in the presence of greatness. To put the matter simply, one has to write a poem of the caliber of a *Paradise Lost*, out of another man's words and into another tongue. That is the aim.

As regards the method, I have used a "measure" which is certainly not as "stately" as blank verse might have been. I have used English rhythm which seems to approximate the Latin rhythm, each in its own way. I have done so in order to keep what a translator can truly keep going, and that is the impulse of the narrative. Very many of the incidental beauties and subtleties must be marred or lost. I can only hope that some traces of them will remain.

But my principal hope is that this translation will make Aeneas, Turnus, Camilla, Mezentius, Dido, Palinurus, and all the other characters in this marvelous poem alive and recognizable beings to us, in this world, now. Their problems are ours. The solutions of our problems are the solutions Virgil so clearly saw and set down in a way only the greatest of human beings can do: in words which are forever valid.

Virgil, I know, is the subject of school exams, like Shakespeare. I suppose this cannot be helped. But the questions to be answered about Virgil are not really "Can you translate 'Sic itur ad astra'?" or "Who won the boat race in Book V?" They are questions which can only be answered by reading his poem as a poem, as an organic whole. My hope is that I have offered some indication of the quality of one of the world's masterpieces: that the deepest questions of human ethics Virgil posed in magnificent poetry are still recognizable and that our responses to them will be natural and inevitable. I therefore offer my translation in the words of Shakespeare's Octavius

According to his virtue let us use him

—hoping that the following line will not also be applicable

With all respect and rights of burial.

—Patric Dickinson

THE THREE APPENDICES THAT FOLLOW HAVE
BEEN PREPARED BY J. SHERWOOD WEBER
OF PRATT INSTITUTE, NEW YORK.

APPENDIX I

Relevant Dates in Roman History

ca. 1184 B.C.—Legendary date of the Greek sack of Troy.

753 B.C.—Legendary founding of Rome, the "eternal city," by Romulus and Remus, descendants of Aeneas, beginning the Rule of Kings, which lasted until 510 B.C.

509 B.C.—Latins defeat Tarquin, eject Etruscans, and establish the Roman Republic in the form of the independent Latin city-state of Rome.

390 B.C.—The Gauls sack Rome.

264 to 241 B.C.—First Punic (Phoenician or Carthaginian) War, as a result of which Rome won Sicily, her first province outside of the Italian mainland.

218 to 201 B.C.—Second Punic War, in which Hannibal, Dido's "avenger," failing to subdue Rome, was forced into a one-sided peace that ended the era of Carthage as a major independent state.

149 to 146 B.C.—Third Punic War, ending with the Roman destruction of Carthage.

111 to 31 B.C.—Rome is plagued by an era of wars, mostly civil, and of brutal proscriptions during careers of Marius and Sulla, Julius Caesar, Pompey, Antony, Brutus, Cassius, Octavian.

70 B.C.—Birth of Virgil (Publius Virgilius Maro) near Mantua.

63 B.C.—Birth of Octavian Augustus, Caesar's grand-nephew, adopted son, and heir.

49 to 46 B.C.—Caesar wins civil war against Pompey.

44 B.C.—Caesar's assassination sparks a civil war pitting Mark Antony and Octavian against Brutus and Cassius.

42 B.C.—Mark Antony and Octavian defeat Brutus and Cassius at Philippi.

31 B.C.—Octavian defeats Antony and Cleopatra at the Battle of Actium, annexing Egypt after the suicides of Antony and Cleopatra in 30 B.C.

30 to 19 B.C.—Virgil supported Augustus and composed the *Aeneid*, dying in 19 B.C. before completing it to his satisfaction. Octavian Augustus "published" it nevertheless.

27 B.C. to A.D. 14—In 27 B.C. Octavian assumed the name of Augustus and formally established the Roman Empire, which he ruled as the first Roman Emperor.

27 B.C. to A.D. 180—*Pax Romana* (Roman Peace), two centuries of virtual peace (no major wars) throughout the expansive Roman Empire, ending with the death of Marcus Aurelius.

APPENDIX II

Book-by-Book Outline

BOOK I—Books I through IV have an elapsed time of from six to seven weeks, but they recapitulate events of a much longer period. After announcing his theme (Aeneas' fulfillment of destiny despite many obstacles and vicissitudes) and invoking the Muse, Virgil explains Juno's anger and describes the Trojan landing in Africa. After Jupiter prophesies to Venus the course of Roman history from the founding of Lavinium to the coming of Augustus, Venus guides Aeneas to Carthage, where he is warmly welcomed by Dido.

BOOK II—To Dido and her court Aeneas relates the story of the sack of Troy, explaining the trick of the wooden horse, the actual capture and destruction of the city, and his own escape with a few survivors, including his father, Anchises, and his son, Ascanius.

BOOK III—Aeneas recounts his seven years of wandering (not unlike those of Odysseus in *The Odyssey*), including the landing in Thrace, the building of a city there, and the advice to search farther by the Oracle of Apollo at Delos; the brief settlement in Crete; briefer periods in the Strophades and Epirus; and landings in Italy and Sicily, where Anchises died.

BOOK IV—Dramatizes the tragic Dido-Aeneas love affair: Dido's Venus-manipulated passion, the consummation in the cave, the lovers' neglect of duty, Jupiter's order to Aeneas to depart, the anger of Dido, Aeneas' defense, Dido's efforts at reconciliation, Aeneas' departure, and Dido's curse and suicide.

BOOK V—Books V and VI, which develop action taking a little over three weeks, trace Aeneas' approach to Italy via Sicily and the Other World. After reaching Sicily, Aeneas visits his father's tomb and stages games in Anchises' honor. Disgruntled Trojan women, weary of wandering, burn the ships, most of which are saved only because Jupiter sends a rainstorm. Leaving behind a colony of Trojans, Aeneas leads his hardiest followers in a miraculous voyage to Italy, losing Palinurus, his pilot, on the way.

BOOK VI—Landing at Cumae, Aeneas visits Sybil at Apollo's temple, finds the Golden Bough, and journeys through the Underworld, where Anchises predicts the future greatness of Rome and explains her destiny to rule the world in peace.

BOOK VII—During a four-day period, Aeneas lands again in Italy, sends a mission to King Latinus, and receives an offer of Lavinia's hand in marriage. The Latins—moved by the angry Juno and by Allecto, the Fury, and led by spurned Turnus—clash with the Trojans and begin a furious war.

BOOK VIII—Aeneas, again divinely inspired, seeks an alliance with the Greek king Evander, ruling at Pallanteum, the site of future Rome. Evander provides forces led by his son Pallas and advises Aeneas to seek Etruscan aid. Venus supplies a Vulcan-made shield, wondrously decorated with scenes from the future history of Rome, ending with the triumphs of Augustus.

BOOK IX—During Aeneas' four-day absence, Turnus directs a successful attack against the Trojan ships, fighting his way through the Trojan camp.

BOOK X—During a day-long battle, Aeneas leads the Trojans in breaking the Latin siege but loses Pallas to Turnus' spear. Aeneas slays several Latin chiefs.

BOOK XI—After a twelve-day truce for burial of the dead, the Latins under Turnus suffer a series of setbacks and panic.

BOOK XII—On the last day of the conflict, Aeneas and Turnus prepare for single combat. After further costly Latin reverses, Aeneas finally meets and slays Turnus.

APPENDIX III

Glossary of Gods, Men, Peoples, Places

ACESTES—Trojan-descended king of western Sicily, who twice received Aeneas during his quest.

ACHAEANS—The Greeks; also called Argives, Danaans, Pelasgians.

ACHATES—Faithful attendant and armor-bearer of Aeneas.

AENEAS—Son of the goddess Venus and Anchises, husband of Creüsa, father of Ascanius, and leader of the Trojan quest for their Italian homeland. Aeneas is a Trojan prince allied to, but not descended from, Priam.

ALBA LONGA—Latin town in the Alban hills near Rome, supposedly founded by Ascanius.

AMATA—Queen of the Latins, wife of King Latinus, and a strong supporter of Turnus in the Trojan-Latin conflict.

ANCHISES—Aged father of Aeneas by Venus, for which union he was blinded by Jupiter.

ANNA—Devoted sister of Dido.

APOLLO—Also Apollo in Greek myth; controls many things, including prophecy.

ASCANIUS—Son of Aeneas and Creüsa and founder of Alba Longa; also called Iulus to relate him to the Julian family of Julius Caesar and Augustus.

AUGUSTUS—Born Octavian in 63 B.C.; grandnephew, adoptive son, and heir of Julius Caesar as well as founder of the Roman Empire in 27 B.C. The assumed name Augustus derives from *augeo* (I increase, I strengthen), its adjectival form meaning someone worthy of honor for strengthening something. An "Augustan Age" still symbolizes a period of peace and order.

AVERNUS—A lake near Naples and the legendary entrance to the Underworld.

CAIETA—A headland on the Italian west coast named for Aeneas' nurse.

CAMILLA—Famous warrior-maid ally of Turnus.

CARTHAGE—A Phoenician seaport on the North African coast, founded by Dido; the power rival of Rome until its sack in the Third Punic War.

CREÜSA—Daughter of Priam and wife of Aeneas, who disappeared mysteriously during Aeneas' flight from burning Troy.

CUMAE—A Greek colony near Naples, where Aeneas landed, consulted the oracle Sybil, and entered the world of the dead.

CUPID—The Greek Eros; son of Venus and conveyor of her love darts and potions.

CYBELE—An Asian goddess worshiped on Mt. Ida; also called Phrygian mother.

CYTHERA—A Grecian island; center of Venus-worship.

DARDANUS—The mythical founder of Troy who supposedly migrated from Italy. Aeneas seeks the place Dardanus left.

DELOS—An Aegean island where Apollo was born.

DIANA—The Roman goddess of light; related to, but not the same as, the Greek Artemis.

DIDO—Daughter of Phoenician King Belus, widow of Sychaeus, foundress and Queen of Carthage. Dido (also called Elissa) loved Aeneas and cursed him and his line before committing suicide when Aeneas abandoned her to fulfill his destiny.

ERYX—A Sicilian mountain; also a center of Venus-worship.

ETRUSCANS—Also called Tuscans and Tyrians. Tribe from north of Latium who allied with the Trojans against the Latins.

EURYALUS—A courageous Trojan youth and insepa-rable friend of Nisus.

EVANDER—Former Greek who became king at Pal-lanteum on the Tiber, the future site of Rome; aids Aeneas with forces led by his son Pallas.

FATES—The goddesses who assigned to man his fate. Their names were Clotho, Lachesis and Atropos; they were called the Parcae.

HADES—The Underworld; also called Erebus and Orcus.

HECTOR—The Trojan prince who led the Trojans against the Greeks and Achilles in the Trojan War. He was married to Andromache.

HECUBA—The wife of Priam and mother of many Tro-jan heroes, but not of Aeneas.

HELEN—The beautiful wife of the Greek Menelaus, whose abduction by Paris was the mythical cause of the Trojan War.

HESPERIA—Greek name (meaning "land of the west") for Italy; also called Ausonia.

ILIUM—Another name for Troy; basis for the title *Iliad*.

IRIS—She was one of the gods' messengers.

JUNO—The Greek Hera, sister *and* wife of Jupiter (or Jove). In her anger at the Trojans (resulting from the judgment of Paris, the descent of the Trojans from an illegitimate son of Jupiter, the Trojan threat to her favorite city of Carthage, and other things), she caused many of Aeneas' trials and tribulations.

JUPITER—Father and ruler of the gods. Also called Jove in Latin and Zeus in Greek, he is a more pow-erful figure in Roman than in Greek religion.

JUTURNA—Italian goddess of springs and streams, and sister of Turnus.

LAOCOÖN—Trojan priest of Apollo and Neptune who warned the Trojans against the danger of the wooden horse and was crushed by serpents for his pains.

LAOMEDON—Father of Priam and his predecessor as Trojan king.

LATINS—Inhabitants of Latium.

LATINUS—King of Latium and nominal, weak-willed head of Italian forces during the war with Aeneas' followers.

LATIUM—The coastal district of west central Italy, south of Rome; the territory of Latinus and his Latins.

LAURENTUM—Capital city of Latinus in Latium.

LAUSUS—Son of Mezentius, ousted Etruscan chief and ally of Turnus.

LAVINIA—Daughter of Latinus and Amata, betrothed to Turnus, but destined to wed Aeneas and breed a new race of Latins.

LAVINIUM—Mythical city built by Aeneas in Latium after his marriage to Lavinia.

MARS—The god of war; called Ares in Greek myth.

MERCURY—Like the Greek Hermes, a messenger god.

MEZENTIUS—Exiled Etruscan tyrant, father of Lausus, and ally of Turnus.

MINERVA—The goddess of wisdom; the Greek Pallas Athene.

MT. OLYMPUS—Home of the gods in northern Greece.

NEPTUNE—God of the sea; the Greek Poseidon.

NISUS—*See* Euryalus.

OENOTRIA—Ancient name for the region south of Latium.

PALLANTEUM—Mythical city of Evander on the site of Rome.

PALLAS—Son of Evander and ally of Aeneas in the war with the Latins.

PERGAMUS—Also called Pergamum and Pergama, the citadel of Troy.

PHOENICIANS—Seafaring people from northern Africa and inhabitants of Carthage; hence, also Carthaginians.

PHRYGIANS—Somewhat effeminate peoples of Asia Minor who worshiped Cybele. The Trojans were sometimes called Phrygians as an insult.

PRIAM—King of Troy at the time of the Trojan War.

ROME—The "eternal city" on the Tiber River, traditionally founded by Romulus.

ROMULUS—Also called Quirinus. A descendant of Aeneas, son of Mars, reared by a she-wolf, Romulus (with his brother, Remus) founded Rome in 753 B.C. and became its first king.

RUTULIANS—A tribe of Latins from east of Latium, from which Turnus came; also called Daunians.

SATURN—Father of Jupiter and Juno. Saturn (Greek: Kronos) was driven from Olympus by Jupiter, came to Italy, and ruled during the Golden Age.

SINON—The Greek spy who deceived the Trojans about the wooden horse.

SYBIL—Also named Deiphobe; priestess of Apollo at Cumae, near Naples.

SYCHAEUS—Prince of Tyre and the murdered husband of Dido.

TIBER—The river in northern Latium on which Rome was built.

TROJANS—Inhabitants of Troy; also called Aeneadae and Teucrians.

TROY—The city of Priam in Asia Minor that was sacked by the Greeks in the Trojan War; also called Dardania, Ilium, Pergamus, and Teucria.

TURNUS—Thwarted suitor of Lavinia, hot-headed chief of the Rutulians, and actual leader of the Italian forces against Aeneas.

ULYSSES—Odysseus; hero of *The Odyssey*—to Greeks a paragon of wily resourcefulness, to Romans a symbol of treachery.

VENUS—The Greek Aphrodite, goddess of love, whose bribery of Paris led to the Trojan War.

VULCAN—The Greek Hephaestus; husband of Venus, god of fire and metalwork, who made the shield picturing the future history of Rome that Venus gave Aeneas for his fight against Turnus.

Classics from
Ancient Greece

THE ILIAD
By Homer trans. W.H.D. Rouse
This very readable prose translation tells the tale of
Achilles, Hector, Agamemnon, Paris, Helen, and all Troy
besieged by the mighty Greeks. It is a tale of glory and
honor, of pride and pettiness, of friendship and sacrifice,
of anger and revenge. In short, it is the quintessential
western tale of men at war.

THE ODYSSEY
By Homer trans. W.H.D. Rouse
Kept away from his home and family for 20 years by war
and malevolent gods, Odysseus returns to find his house
in disarray. This is the story of his adventurous travels and
his battle to reclaim what is rightfully his.

THE METAMORPHOSES
By Ovid trans. Horace Gregory
Prized for its splendor and savage, sophisticated wit, *The
Metamorphoses* is a masterpiece of Western culture—the
first attempt to link all the Greek myths, before and after
Homer, in a cohesive whole, to the Roman myths of
Ovid's day.

**Available wherever books are sold or at
signetclassics.com**

S520